THE LOVEDAY REVENGE

Also by Kate Tremayne

Adam Loveday
The Loveday Fortunes
The Loveday Trials
The Loveday Scandals
The Loveday Honour
The Loveday Pride
The Loveday Loyalty

THE LOVEDAY REVENGE

Kate Tremayne

headline

First published in 2007
by HEADLINE PUBLISHING GROUP

1

Cataloguing in Publication Data is
available from the British Library

ISBN 978 0 7553 3350 9

Typeset in Bembo by Palimpsest Book Production Ltd, Grangemouth, Stirlingshire
Printed and bound in Great Britain by Mackays of Chatham plc, Chatham, Kent

HEADLINE PUBLISHING
A division of Hodder He:
338 Euston Road
London NW1 3BH

www.headline.co.uk
www.hodderheadline.c

Acknowledgements

Writing about the Lovedays has made them very much part of my family. How can I not suffer anguish at some of their adventures when the characters are so very real to me? The support of my own children, Alison and Stuart, in understanding the idiosyncrasies of a writing mother is gratefully appreciated. Also the joy and laughter of my grand-childen, Jasmine, Dan, Noah and Megan, who brighten my day when the Lovedays are facing their darkest hours.

To Teresa Chris who is a constant support and inspiration.

To the wonderful team at Headline for the spectacular covers and promotional work. The terrific editors, Jane Morpeth and Sherise Hobbs, who have inspired and encouraged me. And to Celine Kelly who has kept the transition from typescript to print all running smoothly.

And to you my readers for your continued loyalty. Your emails and letters are always a joy to receive

Dedication

Friends come into your life for a reason, a season, or a lifetime. Anonymous.

This book is dedicated to friends everywhere. Especially to Karen Vincent and Verity Reynolds — you know why. And to my greatest life-long friend — my husband Chris.

In my friends I have been truly blessed. At the very least you share your love and laughter, lift me up when I am down, and celebrate my joys. Together we dream of moving mountains and, even if we do not succeed, the journey was always worthwhile. Some of our journeys have been long, and some, through circumstances, short. All have been treasured. I would not be the person I am without having met you. Thank you. You are always in my heart.

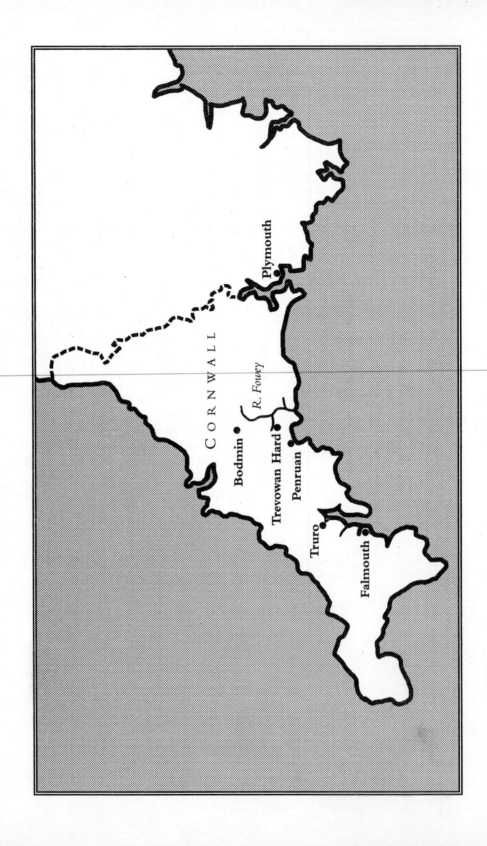

THE LOVEDAY FAMILY

Arthur St John Loveday   **m.**   Anne Penhaligan
b. 1679   **b.** 1691
d. 1742   **d.** 1733

George Loveday   **m.**   Joan Trelawny
b. 1711   **b.** 1722
d. 1785   **d.** 1764

Margaret
b. 1736 –
m. Charles Mercer
b. 1726
d. 1791

Elspeth
b. 1738 –

St John
b. 1740
d. 1744

Edward *(twins)*
b. 1743 –
d. 1794
(1) **m.** Marie Lenoir
b. 1747
d. 1767
(2) **m.** Amelia Allbright
b. 1759 –

Rowena
b. 1743 –
d. 1743

Joshua
b. 1745 –
m. Cecily Truscott
b. 1749 –

Hubert
b. 1746
d. 1777

William
b. 1747 –
d. 1794
m. Lisette
Marquise
de Gramont
(*née* Riviere)
b. 1771
d. 1794

Thomas
b. 1758 –
m. Georganna Lascalles
b. 1768 –

Tamasine
b. 1778 –
m. Maximilian Deverell
b. 1770 –

Richard Allbright
b. 1781 –

Rafe
b. 1791 –

Joan
b. 1794 –
d. 1796

Japhet
b. 1763 –
m. Gwendolyn Druce
b. 1764 –

Japhet Edward
b. 1794 –

Druce
b. 1798 –

Hannah
b. 1768 –
m. Oswald Rabson
b. 1763
d. 1796

Peter
b. 1771 –
m. Bridie Polglase
b. 1777 –

Michael
b. 1798 –

Davey
b. 1787 –

Abigail
b. 1789 –

Florence
b. 1790 –

Luke
b. 1792 –

Adam
b. 1767 –
m. Senara Polglase
b. 1768 –

St John *(twins)*
b. 1767 –
(1) **m.** Meriel Sawle
b. 1771
d. 1796
(2) **m.** Felicity Barrett
b. 1772 –

Rowena
b. 1788 –

Charlotte Barrett
b. 1792 –

Nathan
b. 1792 –

Joel *(twins)*
b. 1794 –

Rhianne
b. 1794 –

Sara
b. 1796 –

Prologue

Adam Loveday was running hard. It was night, and the moon gave little light through the foliage of the wood. The tree trunks were dark cathedral pillars, their branches linked overhead like a vaulted ceiling. He veered to avoid them, the ground mist swirling upwards blurring his vision. Around him the bracken was waist high, hampering his speed. Impatiently, his hands pushed the fronds aside and he cursed the closely packed stems that wound around his legs, threatening to trip him with every step. A man could easily hide here and a pursuer pass within a few feet and not see him. But this was not the time for hiding.

He paused briefly to get his bearings. Every sense was alert to danger. His heart was thundering in his chest, almost suffocating him in its intensity, and the night air fanned the sweat that drenched his body. No landmark was recognisable amongst the towering oaks. He swung round, scanning the landscape. His eyes, accustomed to the darkness, detected a thinning in the trees to his right. On the wind blowing from the direction of the moor he could smell the dankness of peat and gorse. That way lay treacherous bogs that could suck a man into their cold embrace if he lost his way on the secret tracks.

Fear tightened his throat, tasting bitter as bile, and his rasping breath echoed in his ears. It was not caused by panic that tonight could end in his death, although that was a possibility; it was dread that retribution would be denied him. Defeat was not an option he would consider. Too much depended on the outcome of this confrontation. Loyalty to his family made his own life insignificant. He owed it to those dear to him who had sacrificed their lives to uphold the family honour and pride. Tonight justice demanded revenge.

Ahead of him the sound of a body crashing through the undergrowth was easily discernible. It was closer, the pace unrelenting, driven by desperation.

There could be no escape. Destiny had dealt its hand. The confrontation was long overdue.

He increased his speed. The mist thinned, revealing the figure of a thickset man. Adam raised his pistol and drew back the firing hammer. 'Stop or I shoot!'

The form lunged into the veil of surrounding bracken, diving to the ground. The thickening mist further obscured Adam's vision and an eerie stillness hung over the wood. Then a burst of coarse laughter was followed by a challenge.

'Loveday, are you ready to die!' his tormentor bellowed.

Adam clutched the pistol, his arm outstretched ready to fire as he slowly circled, searching for sight of his enemy.

Without warning the figure attacked from behind. Adam's legs were kicked from under him and he fell to the ground. Instinctively he rolled, but as he came up on his knee to rise, a pistol was cocked close to his ear. Time spun out and expanded with ethereal slowness. Harry Sawle's face was a foot from his own, the pistol barrel cold against Adam's temple. Hatred contorted the smuggler's features. They had been adversaries for years. Was this how it was to end? It was Adam's last thought before the trigger was pulled.

There was no blinding flash, just an ominous click. The weapon had misfired. Adam sprang to his feet, his hands reaching for Sawle's throat, and the two men fell to the ground with Adam's weight on top of the smuggler. His fingers pressed harder. Sawle's eyes bulged with terror, his hands on Adam's arms rapidly losing their strength. This was the moment of Adam's triumph. Sawle would die for his part in Edward Loveday's death, and for the brutality he had inflicted on other members of Adam's family.

'Adam, stop!'

The voice shocked him into loosening the pressure of his fingers. Sawle lay unmoving on the ground beneath him, but his harsh gasps for breath told that he was still alive. Adam stared at the shadowy figure emerging out of the mist.

'There is no honour in murder. This man is not worth you endangering your immortal soul. Only the law can judge him and claim his life.'

Adam cried out. He was shaking violently as he stared into the darkness where the vision of his father had been. But now there was no man. No mist. No trees. No body lying prone beneath his hands. Only a memory of mocking laughter.

'Good Lord, Adam, you look as though you have seen a ghost.' His

2

wife Senara was gently shaking his shoulders as she sat up in bed next to him.

Adam groaned and shook his head. The dream had been too real. It haunted him still. 'I had hunted down Sawle. The time for revenge had come. I had his throat between my hands and the moment of his death was upon him. Then my father appeared. Real and solid and no ghost. He told me that was not the way. He was angrier than I had ever seen him. He told me that the law should deal with Sawle; that I must not have his blood on my hands.'

'Edward was a wise man. When revenge is governed by hatred, it can bring no good upon the perpetrator. The feud between Sawle and your family has raged for a decade. This dream is an omen.'

'You would say that.' He placed a trembling hand on his brow. 'You see omens and premonitions in everything.'

'You may mock my gypsy blood, but I am rarely wrong. I believe in an afterlife. This was Edward's way of warning you. If you kill Sawle, then you will be guilty of murder and will face the noose. Nothing will stop you pursuing the smuggler for his crimes against your family, but only the law can judge him and mete out justice.'

She gripped his arm, her eyes round with fear. 'Promise me you will heed this dream.'

Adam would give his life to spare the woman he loved suffering, but he would give her no false promises.

'I will remember the dream.'

He did not tell Senara that the dream had also shown that Sawle would do everything in his power to kill him.

Chapter One

May 1799

The black-painted hull of the cutter sliced through the waves with a speed few others of its class could match. The dozen sailors were hardened and experienced and kept a wary eye upon the coastal waters for any sign of danger. All but a single sail had been trimmed, for the sliver of moon in the midnight sky turned the canvas to ghostly spectres and could reveal the ship's position. And this was a ship whose illicit cargo needed to be landed in secret. Fortunately, tonight the banks of cloud would hide the moon for most of her voyage and the cutter would escape detection by all but the most vigilant of her enemies.

Since entering British waters, the crew of *Sea Mist* had been nervous, and extra men had been posted on watch to warn of any lights from a patrolling revenue ship. Captain Ezra Lerryn knew these Cornish waters well. He gave a wide berth to the headlands with treacherous undercurrents that could drive a ship on to the spikes of granite rocks hidden beneath the water, and navigated with expertise the shallows where a vessel could run aground. He needed no map to show him the concealed inlets and coves that were the salvation of their clandestine trade.

He scanned the dark outline of the land where small bays and jutting headlands were protected by high cliffs. His landing site had been chosen so that the pack ponies could reach the beach. It was a small cove they often used, but that made it more prone to excise patrols, on either land or sea, lying in wait to ambush them. This stretch of water from Falmouth to Plymouth was regularly patrolled. *Sea Mist* approached Gibbon Head with the stealth of a sneak thief, all lights doused on board.

Ezra Lerryn began to breathe more easily and wiped the droplets of spume from his bushy beard. Soon the longboats would be lowered to ferry their cargo ashore. Even so he remained vigilant, his deep-set eyes focused on the shore. The men had been ordered to silence; sounds carried great distances at night. The cove was almost within hailing distance but the moon was behind a cloud, concealing any movement on the beach.

Without warning, a flash of light illuminated the headland and the accompanying boom of a cannon startled him. He swore savagely, angered by the incident. This could be their undoing, but he had weathered other such attacks. All was not yet lost.

'Damn their eyes, the revenue bastards be on to us!' His gut knotted with tension as the moon was uncloaked and its light showed the silhouette of the vessel that had fired on them. This was no ordinary revenue ship they could easily outrun. He cursed their ill fortune. They had been sighted by *Challenger,* the sister ship to *Sea Mist,* built in the Loveday shipyard. Only *Challenger* could match the smuggling vessel in manoeuvrability and speed.

'Hard to port and get us out of these waters,' shouted Captain Lerryn, desperate to escape.

The sailors, aware of the danger, were clambering up the rigging to unfurl the sails. The tiller responded and the cutter began to turn about, but tonight both wind and fate were against them. *Challenger,* already under full sail and with the wind in her favour, bore down on them like an avenging fury. Lerryn would never concede defeat. He had the strength, physique and volatile temper of a bull. This was a duel of skill and tenacity that was long overdue. Reputations and livelihoods were at stake. Ruthless men captained both ships, and neither would yield until there was a victor and a vanquished.

Ezra Lerryn was a seasoned sea dog with thirty years' experience as a free-trader, and was confident in his ability to outrun the revenue ship. No excise vessel had ever come close to him since he had commanded *Sea Mist.*

The craggy features of his second-in-command, Walter Finch, were thrust close to his face as he shouted against the wind: 'Do we ditch the cargo, Cap'n?'

'Damn their eyes! I bain't lost a cargo and I won't lose this 'un.'

Finch shook his head, his voice whistling through the gap in his front teeth. 'She be gaining on us. Better to lose the cargo than the ship be impounded as a free-trader with the goods on board.'

Lerryn lashed out, swiping Finch across the mouth. 'Lily-livered varmint! It be you I'll throw overboard at any more such talk. No preventive men have got the better of me.'

'Then you'll get us all hanged.' Finch ducked another vicious punch aimed at his head, then yelped in fear as another cannon shot splashed into the water close to their starboard side. 'There bain't no outrunning that demon ship.'

'To arms!' Ezra yelled in defiance. 'To arms, men! They bain't caught us yet.'

A shout carried across the water. 'Heave to! This is the King's ship *Challenger*. Heave to, or we fire again!'

The command chilled Finch's blood, and as he ran down the deck shouting orders for the cannon to be run out, he saw that *Challenger's* lights were now ominously close. Several of the sailors were lashing brandy kegs together in preparation for throwing them over the side. They were weighted to sink just below the water. It was a common ruse by smugglers, for if there was no cargo on board there was no evidence to incriminate them. They would then return the following night to haul in the kegs.

'Leave the cargo be,' bellowed Ezra Lerryn.

With the force of fear of capture turning his guts to water, Finch lashed out at the sailors with a belaying pin. 'Forget the kegs! Get to the guns. Blast the revenue ship out of the water, or we be done for.'

Two of the cannon were fired but their shots fell wide of the mark. Ezra Lerryn screamed abuse at his men. The crew were terrified, making their movements clumsy. Arrest meant prison and either transportation or hanging. Those who were religious uttered prayers; others cursed the poverty that had forced them into this dangerous life. The nightmare continued as a shot from *Challenger* whistled overhead and shattered the mainmast. Sail and wood crashed to the deck and the air was filled with the cries of three wounded smugglers writhing in agony. Splinters from the mast, lethal as arrows, had speared the men.

As the moon scuttled behind a cloud, Captain Lerryn ordered: 'Get those cannon reloaded and man the swivel guns! They bain't taking us or our cargo.'

They were brave words, but Lerryn knew that if he lost the cargo he'd be a dead man anyway. The owner of this ship had warned him of such a fate when he took command, and Harry Sawle never made idle threats.

Lerryn was prepared for a long sea chase and if need be a bloody battle. However, he was not prepared for the next cannon ball from *Challenger* landing on the quarterdeck, splintering the planking. A shard of wood exploding upwards was driven into Lerryn's throat, puncturing his larynx, and another fragment blinded Finch, who fell screaming to the deck clutching his bloody face.

As the captain writhed in his death throes, the crew panicked. A cannon ball smashed through the ship's railing, mortally injuring another man. Without a captain, and with the second-in-command wounded, the smugglers were thrown into chaos. One man was dead and five were badly injured.

Under the skilful command of Captain Ambrose Pinsett, a local man from Helston, *Challenger* was brought alongside. Revenue men armed with rifles trained their weapons on the smugglers.

'In the King's name surrender, or you will be shot for resisting arrest,' ordered Pinsett.

The smugglers knew they were beaten, and only two of them put up any sort of fight as *Sea Mist* was boarded. One jumped overboard and was shot in the back as he tried to swim ashore. His body was dragged back on board with a grappling hook. The rest of the men were clapped in irons and put in the hold. The demasted cutter was then sailed in triumph to Plymouth by Pinsett and his men.

The repercussions of that night would unleash a storm of retribution that would wreak havoc upon the local communities for many months to come.

Chapter Two

The early-morning mist still hung over the river inlet as Adam Loveday rode into the shipyard. The shipwrights were already at work on scaffolding around the two vessels under construction. The merchantman *Pride of the Sea* was moored at the dock, and work on her fitments and rigging would be finished next month.

Adam stabled his gelding, Solomon, and as he walked across the yard he paused to study the merchantman. She was the largest ship yet built in the yard to his own design, and every day that he had watched her rising from a skeletal hull to her present majestic three-masted glory, he had experienced a fresh swell of pride. She was aptly named and was certainly the pride of the shipyard.

The Loveday yard had been in Adam's family for four generations, and such prestigious ships would bring acclaim and prosperity. But that was still in the future. Adam had built the ship with his own money, as his share of the costs in a partnership of investors who were to trade with the new colony in Sydney Cove. It had been a risky gamble. The voyage could take between eight and ten months and involve many hazards, but Adam had been determined to be part of the venture and was confident that it would succeed. In the mean time, the yard still struggled to pay the wages of the shipwrights and settle the creditors' bills.

Adam surveyed the second ship, in its wooden cradle. The cutter had been commissioned by the revenue service and was the fifth the yard had built. The hull and outer shell were almost complete, but Adam frowned as he regarded her. He had hoped this ship would ease the financial burdens of the yard, but the excise office had been slow to honour their payments. The government had declared that the war with France had depleted their coffers and had only paid half the amount of the costs so far incurred. Lack of money had given Adam many sleepless nights this winter. There were not only the wages for the yard to be met, but also those for his estate at Boscabel. When he had bought the land and house it had been deserted and neglected for years. It had taken all his spare cash to renovate the property so that it was fit for his wife and four children to inhabit. At eighty acres, the estate was by no means vast, but three fields had been ploughed for crops and another two cleared of weeds and brambles for grazing. A cook, two general maids and a nursery maid worked in the house, and seven estate workers lived in three tied cottages. If the Admiralty did not pay him by Midsummer's Day for the work completed on the new cutter, he could not meet the next quarter's wages. Forty shipwrights and carpenters and ten apprentices now worked at the yard, and Adam feared he would have to raise another bank loan to meet his obligations.

He pushed his worries aside. He was an optimist and believed that the money would arrive. To any outsider the yard looked prosperous. It had been established fifty years ago and in those days had built fishing luggers. Now it was one of the largest in the county. There was a sawpit, a forge, three carpentry sheds, and for the welfare and benefit of his workers, a kiddley that doubled as an alehouse and general store. His father, Edward Loveday, had seen a greater vision for the yard and had faith in the designs Adam had shown him. In recent years they had built brigantines, cutters and now the three-masted merchantmen. More shipwrights had been employed and these lived in a score of cottages that had been built for them to rent. Also under Edward's ownership a dry dock had been built, and a schoolhouse for the children. There was also a grander residence, Mariner's House, where Adam had lived in the first years of his marriage and which was now the home of the overseer, Ben Mumford, and his family.

'Ahoy there!'

A shout from the river drew Adam's attention and he saw a mast appear through the branches of the trees on the bend of the river. Curious, he walked down to the landing stage and was startled to recognise *Sea Mist*, her mainmast shattered. Any misgivings he felt that Harry Sawle would be demanding her repair were dispelled at seeing a middle-aged naval lieutenant standing on deck. The officer leaned heavily on a walking cane. Beneath his naval wig and bicorn hat, his florid features had been distorted by a seizure, and his stout figure was easily recognisable. Adam had met Lieutenant Shaver on previous occasions. He had no great liking for the man, who was conceited and arrogant.

The officer gripped the shoulder of a young sailor with a fleshy hand as he walked precariously down the gangplank, one leg dragging. In the seven months since Adam had last seen him, the man had swollen in girth and his eyes were bulging and rheumy. His voice was slurred as he answered Adam's greeting.

'*Sea Mist* was apprehended two nights ago and was damaged in our pursuit,' he informed Adam. 'She was carrying contraband and has been confiscated. Once repaired, she will be put into service against those who continue to flout the law.'

Adam appraised the cutter; even without a closer inspection, he could see that the damage was extensive. Half the decking and ship's rails would also have to be repaired, as well as the mast. 'If you want the work done at once, it will mean we cannot continue with the new ship.'

'In the circumstances, that would be an agreeable solution.'

Adam was alerted by something in the officer's voice. 'What circumstances?'

Shaver shifted his weight and glanced around the yard. 'Do you not offer me a seat, Loveday? I find it painful to stand.'

'My pardon, Lieutenant. Join me for refreshments in my office and we can discuss this matter in comfort.' Adam knew evasion when he heard it, but chose not to press the point at this moment. The repairs would be welcome extra work for the yard.

He slowed his pace to the officer's unsteady gait. Shaver leaned heavily on the sailor and his walking cane, and wheezed: 'How soon before the cutter can be repaired and patrol our waters?'

'I cannot say without a full inspection, but it could be two months.'

'So long! I thought your yard more competent.'

'My yard's reputation lies in the quality of our work. I will not compromise on that.' Adam opened the door of the whitewashed single-roomed office and stood aside for Shaver to enter.

The office held a desk, two wooden chairs, and a leather armchair by the fireplace. A large chest of drawers contained the plans of the ships previously built in the yard, leatherbound ledgers and order books, and also small wooden models of the ships Adam had designed. There were also paintings done by either a local artist or Adam himself of every ship of significance built by his family. The paintings were a visual record to impress new customers. Shaver did not even glance at them.

The officer shuffled to the comfortable armchair before the hearth and sat down with a sigh. The sailor was dismissed and Shaver snapped at Adam: 'Send a full report and costing to Plymouth. It is necessary for you to start work immediately.'

Adam took exception to Shaver's tone. His dealings with the officer in the past had always been confrontational. He curbed his sliding temper

11

and poured the lieutenant a glass of brandy from a decanter on a side table, but abstained himself. It was too early in the day to take alcohol and he wanted a clear head when dealing with this man. Shaver might appear to be past his prime, his body swollen and decrepit, but he could sway any future dealings with the revenue or the Admiralty.

'When was the cutter apprehended? Who was aboard her?'

'Two nights ago. The contraband of brandy and tobacco is stored in the customs house at Plymouth with a double guard to ensure it is not stolen. A dozen men were on board. Three were killed and five wounded when they resisted our boarding. The crew were taken in chains to Bodmin. Who is the cutter's owner? Is it the arch-smuggler Harry Sawle?'

'Sawle commissioned her as a merchant ship.' Adam had remaind standing, and looked down at the officer from his six-foot height. He swept a hand through his dark hair, held back at the nape of his neck with a black ribbon.

'She was always intended for smuggling!' Shaver erupted. 'You are as guilty as those knaves for building her. No decent man would have dealings with such vermin.'

'I build ships, not act as judge on a man's character.' Adam hooked his thumbs into the waistband of his breeches. 'Sawle paid his dues on time. I am owed money for the construction already done on the new cutter. Until I am paid what is owed on her, no further work will continue on either vessel. And when I submit my costing for *Sea Mist*, I expect to be paid half on commencement and the balance before she leaves the yard.'

'You always were an upstart, Loveday.' Shaver's jowls turned an apoplectic puce. 'You cannot hold the revenue office to account in this manner. We are at war with France. It is your patriotic duty—'

'My duty is to meet the wages of my shipwrights and carpenters, or their families will starve.' Adam cut across his bluster, angry that the service would see him bankrupt rather than honour their contract. 'If you do not agree to my terms, then the repairs must be done by another yard, and that work will be inferior. *Sea Mist* is a fine ship. She was launched hardly more than a year past. Her rigging was specially designed. Another yard has not the knowledge to re-rig her so that she maintains her speed.'

'The work must start at once,' Shaver sprayed spittle in his agitation and helped himself to a second brandy. His belligerence was worse than Adam remembered, and his own pride rebelled at the man's pompous attitude.

'Not without payment and a signed contract,' he returned. 'To speed matters you can return to Plymouth with my costing. My inspection and report should be ready in about two hours. I have all the figures for the materials to hand. I will then have some men row you and your crew back to Fowey, where you can take ship to Plymouth.'

'It does not do to hold a government office to ransom, Loveday.' Shaver glared, his eyes narrowing with disdain as he studied the younger man. His lips set into a sneer as he took in Adam's lean figure and the gold ring in his ear. 'You always did look more like a pirate than a naval officer.'

Adam raised a brow, more amused than ruffled by the snide comment. Shaver's uniform was splattered with sea spray, the gold braid tarnished and the white of his waistcoat stained with brown flecks of snuff. Adam was aware that he himself had come to the yard to work, and although his dark green jacket was of the finest cut and cloth, it was not in the latest cutaway mode. Beneath it he wore a long brown leather waist-coat and black breeches and riding boots.

'I will inspect *Sea Mist* now and will send Pru Jensen to you from the kiddley. She will provide you with any refreshments you require. I recommend her pasties; they cannot be beaten. Your men can spend the time in the kiddley if you wish to take my report back with you.'

'Aye, since time is of the essence I shall partake of Mrs Jensen's fine pasties. But I want your word that the work will begin at once.' Shaver poured himself another brandy and did not meet Adam's gaze.

There was something about the officer's manner that made Adam uneasy. His belligerence was offensive. And since *Sea Mist* was the fleetest of the smuggling vessels that had plied these waters, why was there such a rush for the repairs?

'The work will begin as soon as the payment due on the new cutter is received, along with half the cost of the repair work.' Adam refused to back down. He had an uncomfortable feeling that the Admiralty would use the excuse of the war to cancel the order for the cutter. With *Sea Mist* in their possession, they would have another ship to patrol the coastal waters.

The feeling persisted whilst he surveyed the cutter and made a list of the work required. Fortunately there had been little damage below the main deck other than replacing some panelling. He returned to his desk and wrote up his report and costing while Shaver held a stony silence and ate a meal of two pasties and half a roast chicken washed down with three quarts of ale. Half an hour later Adam sanded the parchment and held it out to Shaver. The lieutenant scanned it and his lips tightened at the total cost.

'Is this the best price you can offer?'

'There is no great profit in it for me. For the cost of these repairs the revenue office will have procured one of the fastest ships in these waters for a fraction of its original price a year ago.'

Shaver heaved himself to his feet. 'Summon Seaman Jones to help me back to the landing stage and have us rowed to Fowey.' He did not address another word to Adam as he boarded the yard's dinghy.

Adam called Ben Mumford to his office. The overseer wiped the worst of the mud from his work boots as he entered. In his fifties, Mumford was two decades older than Adam, and Adam valued his advice and experience.

'Did the Admiralty pay what was owed?' Mumford enquired, rubbing a sheen of sweat from his bald head. 'We'll be stretched to continue work on the cutter and the merchantman if *Sea Mist* is to be repaired. And that bain't a job that will do us any service. There were rumours this morning afore she arrived that she'd been taken by the preventive office. Sawle bain't gonna like that. Sooner she be out of this yard the better.'

'I agree, but we do not work on either cutter until we are paid for both the work done and half the cost of the repairs. And I have an uncomfortable feeling about the urgency they are insisting upon.'

'Do you think they mean to renege on the other cutter, Cap'n Loveday?' Mumford used the courtesy title given to Adam from his days of captaining his own brigantine, *Pegasus*, which had been built by the yard. 'The contract be binding.' He was outraged.

'We shall see what payment arrives at the end of the week.'

The door opened and Adam's wife walked in, her expression drawn with worry. She had accompanied Adam to the yard and gone immediately to the room set aside for anyone needing the herbal remedies she had learned from her gypsy grandmother. A group of women from the yard and nearby villages had been waiting for her attention.

'What has happened to *Sea Mist*? You are not doing work on her for Sawle, are you?' Senara's voice shook with the depth of her concern. 'He will bring trouble to us if you have dealings with him.'

'She has been confiscated by the excise office. They are paying for her repair.' Adam went to his wife's side. 'Sawle is not involved.'

'How can he not be involved? It is his ship.'

'I cannot refuse to repair her.' Adam was resolute.

Ben Mumford excused himself, and once the couple were alone, Senara voiced her fears. 'Adam, I have a bad feeling about this.'

Adam held up his hand to halt her words. 'My love, I do not need to hear one of your premonitions. They have been proved right too often. I need the goodwill of the Admiralty and the revenue service to honour their contracts.'

She paced to the window to stare at the smuggler's cutter. Her voice was ragged when she spoke. 'Harry Sawle will be furious his ship has been impounded, and if you repair her for the excise men he will take that as a strike against him. It is not wise to cross him over this. There is enough bad blood between you.'

'I do not fear Sawle.' Adam ignored her words of warning. 'He hates us. And I have vowed to bring him to justice for my father's death and the attack on my cousin Peter last year. Sawle has stayed away from Cornwall until now. If this incident brings our feud to a head, then so be it. It is long overdue. And I do not fight him alone. My family will support me.'

He came to her side and turned her towards him and held her in his arms. 'We have right on our side.'

'Sawle believes the same.' She put her hands on his chest, her eyes wide and beseeching as she gazed into his handsome face. She shuddered as though a ghost had walked over her grave.

'If your twin and cousins were here, they would collaborate with you to bring your enemy to justice, but St John is in London with Felicity. She would not take kindly to cutting short their planned stay to place your twin's life in danger. Uncle Joshua would not shirk a fight, but he is no longer young and should be upholding law and order, not pursuing a vendetta. How can he preach from the pulpit the Christian ethic of turn the other cheek and love thy fellow man, and then take up arms? For that is what it will come to.'

Adam cupped her face in his hands and stroked her rich brown hair. Despite bearing him twins and two other children, she was still as slender and lovely as the day he had met her. He kissed her nose. 'You worry too much.'

'And you are not invincible, my love. Where is your family at this moment to support you? Your cousin Peter is a parson, and he also has a wife and a baby to provide for. Unlike his brother Japhet he is no swordsman. And Japhet cannot help you from Botany Bay. Please reconsider taking on these repairs.'

'I have given my word.'

She laid her head on his chest and closed her eyes to combat her rush of fear. If Adam had given his word, he would not break it. It was a matter of honour.

'Peter was attacked and left for dead by Sawle's henchmen,' Adam reminded her gently. 'Those men must be brought to justice.'

15

'Your family's hot blood can be a curse.' In her fear, Senara lost her usual calm and her voice rose. 'It has made pioneers and adventurers of your ancestors. No one disputes their courage. But Harry Sawle is not going to wait until your family are here to support you. He will strike when you are most vulnerable.'

'I do not see that I have any choice.' Clearly Adam's mind was made up, and he went on without hesitation. '*Sea Mist* must be repaired whatever happens. Sawle is capable of trying to steal her back, but the work will take several weeks. A damaged ship is no good to him. He knows we are the best yard to repair her. By the time the cutter is seaworthy, St John will be back at Trevowan.'

Senara was not convinced. 'If that ship is repaired and impounded, Sawle will not rest until either you or he are dead. Nothing is worth that risk.'

Chapter Three

The news of the capture of *Sea Mist* ran like quicksilver through the local community. The law-abiding nodded in satisfaction that evidence had finally been found to hang one of Cornwall's most notorious smugglers. Harry Sawle might not have been on board, but as the owner of the vessel he was responsible for the cargo she carried. For more than a decade Sawle had ruled the district with terror, his cut-throat henchmen dealing out brutish retribution to any who crossed him. He was universally hated and feared. No one would celebrate or refrain from jumping at shadows until the smuggler leader was arrested and dancing at the end of a rope.

The families of *Sea Mist*'s crew were not so jubilant. They feared for the lives of their menfolk. For generations free-trading had been a way of life to the coastal villages. Taxes on tea, tobacco and brandy were extortionate. What harm did running such a cargo do, aside from providing a little comfort to those who would otherwise be unable to afford such pleasures?

Sawle had been in a different league to the smaller smuggling bands doing the occasional run. He made his fortune by landing silks, lace and exotic spices as well as the more common contraband, but each year he became greedier for higher profits, which resulted in greater risks for his men.

With the crew of *Sea Mist* arrested, many wives and children would face starvation next winter without a bread-winner to provide for them. The villagers of Penruan, the fishing village where Harry Sawle had been born and raised, and where his brother and mother still lived, feared not justice but reprisal from the smuggler. No one even remotely connected with Harry Sawle would sleep easily in their beds. Fortunately, none of the local fishermen had been part of *Sea Mist*'s crew on the night she was taken. The men of Penruan, Trewenna and Polruggan used by Sawle had been ordered to act as tubmen to help bring the goods ashore and get them away on the pack ponies or carts. They had seen *Challenger* laying in wait offshore when they arrived at the cove and had remained hidden, watching the sea battle from a distance. The capture of *Sea Mist* had been a severe blow. Fishing and labouring work had been scarce through the winter and spring, and their families were gaunt and hungry. After their relief at escaping arrest by the preventive officers, the tubmen's mood turned to resentment that another night's wages had been lost. And some of that anger was directed at Adam Loveday and his family.

Living on their large estates and in their grand houses, what did Adam and St John Loveday know of poverty and hardship? Before *Challenger* had been built there had been regular work for the tubmen, and their families had thrived.

As their stomachs growled with hunger and they returned to their cottages to hear their children grizzling from lack of food, they forgot that many of them had been given work by the Loveday family throughout last summer and harvest. And that Senara had nursed their children through sickness without payment for her time or the healing herbs she had picked and prepared. With no money to pay for a physician, some of those children would have died. Many villagers also lived in cottages owned by the Lovedays. When the rent could not be paid, no one had been turned out into the street as happened with other landlords.

Adam, St John and their cousin, the widow Hannah Rabson, who ran her late husband's farm, had all donated flour and vegetables to the villages of Penruan, Trewenna, Polruggan and Polmasryn when the weather had been bitterly cold. These villages comprised the parishes of father and son the Reverend Joshua and Parson Peter Loveday, and their wives had baked bread and made soup for the needy of the community. The villagers accepted charity as a bitter pill to swallow. They might be poor, but they were proud. Working for Sawle had enabled them to hold their heads high and provide for their families.

On hearing of the confiscation of the cutter, only one woman shed a tear. Sal Sawle had long despaired of her second son. Her love for him had been stifled by his acts of cruelty and violence, but no mother could rejoice in a child's downfall. Harry was too like his father. Reuban Sawle had been vicious and evil in his later years, when he had organised the local smuggler gangs, and he had died unlamented by his family and the community.

In the kitchen of the Dolphin Inn, run by Sal's oldest son, Clem, Clem's wife Keziah saw her mother-in-law wipe her eyes. She stopped scrubbing the floor, threw the brush into the bucket of soapy water and stood up to put her arms around her.

'No good will come of this day, Kezzie,' Sal moaned.

'You must not take on so, Ma. Mayhap now he's lost the ship, Harry will see the error of his ways and give up the trade.'

Sal gave a sigh that was dragged up from her stout boots. 'That devil will never give up. This will make him mad for vengeance. Bain't he brought enough shame upon us?'

'There's a warrant out for his arrest. If he has any sense he will stay away from Cornwall,' Keziah reassured her. But even she did not believe that.

Sal moved away from Keziah, embarrassed by the show of affection. She had received so little of it in her life. She flopped down on to a wooden kitchen chair and stared at her amber-haired daughter-in-law. 'Harry be my shame. He should have died at birth for all the pain he's brought to these parts.'

'But you have Clem and Mark to be proud of. Clem has given up the fishing to run this inn. It thrived when you were younger. This is your pride as well.'

'Clem and Mark are good men,' Sal agreed. 'But I had my share of bad 'uns. Especially that daughter of mine. I used to be so proud of her before she tricked St John Loveday into marriage by getting herself with his child. Rowena was the only good thing to come out of that ill-fated union.'

'Come on, Ma, don't you be upsetting yourself over all that. Let the dead rest in peace. And Harry knew the risks when he took up the trade. He's lost his ship but he's managed to keep his freedom.'

'But for how long? This is the proof the authorities needed to bring him to trial.' Sal sighed and sank her head into her hands.

'Then he should stay away from here.' Keziah tossed back the long corkscrew curls of her hair, a fierce light in her eyes. She had no time for her brother-in-law and his life of crime. In her opinion, if you broke the law then you took the consequences. She was a large-boned woman with strong principles. As well as the inn, she and Clem had a cottage high on the side of the coombe where they lived. Clem had given up smuggling when they married and concentrated on fishing. When he took over the inn he rented his boat to a man in the village. Keziah also kept a herd of goats and was famous for the cheese she made and sold in local shops and markets. Sal lived with them, looking after their young son Zach when Clem and Keziah were working in the inn of an evening. Keziah had refused to marry Clem until he had given up his involvement with the smugglers. She thanked God every day that he had never fallen from grace.

'I fear what Harry will do when he learns his ship has been taken,' Sal moaned. 'There'll be no reasoning with him. I thought when you and Clem took over the inn that things would change and the Sawles could be respectable again.'

'We be respectable now, Ma. People know that. As for Harry . . .' Keziah shrugged and her voice became harsh. 'He made his choices. He wanted power and he wanted easy riches and he didn't care who got hurt in the process. He made his bed and now he must lie on it.'

'He stayed away 'cos it suited him.' Sal's voice cracked with pain. 'St John Loveday put a price on his head with a warrant for his arrest. He'll exact punishment for that. He won't let it rest. And what of us? Harry saw the Dolphin as his. There'll be a reckoning with Clem for taking over when Harry's man were arrested for storing contraband in the cellar.'

'Mordecai Nance were hanged for his crimes, which included murder.' Keziah returned to scrubbing the flagstones, the water splashing up the sides of the Cornish range in her agitation. 'His no-good wife turned the Dolphin into a bawdy house and she had a cache of trinkets stolen from the villagers in the cellar. She's now on the high seas bound for Botany Bay.'

'Harry were behind their crimes. How many more lives will he destroy?' For the old woman to speak of her pain showed her distress. Usually Sal kept her condemnation of Harry's exploits to herself, maintaining a silent dignity on the subject.

Keziah sighed. Sal had changed in the months Harry had been away. She had put on weight and her apple cheeks were rosy with health. She took more pride in her appearance: her grey hair was scraped back under a white linen cap and she wore a new brown skirt and bodice. 'The inn were yours, Ma. Harry never helped with the running of it. You gave it to Clem. He be the eldest and that be your right. Harry brought the Dolphin to disrepute,' she added. 'In the six months Clem has been in charge, it no longer has an unsavoury reputation. We even take in two lodgers now, and carters stop overnight to break long journeys.'

Sal patted her hand. 'That be as much down to you. You've been the saviour of my Clem, or he would've gone the same way as Harry. And you've made the inn a homely, welcoming place again. It could never be that in Reuban's day. That husband of mine were a miserable bugger without a kind word for anyone.'

'Don't fret, Ma.' Keziah picked up her wooden bucket and threw the dirty water out into the inn yard. 'Clem is more than a match for his brother.'

Although Adam had made light of his wife's words of warning concerning *Sea Mist*, the presence of the cutter loomed ominously over the yard. Finishing his paperwork in the office for the day, he placed the ledgers and work inventories in their drawers. As he closed the door behind him, his gaze lifted to the ship moored by the landing stage. He was proud of all the vessels they had built, but this one had never sat easily with him and now she was back. Would he and his family ever be free of Harry Sawle's malevolent spectre?

It troubled him that he had agreed to build the cutter for Sawle in the first place. His father had been shot by excise men when Sawle had stored contraband on Loveday land. Edward Loveday had later died from his wounds, and Sawle had then wanted a cutter to rival the speed of the excise ship built in this yard. Adam should have told the smuggler to go to the devil, but the yard was in dire financial straits, and losing the family business would have been a greater betrayal of Edward Loveday's memory than taking Sawle's money to save it.

Adam frowned as the mist rolled up the river on the afternoon tide. Sawle had become his nemesis in recent years. As youths there had always been antagonism between them. Harry had resented Adam and St John's wealth and status in society. When his father had begun to drink to excess and became incapable of running the smuggling gang he had organised from the Dolphin Inn, Harry had taken over. He had increased the number of men who worked for him and made more landings on beaches all over Cornwall. Like Reuban, he ruled by brutality and fear.

Their lives had become interlinked when Adam and St John had vied for the attentions of Sawle's beautiful younger sister Meriel. Adam had succumbed to the temptress's charms whilst on leave from the navy. He had been recalled to duty, and when he returned home several months later it was to discover St John married to a pregnant Meriel, their marriage forced on him at gunpoint by Sawle. Determined to one day be mistress of Trevowan, Meriel had seduced St John, who had been weak and easily manipulated. When his allowance did not stretch far enough to buy Meriel the jewels and fine gowns she demanded, he had joined Sawle in his smuggling ventures, with disastrous consequences.

The memory of those troubled days still roused Adam's anger. Sawle had exploited St John, and his brother had been arrested for the murder of a rival gang leader. Fortunately St John had been found innocent. It was obvious to Adam that Sawle had killed the man and would have let St John hang for his crime had he been convicted. Not content that her greed had almost been the death of her husband, Meriel remained dissatisfied that the riches she wanted from life eluded her, and had compounded Harry Sawle's betrayal with her own. When her beauty attracted the Earl of Wycham, she abandoned her daughter and husband and ran off with him, leaving St John to face the shame and ridicule of a cuckold. Later deserted by Wycham and diseased from her short time as a courtesan, Meriel returned to Trevowan rather than die on the streets.

Even in death, however, she added fuel to the vendetta between the two families. St John had been absent from Trevowan on her return and she had been buried in the family vault. On his homecoming he was furious that his treacherous wife had been laid to rest with their ancestors, and had her body removed and interred with members of her own family. Sawle had seen that as a further insult, and his hatred for the Lovedays intensified. He had attacked all of them by any means in his power, but had always managed to escape justice.

Adam knew that while Harry lived there would be retribution. The capture of *Sea Mist* and her arrival here would bring matters to a head. Aware that his family were in danger, he intended to place guards at night in the yard and on his estate.

His mood remained introspective as his gaze travelled over the yard, where the shipwrights and carpenters were packing away their tools for the night. He moved towards the merchant ship, his experienced eye studying the work carried out that week. He loved the familiar smells that came from her hull: the scent of freshly cut timber, and pitch and rope from her caulked planks. She rose majestically from her supporting cradle, pulleys in place to raise the timber over her sides for the decking and partitions. There was a part of him that ached to sail on her maiden voyage to the far ends of the oceans. He had never lost his love for the sea and the adventure it had brought him.

After leaving the navy, he had captained *Pegasus*, the first ship designed by him that had been built in the yard. In those days he had worked as an agent for the government, sailing to France in the early days of the Revolution. He had rescued aristocrats fleeing for their lives and brought them safely to England, and had fought several sea battles against the French. That war was still going on. If he had stayed in the navy, he would be in the thick of it, fighting with Nelson at Cadiz and the Battle of the Nile. The fact that Nelson had lost his arm two years earlier in the battle to secure the island of Tenerife only added to Adam's respect for the English commander.

News of the victories of the courageous admiral fired his blood, and there had been momentary regret that he had not been a part of them. But the shipyard had a stronger hold over him, and once he had married Senara, he had been loath to spend years at sea away from her. He was the father of four children, two boys and two girls, a family any man would be proud of. He had great hopes for the boys. Nathan, at six the eldest, was already asking to accompany him to the yard, and loved to hear stories of his adventures at sea. Joel had a wilder streak that often reminded Adam of the boy's uncle Japhet. That gave him some misgivings. Japhet was the black sheep of the family – a lovable, charming rogue, a crack shot and an expert swordsman. Their buccaneering great-grandfather would have idolised him, but Japhet had been governed by the wildness of his blood rather than by wisdom, and had paid the price with his arrest and trial for highway robbery. Yet Japhet had more than his share of the Loveday charm and luck. He had been pardoned, and from his letters was prospering in his new life on the other side of the world.

Adam hoped that Joel would have the wisdom to temper the wild streak in his blood and that fortune would always bless him. As to his daughters, Rhianne was an angel in comparison with her twin, while the toddler Sara seemed to have inherited the gypsy beauty of her mother, although she was showing a headstrong need to compete with her older siblings. Adam smiled at memories of nursery battles in his home. Whatever the future of his children, it would not be without adventure; they were all too feisty to be satisfied with a conventional life.

Thoughts of his children roused his protective instincts. For their future to be safe and secure, Sawle had to be dealt with. It was as well that *Sea Mist*'s capture would bring things to a head.

Adam knew how Sawle's mind worked. The smuggler was ruthless, brutal and without mercy. For himself Adam felt no fear, but his family were his Achilles heel. His courage was a match for anything Sawle could throw at him, and though justice would make him see this vendetta through to the bitter and if necessary bloody end, he had inherited his father's wisdom and patience. To triumph over Sawle they would have to plan carefully and keep one step ahead of him.

His eyes narrowed as his stare returned to the damaged cutter. What would Sawle do once he learned of its capture? How would he react? Where and when would he show his hand? Of one thing he could be certain. It would not be long before Harry Sawle returned to Cornwall, plotting his revenge on all who had crossed him.

It was another week before Harry Sawle learned the fate of his ship. He was drinking in a pub in St Peter Port in Guernsey. The island was a favoured haven for importing French brandy, and many agents for the English smugglers sailed their cargoes from there. Harry had been a frequent visitor in recent months, for Guernsey was also a haven from British taxation and a number of wealthy merchants from London had retired there.

Harry's success as a smuggler was due largely to the speed of *Sea Mist*. Her sister ship, which was owned by his Guernsey agent, had also been built in the Loveday yard. But success bred jealousy amongst other free-traders, and when the bearded captain Simeon le Grand strode into the tavern and heard Sawle boasting of his expertise, he roared with laughter.

'You are not so clever, Englishman. I hear that the preventive men took your fine ship *Sea Mist*. Ha! Ha! You boast in vain.'

Harry had been drinking heavily and reared to his feet to launch himself at the Frenchman. 'You lying French pig. No ship can take *Sea Mist*.'

'English dog! Why should I lie? Your cargo rots in a custom house and your men moulder in prison. Your fine ship had its mast shot away. She is not so fast now.'

Several other captains drinking in the low-beamed taproom jeered at Harry's misfortune. He was the least popular of the men who frequented the tavern. But they had sensed a fight, and others, eager for entertainment, taunted le Grand.

Le Grand ignored them. He despised Sawle for not captaining his own ship and for paying henchmen to do his dirty work. 'A pox on your scurvy ship and her crew. If the preventive men have her, she will put us all out of business.'

'You lying knave.' Harry lunged at the French captain, who side-stepped, increasing his anger.

'I do not lie!' le Grand bellowed. He was a head taller than Harry and three stone heavier. He had been the most important smuggler in St Peter Port until Sawle arrived, and he hated the Englishman with a passion.

Fury flamed through Harry's blood. No one mocked him. Le Grand was no exception. The sailors' drunken jeering goaded him further. It was time the man learned his place. A dagger secreted in Sawle's sleeve suddenly appeared in his hand, gleaming briefly in the weak candle-light. He pushed against le Grand, then spun on his heel and marched through the sniggering crowd.

'The Englishman has no fight in him,' scoffed a portly sailor. 'He is all hot air.' His words ended in a grunt as the knife embedded itself in his gut, but the other men were too engrossed in their ridicule to notice.

'No one mocks me!' shouted Harry as he left the inn. In moments he had disappeared in the labyrinth of dark alleys along the waterfront, and the jeers in the inn had fallen silent as the large figure of le Grand teetered over backwards to crash to the floor. A four-inch gash in his stomach spilled his guts on to the sawdust.

The second sailor held up a blood-soaked hand that had clutched at his belly. 'The bastard has done for me.' He died moments later as his doxy, heavy with his unborn child, held him in her arms, screaming curses at the Englishman who had fled the inn. The tavern was in uproar.

'Get the bastard!'

'Kill the English pig!'

The sailors bayed for Sawle's blood, but most were too drunk to pursue him, and stumbled against each other, hindering pursuit. The rest had seen too many violent deaths in portside taverns to care.

Sawle ran through the streets and banged on the door of his Guernsey agent. Once inside, he gasped: 'Get me on the first ship bound for Cornwall.'

Chapter Four

The newly married couple, St John and Felicity, were returning from a delayed honeymoon in London. They had been away from Cornwall for four months, staying in St John's stepmother Amelia's London home. Their two children – St John's daughter Rowena, who was ten, and Felicity's six-year-old Charlotte – had accompanied them. The girls, with their blonde hair and blue eyes, could pass for sisters, and despite the difference in their ages they had formed a close bond. Unfortunately, the same could not be said for their parents. The atmosphere in the coach between the adults had been strained.

The journey had taken longer than usual, with far more stops than St John had planned. London had presented him with the temptation to follow his passion for gaming. Felicity did not approve of such pursuits, especially when he indulged in them to great excess with little success and his debts mounted. St John was not a man to stifle the fire that consumed him when playing at cards or dice. He had been too long denied the pleasures of the tables after inheriting Trevowan and the failure of the first harvest. He had chosen Felicity as his bride because she was wealthy, pretty and, he had thought, easy to control.

Felicity had married St John for love and in the belief that he would honour his vow to reform. She had known him for many years, and had fallen long ago for his dark, handsome looks. She had begun to hope that her interest in him was reciprocated. Then the scheming Meriel Sawle had set her cap at him and St John had been seduced into a disastrous marriage. On the rebound from her unrequited love, Felicity had married a naval captain, Charles Barrett, and had been miserable. He was a wastrel, a gambler, violent and abusive. She had not mourned him when he died during a battle with the French fleet. Then, after Meriel's death, she had met St John again and realised that she still found him irresistible. In the intervening years she had heard of his reputation for drinking and hard gaming, traits she deplored. She had no intention of marrying a wastrel. During the next months, however, St John changed his ways, and she accepted his proposal.

The first time he had abandoned her to spend the night at the gaming tables they had been married but a month. He had lost two hundred guineas and had returned to her bed intoxicated. Appalled that her worst fears had been realised, she had quarrelled with him all night. There had been a frostiness to their marriage ever since. She hoped that now they were returning to Cornwall, matters would improve. She was wretched and did not want a loveless marriage.

The journey from London had been made bearable for Felicity because Amelia and her son Rafe accompanied them. At nearly seven, Rafe had little patience with the two giggling girls. Rowena, who adored him, did not like him being left out and tried to include him in any game, but Charlotte resented her new friend's attention being given to another and would sulk if she was ignored.

Amelia usually spent six months of the year in London, but she had declared that this would be her last visit for some time. A governess had been interviewed in London and would be at Trevowan in a few weeks to educate the children in their home. Since the death of her youngest child, Joan, Amelia could not bear the thought of sending Rafe away to school. She also missed her eldest child, Richard Allbright, who had been at sea as a midshipman for two years. The continuing war with France meant that he would be facing enemy action, and she was alarmed that he might be harmed in some way.

It was late in the afternoon when the coach pulled into the drive of Trevowan. The sky was grey and overcast and the gables of the stone house on the clifftop appeared bleak and forbidding, very different from how Felicity remembered them during St John's courtship. She suppressed a shiver of unease. A bitingly cold wind off the sea whipped the hood of her cloak from her fair hair as she stepped to the ground. She clutched the edges of the fur-trimmed velvet close together as St John marched ahead, barking orders to the servants. The children were squealing with excitement at spotting Bodkin, Rowena's cat, darting into the house, and set off to chase it.

Amelia linked her arm through Felicity's. She frowned in her stepson's direction, clearly annoyed that he had abandoned his wife in such a rude manner.

'St John will be eager to ensure that the house is warm and welcoming for you,' she said, making excuses for him. 'May can be such a damp month.'

Felicity did not answer and kept her head bowed, refusing to show that she was upset.

'You must not take his moods too much to heart,' Amelia stated. 'He is concerned that he has been so long away from the estate. He will be eager to consult Isaac Nance, the bailiff, to ensure that the crops were sown on time and that the livestock produced the lambs and calves anticipated.'

'Nance is experienced in his work, is he not?' Felicity was embarrassed at her husband's neglect, and her voice was clipped with anger. 'He was St John's father's bailiff for a score of years before his death. He knows what needs to be done.'

'But even the most trusted servant is best kept a watchful eye upon.'

The household servants – three maids, a footman and the cook – had assembled hurriedly in the entrance hall to greet the family on their return. Felicity forced a tight smile to conceal her feelings of pain and rejection. Amelia was trying to be kind, but she did not believe her. St John was still angry that she had criticised him.

The plump figure of Winnie Fraddon, the cook, bobbed a curtsey. 'Welcome home, Mrs Loveday. There be refreshments waiting for you in the winter parlour.'

Mulled wine, tea and fresh-baked biscuits were laid out for them, and despite it being May, a fire had been lit against the dampness in the air. St John was nowhere in sight and the children could be heard running along the corridor upstairs. Amelia shook the travel dust from her dress and sighed as she sank on to a padded day bed. There was an attractive colour to her firm cheeks and little grey marbled her luxurious auburn hair.

'It is a relief to be free of a constantly jolting coach. And London is always so hectic. Are you glad to be back in the country, Felicity?'

'I am content with a quiet life. London was a whirlwind of entertainments, which were exhausting at times.' She rubbed her brow, then took her smelling salts from her reticule and leaned her head back on the chair as she inhaled them. 'Long journeys always give me headaches. If you will excuse me, I shall retire to my room.'

Her head was pounding and she wanted time on her own to reassess her emotions and the unsettling change in her husband since their marriage. Surrounded by the Loveday cousins in London and the perpetual plays, soirées, dinner parties and dances they had attended, there had been little time to spend a peaceful moment alone. Trevowan would be equally demanding of her time and energy. And once word reached the other members of the family, there would be a stream of visitors eager for news of the relatives in London and the sights they had seen in the capital. She would need all her strength to paint on a smile and pretend that her short marriage was blissfully happy. At present she did not have the energy to even contemplate a reunion with the vibrant personalities of the Loveday family.

But there was not to be a reprieve. Before she could rise from the couch, the strident thud of a walking cane on the approach to the winter parlour warned her of the arrival of Elspeth Loveday.

'So you have returned!' St John's spinster aunt declared by way of a greeting. 'You missed some fine hunting. Where is that nephew of mine?'

'St John is closeted with Nance, I believe,' Amelia remarked.

'Glad to hear he is throwing himself back into work.' Elspeth limped to a chair and her piercing eyes regarded the two younger women over the top of her pince-nez. Her long days in the saddle had left her without any spare flesh on her slim figure. She was wearing a new dark blue riding habit, and her grey hair was pulled back and hidden under a black lace headdress.

'You look tired, Elspeth,' Amelia observed. She had always been in awe of this woman. At sixty, her sister-in-law could wither another's self-esteem with a single comment. 'Should you ride so often? It looks as though your hip is paining you.'

'The day I stop riding they can seal me in my coffin,' snorted the matriarch. 'Senara's balm eases the pain. It always has. You look pale as a cod's head, Felicity. Did life in London not agree with you? Can't abide the place myself. Too many preening fops and no decent place to ride. Rotten Row is a social parade ground.'

'The journey was tiring.' Felicity found the stare of St John's aunt unnerving. There would be no secrets in this closely observed house, and she feared her ridicule.

'Has St John not been caring of your welfare?' Elspeth pounced with uncanny aptitude on the situation between the couple.

'He has been most solicitous,' Felicity said defensively.

Elspeth heard the tremor in her voice and cursed the selfishness of her nephew. Felicity looked close to swooning. Elspeth had no patience with women who fainted away at the least provocation. She had thought Felicity had more mettle.

'Travelling is most vexatious, especially with bickering children.' Amelia poured tea from the silver pot, as Felicity had shown no sign of carrying out her duty as mistress. She handed a cup to the younger woman. 'Drink this, my dear, it will restore your spirits.'

'You have been gently reared, Felicity,' Elspeth declared. 'That is what my nephew needs in a wife. He and Adam missed a refined upbringing. I did my best after their mother died at their birth, but

I was something of a hoyden, or so my father constantly informed me when he was alive. Edward was twenty years a widower. He was busy with the shipyard and the estate. I ran the house, but gave the twins the freedom I would to any young colt. I did not want to break their spirit.' She gave a dry laugh. 'They both learned to take their fences head on without fear. I thought that was all they needed to stand them in good stead. But they can be rather unruly, to the thinking of many of our neighbours. Adam is not received by some of them for marrying beneath his station.'

'You do yourself a disservice, Elspeth,' Amelia replied. 'St John and Adam are not without their sensitivities and have the manners of true gentlemen. St John has chosen well in Felicity.' She smiled. 'As a loving wife, she has the strength to guide him against unwise associations.'

Elspeth sucked in her lips and fixed the younger woman with a forthright stare. 'St John needs his wild blood taming. Amelia will tell you it takes time for a woman of certain sensibilities to feel settled within our family. My advice is to take us as you find us.'

Felicity slept badly, and when she awoke St John had already dressed and left their chamber. He had not come to bed until she had fallen asleep. Her heart was heavy and she put her hand to her mouth to stifle a feeling of nausea. To take her mind from her unhappiness, she attended to the letters that had been delivered in her absence. There were two from her mother. Sophia Quinton was impatient to visit her and hear all the news from London. Two others were further well wishes from friends who had been unable to attend the wedding. Felicity put her mother's letters aside. Sophia could be overbearing at times.

After luncheon she broached the subject of her mother visiting them to St John, who was reading the *Sherborne Mercury* in the orangery. Amelia and Elspeth were also reading.

He scowled. 'Am I not surrounded by twittering women as it is? I get no peace from their demands. Elspeth wants the roof of the stables re-thatched as it has leaked all winter. That is a vast expense. And Amelia expects me to buy our own coach and horses.'

Felicity glanced at the formidable aunt, who was studying her nephew. Elspeth declared sharply, 'If the thatch is not repaired the timbers will go rotten, then you will have an even greater expense on your hands.'

'But we have a coach,' Felicity objected.

'It is Amelia's.' His manner became sullen at her indignation. 'When the harvest failed I needed to sell it and the horses to meet wages and the creditors' bills. She paid me the money from her income from her London properties. She rarely rides and uses it frequently.'

'But you are welcome to use it whenever you need to,' Amelia was quick to reassure.

'You have always been generous, but there will be times when that will inconvenience you, Stepmama. We need a carriage of our own.' St John folded the news-sheet and put it aside in preparation for leaving the room.

'Had I know that, I would never have given Mama my carriage and horses.' Felicity was aghast.

'Then tell her you need it back,' St John snapped.

'That would upset Mama. And how would she be able to visit us? We would have to send a carriage for her journey.'

St John's eyes narrowed. 'There is nothing so unattractive as a person who is mean with their money. You have ample income to provide us with a carriage, do you not? If you do not wish for such an expenditure, then if Amelia is using the carriage to visit her friends, we will ride on horseback.'

'But Charlotte cannot ride far!' Her lips set into a mutinous line that St John found distasteful.

He shrugged and stood up. 'I am riding to Trewenna to discuss a legal matter with my uncle. I shall not be back until this evening.' He marched from the room without asking her to join him.

Felicity felt tears sting her eyes and hastily brushed them aside. She did not understand what she had done to make her husband change so drastically in his attitude towards her.

Amelia was distressed by the harsh exchange of words. She hated dissension, and in the last month there had been an increasing coldness between the couple. 'You are, of course, welcome to use the coach whenever you wish, my dear. You must not mind St John. The debts on the estate have been a great source of worry to him. He is generous by nature and would want you to have the best of everything.'

'But I do not have an unlimited income,' Felicity admitted. 'We spoke about renovating some of the rooms and paying for a governess for the children, but expenses such as a carriage will soon deplete my late husband's savings.'

'I thought you had a fortune at your disposal,' Amelia said with surprise.

The colour drained from Felicity's already pale features. 'In Truro I could keep my daughter and myself in some modest style. But two thousand pounds will not last for ever.'

Elspeth cleared her throat and for once seemed to be carefully weighing her words before she spoke. 'Does St John know the extent of your fortune? From something he said earlier, he seems to be under the impression that it is two thousand a year.'

'Then there has been a very grave misunderstanding.' Felicity stood up, her eyes glittering with fury. 'Two thousand pounds is no little fortune. To even think that I was in possession of two thousand a year is absurd. My late husband inherited some money, but he was a naval captain, not a landowner. Such money if used and invested wisely will keep us in comfort and help to return Trevowan to its former glory.' Her whole body trembled as she expressed her emotion. 'But St John was never interested in my money. He told me he married me for love.'

'I am sure that he did, my dear,' Amelia hastily assured her. 'But he must be told the truth at once. It could seriously change his plans for the work needed on the house and investment in the estate.'

'We are due to travel to Truro next week to visit my banker.' There was now a steely edge to Felicity's voice. 'He will be informed of my financial status then.' She left the room rather hurriedly and Elspeth watched her with a frown.

'St John must be told,' she announced. 'He won't like this, but he must curb his expenditure at once. What possessed him to spend so long in London? The cost of the honeymoon must have been crippling.'

She hobbled from the room and accosted St John in the hall before he left. Amelia held her breath at the angry sound of raised voices that soon came from his study. Moments later the side door leading to the stables banged shut as St John stormed from the house.

Chapter Five

St John rode from Trevowan with a devil on his shoulder. Anger formed a red mist around him and he gave the gelding its head as he left the road to Trewenna and took off across the moor. He rode for an hour, the wind whipping his face and flecks of foam from the horse's neck splattering his breeches, until the gelding finally slowed and stopped to drink at a stream. St John flung himself on to the heather and glared at the sky.

'Why does fate continue to mock me?' he shouted, shaking a fist at the scudding clouds. 'What use is this wife to me now? Damn her, I thought her rich.'

His mind whirled with angry thoughts and the injustices of life. He had wed Felicity with the intention of restoring Trevowan to greatness. He had been tricked. Though she was hardly a pauper, two thousand pounds was well short of the fortune he had been led to believe would be his on their marriage. He had been too hasty in his choice and now he was stuck with a bride he did not love and who had no money to provide him with a life of ease and gambling. And Felicity had shown herself to be far from the compliant bride, amenable to all his wishes. Beneath that sweet smile was a backbone of steel. His first wife had been a shrew. He would not tolerate another.

He felt in his pocket for his hip flask and cursed to find that he had left it at home. Without even a drink of brandy to soothe his mood, his thoughts soured. He did not want to return to Trevowan. The place was filled with women demanding his time and attention. He could visit friends, but when he rose from the ground to remount, he saw that his breeches and jacket were soiled from his hard ride and were unfit to pay a social call.

The lack of expected wealth from his bride turned his mind to other financial matters. There was still the inheritance from Uncle William, which could yield a tidy sum. Uncle Joshua was executor of William

Loveday's will. He might have heard from the lawyer that the money had been released whilst St John had been in London. William Loveday had drowned three summers ago, and his wife, Lisette, had disappeared at the same time, though her body had never been found. It had meant that no money could be released from William's estate until proof was found that his wife no longer lived. Some months ago, evidence had come to light that she had indeed died with her husband.

Before she had wed Uncle William, Lisette had been married to a French marquis who had died in the early days of the Revolution in France. She had brought to England a vast amount of jewellery set with precious stones sewn into her petticoats. These would be worth a great deal. Uncle William had bequeathed his estate to his two brothers, and on Edward's death, St John had become the heir to his share. He would visit Uncle Joshua at Trewenna. The inheritance would help to lessen his disappointment over Felicity's income.

His aunt and uncle lived simply on Joshua's stipend, and employed only one maid, who showed him into the parlour. Aunt Cecily appeared within minutes, her round face alight with pleasure.

'Nephew, we did not expect you back for another week. How was London? Is not dear Felicity with you?' The questions tumbled forth.

'The journey tired my wife,' St John replied evasively.

'The roads can be atrocious and Felicity has a delicate constitution, I believe. I will call on her tomorrow at Trevowan. You must tell me all about London and how your dear aunt Margaret and cousin Thomas fare.'

St John restrained his impatience and replied in a perfunctory manner. 'Everyone was well and London was most enjoyable. Rowena was good with Charlotte, despite the difference in their ages.'

'She needs brothers and sisters,' Cecily remarked. 'It was Felicity's first time in the capital, was it not?'

'It was. I think she found it overbearing at times. The noise takes some getting used to.'

Cecily frowned at the sharpness of his tone, but did not comment. 'Joshua will not be long. He is with the churchwarden. I sent word to him that you are here. Have you seen Adam since your return?'

'No. There has not been time.' He was regretting coming; his aunt's questions were irritating him. 'There was a family matter I wished to discuss with Uncle without delay.'

'I hope you will join us all at Boscabel after church on Sunday, or do you wish us to dine at Trevowan? You do intend to follow your father's tradition of a monthly family gathering, I trust.'

'Of course, but I had not given this week much thought.'

'Then it would be easier for us to dine at Boscabel. Felicity may wish for more time to prepare for her new role as hostess. There are so many in the family now.'

St John found his resentment returning that Adam had taken on many of the roles of their father and that Boscabel was as much a family meeting place as Trevowan. The old rivalry resurfaced. 'Trevowan is the family home. Such meals will take place there now that I am again in residence.'

Cecily sighed. 'This is not a matter where there should be competition between you. I thought you and Adam had put such silliness behind you.'

To St John's relief his uncle called out from the hall and came into the parlour to take his hand in a hearty handshake. 'Welcome back. How is your dear wife?'

'The journey exhausted her. She sends her regards to you both.'

Joshua eyed his nephew's attire. 'You look like you have ridden hard. All is well, I trust?'

'The children did not travel well. The journey took a week. I needed to get out on the moor after so long cramped in a coach.'

Cecily excused herself. 'I will leave you two to talk.'

'Sit yourself, nephew.' Joshua gestured to a chair. 'You look tired and somewhat out of sorts.'

St John was too pent up to sit, and paced the room. The parlour was small and cluttered with heavy, old-fashioned furniture, which impeded his strides. 'Have you heard anything from the lawyer about Uncle William's estate?'

'I had reason to visit Bodmin and called on him a sennight past. But why such haste from you on the subject? Did you incur debts in London? I thought you had put your gaming behind you.'

'I have little joy in my life except my gaming. Why should I curtail it?'

Joshua was taken aback. 'A man but recently wed usually has many joys and blessings. Your words disturb me, nephew. Is your marriage not all you had hoped for?'

'I was misled.' He stopped pacing and punched his fist into his open palm. 'I had it on good authority that Felicity was in possession of a sizeable fortune. That is not the case. There is scarcely enough to invest in new stock for Trevowan and repair the stable roof. We also need a carriage and horses of our own.'

Joshua steepled his fingers and regarded him over the top of them.

'I thought you held your wife in great affection. To hear you so out of countenance with your situation is disturbing. Felicity is a woman of beauty and refinement. A worthy mistress of Trevowan.'

'I needed a wealthy bride.' St John's frustration burst forth. 'Since Father gave half my birthright to Adam, the shipyard no longer contributes an income to the estate. I have loans to repay.'

Joshua stood up, his expression stern. 'You do your wife a grave disservice by your tirade. Did she lie to you about her fortune?'

'Of course not! It was never mentioned. It would have been crass of me to have broached the subject. I knew only that she had a comfortable income and her needs were never extravagant.' St John suppressed the urge to run his finger under his stock. He was sweating in his agitation and anger.

'Then you are fortunate. It displeases me to hear you deride her in this manner. Your father would have been similarly appalled.'

St John bit his lip; his anger had made him incautious. He should not have allowed his resentment to show. He did not want his family to ridicule him for his choice of bride. He defended his outburst: 'It is for the future prosperity of the estate that I am mortified at her lack of money. I owed it to Father that having once wed unwisely, this time I would make amends.'

Joshua picked up his long-stemmed clay pipe and filled it with tobacco. He put a taper to the embers burning in the fireplace and drew sharply on the pipe several times before answering. A swirl of blue smoke surrounded his head. 'Edward would have been pleased with your choice. Felicity comes from a good family. He would want you to be happy.'

'I only found out this afternoon,' St John went on, taking no comfort in his uncle's remark. 'It was a shock. How am I to repay the loans on the estate, and soon the quarter-day wages will be due.'

'So that is why you are eager to learn of William's bequest. Sit down, I will not discuss this whilst you pace like a caged lion.'

St John sat by the window with ill grace. Joshua continued to regard him with a serious expression. 'As your father's heir, you are entitled to his share of William's estate. But I am the sole executor. It was William's wish that all his nieces and nephews receive a bequest. Nothing was stated as to its value, as he would not have envisioned that he and his wife would die at the same time. Lisette was much younger than him. I think it is only right that each of the wives of you, Adam, Japhet and Peter receive an item of Lisette's jewellery. Also your cousin Hannah.'

St John flushed with renewed anger. 'That will reduce considerably my father's share of the legacy.'

'As it will my own portion,' Joshua reminded him sharply. 'But it is a question of fairness, not greed, is it not? Your father would have wished everyone in the family to have something to remember William by.'

St John stared at the floor. This was a severe blow, but to refuse his uncle's request would put him in a bad light with the family.

Joshua went on. 'The jewellery will be apportioned so that the value is equal for all the women. I trust you will agree.'

He could not bring himself to speak but nodded his assent.

'I have the jewellery hidden safely here. We shall ask the ladies to select a piece on Sunday. Then the rest will be sold and the proceeds divided between us. The remaining jewellery should fetch a thousand guineas, and there is also William's savings, which came to several hundred pounds.'

It fell short of the inheritance St John had hoped for, but it was a balm to his wounded pride and would allow him to pay off the loans raised against the estate. He stood up to leave and Joshua walked with him to the door.

'Do not let your disappointment cause a rift in your marriage. Felicity will be a loyal and loving wife.'

The advice did not pacify St John's anger. Felicity had duped him. Again a woman had played him false and toyed with his affection. He had married to gain freedom from the financial shackles that bound him to Trevowan and denied him the life of ease and pleasure he desired. Now the chains were even weightier, with a larger family to provide for.

He returned to Trevowan in an ill mood. The house was inordinately quiet. His aunt's horse and the two girls' ponies were not in the stables. Elspeth must have taken them riding. He suspected Felicity was sulking in her room. Let her stay there. At least in his study he had the comfort of the brandy bottle.

The half-filled glass was poised on his lips when the door to his study opened and Felicity walked in.

'I trust your ride cooled your temper, husband.' She eyed the glass in his hand with distaste.

St John drank down the contents in one gulp and refilled it. His mood was mutinous and he would not tolerate a lecture. Felicity sat on the chair by the hearth and smoothed her muslin gown over her knees. 'The children are riding with Elspeth, and Amelia has taken Rafe to visit Hannah. He was inconsolable when the girls went riding and is demanding his own pony. He is six months older than Charlotte, and Elspeth upbraided your stepmother for not providing her son with a pony before now.'

'It is an extravagance when she spends half the year in London. Rafe can ride Rowena's pony. The upkeep of the stables is high enough as it is.'

'Amelia has spoken of spending more time at Trevowan now that a governess has been engaged for Rafe's education.'

St John suppressed his irritation at the added expense his stepmother's residence would incur. 'I have been going over the estate accounts. A governess is not a necessity. The children can attend the school at Trevowan Hard. Hannah's children do very well there. Bridie is as good a teacher as any. When Rafe is older, he will be sent to my old school.'

'This is not about school fees, is it? Amelia will happily pay the governess's wages.' Felicity's eyes hardened and there was a condemning set to her lips. 'Elspeth informed me that you believed I had a vast fortune at my disposal. If you married me for my money, you must be sorely disappointed in your choice of bride.'

'Trevowan was in debt.' He drank down the second glass of brandy.

'Then your courtship was a lie.' Her slender body quivered with affront. 'You professed your love and devotion to win my hand. You are a blackguard and a liar. You declared you had renounced your wastrel ways, your gaming and drinking. I trusted you.'

'And I trusted you to bring a fortune to our marriage bed.'

His cheek flamed with fire from the force of her slap. He grabbed her wrist and jerked her close to his body. 'Do not ever raise your hand to me again, madam. Or you will regret it.'

Her violet eyes blazed with a fury that matched his own. It shocked him. He had thought her meek and compliant.

'Do not ever treat me with less than the respect I deserve as your wife. Or *you* will regret it, sir. My father and my first husband were bullies, wastrels and philanderers. I will not tolerate such a marriage. I will leave you.'

'Then you will go penniless.'

'There you are mistaken.' She wrenched her wrist free from his hold, her stare glittering with defiance. 'My marriage portion is tied up in investments that yield a quarterly income. I have seen too often how gaming can deplete the family coffers and security. I would not put my daughter's future at risk, or that of an unborn child.'

She was halfway to the door before the full impact of her words filtered through his fury and resentment.

'Did you say unborn child? Are you with child, Felicity?'

She gripped her hands over her waist as she turned to face him. Her head was tilted at a proud and stubborn angle. 'I wanted to be absolutely sure before I told you.' Her lower lip trembled and she caught it between her teeth and took a sharp breath before continuing. 'I wanted such an announcement to be the happiest of moments. Not like this. Not with you hating me . . . regretting our marriage.'

His anger deflated. A child changed everything. He would have his heir at last. A son! Felicity was carrying his son. He moved towards her and clasped her hands. 'You are truly with child?'

'I do not lie.' She sounded cold and unresponsive.

'Then this is the most joyous of days.' He bent to kiss her, but she turned her head aside so that his lips brushed her cheek.

'How can it be joyous when it traps us in a marriage that is now repugnant to us both? You lied and made false promises to me. And it was my money you wanted, not me as a woman. Now it seems I have wed a drunkard and a wastrel, something I vowed never to do.'

'I did not lie,' he blustered. 'I was angry at what I thought was a deliberate deception played upon me. I have been a fool.'

Her eyes remained hooded and her voice was thick with distrust. 'You do not love me. It is you who deceived me.'

Her body was stiff with recrimination. His mind sped back to the years of bitterness in his marriage to Meriel. That had been a living hell. He did not want a return to that. He was indolent and liked his creature comforts. He had thought that he wanted a compliant wife, but would he have respected Felicity if she had proved to be easily intimidated? She had shown an unexpected side to her character in the way she had stood up to him. Their confrontation had strangely excited him.

'How callous you make me sound.' He drew on the Loveday charm now to win her support. 'These last weeks in London have been some of the happiest of my life. Your grace and beauty won the hearts of all we met. That made me so proud. You belittle yourself if you think even for a moment that I am not your devoted servant.'

She stared hard into his eyes and persisted: 'But do you love me?'

'My dearest love, I love and adore you.' The lie tripped easily off his tongue. Those first weeks of marriage *had* been happy, and Felicity was carrying his child. In that moment she was the most ravishing, most exciting woman he had ever met.

Chapter Six

Senara rode to the shipyard with her husband. It was her morning to tend any patients who needed her remedies to heal their ailments. They came from the nearby villages, unable to afford the fees of a physician. The cold and damp of the late spring weather had brought a return of a morbid fever that had struck many families, and a pernicious cough had laid low several of the women and children, continuing to plague them despite all Senara's efforts.

As they left the stable, Adam was hailed by the overseer, Ben Mumford, and went down to the jetty to inspect the work being carried out on *Sea Mist*. The money owed from the excise office had been received the previous day, so the work could begin. Senara shuddered at the sight of the cutter. It was as if the vessel was tainted by its owner's evil.

The stable lad who attended the yard horses used for moving timber approached leading one of the large beasts.

'Mrs Loveday, Duchess kicked out at some fencing. She's hurt herself real bad.'

She examined the animal. The leg was swollen, badly bruised, and it was bleeding. 'Wash it well, lad, and settle her in the stable. The wound is not deep but it will need a poultice and binding. I shall tend to her shortly.'

She was carrying a large pouch of herbs that she had picked in the woods at Boscabel that morning whilst the dew was still on them. They would be used in the remedies she made up in the workrooms that Adam had built on to Mariner's House. Senara had learned her skills with herbs at the side of her gypsy grandmother, and though some of the villagers regarded such knowledge with suspicion, they were glad to call on her in times of sickness and hardship.

Five women and three children were sitting on the stools, awaiting her. Charity Mumford was treating a patient in the smaller room, where dried herbs hung from the rafters and rows of potions, balms and tinctures in clay pots were stored on shelves. There was a row of copper saucepans and dishes; a large wooden washing bowl and draining board in one corner; and an iron wood-burning stove that heated water when Senara was distilling her potions.

The room smelled of lavender, comfrey and calendula, but all the herbs had their own fragrance that collected in the air. She greeted the patients and put on a clean apron to cover her skirt.

'Does anyone need me to attend to them urgently, Charity? Duchess has injured her leg and I must return to the stables.'

Charity was tending to Seth Wakely. The portly woman in her white cap and apron was chatting as she worked, her easy manner putting any nervous patient at their ease. Seth had lost one leg below the knee whilst serving in the navy with Adam, and his stump was rubbed raw from his peg leg. He was an experienced carpenter and Adam had not hesitated to offer him work. Now he carved the fine figureheads on all their ships.

The overseer's wife looked up at Senara. 'There be only Rosie Pascoe I think you should examine. Bit of women's trouble,' she mouthed.

Senara nodded. 'Your leg looks painful, Seth,' she said, glancing at it. 'Charity will make you up a poultice every evening and send it over for your wife to heat and place on it of a night. That should clear the infection in a few days. Leave off the peg and let the air get to the wound as much as you can. Just cover it with a cloth whilst you sit working at your bench so no sawdust gets into it.'

Seth hobbled out on a pair of crutches and Senara turned to Rosie Pascoe, a farmer's wife who had walked the three miles to the yard. She had been married ten years and feared she was barren, as she had never conceived. She was stick thin and her menses were erratic. Senara prescribed a sedative. The young woman was too eager to please and worried over every small detail, so that her nerves were constantly overset. Senara also gave her a tonic that would enrich her blood. Both remedies had helped women of her nature to conceive in the past.

On her way to the stables, Senara passed her sister Bridie driving the dogcart through the yard to the schoolhouse, where she taught the children four mornings a week. Bridie also had her parish duties at Polruggan, where her husband Peter Loveday was the parson. Their mother, Leah, also lived in the parsonage and looked after baby Michael while Bridie attended to her work.

A group of children were standing outside the school, and after an exchange of greetings Bridie hurried inside to ring the bell to summon any latecomers.

The morning passed quickly for Senara. Once Duchess was dealt with, she found Charity Mumford tending competently to the last few patients, and this left Senara free to prepare a fresh batch of cough linctus and also an unguent to ease the pain of the swollen joints of the older residents due to the dampness of the climate.

As she worked, she was aware that most of the talk from the women was of Sawle's influence in the district. Patience and Beth Wibbley, cousins from Trewenna, were sharp in their comments.

'What do Cap'n Loveday be about having that ship in the yard for repairs?' Beth grimaced. 'No good will come of it.'

'Sawle be a devil. I thought we were done with him in these parts after his henchmen were hanged at Bodmin.'

'*Sea Mist* were built here,' Charity defended Adam. 'Who else will repair her? Sides, it wouldn't be right for her to go elsewhere. We need the work.'

'It will bring Sawle back, you mark my words.' Beth shook her head, her florid jowls wobbling in her distress. 'There be bad blood between he and Cap'n Loveday for all that ship were built here.'

'Sawle won't take kindly to the preventive men taking his ship.' Patience sucked in her ample cheeks. 'And it don't bear thinking about what he be capable of when crossed. There's been many a body washed up on the beach with its throat cut.'

The words added to Senara's fears. Adam could take care of himself and was a match for Sawle in any fight, but the smuggler had once tried to steal *Sea Mist* when she had first been launched. Adam had overcome his men and Sawle had later denied he had ever tried to steal the ship. He had also threatened to set fire to the yard if Adam built another cutter for the revenue office.

Harry Sawle did not make idle threats. The half-built cutter had eaten up all Adam's spare money, and the payment received yesterday would only meet their creditors' bills. Senara had an uneasy feeling that the excise would find excuses to break their contract. Once *Sea Mist* was repaired, they did not need the new cutter to patrol the waters. She had warned Adam not to proceed with any further work on her until they had received the next payment from the excise office. The Loveday yard would not be the first to go bankrupt because the government did not honour its commissions. She would be glad when the work on *Sea Mist* was finished and the cutter no longer cast its sinister shadow over the yard. She could not believe that Sawle would allow his ship to be taken without some form of retribution.

A chorus of young voices outside proclaimed that school was over for the morning. Senara finished labelling the last of the new remedies in their pots and walked outside, lifting her face in welcome to the warm sunshine. Across the yard Bridie was speaking with Adam's cousin Hannah, whose children attended the school. Like the Loveday men, Hannah was tall, with dark hair and striking features. She had a natural grace and beauty, her passionate nature evident in the full curve of her lips, and the proud set of her chin also showed courage and strength of character. Since the death of her husband two years ago, she had run the farm as competently as any man, and if any worker thought himself above taking orders from a woman, he soon found he had met his match. Hannah could be formidable, but unlike Elspeth she had a softer, more compassionate side to her nature, and she also had a good head for business.

Senara noticed that Bridie seemed eager to reassure her sister-in-law over some matter. Hannah's four children could be a handful. As Senara approached them, Hannah was saying, 'But I feel that I am letting you down by having the children attend the governess at Trevowan.'

Bridie laughed and shook her head. 'The school here was to give the villagers the chance to learn to read and write. Davey is eleven and has a lively mind. I am often at a loss as to what lessons to give him. He needs a tutor who has been to university. Abigail is also bright, and even little Florence at eight is showing signs of overtaking her elders in her writing.'

'Perhaps Luke should start here next year when he is seven.' Hannah still looked concerned.

'Luke must be with his cousins and brothers and sisters,' Bridie reassured. She smiled at Hannah. 'If I was not married to your brother, you would not hesitate to send them all to Trevowan.'

Hannah turned to Senara. 'Have you thought how Nathan will be educated? He is six now, the same age as Luke, and Felicity's daughter Charlotte.'

'Adam has talked about engaging a tutor for the children when the time comes.'

Hannah looked happier. 'I did not want to offend Bridie. She has done such wonderful work with the children here.'

'I am not offended,' Bridie assured her. 'And I should be getting back to Michael. He has another cold and finds it difficult to shake them.'

'He is not feverish, is he?' Senara worried at the fragile health of her nephew. He had been born early and was a frail and sickly child. But he had survived the winter and had proved he was a fighter. That was a good sign.

Bridie's face softened at mention of her son. 'He has no fever and is sitting up on his own now.' A distant clock in a church tower chimed the half-hour and she frowned as she added, 'I must make haste; there is a meeting with the lace-makers this afternoon at the parsonage.'

'I worry that Bridie does too much,' Senara said as she watched her sister limp to the stables to collect the dogcart. Her back had been twisted since birth, but she never complained of the pain she must constantly suffer.

'Bridie has won the respect of the village women by her diligence, and that was important to her after she wed Peter. It is not easy being a parson's wife. She has performed wonders to organise the lace-making, and the women sell their goods in the market. There was less hardship in the villages this winter because of her foresight and caring.'

'There was rarely enough money in our childhood,' Senara replied. 'We were often hungry. I was so proud when Bridie took up learning at the school here. She taught me my numbers and letters, for it would not have been appropriate for Adam's wife to be seen to be illiterate.'

She did not like to think of those days, having an odd superstition that to talk of past hardships was to somehow attract them again in the future. She understood Bridie's need to be accepted by the local community and to do everything she could to better the suffering of the poor.

Hannah had also fallen silent and had been staring at *Sea Mist*. There was a tightness about her lips when she spoke. 'That ship will bring her devil master back to our shores. Even the price on his head will not keep him away.'

Hannah had every reason to hate the smuggler. He had visited her farm of a night to frighten her into allowing his men to store contraband there. When she had refused, he had disregarded her orders and stored illicit goods on her brother's land, which she was managing in Japhet's absence. Furious at his audacity, she had summoned the excise officers to confiscate the goods and lie in wait for the smugglers to return. As a consequence, several of the tubmen had been arrested. In retribution Harry Sawle had attacked his brother Mark, who worked on her farm, and left him more dead than alive.

Seeing his ship here caused the hairs on the back of Hannah's neck to rise with apprehension. If *Sea Mist* was here, she was certain that Sawle would not be far away. She touched the dagger she always carried in a belt around her waist. It might not be stylish, but in his hatred of the Lovedays Sawle would strike indiscriminately at man or woman. She was accomplished with the weapon, and also with a pistol, taught by Japhet, who had led his own unconventional lifestyle.

44

'There has been no word or sign of Sawle, has there?' Her voice cracked with tension.

'No, thank heavens.' Senara folded her arms across her chest and glared at the ship. The shipwrights were shouting as they hauled on pulleys to lower the new mast into place. 'I wish Adam had not agreed to the repairs. The sooner they are done and the ship leaves the yard, the happier I will be.'

Hannah called to her children, who were playing tag with others from the yard. They were stamping in the puddles that had not cleared from last night's rain. Senara walked with her to the farm cart and changed the conversation. 'Is the calving finished on the farm?'

'Almost. There are still a few cows who are due in the next week or so.'

'Did you lose any calves?'

'Only one so far. I need to increase the milk herd and would prefer not to have to pay market prices. Fortunately eight were heifers.'

'That is good news. And your new overseer, Toby Keswick, how is his work?'

'Sometimes he can be stubborn and think he knows what is best.' Hannah laughed. 'Such is the way of men. I have no complaints. He worked at Traherne Hall for many years, though he is not as competent a stockman as Mark. His wife Lillith has taken over the buttery and is running it efficiently.'

'You were lucky that Sam Deacon continued at the farm so long after Oswald died. It must be hard for you with him gone.'

A veil was drawn over Hannah's usually expressive face. 'Sam had his duty to his family. He was no ordinary farm labourer.'

'I always thought there was a military bearing about him.'

'There was.' Hannah remained infuriatingly enigmatic.

'Have you heard from him since he left?'

'I did not expect to.'

Her words were too sharp, and Senara guessed that Sam, who was certainly not the common farm labourer that he had seemed, had meant more to her than she would admit. Though Hannah had been deeply in love with Oswald, who had died so young, she was a vibrant, passionate woman and was certainly not meant to be a grieving widow all her life.

Hannah herself did not feel there was anything lacking in her life. She loved her home and children and enjoyed her work. With so large a family living close by, she was never lonely during the day. If of a night an emptiness or restlessness haunted her dreams, she dismissed it as irrelevant. The compensations of her life far outweighed any disadvantages.

On the drive home to Rabson Farm, the children chatted excitedly in the back of the cart and she questioned them about their day. Farm work began shortly after dawn and continued past dusk. This was her time for the children, for once they returned to the farmyard, there would be a dozen chores awaiting her. As they turned through the open gate in the dry-stone wall, the farm spread across the valley before them. The house was partly timbered, with later additions in stone. Oswald's family had lived here for generations, and she had loved it from the moment her husband had carried her over the threshold. It was young Davey's heritage, and she was determined that it would prosper under her management.

The children jumped to the ground as she drew up by the stable. Mark Sawle had been raking the soiled straw from the stalls into a hand-cart to carry to the manure heap. His young bride Jeannie washed out the milk churns at the yard pump and stacked them to dry in the afternoon sun, and Hannah could hear the milkmaids, Tilda, Bessie and Fanny, laughing as they worked in the buttery.

Mark came forward to unharness the horse and put her in the meadow to graze. He was very different from his brutal older brother: hardworking, considerate and with a gentle manner that made him good with the horses and livestock. Hannah had never regretted hiring him and he had proved his loyalty on many occasions.

The plough horses and Japhet's Arab mare Sheba were grazing in the paddock. Sheba lifted her head and neighed at Senara's return. Did she remember her master? Senara wondered. Japhet had left his prized mare in her care when he had been arrested for highway robbery. After a harrowing year in Newgate, he had been convicted at his trial. They had always hoped for a pardon, and his wife Gwen had influential family and friends at court, but just as it seemed he would be reprieved he had been transported to Australia to serve fourteen years in the new penal colony. When his pardon was finally granted, Gwen had not hesitated to sail to Australia to deliver it. The family had hoped for Japhet's return the following year, but he had seen the colony as a chance to make his fortune and had remained a free man in the growing community of settlers.

Hannah suppressed a sigh of regret. She adored Japhet and missed him dreadfully, but she was certain that he would prosper in his new life. She stared across the meadow to the milk herd. The calves had been separated from their mothers and put in another field on the far side of the farm.

After Oswald's death it had been easier to increase the herd and cut down on the raising of crops, which required more intensity of labour throughout the planting and harvest seasons. She hoped that her late husband would approve.

Toby Keswick was at work on the hedging. The old wood had been spliced and bent over to form a solid barrier. He was competent enough, but often needed reminding of the work required that week. It had been so different when she had Sam to rely upon.

But Sam was gone, she told herself sternly. He had no place here now. He had been a rock during the last months of Oswald's illness and after his death. Hannah had carried on but she had been swamped by a grief that could still lance through her heart to this day. Sam had been more than an overseer; he had been a good friend and adviser, and she had been shocked how much she missed him when he left. But those feelings were inappropriate. She was still in love with Oswald and there was no place in her heart for another.

Yet she could not help but wonder what had happened to Sam. A mysterious visitor had arrived at the farm with news of his family, a family, it had turned out, who were far more illustrious than the Lovedays, and duty had taken him to effect a reconciliation with his father.

Sam had been a match for Harry Sawle in strength and courage and she had felt safe knowing he was close at hand. She felt more vulnerable with only Toby and Mark to protect her. With the possibility that Sawle was back in the district she must be more vigilant and alert to possible danger.

Chapter Seven

Hannah had spent all night attending a difficult calving. At one point she thought she would lose both the cow and its young. Mark had been proficient dealing with the other births, but any complications had been left to her. She hated to see an animal suffer, but the cow was giving birth to twins and had been in labour all day and was now extremely weak. She racked her brains to think how Oswald would have dealt with such a birthing.

'Best you kill the cow and we cut the calves out of her,' observed Toby Keswick, who was leaning over the stall scratching his patchy beard.

Hannah knelt on the straw, an oilskin apron tied around her waist, as she examined the labouring animal. The hooves of one of the calves were doubled up under it at an unnatural angle and she had been unable to straighten them.

Toby rubbed his large stomach, which was grumbling from lack of food. Aggie had brought them all a mug of ale, but it was long past the usual time to break their fast, as Hannah had insisted that they remain with the cow. Mark Sawle squatted at her side. His normally spiky hair was flattened to his scalp and dark with sweat.

'We need to get a rope under those legs, Mrs Rabson,' he advised. 'With respect, you be too gentle with her.'

Hannah sat back on her heels and dragged a blood-smeared hand across her brow. 'Oswald would have known what to do,' she groaned.

Mark cast a baleful glare at the overseer. 'So would Sam Deacon. You said you were a skilled herdsman, Toby. You know little more than myself. You lied at the hiring fair. Mrs Rabson needed a strong, experienced man . . .'

'Now you listen here!' snarled Toby. 'I never had no complaints from Sir Henry.'

'But he had an experienced bailiff and stockman who gave you orders,' Mark returned.

'There is no point in bickering.' Hannah lost patience with her farmhands. 'Take over, Mark.'

The two men had never got on. Toby thought he knew best in everything and Hannah had constantly to call him to order and point out the correct way to treat the animals. It had been obvious within a few weeks that he did not have the experience he had claimed. But he worked hard in the fields and had a good general knowledge of farm work, and needed little supervision.

The cow was lying inert on the straw, slavering at the mouth. She gave a low groan and rolled her eyes. Then her swollen body shuddered, and her head lifted slightly then fell back on to the ground. Hannah groaned inwardly, her voice barely a whisper as she gasped: 'Oh Sam, where are you, I could do with you here now.'

'We be losing her,' declared Mark.

Hannah knelt to cradle the animal's head. The cow was a valuable beast and would have been expected to produce many more calves in her lifetime. This was only her second pregnancy. To her dismay, Hannah saw that the animal had stopped breathing and her eyes were glazing over.

'Get the calf out fast, Mark. Maybe we can save it.'

He slashed with his knife and hauled the calf on to the straw, still in its birth sac. Hannah wiped the inert body, clearing mucus from its mouth. She worked swiftly. This was something she had done scores of times. When the animal did not move, she took up a threadbare blanket and vigorously rubbed it whilst Mark continued to work on the mother, drawing out the second calf. A glance showed Hannah that that one at least was moving. Her arms were aching as she continued to rub the first calf, but it showed no signs of life.

'Let me, Mrs Loveday.' Mark picked it up and held it by its back legs, then gave it several rough shakes, and when he laid it on the ground again, the small body gave a perceptible quiver. Hannah continued to massage it until its breathing became stronger. Its twin was laid at its side and the two lifted their heads, searching for their mother.

'At least we've saved the young 'uns,' Toby commented, as though he had done all the work.

Mark ignored him and wiped his hands on a bunch of straw. 'It will not be easy feeding them by hand. They'll want regular suckling through the night. Jeannie will help me. We'll sleep in the barn for a couple of nights.'

Hannah stared sadly at the cow's carcass. 'Deal with her, Toby.'

The calves were moving more confidently in the straw. Mark ran a hand over them. 'The one who caused all the trouble is a bullock. At least the other is a heifer, though it will be two years before she is producing milk to replace that of her mother.'

'That is the way of farming sometimes.' Hannah shrugged off her disappointment.

As she walked swiftly from the cowshed, she found that she was shaking. She was shocked to the core that in her moment of great need the name she had called was that of Sam Deacon and not that of her husband.

Too shaken to return to the farmhouse, she entered the stables and went to Sheba's stall. The Arab mare nuzzled her hand, searching for an apple. She absently stroked the sleek neck. Usually she could not be near the horse without her thoughts focusing upon Japhet, but now it was Sam's image that filled her mind.

'This is insane,' she groaned. 'I still love Oswald. Sam was just a friend.'

But a friend who in recent weeks too often entered her dreams, mocked an inner voice. She must banish her memories of him. He was lost to her. Annoyed that her thoughts would not be dispelled, she went to the farmyard pump and sluiced water over her face and hands. She could hear Lillith singing as she turned the butter churn; by now the milkmaids would be separating the whey from the curds for the next batch of cheeses. This was a range of produce she would build in the future to be sold in the markets as well as the local kiddleys. Many of the small alehouses sold basic general provisions, and she had spent the winter travelling to these to win orders for a regular delivery of her cheese, butter and milk. She had been successful, and now she had plans to expand her milk herd. Only one arable crop had been planted this spring, and two of her fields had been left to provide hay for the winter feed for the livestock.

She heard a scuffing sound and glanced across the yard to see her youngest child, Luke, looking forlorn and wandering around the yard kicking at stones.

'Why are you not playing with your brother and sisters, Luke?'

'They don't want me. Davey is carving a wooden duck and said I would hurt myself, and Abbie and Florence are playing with their stupid dolls.' He gave a long, heartfelt sigh. 'I wish Charlie was here. It's not fair he had to go away. Why do people go away, Mama?'

His lower lip trembled as he continued: 'Papa went away. And Uncle Japhet, though I don't remember him well. Aunt Tamasine left us after she married. She was always such fun. Then Sam took Charlie away

50

and Charlie was my best friend.' He sniffed and cuffed a tear from his eye. 'Abbie and Florence can be mean. They won't climb trees and they won't play soldiers with me. They just play with their silly dolls.'

'They are not mean.' She hugged him. 'They are just more grown up than you and play different games. Aunt Tamasine has not gone for ever. She came to visit us when Uncle St John was married. And you know that your papa is now in heaven watching over you. Aunt Tamasine and Uncle Japhet will come back, I promise.'

'What about Charlie? He was my bestest ever friend.' He continued to sniff and his voice was accusing.

Hannah took out her handkerchief, wiped her son's face and kissed his cheek. 'I do not know if you will see Charlie again.' She felt her throat tighten with longing for Sam's adopted son, who was the same age as Luke. 'His family live a long way away.'

His body was tense and she felt him fighting to control his tears. 'I know Papa is in heaven and I will not see him again. But Charlie is only little like me. It wasn't fair Sam that took him away. I hate him. I thought he was nice but he wasn't – not to take Charlie away.'

'Many people will come and go in your life. Some will be lifelong friends; others are just fleeting and are with you for a short time. They all leave their special mark. You have to learn to treasure the moments you have with them, for each of us must lead our own lives. Friends are wonderful, but you have to learn not to rely on them for your happiness. Learn to be a friend to yourself and you will never be lonely or bored.'

He wriggled from her hold. 'Does that mean you are happy and do not miss Papa? Or Uncle Japhet or Sam? I see you crying sometimes when you stroke Uncle Japhet's mare.'

Trust a child to speak a simple truth and twist your words back upon themselves. She could not help smiling, and ruffled his dark hair. 'It is foolish of your mama to cry, for I have my memories and they are wonderful.'

He put his head to one side. 'They are not the same as having those people here, are they?' With wisdom above his six years, he ran to her and threw his arms around her thighs. 'I love you, Mama. But will you promise me that you will never go away? You will not leave me, will you?'

She had not realised the depths of his fears, which must be very real, for he had lost so many people he loved and cherished.

'Mama will never leave you, not until you are fully grown, and then you'll be the one leaving this farm for a new and exciting life of your own. Go and find Aggie; she is baking muffins. Tell her I said you could have one for being such a brave boy. You are lucky to have your cousins Rafe and Nathan close to you in age. Tomorrow I will bring Nathan back from Boscabel to spend the day with you.'

Her words seemed to satisfy him, and he ran off into the kitchen, making a clicking sound and pretending he was riding a horse. Hannah straightened. She too missed young Charlie, who had grown from a toddler to a lively, adventurous child in the three years he had lived at the farm. It was because of him that Sam had left. The boy's birth had caused a rift in the family that had to be settled.

She stared into the distance, where a flock of ducks flew in a large V across the cloudy sky, and mentally shook herself. Sam and Charlie are gone, she told herself fiercely. If our paths are meant to cross in the future, they will. Now I have a farm to run, children to feed, the end-of-the-month invoices for the milk, butter and cheese deliveries to be written, the accounts to put in order and a pile of clothes to be sorted for the washing. Her work would chase away any shadows of sadness from her mind. She would not dwell on those who were no longer around her; she had a loving family and four adorable children, even if Abigail and Florence could be heard bickering in their bedchamber.

For the rest of the day she was too busy for her thoughts to dwell upon the past. A revised delivery schedule had to be arranged to fit in all the new orders. By the time the newly born heifers were producing milk, she would have increased her profits for the farm by a third.

It was a long time since she had felt so elated and confident that she had made the right decision, and for the first time in months she slept peacefully, without nagging concerns for the future of the farm.

It was a shock the next morning when a distracted Mark Sawle burst into the kitchen as the milkmaids were about to start the milking.

'Mrs Rabson, the calves be mortal sick. Three be dead and the others be lying on the straw and won't rise or take their feed.'

Now the calves were separated from their mothers, they were housed in a separate barn. She was appalled when she entered and discovered the condition of the animals. They were lying in their own excrement, which was streaked with blood, and their breathing came in hard, rasping gasps.

'Ride Sheba to bring Senara Loveday to examine them. Tell her what has happened. I trust her skills with animals, but this is a murrain like none I have seen before.'

When Senara galloped into the farmyard, Hannah was leaning on the door of the barn, her head on her raised elbow in a gesture of despair.

'They are dead. All dead, Senara. If it spreads to the herd, we are ruined.'

'At least they were isolated,' Senara reassured her. 'I will examine them and let you know what I find.'

Hannah stayed at her side as she carefully examined each calf. Their tongues and stomachs were swollen, but not from any disease she had encountered before. There was also a strange tinge to the colour of their tongues, and their eyes looked liverish and yellow. She inspected their stools and her frown deepened. Then she knelt once more at the head of a dead calf and opened its mouth to peer closely inside.

'Heaven forbid it is a new strain of disease that could sweep through all the herds in the county. That would bring ruin to many farms.' Hannah was grey with worry.

Senara continued to stare at the carcasses for some minutes without speaking. 'I would stake my reputation as a wise woman that this is no disease. It looks as though they were poisoned.'

'Poisoned! But that is impossible. How could they have been poisoned?'

'If someone had a grudge against you they could steal into the barn at night and administer some lethal potion.' They exchanged significant glances and Senara added, 'I will check the rest of your herd. But as a precaution the carcasses and bedding here must be burned and the barn floor scrubbed.'

To her relief there were no adverse signs in the remaining herd, but when they sat at the kitchen table both women were pale and drawn.

'It is still too early to be absolutely certain that it was not some new murrain that struck the calves. If it was, it will not be isolated to this farm. If there are no further outbreaks in the next two days, we will know it was poison.'

'There is only one person capable of such an act,' Hannah declared. 'Sawle must be back in the district. This is a warning to us all. I was the cause of him losing a cargo of contraband when I informed the authorities that it was stored on Japhet's land. An eye for an eye. That is Sawle's way. The loss of the calves will affect my income. I cannot afford to replace them.'

'The consequences could be worse if it was not poison but an infection.' Senara did not want to frighten Hannah but she had to state the truth. 'Even so, the farm should be patrolled at night.'

Hannah agreed. Last time Sawle had threatened her, Sam Deacon had been steadfastly at her side. She would give much for his strength and reassurance now.

On the other side of the Tamar valley, Sam looked west across the river at the setting sun. His wheat-gold hair turned coppery as the sky was streaked with banners of red and gold, and his skin was tanned from his life on the land. It was a perfect sunset, which heralded a clear day on the morrow. Was it a good sign? The last months had been frustrating as he sought to end the rift in his family. So far all his attempts had been hopeless.

As he gazed across the Cornish border towards the southern coast, he wondered if he would ever succeed. He had learned much of family pride and loyalty in his days serving Hannah Rabson. He had witnessed how honour could be both a blessing and a curse. Yet despite all their trials and tribulations, the Lovedays had won through. They had been his hope and his inspiration that his own family would finally see reason.

With the memory of those years he found the image of Hannah etched into his mind. She was incomparable, a woman unparalleled in his estimation. A woman worthy of love and devotion. The hardest decision of his life had been to leave her and bring Charlie back to the land of his forefathers.

Charlie lay on the banks of the Tamar watching a heron fishing in the reeds. The boy was brown as a berry, with hair the same colour as Sam's. He passed easily for his son and was oblivious of the havoc his existence had caused. Yet a more lovable child it would be hard to find. When Sam had done his duty by the scrap of newly born humanity, he had never expected to love the boy so profoundly. Indeed, so profoundly that he would sacrifice his own life and happiness. He had taken his sister's baby from the orphanage to give him a chance of a better life.

It had not been easy finding work and caring for a baby. Sam had resigned his commission as captain in the King's Own Hussars and changed his name from Deighton to Deacon to protect Charlie's identity. Charlie had thrived and was accepted as his son as he travelled from village to village. Only when he worked for Hannah had he been persuaded to stay for longer, respecting her determination to run the farm throughout her husband's illness and death.

Hannah had needed him and Charlie had blossomed in the security of a caring home and the company of other young children. Sam had stayed to protect her when Harry Sawle had tried to victimise her and she refused to be manipulated to his will. it had been his undoing. A force greater than his own will had discovered his whereabouts, and now Charlie was to face the consequences of a twenty-year feud between two irascible titans and a tragic love affair between cousins.

Charlie's grandfathers were brothers who hated each other with a vengeance. Both had loved Sam's mother, Lady Isabella, and Hugo Deighton had won her hand. His brother, Lord Eastley, had never forgiven him. The romance between Hugo's daughter Catherine and Eastley's only child and heir Reginald had been ill fated from the outset. Neither family would accept it and the couple had run away together. When on Lord Eastley's orders Reginald had abandoned Catherine rather than lose his inheritance, Catherine had found herself pregnant and unable to bear the shame. Two days after Charlie was born she had hanged herself. Sam had been searching for his sister and arrived too late to save her. Outraged at the way she had been treated, he had challenged Reginald to a duel and his cousin had died at his hand.

Neither of Charlie's grandfathers would acknowledge Charlie, and Sam had been banished from his family home.

Then last year Lord Eastley's lawyer had found Sam and informed him that his lordship now intended to adopt Charlie and make him his heir. Sam, however, had no intention of allowing Charlie to be part of a web of deceit. The true heir to Eastley's estate was his own father, Hugo Deighton, and then Sam's elder brother Richard.

So far he had not spoken to his lordship; all their dealings had been through the lawyer. As Charlie's guardian, Sam had refused to hand the boy over into his paternal grandfather's clutches, distrusting his motives. His suspicions were compounded when the lawyer had informed him the previous week that Lord Eastley had in his possession proof of Reginald and Catherine's marriage. Sam did not believe him. If the couple had married, why had Reginald deserted her?

So far, Sir Hugo Deighton had refused to see Sam. That must change. Hugo was Eastley's heir, but his lordship was now threatening court action to prove Charlie was legitimate. His lordship clearly had no love for the boy, and was only using him to strike at his brother. He had vowed that he would see his home burned to the ground before Sir Hugo or his sons took possession.

How could Sam allow Charlie to be used in this manner? His future might be assured, but at what cost? He would be brought up in a home without love, and Sir Hugo would never accept him as anything but a usurper and his enemy.

Chapter Eight

When Adam learned of the poisoning, he asked St John and Peter to meet him at Trewenna Rectory to discuss ways to ensure that Hannah was not in danger. The day was overcast and little light penetrated the small window partially covered with ivy. Not wishing to upset Aunt Cecily, Adam told her it was a legal matter the family needed to discuss, and the men sat around the table in the dining room. When he related the death of the calves, St John shot from his chair, his face dark with fury.

'Several of my calves were found dead yesterday morning. Nance thought it was through sickness and isolated the others. Are you sure Hannah's were poisoned?'

'I enquired at Traherne Hall and some of the other estate farms,' Adam stated. 'No other calves have died. If this is Sawle's way of warning us, he is wily enough to make it look like an act of nature. I suppose you've disposed of the carcasses?'

'I had them burned. I could not risk an infection spreading.'

'And have others sickened?' Joshua persisted.

'No, thank God. It could wipe me out financially if I lost the herd.'

'Then poison seems to be the cause,' Adam continued. 'And if Sawle is involved, not only do we have to protect our property. He must be hunted down.'

Joshua was clearly worried about his daughter. 'Hannah is stubborn. She will not accept too obvious protection from us.'

'At least she has agreed to hire a nightwatchman,' Peter added. 'Father and I will visit the farm more often.'

'If it is Sawle,' St John rounded on his twin, 'this has come about because Adam is repairing *Sea Mist*. It is a deliberate provocation. You should have refused the work.'

Adam stood up to confront his brother from across the table. 'I had no choice. The excise office could have cancelled the order for the new cutter. The yard needs that income.'

'Because you have put all your money into building that damned merchantman,' St John fumed, 'to line your own pocket and those of your investors. I thought we were shipbuilders, not financiers.'

'I *am* a shipbuilder.' Adam's knuckles whitened as he rested his hands on the table. 'And I run the yard how I see fit. The money from the investors is the security for its future.'

'Please, let us not quarrel,' Joshua interceded. 'Both of you sit down so that we can discuss this rationally. Our concern is for the safety of our family and property. And Hannah is the most vulnerable.'

Adam swallowed his anger at his brother's outburst. 'Uncle is right. But though this smacks of Sawle's handiwork, I have contact with men who would inform on him. They have not reported seeing him in Cornwall. He would be a fool to return now that there is a price on his head.'

'Your spies are probably also in Sawle's pay,' St John sneered. 'And he would kill them if they gave evidence against him. You cannot trust anyone where Sawle is concerned.'

'St John has a point,' Peter advised. 'The price on his head should have enticed someone to come forward with information. It is a great deal of money.'

'Not if it places their own families or lives in danger,' Adam observed.

'So what do we do?' Joshua pressed.

'Keep alert,' Adam counselled. 'I'd add another fifty guineas to the reward, but that would only show Sawle that we fear his retribution. I shall increase the night watch at the yard and have a man patrol Boscabel of a night. And Uncle Joshua and Peter should also take precautions. A dog would warn you if anyone were prowling around the churchyard or grounds. Senara took in a couple of strays last winter. You are welcome to have them.'

'Are they house-trained?' Peter asked. 'I do not want some mangy cur around Michael.'

'No, but they are meant to be guard dogs and sleep outside.'

'I shall think on the matter,' Joshua informed him. 'As you know, your aunt is nervous of dogs, especially if they have been strays. She was bitten as a child. But I shall carry a dagger at all times. A pity that it would be incongruous for a preacher to carry a sword. It would give me great pleasure to run that brigand Sawle through, given half a chance.'

His words brought a chuckle from the others. In his rakehell days before taking the cloth, Joshua had been an accomplished swordsman. The death of an opponent in a duel had shocked him into changing his lifestyle and entering a seminary.

'We would all do well to carry arms after the way I was abducted last year,' Peter cautioned.

Joshua studied the twins. He did not want to encourage a war against Sawle. As far as he was concerned, if the smuggler stayed away from his old home and haunts, that was the best solution. From the stubborn set of his nephews' chins, it was obvious they would start a manhunt if their old adversary were behind any trouble in the district.

'We may know more of Sawle's dealings and whereabouts by Sunday,' he advised. 'In the mean time, I think we should play it calmly for now and take what precautions we can. What do you intend to do, St John?'

'I agree with you, but I do not wish my wife to be upset by any talk of that villain. It would greatly distress her, and it is my pleasure to inform you that Felicity is with child.'

'That is splendid news,' Adam replied with a smile.

'Congratulations.' Both Peter and Joshua were effusive in their good wishes.

'Trevowan needs an heir. I pray it will be a boy,' St John answered with a smug air. 'I have no intention of working all my life to improve the estate only to hand it over to my half-brother.'

'The Lovedays predominantly sire sons,' Peter said proudly. 'Little Michael is a blessing for which I daily thank God. You will have your heir, I am sure.'

Joshua cautioned: 'All the more reason that this matter is dealt with by the letter of the law and not as some personal vendetta.'

On Sunday morning Peter Loveday finished ringing the bell to summon his congregation to morning service. His churchwarden had sent word that an attack of gout had confined him to his bed. As he entered the church from the bell tower, Peter froze in shock. Bridie sat in the front pew wringing her hands, her face white with tension. She was the only person present. Leah was absent, tending to Michael, who was fractious and teething.

'Where is everyone?' Peter demanded.

His wife shook her head. 'When no one had come in, I went outside. The village seems deserted.'

'This is an abomination!' Peter flushed at the extent of his outrage. 'Where are the villagers?'

'I have no idea.'

Peter gripped his Bible close to his chest and struggled to control his composure. This was a ploy to insult and discredit him. 'We will pray for the salvation of our village, wife.'

Bridie dutifully bent her head, but her mind was racing with fear. This had never happened before. There was no sickness in the village. Usually a score of people attended the morning service. The men resented Peter's sermons condemning the smugglers, for many supplemented their farm or mining wages working in the trade. But this smacked of insurgency. To forgo church on a regular basis was to endanger the soul, and was also against the law of the land. If the villagers dared to miss the church service, what else lay behind their actions? Had Peter's sermons alienated his flock more than she had realised?

With a shiver of alarm she remembered the ordeal that Peter had suffered when Mordecai Nance had been in charge of Harry Sawle's smuggling runs. Her husband had been abducted and beaten, then taken to a cave on the moor and left to die. Only his courage and wits had saved him. Fortunately Nance had been caught and hanged for his crimes, but if the villagers now sought to rebel against Peter's sermons, it boded ill for their future – even their safety.

But Bridie could not believe that the women of the village would have turned against them. Since her marriage she had worked hard to win their trust. She thought she had succeeded, and their absence today was a bitter blow. Not only did she tend the sick and dying, and distribute clothes and food that had been donated to the parish; the lace-making classes she had arranged earned additional income. She felt betrayed.

Peter prayed for the souls of his flock and their misguided ways. As time stretched on, Bridie became more nervous.

'This is pointless.' She interrupted her husband's prayer. 'No one is here. The church is cold and Ma should not be left too long with Michael while he is teething. He has been crying all morning. We can say our own prayers in the warmth of the parsonage.'

'I will not abandon my duties.' Peter's jaw set in a stubborn line. 'Go to Michael if your mind is uneasy. I will remain here until the service would normally be over.'

Bridie glanced towards the oak door. The empty church made the hairs rise on her neck. She could not leave her husband. What if this was some trick by Sawle's men to attack Peter in some physical way? He was unarmed. Though he often carried a dagger since the attack, he refused to bear weapons in the Lord's house. Yet that was the very place the smugglers had set on him last time.

'I will check on Michael, but I will return.'

She hurried out of the church. Leah was dozing by the kitchen range and started at her unexpected arrival. Michael was sleeping in his crib. His thumb was in his mouth and he was sucking noisily. Bridie's heart swelled with love. He was so precious, so adorable, but he was tiny, having been born prematurely, and she fretted that he should be gaining more weight.

'Michael is well,' Leah observed. 'What are you doing here? The service is not over, is it? Or did Peter lose his voice? His sermons are never shorter than an hour. You have been away half that time.'

'The church is deserted. And there is no sign of anyone in the village. There was no word that there was a fair in the area or something that would tempt the congregation away.'

Leah sucked in her mouth. 'Happen they sought to teach their parson a lesson to keep his sermons short or they will go elsewhere.'

'I thought they had accepted us, especially the women.'

'Were not some absent from the last two lace afternoons?' Leah eyed her daughter sadly.

Bridie chewed her lip. Her mother was right. Excuses had been made, but the gathering was intended as a supportive group. The lace was then sold to a shop in Bodmin or, if it was not up to the shop's standard, at the market.

'I will return to the church,' she informed her mother. 'There is something I need from upstairs first.' She ran to the bedchamber she shared with her husband and drew out a primed pistol from a drawer. After the trouble with Nance last year, Peter had shown her how to use the weapon. She thrust two daggers in their leather sheaths into a pocket of her gown and carried the pistol hidden in a fold of her skirt. If the smugglers caused trouble, they would find her prepared.

When Bridie had left the church, Peter broke off from his prayers. Hot anger swept through him. How dare the villagers insult God in this manner? How dare they so insult *him*, the shepherd who cared for their souls? It was an abomination. An affront to God. It could not be tolerated.

In his agitation he paced before the altar in long, forceful strides. Every missing member of the congregation would be called to account for their actions this day. They would hear the wrath of the Lord through him. His duty was clear: to bring them back into the fold.

He was of a mind to bang on every door in the parish and demand why they had absented themselves. His rage blazed to a greater fury. But he had no need to question his parishioners. He knew who was behind this. Someone they feared more than God. The Lord might punish them in the next life, but Harry Sawle would wreak a terrible toll upon them in this one. Maiming or death was Sawle's retribution on any who dared to thwart his orders.

He wrestled to bring his fury under control. Outrage impelled him to hunt down Sawle and call the blackguard to account for setting his henchman Nance on him last year. He still smarted at the shame of his abduction. He knew he was regarded as the weakest of the Loveday men because he had spent his early manhood preaching instead of whoring, fighting and kicking up his heels. But he was not afraid of the smuggler. Even though he might not be the match for him in brawn or street fighting, he was no coward. Sawle, though, was devious, cunning and evil. He was the devil incarnate in their midst.

Peter did not possess that decree of low cunning. There was a naivety about him instilled by his religious piety. He had not frequented dens of ill repute or the streets where violence and debauchery reigned. He knew that men were capable of great evil but had no experience of pitting his wits against a deviant mind capable of any atrocity to achieve its own selfish ends.

His cousins had lived more worldly lives. St John had been in league with Sawle and must know something of his mentality. Adam, during his years in the navy, had mixed with the roughest of men who had been pressganged into service. But even they were innocents against the full might of Sawle's malevolent reasoning.

Peter heard the sound of his wife's light steps enter the porch of the church and composed himself to kneel in prayer and speak under his breath: 'Dear Lord, guide me. Give me the strength and the wisdom to outwit the demon who would destroy us all.'

Chapter Nine

Uplifted by the news that Felicity was with child, St John was prepared to be gracious when he joined his family for a meal at Boscabel after attending Uncle Joshua's sermon at Trewenna church. The women were joyous in their congratulations, bringing a delicate flush to Felicity's cheeks. They then clamoured for news of the family in London and the sights the couple had enjoyed during their honeymoon.

St John spoke warmly of the events and plays they had seen, and complimented Aunt Margaret and his cousin Thomas for their hospitality. His gaze, which continually lingered on his wife, spoke of the depths of his affection.

Felicity was heartened by her husband's tender manner. She had resolved to put aside her disappointment at his attitude over her income. The baby had healed the rift that could have torn their marriage apart. The sickness that accompanied her pregnancy was easier to bear now that she was assured of St John's devotion. This morning he had presented her with a magnificent diamond necklace and bracelet from the collection of jewels from his uncle's estate.

'You deserve the best, my love. I regret that the jewels cannot all be yours,' he had said as he placed the necklace around her neck and kissed her nape.

'These are beautiful. But should not the jewels be shared equally in value between the Loveday women?'

He brushed aside her concern. 'Uncle Joshua agreed that these should be yours. The others will make their choices after luncheon today. Then the rest will be sold and my share will free the estate from debt.'

The old hall at Boscabel was large enough to seat the whole family, and today eleven adults were present; the twelve children from the marriages of the cousins had been fed in the nursery and their afternoon naps or games would be supervised by two nursery maids.

Felicity felt a twinge of guilt after the meal when Uncle Joshua laid the remaining jewellery on a strip of velvet on the dining table. Clearly her necklace and bracelet were the most expensive items from the collection. The spread of jewels brought a gasp from the women.

'I had no idea Lisette possessed so many trinkets,' Elspeth announced. 'And all those years dear Edward supported her when the estate and yard were struggling to survive. The ungrateful baggage could have saved this family from much unnecessary hardship by parting with some of these.'

'She sold several pieces to spend a fortune on new gowns before Edward, as her guardian, had the jewels put into the custody of the bank.' Cecily was equally condemning.

'The minx was selfish as well as ungrateful.' Amelia shook her head. 'I want nothing that belonged to her. She brought only shame and pain to our family.'

Bridie shifted uncomfortably. She still felt out of place in the grand Loveday houses and was painfully aware of her own humble roots. 'I know Lisette could be difficult, but it does not seem right on this occasion to speak ill of the dead.'

Elspeth gave a derisive snort. 'I am not a prude, but her conduct was not to be tolerated. She was mentally unstable and her behavious was immoral and without a shred of decency. My dear brother William was gulled into marrying her, and for years before that she created distress and scandal for our family in repayment for us giving her a home.'

'Aunt, let Lisette's soul rest in peace,' Hannah said gently. 'She was the twins' cousin, the niece of their French mother.'

'Dear Marie was the sweetest of women,' Elspeth continued, her piercing stare sweeping over the faces gathered round the table. Nothing would halt her when she had set her mind upon a subject that roused her indignation. 'I am not saying her family was unstable – just that ungrateful baggage. Adam risked his life to save her from the Revolution and bring her to England. Precious thanks we got for it.'

'Elspeth, we are all aware of Lisette's faults,' Joshua interrupted. 'Let us not drag up the past. She is dead.'

'And because of her so is dear William,' Elspeth snapped.

'May they rest in peace.' Adam spoke firmly. He did not want the scandal of Lisette and her husband's death resurrected. It would lead to argument, and there were more weighty matters to be discussed this day.

He conceded that their French cousin had been wanton and head-strong, and they had all been shocked when the truth of the couple's deaths had been discovered. Lisette had been having an affair with her brother. William had discovered them together and fought Etienne in a duel. Terrified that her brother would be killed, Lisette had thrown herself between the men and had been shot. William had then killed her brother and taken the bodies out to sea in a dinghy before drowning himself.

Adam was not the only one who was impatient for the matter of the jewels to be resolved. Joshua was finding the accusations difficult. Elspeth was being deliberately antagonistic and he glared at his older sister.

'Elspeth, let our brother rest in peace. It is in William's memory that you should select a piece.'

Elspeth shook her head. 'Not I. There is blood on those jewels. Because of that wanton wretch, William took his own life. I want none of it. Sell my piece and use the money to buy two plough horses for Trevowan.'

Senara also declined to choose. 'I could not wear such gems. Lisette's life was blighted. I feel they would bring bad luck, for they came from her unhappy first marriage to the Marquis de Gramont, who was killed in the early days of the Revolution in France. Lisette was lucky to escape with her life but her ordeal affected her mind.'

'That is superstition.' Elspeth waved a hand in dismissal. 'In my opinion Lisette was always highly strung.'

'But I would not feel comfortable wearing anything she owned.' Senara glanced at her husband. 'If Adam wishes me to have a piece and it is sold to improve the livestock here at Boscabel or pay the wages at the yard, that is another matter.'

Adam took her hand and squeezed it. He also felt that the jewellery was tainted. It had never brought Lisette happiness. The money from the sale would ease his present financial burdens.

'I agree with my sister,' Bridie added. 'Such jewellery is inappro-priate for a parson's wife. 'Though Peter may wish to use the money from the sale of it to serve the parish.'

Cecily threw up her hands, appalled at the sacrifice Bridie proposed. 'The money should be used for yourselves. Peter's stipend as a parson provides for no luxuries. You could engage a servant. Your mother has worked hard all her life and I know she prides herself that she helps you in your work at the parsonage, but she has enough to do caring for Michael when Bridie has duties to attend.'

'I agree with my mother,' Peter answered. 'Most of the furniture in the parsonage is riddled with worm and should be replaced.'

Hannah also had a stubborn set to her jaw. 'I too would prefer for the jewellery to be sold. I need to replace the dead calves.'

A heated discussion followed on the best way to sell the jewels until Joshua rapped his knuckles on the table to silence them. 'I shall take them to a reputable jeweller in Truro. It would please William that they bring aid and comfort to you all. That is what counts. Pieces will also be set aside for my sister Margaret in London and of course Japhet's wife Gwen. I also think Edward would expect Tamasine to be included.'

'My half-sister hardly knew Uncle William and his wife.' St John baulked at this new incursion into the inheritance. 'Did she meet them? I was in America at the time.' He had not expected so many of the women of his family to be included in the legacy.

'Would you deny your half-sister?' Elspeth rounded on him. 'If your father was alive he would have included Tamasine.'

'She is hardly a pauper. Her husband is an extremely wealthy man,' he raged. He was horrified at the shrinking percentage he would be eligible to from his uncle's estate. Could they not see that he did not want the money for himself but for the good of the estate – the home where they had all been born?

'Would you then deny your Aunt Margaret or Gwen?' Elspeth glared at him over the top of her pince-nez. 'Deny one and you begrudge us all. William had pride in all our family. None of us seeks to benefit from his death.' The stalwart's woman's eyes glittered with unshed tears. 'William's life in the navy took him away from us for so many years. You shame his memory. You shame us all by your clutchfist ways.'

'Are you not content with the inheritance of Trevowan?' Adam could not contain his rage. 'This is petty, and Father certainly would not have countenanced your objections to treating the whole family as equal.'

St John stood up, his face crimson with anger, and rounded on his twin. 'As usual I am in the wrong. You are jealous that as Father's heir I am entitled to a larger share than yourself. Would you not have Trevowan free of debt?'

'Aye, if that is what you would spend the money on and not gamble it away,' Adam flared, his body braced and bristling for a fight.

Joshua also rose to his feet and put a restraining hand on St John's chest. 'Calm down and let us discuss this in a reasonable manner.'

St John shook off his uncle's touch and marched to the end of the table. 'Do as you will. I would not deny any member of my family what is legally theirs. Uncle Joshua is William's executor. It is for him to carry out his brother's wishes.' He held out a hand towards Felicity. 'Come, wife. My family have shown their disregard for your sensibilities by this tirade against me.'

'St John, there is no need to leave.' Amelia glanced apprehensively at Felicity and added, 'You must forgive our heated words, Felicity. For two years we were all upset by the mystery that surrounded William's death and his wife's disappearance. And learning the truth of it just a few months ago was extremely distressing.'

'St John explained the circumstances of the deaths.' Felicity spared Amelia's feelings, though she had been shocked at such deviant behaviour by a member of her husband's family. She rose to join him and placed her hand in his. 'However, I am unused to such heated debate. And this is clearly a family matter that should be settled between yourselves. You judge St John harshly and I believe unjustly on his past exploits. This year has he not taken his responsibilities seriously and forsaken his wild days of drinking and gaming? You should be proud of him, not condemn him with such venom. I thought you prided yourselves on your family loyalty. You do him an injustice.'

Amelia was taken aback by the outburst but quickly recovered her composure. If St John walked out in a temper it would cause another rift within the family. She wanted Felicity as an ally not an enemy. Her stepson's wife had shown strength of character today that she had not thought she possessed. She would be the saving of St John from the reckless, wayward side of his nature.

She smiled at Felicity. 'My dear, I pray you are not overset by our unfortunate comments. Your loyalty to your husband is commendable. And you do right to remind us of the reformation of St John. You must not let the overheated words of a family discussion upset you. The Lovedays are a passionate brood and tempers sometimes run high, but harsh words are soon forgotten.'

St John continued to glare at the gathering, his body stiff with affront.

Adam also saw the wisdom of pacifying his twin. Peter had told him that no one had attended his service that morning. He too felt it was a warning to the family that they were not invincible. St John still had not been appraised of these latest developments.

He swallowed his anger at his brother's avarice. There were no secrets within such a close-knit family, and Elspeth had told him of St John's disappointment that Felicity was not the rich bride he had anticipated. St John was a fool not to count two thousand pounds as fortune enough when his wife had so many other fine qualities.

The truce between Adam and his twin had been fragile, the rivalry since childhood too deep to be easily bridged, but he did not want the old antagonism to return over today's dispute.

'Let us not quarrel, St John. Uncle's death upset us all. The past has gone and cannot be altered. Let it not spoil the present. You have a greater treasure in your new wife and expected child than any money can bring. This should be a day for rejoicing, not arguments.'

Senara relaxed, relieved that the tension in the room had eased. The family needed to be united more than ever before now that Sawle could be close at hand. She had woken this morning cold with the sweat of premonition that the smuggler was not far away. In her dream a black panther had prowled through the yard and family properties, spraying its scent as a warning that it regarded itself as a triumphant predator upon their lives.

Once the women had adjourned, the men remained in the hall sipping their brandy and enjoying cigars. After several glasses of wine and brandy, St John's mood had mellowed, until Peter mentioned, that his service had not been attended.

'Is this not proof that Sawle has returned to plague us?' flared St John. 'We must strike before he does any more harm to us. So far his actions have been warnings.'

'We have no proof that he was behind the death of the calves or the congregation not attending at Polruggen.' Joshua played down the incidents. 'We could be jumping at ghosts. Cows get sick and die. There could be a simple explanation why the villagers did not attend church this morning. Most importantly, there has been no sighting of Sawle or even of a stranger who could be acting on his behalf.'

'We must be prepared.' St John refused to back down. 'This is just his way of firing a shot across our bows. The authorities should be informed and a search made for him.'

'I agree with Uncle Joshua,' Adam said. 'To order a search would be to show that we fear Sawle. He would relish such notoriety. Instead a discreet check should be made on his old haunts. If anyone is carrying out his orders, it is no one that we know. Most of the senior members of his smuggling gang were arrested and imprisoned last year.'

'It is fine for you to play it down.' St John was scathingly sarcastic. 'He has not touched any property of yours. Yet it is because you have that damned ship of his in your yard that he has returned.'

'Papa, with respect, I think St John is right.' Peter voiced his own concern. 'He will not strike at Adam yet. Not if it could mean jeopardising the repair of his ship. These incidents are indeed warnings. We should not ignore them.'

'The preventive office have confiscated *Sea Mist*. It is no longer Sawle's property.' Joshua drew sharply on the long stem of his clay pipe and blew a cloud of smoke into the room before continuing in the voice that delivered his most severe sermons: 'I know your fiery tempers and how your blood will be crying out to bring this knave to justice. This matter could get out of hand. We have no proof against Sawle.'

'Do you think the blackguard will allow the excise office to take his ship without retribution?' St John scoffed. 'Sawle will not take any revenge upon Adam until after it is repaired and by some means is back in the smuggler's possession.' He gave a derogatory laugh. 'Fine revenge that would be to snatch it from the yard before the revenue office have paid Adam for the work. He will have his ship repaired without paying a penny. Neither will you receive payment from the revenue office if you have lost them possession of the cutter.'

Adam battled to check his temper. It was a possibility he had considered and it worried him, but he did not have a choice. If he did not complete the repairs, he doubted the excise office would honour the contract for the half-built cutter. 'The yard will have armed men on watch at all times until *Sea Mist* is safely delivered to its new owners.'

Peter was not convinced. 'All the more reason why Sawle would want to capture her. To show you that he is the more wily opponent.'

'He wants us all ruined,' St John snapped.

The cousins argued heatedly until Joshua struck the table with the palm of his hand. 'These are matters that may come to nothing. We might be a match for Sawle's brigands, but what about Hannah? She is my main concern. She must be protected but as unobtrusively as possible.'

The younger men fell silent, aware that a woman, even one as feisty and brave as Hannah, would be powerless against such an enemy. Joshua studied each of them, his expression drawn with anxiety. 'Hannah has spoken little of her fears, but she must know the danger.

69

She was responsible for the seizure of Sawle's cargo hidden on Japhet's land and for several of his gang being arrested. I will pay for men to keep an eye on the farm of a night. That should put her mind at rest.'

'That is a wise suggestion. Hannah must not be put at risk. But we could look foolish if we over-reacted to this.' Adam rubbed his chin. 'A few sensible precautions are all that are needed. Sawle wants us to suffer for what he has lost. He would see us ruined first and then lose face in the community.'

After a long discussion it was agreed to play the matter down. Peter remained unsettled and addressed his father: 'How do I deal with the villagers not attending my services? They should be brought to account. It is an abomination.'

'It has been done to humiliate you.' Joshua tapped his fingers together as he considered the matter. 'I think you should ignore it for now. See what develops in the next week.'

'But I am in neglect of my duty by allowing my flock to place their souls in danger.'

'Sawle is playing upon your religious fervour.' Joshua regarded his son with a frown. 'I advise that you do nothing, Peter. Let this blow over and they will come back to the church.'

'But it is an insult to God as well as our family.' Peter was white-lipped as his anger erupted.

'Then see it as a test of faith, my son,' Joshua advised. 'Pray for guidance, for compassion and for tolerance. The villagers have been in Sawle's pay in the past. They would have no choice but to obey him. He wants you to rant at your parishioners so that he can ridicule you.'

Peter's eyes glittered with determination. 'I will not fail my God. They must be shown the light.'

Joshua sighed. 'I strongly advise you to heed my words. It is for God to judge, not his servants. The villagers will not risk their souls to appease Sawle. Does not the Bible say, "Be not overcome by evil, but overcome evil by good"?'

Peter did not look convinced, and Joshua added, 'The good book also says, "God is not mocked; for whatsoever a man soweth, that shall he also reap." Pray for your parishioners, my son. They will return to the fold.'

Peter accepted that his father spoke wisely, but it would surely be a harder test of faith not to go amongst the villagers and preach to them of damnation. Two years ago it would have been impossible, but his marriage to Bridie had shown him a more compassionate way.

'The Good Lord looks after his own,' he said and bowed his head in a silent prayer. 'Our rewards are in Heaven.'

Chapter Ten

If Harry Sawle could have heard those words, he would have chuckled and added, 'The devil also looks after his own and his rewards are on this earth. That is what matters.'

Their enemy was closer than they realised. Sawle was hidden in the thick foliage of an oak tree, watching the family through the tall windows of the dining hall at Boscabel. The windows were open, and hearing the raised voices of the Lovedays, he grinned sardonically. Their words were indistinct, but from the heat of the conversation he guessed they were discussing the events he had ordered his men to carry out. Peter Loveday's feathers were most noticeably ruffled as he paced the floor and waved his arms. His father took a long time to pacify him. Nothing roused this young bantam cock more than his religious fervour. He was clearly outraged that no one had attended his service that morning.

It proved to Harry that he still had the power to make the villagers obey his commands, no matter how outrageous they might appear. That power was intoxicating. He had craved to be noticed and to control the lives of others. All his life he had witnessed how men of power and property had mastery over their servants and minions. From an early age he had rebelled at the inequality between rich and poor. That the inn provided the Sawles with a better income than the fishermen of the village earned meant little to him. As soon as he was old enough, he and Clem had been given a fishing sloop by their father and were expected to go to sea in all weathers. Often, after ten or twelve hours at sea, they would return home and with only a few hours' sleep would be hauled from their beds and used as tubmen when a cargo was landed. If they protested they were beaten with the buckle of Reuban Sawle's belt. If their immature bodies were weary and they dropped a cask of brandy, which smashed on the beach, they were struck so hard by the smuggler in charge that their ears rang for hours afterwards. They then received another licking from Reuban when he learned of their weakness. There had been countless nights when Harry had cried himself to sleep, his legs drawn up as he hugged his body against his pain and his misery. But he and Clem did not stay weak for long. Carrying the heavy casks and hauling in fishing nets soon built up their muscles. The constant beatings made them resilient and they learned to conquer their fear of pain.

Harry never forgot the power his abusive father had once had over him. A natural fighter, he had turned from his role of prey to that of hunter. To boost the self-esteem that his father had tried so steadfastly to crush, he began bullying the children of the village. He made them swear allegiance to him, and on feast and fair days they were ordered to become pickpockets, working in the crowd. Any plunder would be surrendered to Harry. If they failed to steal anything he saw it as disobedience and dragged them down to the beach, stuffing sand in their mouths or forcing their heads under the incoming tide until they half drowned. They never defied him again and were too terrified of the revenge he would exact upon them to speak of their ordeal to anyone in authority.

In his hiding place in the tree Harry flexed his hands and then balled them into meaty fists. The knuckles were scarred from the scores of beatings he had given out over the years. They had made him the undisputed ruler amongst the smugglers. He no longer had to use his fists, unless he wanted the pleasure of hearing bones crunch or flesh cave in beneath them. Now he paid others to do his dirty work.

Harry knew he was not the most respected man in the community, but he was the most feared. That was accolade enough. He had also become rich, certainly richer than St John Loveday. Then within a year everything had changed and he had been brought close to ruin.

His blood boiled with the force of his anger. The rage was demonic in its intensity. There was no place in his heart for compassion or mercy. A burst of easy laughter from within the house jerked him from his malignant reverie. He saw their amusement as a further affront. It was time the proud Lovedays were brought to heel and learned that no one crossed Harry Sawle and lived to tell the tale. His revenge would be sweet, but he knew it was a dish best served cold. And this was no single vendetta.

He could pay thugs to kill his enemies, but that would be too easy for these adversaries; he wanted them to suffer first. Adam thought he had triumphed over him by building the new revenue cutter, and it was a further insult to learn that he was repairing *Sea Mist* for the authorities.

A sardonic grin puckered his scarred cheek. The flesh was blackened from a musket misfiring during a confrontation with Senara Loveday. Every time he caught his reflection in a mirror he was reminded of his hatred for that family. Let Loveday pay out for the repairs, but it would not be the preventive officers who claimed the cutter. There would be no payment for Adam, and with the debts of the yard amassing, he could lose everything he and his father had worked for. And that would be just the start of his revenge, Harry vowed. There would be more – much more.

Had he not poisoned the herd at Trevowan and also the calves at Hannah Rabson's farm? She had been repaid for the cargo she had lost him. St John had also tasted his wrath for daring to issue a warrant for his arrest. That arrogant pride must be humbled and St John humiliated before he met his end.

Then there was Peter. The Loveday that Harry had dismissed as a pious weakling. The parson had proved his mettle last year and showed that he could be a formidable opponent. More fool him that he had not learned his lesson, and continued to preach against the evils of smuggling. Harry glowered as he watched the young preacher pace the floor, addressing his elders with a confident air. His manner was that of a general on the battlefield whose troops listened to him with respect. The image deepened the smuggler's scowl.

'Have your moment of glory, preacher. It will serve you to no avail,' he ground out under his breath. 'How strong is your bravado when we meet face to face?'

Harry had already proved that the parson's religious fervour could not keep the parishioners in his church. That was but the beginning of his planned downfall.

His eyes narrowed and fury scorched his gut. A few feet away Adam Loveday held court, as proud and influential as any lord of the manor. He was one of the most respected and liked men for miles around. It never entered Harry's head that Adam's house had been a partial ruin, with half its roof missing, and that only the skill of the yard's carpenters had made it possible for it to be restored. He saw only its present glory. The replenished livestock and the acres of fields that had been arduously cleared and put under the plough again proclaimed to Harry his enemy's position and influence.

The smuggler spat on to the grass below him. Again he ignored the fact that Adam had worked hard for every penny spent on his new estate and in the yard. His success proved that he, out of all his family, had the most to lose. Harry grinned evilly. Was that not how it should be, and would if not make this vendetta all the sweeter?

Adam was his main adversary – his greatest threat. They had been enemies for most of their adult lives. Adam had dared to pit his strength and wits against Harry and had never backed down from a fight, and for all his fine manners he had usually emerged the victor. That would now end. Adam Loveday would suffer at each persecution inflicted upon his family by Harry's men. He would be the one who paid the highest price.

Sawle watched as the men left the old hall. His punishment upon each of them must be carefully planned. He knew his victims well, their strengths and their weaknesses. Each would pay in full for their treachery against him.

Peter was further tested that evening. His second parish, Polmasryn, was three miles from Polruggan, and he was uneasy as he arrived there to take evensong. In the early-evening light the village looked eerily deserted. On a fine evening the men would usually be gathered around the lychgate to talk and half a dozen children would be playing in the single street.

This was a sinister echo of the events in Polruggan that morning. His temper flared that the villagers dared to so insult him and the Lord his God in this manner. Following on the tail of his anger was a sick dread that he had somehow failed his flock.

He drew a deep breath and prayed that nothing would be amiss tonight. The sun hovered above the tops of the trees, bathing the church in a golden glow. The sunlight was reflected in the plain leaded windows – the ancient stained glass had been smashed during Cromwell's austere reign. He tethered his horse where it could graze behind the church and patted its neck, saying stoutly, 'There is nothing sinister afoot. This is a perfectly ordinary evening.'

His step was firm as he marched towards the entrance. There was another half-hour before the service. He found Will Brennick, the church-warden, dozing in the porch. His thin face was heavily pockmarked and his penchant for illicit brandy had made his nose red and bloated. He was dressed in his Sunday-best trousers and jerkin but his shirt was dirty and crumpled and there were several ripe boils on his neck. Will was surly and unwelcoming as he started awake and swayed to his feet.

'Evening, Parson.' He was stooped from his years working in Sir Henry Traherne's tin mine and resented all forms of authority since the mine had been closed.

'You were sleeping when there is work to be done,' Peter snapped. 'Ring the bell to summon the congregation.'

Peter went inside. After the warmth of the sun he was struck by the chill of the interior. The church smelled musty. It always did. The bell rang with a hollow clang, the space between each peal laboured.

Peter opened the large Bible on the lectern at the passage he had selected and spread out the sheets of his sermon. Then he lit the candles on the altar and went to change into his vestments. On his return he was disheartened to find that the pews were empty except for the two elderly Crouch sisters, dressed in black. The daughters of old Dr Crouch had never married and lived in genteel poverty, making extra money by selling their honey and eggs at market. Both were deaf, so his Bible reading and sermon would be wasted on them, and they always dozed through most of the service.

His fingers drummed upon the smaller Bible he pressed to his chest. The minutes passed slowly, the clanging of the bell sounding more like a funeral knell with each peal. Still no one appeared. When the bell fell silent, Will Brennick shuffled into the nave and slumped into a pew.

Peter decided that the only way to deal with the situation was to act as though everything was normal. He raised his voice to loudly sing the hymns and addressed the back of the church during his Bible reading. The effort to appear calm was exhausting. He wanted to shout and rail at the abomination he believed had been deliberately perpetrated here. He kept his sermon short, and when he finally stood at the door to speak with the Crouch sisters, they passed him in silence and gave only a cursory nod to acknowledge his presence.

Brennick wrapped a muffler around his neck despite the warmth of the evening and did not meet Peter's eye.

'Where are the parishioners, Mr Brennick? Is this some ploy to shame me into not preaching upon the ills of smuggling?'

'I did hear there were a lay preacher who be popular. He gives his sermons in the shelter of the tor on the moor.'

'Who is this man?' Peter disliked the thought of unordained opposition, although for many years before he had been conferred with Holy Orders he himself had spoken God's word in towns and at fairs.

'Jeremiah Slater, I believe he be called.'

Peter snorted in disgust. 'He is a drunkard and works for Sawle. He is no preacher.'

'He has seen the light, so he do say.' Brennick shuffled forward, intent on ending the interrogation. He shot Peter a sly look. 'You gonna call your congregation to account, Parson?'

'They have not neglected their duty to the Lord,' Peter replied loftily whilst inwardly he fumed. Obviously Sawle had been behind this, but he refused to rise to the smuggler's bait. It was a five-mile walk to the tor and another five miles back. He doubted the villagers would keep up for long such a trek on their only free day in the week.

However, his pride had been stripped raw. On his father's advice he had curbed his own over-zealous preaching and shortened his sermons, and he had begun to hope that the villagers respected his guidance. To castigate them for listening to another preacher would make him appear foolish. He would play a waiting game, certain that his parishioners would return to the fold.

He tried to remember how his brother had dealt with an underhand adversary. Japhet was quick to use his sword in retaliation but he also had a sharp and cunning mind, and had often related his tales of roguery. Peter had pretended to despise such exploits, but he had secretly admired Japhet's understanding of his fellow man. Japhet had known how to play a waiting game, how to cool his temper and plan his triumph. Peter wished he had paid more heed to his brother's reminiscences instead of condemning him. He needed to call on such cunning now. He baulked at sitting back and allowing Sawle to believe he had won in this matter.

He rode home deep in thought, recalling some of Japhet's exploits, and through a sleepless night considered how his brother would have dealt with Sawle.

Chapter Eleven

Japhet would have been humbled by his brother's faith in him. For years Peter had condemned him for his way of life, and Japhet had resented his brother's sermons. Peter's piety had been beyond his understanding. It was not the Loveday way; even his father, whom he respected as a preacher, did not judge Japhet as fiercely as Peter had done. Eight years the elder, Japhet had been angered by his brother's narrow-mindedness. He had despaired that Peter was the runt of the family, using religion as a prop to bolster his own importance. Joshua's letter that had arrived on the last ship from England had praised Peter and commented on his change since his marriage.

'There is hope for him yet, Gwen,' Japhet had laughed as he sat with his wife discussing the family news. He fingered his dark goatee beard and his hair, unrestrained by a ribbon after his evening swim in the river, curled in soft waves to his shoulders.

The letter had been the first they had received from home, and afterwards he had taken a long walk. He had been unprepared for the depths of emotion roused by missing his family. But he did not regret his decision to settle here and make his fortune. He did not believe in regret. Whatever mistakes he had made in life, they had been his choice and he faced the consequences with head held high and the determination to make something good out of any bad.

England was another world. Australia was a fresh beginning, a place where Japhet could use his wits. He had found that many of the skills he had accumulated over the years were in great demand here. That did not mean life was without its problems. The colony was only thirteen years old and the convicts and ticket-of-leave men outnumbered the settlers.

The Lovedays' position in society had given Japhet his knowledge of running an estate and how to command and get the best from the men working for him. His years earning a living as a horse dealer and handling livestock on his sister's farm had also been an asset. Even his experience as a gambler and his dealings with the baser side of man's desires had made him a shrewd judge of character. As a youth he had enjoyed spending time in his uncle's shipyard and had learned many carpentry skills. And whether a man was gentry or peasant, he was at ease in their company. His quick wits and agile mind had got him out of many a difficult situation during the years he had walked a tightrope close to the wrong side of the law. When he saw an opportunity to improve his lot he did not hesitate to take it. He was fearless against risk and danger. Few men could best him in a street fight and he had fought many duels, with both sword and pistol, and emerged the victor.

However, life in New South Wales presented him with different problems. Here he had to pit his wits against not only the restrictions of living in a penal colony but the elements themselves. In the topsy-turvy seasons of this continent, the summer they had endured had been hotter than he thought a man could rationally bear, especially when forced to continue his work through the heat. Forest fires were frequent, endangering lives and homesteads. And when the rains came they were heavier and more violent than any storms he had experienced in England, causing the rivers to flood.

A natural leader of men, Japhet had made many friends amongst the settlers, who valued his advice, but he had also made enemies. Many of these were amongst the militia. The New South Wales Corps were mostly corrupt and had the power over life and death in the colony. So far Japhet had triumphed in his clashes with them.

He was aware that victory against an authoritative figure could soon turn hollow. There were officers in the corps who resented the fact that Japhet's wife had relatives with positions at the King's court in England. Gwendolyn had spent the year Japhet was in Newgate working to gain his pardon, and once it was granted had followed him to Australia with their son. That she had soon charmed governor John Hunter had also won them enemies. Yet Hunter had little control over the militia, especially the monopoly they held appropriating the government supplies arriving from England and selling them at extortionate prices. When Adam's ship *Pegasus* had arrived in Sydney with a cargo of farm and household tools, dry goods, livestock and cloth, Japhet had been determined that his cousin would not be cheated out of his profits. He had taken charge of the goods and opened a shop in Parramatta, where he had been challenged by the officers. Japhet had faced the confrontation and won the upper hand. He knew he had been lucky that time. But with Adam resolved to trade with the colony,

Japhet was equally determined to protect his cousin's interests and also to profit from the venture by being his agent.

For this to succeed in the long term, he'd had to win over the most corrupt officer in the corps. Japhet believed in keeping his enemies close and under watch. Captain Julius Haughton had tried to threaten him, insisting he pay him dues from the store he had opened or he would be arrested on trumped-up charges. Japhet had called his bluff. But knowing that Haughton was an officer without honour and also a bully who would make trouble for Japhet and his family, he could not allow the feud to fester between them. Life in the colony was too precarious to provoke an ongoing confrontation with the military. Should any dispute come to a head and a fight break out, a civilian could be arrested and hanged for striking a soldier. Japhet doubted he could control his wayward temper and not come to blows with the officer in the future, so he had decided to offer the captain a partnership. It had helped that Gwen's family were acquainted with an aunt of Haughton's and the officer would be loath to have his underhand dealings made known in England. Even so, Japhet did not trust the man, but whilst Haughton made a profit from their partnership he would stop the other officers acting against their ventures.

Japhet was at the sawmill he had built, which had been another profitable enterprise. A wooden framework had been erected to shelter the convicts from the heat of the sun, and this also enabled them to work longer hours. Three sawpits had been dug and the men worked in pairs wielding the long saws that cut through the timber. Two other convicts stacked the timber into piles and another two drove the wagon to deliver the orders to Parramatta township, which was rapidly expanding in size. They also cut into planks the trees felled by the settlers as they cleared their land.

Usually a settler was allowed only two male convicts to work for him, and this was where Haughton had contributed his share of the partnership, by supplying extra men to the mill.

Two hours later, when Japhet returned to Trewenna Place, his homestead on the Hawkesbury River, he was disgruntled to see Haughton's grey gelding tethered in the shade of a tree. This was the third time the officer had called in two months, and Japhet was wary of the man's pretence at friendship.

The officer was lounging in a chair on the cool veranda that ran across the front of the house. Captain Julius Haughton wore his uniform like a badge of honour; his curled blond hair and wide side-whiskers accentuated his natural arrogance. Japhet supposed that many women would find him handsome, but there was a weakness to his chin and his features were rather boyish for his thirty years, betraying his indolent nature. Gwendolyn was seated opposite the officer, and must have received warning of his company. When Japhet had left that morning, she had been wearing her oldest gown, as she intended to bottle preserves. She was now in her blue muslin, one of the latest high-waisted styles she had brought with her from England. Her dark hair was dressed simply in a chignon with a single curl falling over her shoulder.

Her poise and the way she sat at ease entertaining their guest roused Japhet's pride. Even at the ends of the civilised world Gwen was the epitome of an English lady at her leisure. Yet she was capable of working as hard as any of the servants in the house and on the farm. It was these qualities that had captured Japhet's heart where greater beauties had failed.

The maid Eadie, who had accompanied Gwen on her voyage from England, was sitting sewing at the far end of the veranda and also keeping a watchful eye on his son, Japhet Edward. His second son, Druce, would be sleeping in his crib at this time of the afternoon.

As he approached the house, his experienced eye noted the six mares and their foals grazing in the paddock. When he had become betrothed to Gwen in England they had planned to run a stud farm breeding Arab horses for racing or the gentry. When he had been arrested on his wedding day, those plans had been laid aside.

Such fine animals had no place here. Not yet anyway. One day it would be a thriving community. Perhaps in as short a time as twenty years, though Japhet had no intention of remaining here for so long. He bred workhorses but it was no more than a sideline. He was also establishing a herd of beef cattle and had planted some Indian maize and wheat.

He intended to make his fortune as quickly as possible, hopefully within another three years, and return to England a wealthy man. Too many tattle-tongues had been quick to wag that he had married Gwen for her money. She was joint heiress to her father's estate with her sister Roslyn Druce, who had married Sir Henry Traherne, whose estate abutted that of Trevowan.

Japhet, who never usually cared what people thought of him, had been stung by the gossip. Gwendolyn deserved better. He had married her for love. She was the sweetest, most loyal and loving companion and she had a wit to match his own. He wanted to prove that he was worthy of her loyalty and devotion. Those gossips would eat their words when he returned to England.

His homestead had a barn, a storehouse and an outhouse for the convicts. With so many transportees working for him, there was an element of danger in their presence, but Japhet had earned a reputation amongst them for being hard but fair. They knew that if they did right by him he would treat them humanely and with respect. But if they disobeyed his orders or were lazy they were returned to the compound or dealt with severely by Japhet himself. He had fought several troublemakers with his bare fists and emerged the victor – that was the language the convicts respected and understood. That his own sentence had been for highway robbery made him a High Toby in the criminal cant: an elite status amongst criminals.

At the sound of his arrival, Patch Evans, the one-eyed convict who kept a close watch on the security of the farm and protected his family in Japhet's absence, emerged from the side of the house. He had been mending the chicken coop, which had been damaged in a recent storm, whilst keeping an eye on Haughton and Gwendolyn.

Japhet did not think that Haughton was fool enough to press any unwanted attentions upon his wife, but the man was a womaniser and kept two convict women in Sydney who had borne him three children between them. Such arrangements were common among the soldiers. Japhet knew that Haughton was also wary about their partnership and regarded his position in the military as superior to Japhet's standing in the community. If the officer thought for a moment that Gwen would entertain his advances, he would relish making her his mistress as a means to lord it over his partner.

Gwendolyn had risen at Japhet's arrival, and the warmth of her welcoming smile dispelled his unease at Haughton's visit.

'How fortunate that you could put aside your work at the mill, my love,' she said. 'Is it not kind of Captain Haughton to ride so far out of his way to call upon us?'

He knew his wife did not like or trust the officer any more than he did himself, but Gwen also believed that his goodwill should be nurtured.

'Captain, it is always a pleasure when you honour our humble home.' Japhet brushed some clinging sawdust from his breeches. 'There is much work at the mill. The last two men you sent to me have learned their craft well.'

'It has been some weeks since we last discussed business, Loveday. Your cousin's ship will be arriving soon with another cargo. Some of the officers resent the arrival of merchant ships that seek to profit by trading with the settlers. A vessel docked yesterday, but the captain has sent word that no goods or livestock will be landed unless you act as agent to his investors. He carries a letter concerning this from the chief investor, Sir Gregory Kilmarthen, addressed to the governor. Kilmarthen escorted your wife here, I recall, and has been busy since his return to England.'

'He is a close friend of our family and has many links with the English court.' Japhet was elated by this news but showed nothing of this in his expression. From the tightness in Haughton's face, the officer was clearly displeased.

The captain's fair skin was reddened and sore from exposure to the sun, and he flushed even deeper as his anger erupted. 'This places me in a difficult position. Kilmarthen was warned to stay out of interfering in the way cargo arriving from England are sold here.'

'Our government believes in free enterprise.' Japhet fingered his goatee beard. 'It is what made Britain great. A prosperous colony benefits everyone. The officers are your concern,' He leaned against the rail of the veranda and folded his arms across his chest. He was in his shirt-sleeves and his arms were tanned from the hours he spent working on the land. His complexion was equally swarthy, and his dark hair curled to his shoulders, giving him an untameable air. 'Sir Gregory was appalled at the monopoly the corps had established to deal with merchant ships. No investor will risk their capital if they do not receive the profits they expect from such a venture. The officers' greed could bring this colony to its knees, and if the harvest failed, many would die. There is enough profit for the corps in the rum trade. They still maintain a monopoly on all imported spirits.'

'I cannot vouch to control the other officers.' Haughton stood up to pace the narrow space.

Gwendolyn also rose and gestured for the maid to enter the house. 'Gentlemen, I will leave you to discuss your business. Will you stay to dine with us, Captain?'

'Regrettably no, Mrs Loveday. I must return to Sydney.'

As Gwendolyn left the men, the officer's gaze lingered too long on her departing figure for Japhet's liking. He curbed his need to call Haughton to account. There was no point in antagonising him when the matter of the ship's cargo must be resolved.

'Will the officers cause problems if the livestock on board are auctioned at the docks?'

'They are threatening to arrest any settler who tries to buy from you.'

'Do they not understand what it will mean when news of their conduct gets back to England?' Japhet fumed. 'Are they really so short-sighted?'

'This is far from an ideal posting. They hate the heat and regard the convicts as scum. Many feel they have been condemned to a form of penal servitude themselves. They also resent the fact that you have the governor's favour, and now it is flung in their faces that you have influence in England. I tell you, Loveday, there are some who would see you dead before you prosper in this manner.'

The threat did not perturb Japhet. 'The military are not above the law. If I was killed, my death would be brought to the notice of the Prime Minister in England and every officer who had threatened me would be under suspicion. Governor John Hunter may have little sway over the military here, but his word carries a great deal of weight back home. There is talk that he will be replaced soon.'

Haughton regarded Japhet through narrowed eyes. 'But you would still be dead.'

'And as my partner, where would you be, Captain?'

Haughton dropped his gaze and Japhet gave a dry laugh. 'I do not fear an honourable death, Captain. This is a matter of trust and loyalty. You will prosper from the profits of this cargo and from other ships. Your part of the bargain was to keep the military off our backs. There are several ticket-of-leave men in my pay who are more than a match in slitting throats for any of your soldiers. They will defend my interests and go on to establish a life of position in the colony.'

'They cannot fight the might of the corps.'

The arrogance in his tone fired Japhet's heated response: 'As free men they may form their own militia to protect their property.'

'The governor would not condone an uprising,' Haughton sneered.

'I did not say there would be an uprising.' Japhet shrugged, tempering the atmosphere in the room. 'It would do no one's reputation any good. But the corps are outnumbered by settlers and emancipated convicts. They are not invincible.'

Haughton snapped back: 'It is the law that any man who strikes a soldier will be hanged. How else can authority be maintained?'

Japhet guessed that Haughton had faced much derision from the other officers over their partnership. The captain was all bravado, with little courage. He got his way by fear and bullying; it was how the military kept control here. He kept his voice low and reasonable. 'Many laws here were made when it was a colony of convicts controlled by the army. That has changed. More settlers arrive on every ship and with each year more convicts have served their time. With no money to pay for a passage back to England, they will make their life here.'

When the officer still did not hold his gaze, Japhet lost patience with the man. 'You are either for me or against me, Haughton. End our partnership and go back to sharing what profits you can glean from unsuspecting investors. Such prosperity will be short-lived. My way is the only legal, right and decent way forward. What is your decision?'

There was a long pause while the officer wrestled with his greed and his conscience. At last he gritted out in a far from reassuring manner: 'Our partnership stands.'

'Then I shall call on the governor and the ship's captain to discuss my terms. It is for you to muster a loyal band of soldiers to protect the cargo and those who choose to trade with us. Any soldier loyal to us will be rewarded.'

Haughton left, and Japhet entered the house. Gwendolyn, who had remained inside the door listening to the conversation, looked worried. 'Is it wise to take on the military, my love?'

'They cannot maintain their monopoly for ever. I am only dealing with a few ships. They will still have rich pickings.'

'But can you trust Haughton? He is weak. Will he stand up to his fellow officers?'

'I have the measure of Haughton and I can deal with him. He will provide a guard for the store and our customers.'

'But is the money worth the danger to yourself? The farm prospers and so does the mill.'

Japhet took her into his arms. 'You worry overmuch. Fate decreed that I was sent to this land. It is an opportunity to make a greater fortune than I had ever dreamed possible.'

Gwen sighed beneath her breath. When Japhet made up his mind, there was no turning him from his course. He had triumphed over adversity many times and she was certain that he would do so again. She knew that it troubled his conscience that he had brought shame to his family by his arrest. He would return to England a wealthy self-made man or die in the trying. Only that would appease his sense of justice for all they had suffered.

Chapter Twelve

It was not only the Loveday family whom Harry Sawle felt had betrayed him. In the dark he rode towards Penruan. His nocturnal wanderings were the only safe way he could risk travelling. He was lodging in a charcoal burner's cottage in a wood on the moor. The old man was deaf and mute and had two daughters who were not averse to warming Harry's bed.

On his return to Cornwall he had been furious to learn that his own family had turned against him. Clem now considered himself owner of the Dolphin Inn, with their mother's approval. Sal's betrayal cut deepest. He had no great feelings towards his brothers. Mark he considered a milksop and he despised him for toadying up to employers like Squire Penwithick and later Hannah Rabson. He'd deserved the beating his men had given him last year. The pity of it was that he had not died. Clem had brawn, not brains, and had been a good work dog in the smuggling trade before his mealy-mouthed wife had turned him into a lapdog.

He had thought his elder brother had more backbone than to heed a woman's nagging. Clem could have made a fortune continuing as a free-trader; instead he had turned respectable. In disgust Harry hawked and spat on the ground. The very thought left a sour taste in his mouth. Respectability was a means for the gentry to keep the peasants shackled like slaves to convention. It might work for the rich, but where did it get the poor? It kept them in their place, breaking their backs as they worked for a pittance that barely staved off starvation, and meant they had no chance of escaping the squalor of their lives.

From a youth Harry had resolved that would not be his way. He would tug his forelock to no man. In the smuggling trade he ruled as king. He chuckled maliciously. He did not care that those he controlled hated him universally. They were weak. He had no conscience and that gave him power.

Yet for Sal to turn against him and side with his brother hurt like a raw wound anointed with salt. Incapable of loving or even pity, he did have respect for his mother. When his bullying father was drunk and would have regularly beaten the children senseless, Sal had intervened and taken the blows herself. Her face and body might have been beaten black and bloody, but she would not cower beneath Reuban's onslaught and often laid her husband out cold with a skillet or a warming pan. She had never been intimidated by his abuse and had run the inn efficiently, while Reuban rarely lifted a finger and drank all the profits.

His father had had one redeeming quality: he had taught Clem and Harry all he knew about free-trading, and once they were old enough had put them in charge. Harry had thrived on the danger and adventure of the enterprise. He had increased the number of contraband runs, which had made him enemies amongst rival gangs. He took them on, using spies to learn of their landing sites and stealing their cargo. He prospered with each year, and became more ruthless. He took chances others would not dare and he was fearless in his provocation. Even Edward Loveday had swallowed his principles and allowed him to store goods on Loveday land.

Those had been desperate times for the Lovedays. At that time most of their fortune had been lost in bad investments in London. Also Adam had been a spy for the government and had been captured by the French, who had demanded a hefty ransom or he would be killed. To raise the money Edward had come to Harry, who instead of charging interest on the loan, which the Lovedays could ill afford, had demanded that his cargo be hidden on Loveday land.

How Harry had relished that moment of power over a family who despised him. Edward had condemned the trade stridently in the past. But no one was above corruption when needs were dire. The excise men had found the goods and had shot Edward, who had later died from his wound. His death had not troubled Harry. He had been furious that the cargo had been confiscated and he had lost a great deal of money.

Not that the Lovedays had ever been as innocent as they liked to be painted. St John had been happy to supplement his allowance by investing in the trade without his father knowing. The heir to Trevowan had thought himself superior to Harry in those dealings, but he had also paid the price for his arrogance. Harry had killed his main rival, Thadeous Lanyon, and made it look as though St John had been the murderer. At his trial, however, evidence had been found to prove his innocence.

Thoughts of revenge scoured the smuggler as he rode through the night. The moon was bright enough to light his journey, and as he rode he turned over in his mind his own family's treachery. Clem had stolen the inn from him, and with *Sea Mist* taken and another cargo confiscated, Harry was now facing ruin. But how to deal with his brother's disloyalty was more complex. Sal would not abide him harming Clem, who had always been her favourite. His scowl darkened. Brother or not, Clem could not get away with stealing the inn from him. Was he not Harry Sawle, and as such invincible? He had a position to maintain in the community. He would lose face if the tubmen and villagers sniggered behind his back that he could not control his own family.

Caution made him tether his horse outside the fishing port of Penruan and walk through the shadows to the inn on the quay. The cottages set into the sides of the steep coombe wore a ghostly glow in the moonlight. Few had their windows lit by candles or rushlights, a costly expense when the catch had been bad throughout the winter. The tide was out and the fishing fleet tilted sideways with their keels in the mud. The perpetual smell of fish and seaweed hung in the air. There was a rumble of voices coming from the inn. On cold evenings the fishermen would assemble there to mend their lobster pots.

Harry frowned at seeing several horses tied to hitching irons outside the Dolphin. He peered through the window. The red uniforms of the soldiers were clearly visible. There were no longer women selling their bodies in the inn, but Keziah and Sal's reputation for providing cheap quality meals had made it popular. There were also a dozen fishermen drinking quarts of ale and laughing.

Fury twisted Harry's scarred face. Clem was behind the bar, chatting to an officer. His brother looked at ease and far too like the cock of the roost for Harry's comfort. Keziah came into the taproom from the kitchen carrying a tray piled high with roasted chickens and pies. She served these to two well-dressed gentlemen at a corner table. One Harry recognised as the owner of the carting firm based in Trewenna; the other was a farmer from the other side of Polmasryn. Both would be staying overnight. They were respectable, law-abiding men who had certainly never visited the Dolphin in his father's lifetime.

In a few months Clem had transformed the rundown inn into a profitable establishment. Harry bunched his hands into fists, consumed with the need to lash out and hurt someone. His glare settled on Keziah. Clem would never have thought to take on the inn himself. It would have been her idea. She was another woman who believed herself the equal of a man. She had brains, ambition and a gutsy determination. He would enjoy teaching her her place. The corkscrew curls of her amber hair were tied back and her russet work dress was of a good quality and her white apron spotless. As he watched, she paused at the table of soldiers and joined in their laughter. The conversation was jovial and certainly not lewd as he would have expected. Keziah had clearly won their respect. She was a comely, buxom wench, but there was no overfamiliarity from the men. When she turned back towards the kitchen and a serving maid approached with tankards of ale, one of the soldiers fondled the girl's buttocks.

'Leave her alone.' Clem's strident voice cut across the laughter. 'If you want a knocking shop and inferior food, get yourselves off to Ma Bradley's kiddley on the Fowey road.'

Harry grinned, expecting the soldiers to cause a fight, smashing up the furniture and giving Clem a good beating. Instead, although the guilty soldier glowered, his companions made light of it, and one joked: 'I told you this bain't no place to get yourself a woman. Kezzie will be at you with a skillet if you try that on again. But she serves the best food for miles around and you'd go even further to get decent ale like this.'

How had his brother and his wife tamed the military, who were always unruly and ready for a fight with a drink inside them? Harry's mood soured. During his time running the inn, most of the profits had vanished in giving free drinks as bribes to the soldiers to keep their noses out of his business, and the bar had been regularly wrecked by their fights.

The Dolphin looked very different from how he had last seen it. The walls inside and out had been whitewashed, and proper benches and trestles had replaced the stools and the barrels cut in half that had served as tables. A fire burned in the grate and the smell of meat pies wafted temptingly through the crack in the door. The obvious success of the inn increased his anger. Clem had made a fool of him.

He ducked into the shadows as a soldier came out to relieve himself over the side of the quay. When the man went back inside, Harry walked up the hill towards the cottage set high on the coombe. His step was stealthy as he went round the back. He had learned that Clem had not moved into the inn but had kept his cottage, and that Sal lived with them. There was a strong smell of goats from the herd Keziah kept. The curious animals rustled the long grass of the field as they came to the fence of their paddock to see if the stranger had any food for them. Harry snarled at them and waved his hands to shoo them away. Some bleated in discontent. The noise did not trouble Harry. The cottage was set away from the others and the neighbours would not stir. Neither was Sal's hearing as sharp as it used to be.

As he expected, the back door was not locked. A candle glowed dimly in the parlour and his mother was dozing in a chair. He was surprised at how well she looked, her hair neatly hidden under a lace-edged cap, her black widow's dress trimmed with velvet and a small cameo brooch at her throat.

'You be doing all right for yourself, Ma.' His voice had a sharp edge to it. He remained outside the door of the parlour, concealed by the gloom.

Sal started with fright and opened her eyes. 'Who be there? That sounded like my Harry. That you, Harry?'

He stepped into the light and her round, wrinkled face showed no pleasure. 'I knew you'd turn up like a rotting seal on a sand bank.'

'Good evening to you too, Ma. Is that any way to greet your prodigal son?'

'You be better away from here. There be a warrant for your arrest. Bain't you brought shame enough to this family?' She shifted her weight in the rocking chair and folded her arms across her chest.

'A man has to earn his living. And my brother has been taking what be rightly mine.'

'The inn bain't yours. It never were. I'd had enough when Reuban died. Those two villains you hired to run the place turned it into a bawdy house. I were shamed . . . and after how hard I'd worked to make it a home and a decent inn . . .' Her voice cracked with pain.

'It were never decent. Pa saw to that,' Harry taunted. He had not expected Sal to welcome him with open arms, but her hostility added further fuel to his anger.

'The inn were mine after Reuban died.' She lashed him with her venom. 'Clem's made it a place to be proud of.'

'No one takes what be mine,' he warned.

Sal pushed her bulk out of the chair and said accusingly: 'How you gonna run it with a warrant on your head? Left to you, it would've been closed by the authorities for storing contraband. Clem saved it. So don't you talk of what be yours. All that waits for you here is a noose.'

Suddenly the fight went out of her. 'Bain't you done enough harm? Caused enough suffering? You be a fool to come back. I don't want to see me own flesh and blood hang. Get you gone, Harry. There bain't nothing here for you.'

'Not even you, Ma? I never thought you'd turn against me.'

'You be the devil's son, not mine.' She turned her back on him.

Harry instinctively raised his fist to strike her. No one had spoken to him in such a manner and lived. Her head was bowed not from fear of his retribution but from shame, and her voice shook.

'It be best you go, Harry. Do one decent thing in your miserable life. Spare us the shame of seeing you hang.'

His fist dropped to his side. He would not strike Sal, but her rejection closed the only chink of softness that had remained in his evil and corrupt heart. His eyes blazed with a feral light. Damn her! Damn his family! They were all dead to him. But they would live to rue this night.

He stamped through the cottage and came up short to see a white-faced youth staring at him from the bottom of the stairs. He glowered at his nephew. The boy's expression was stark with animosity.

'You made my gran cry. I hate you.'

Harry grabbed the boy and held him high against the wall with his large hands, glaring into the now frightened face. Sal was sobbing into her apron and had not heard the exchange.

'Mention to anyone, especially your pa, that I've been here and you'll be floating in the harbour before the week be out.'

The boy gulped and lost his bravado. Harry released him, and the boy slid down the wall to lie in a crumpled heap. 'Get to bed, or it will be the worse for you. Remember, I bain't bin here.'

Harry kicked the door shut as he stormed out, his gut burning with hatred for the family who had betrayed him. Clem would feel the weight of his wrath. But vengeance needed careful planning, and time, something he knew was not on his side. As he galloped out of the village he could feel the noose tightening around his neck. If he fled Cornwall he might stand a slim chance of escaping it. But to run was not his way. It was the path of a coward, and no one could say Harry Sawle did not stare his demons in the face and go down fighting, leaving a trail of destruction in his wake.

Chapter Thirteen

Another humiliating week followed for Peter. Whenever he passed a parishioner they either looked away in embarrassment or had a smirk on their face. He treated them all the same, raising his hat, offering a cheery greeting and enquiring after their family. This disconcerted them, expecting as they did his anger and recrimination.

Bridie found it harder to face the women. Though she bore them no grudge at the way they had betrayed her husband, it echoed the prejudice she had faced so often as a child. Memories of shouted insults at her hobbling gait, or stones thrown at her to hound her out of a village, brought a return to the nightmares she had suffered in her youth. She had never been confident having always been the butt of abuse and ridicule.

In those days she had known severe poverty and hunger. The attacks had toughened her and made her determined to better herself. It had been a long, slow struggle. Adam had given her the chance of an education when he had arranged for her to attend the school at Trevowan Hard. From the first day it was as though her mind had waited all her life to be released from the constraints of her frail body. Where once she had been starved of food, now she was hungry for learning and the wonderful world reading had opened to her.

She had shone in the schoolroom, and with her new-found knowledge her confidence had grown. Until now. Her love for and faith in her husband made it impossible for her to believe that the congregation would dare to strike at his influential family in this way. Therefore it must be something that she had done that had made them turn against Peter.

When the women who usually attended the lace-making afternoons at the parsonage all sent their excuses, it confirmed that she was the one at fault. That they used the same excuse of illness to keep the children from attending school at Trevowan Hard was equally hard. She knew the children were not ill, for none of the women had called on Senara to tend their ailments. Bridie hid her pain and continued to perform her parochial duties. She visited the families, as she would any sick parishioner, with small jars of preserves or tonic wine that she and her mother had prepared. None of the children had looked ill, but she made no comment and wished them all well. Their mothers were ill at ease in her company, and three had denied her admittance to their cottages.

Gertrude Wibbley, the most outspoken and caustic-tongued, had been the surliest, her bulk blocking the doorway, and it had taken all Bridie's courage to keep smiling. 'I pray little Mary and Jimmy are soon fully recovered. It is a shame for them to miss too much schooling at this time of year, for once the farm work picks up in the summer, they are needed in the fields. If there is anything I can do for your family, you have but to ask.'

When Gert did not meet her eye and made to close the door, Bridie blurted out: 'Mrs Wibbley, if I have done something wrong, or somehow failed the villagers, I am truly sorry. Tell me what it is.'

Through a crack in the door Gertrude replied in a small voice that was far from her usual strident boom: 'It bain't nothing you've done, Mrs Loveday. We all be very grateful for your kindness, but . . .' The hesitation was brief. 'I can't say more.' Then the door was shut forcefully in her face.

So the women were playing this deception against their will. It did not make it any easier to contend with.

That Sunday Polruggan church was again empty during the early-morning service. The streets were deserted and the doors of the cottages closed. It was the same at Polmasryn, where even the Crouch sisters were absent. Will Brennick had earlier sent word that his father, who lived in Bodmin, had suffered a seizure and was dying. He had left to visit him.

'This abomination cannot continue,' Peter ranted at his distraught wife as they left the church.

A drunken voice singing a bawdy song brought an angry flush to Peter's face. David Gorran, a bent and twisted old man with rheumaticky joints, weaved his way precariously down the empty street clutching a clay cider jug. He had once been a farm labourer but in recent years was little better than a vagrant. His mother had inherited a cottage on the edge of the hamlet and he had been her only son. He had never married and had looked after his mother when she was widowed and infirm until she died. He had also been the scourge of the district, and when the drink was in him he often displayed himself indecently to young girls and women. But he had never molested any of them as far as it was known.

'You are a disgrace, Gorran,' Peter fumed, marching up to the man. 'You are drunk on the Lord's day.'

The labourer peered at him blearily and sniggered. 'I be drunk every day, Parson.'

'Why were you not in church? Where is everyone?' Peter's tone was authoritative and brought the old man to a teetering halt.

Bridie had hurried to her husband's side. 'Ignore him, Peter. This is playing into their hands.'

Gorran grinned inanely and swayed backwards and forwards so violently that it was astonishing he remained upright. 'Have 'ee lost someone, Parson?'

'The villagers were not at church today.'

'Happen they've all come to their senses.' Gorran belched and stabbed a finger at Peter. 'Happen they found a more accommodating church, where they bain't judged for trying to bring a bit of comfort to their lives. Happen they be sick of your pious ranting.'

He was drunk and past caution or respect. As Peter struggled to contain his outrage, the old man took another swig from the cider jug. His hands shook so much that a torrent of amber fluid gushed down his chin and on to his chest. He cursed at the waste and became more belligerent as he continued his ranting: 'Anyways, who be you to tell us what be wrong or right? Your family bain't no better. That brother of yours turned villain to rob and steal.'

'Japhet was pardoned.' Peter was incensed that the drunken sot should malign his brother.

Gorran staggered and almost lost his balance but managed to recover. His face convulsed into an ugly scowl. 'Reckon you Lovedays have all sold your souls to the devil.' He leered at Bridie and scratched at his rancid crotch. 'Her and her sister make their witches' brews to enslave us all. Reckon you and Cap'n Loveday were bewitched. What gentleman would wed gypsy blood?'

Before Bridie could stop him, Peter had punched the intoxicated man on the jaw. Gorran crashed to the ground, the cider jug smashing in shards around him. Peter hauled him to his feet to drag him to the village stocks. As parson, he had certain jurisdictions over his flock, especially when they broke the laws of the Sabbath.

'Get the keys from the church, Bridie.'

'This will solve nothing—' she began, but was cut short by his shout of outrage.

'A half-day in the stocks will show the villagers that I will not be mocked. Get the keys, if you will.' His words rapped out like a volley of shots. A vein stood out and throbbed erratically on his temple. It took all his willpower not to lambast this sinner for his heinous words and disrespect.

'Peter, I pray you to reconsider. Gorran is an old man. He but spoke what many must feel.' Bridie's voice broke. There had always been a double edge to Senara's healing remedies. It was not the first time her sister had been accused of witchcraft. It was a word that spread fear through the superstitious-minded. Though witches were no longer hunted down and hanged in the way they had been a century earlier, a woman labelled a witch could be stoned from a village or her house burned to the ground. Any who associated with her would be reviled and similarly condemned.

If Sawle had wanted to find a way to destroy the Lovedays in the community, such rumours about Bridie and Senara could bring trouble to the family. Senara was no sorceress; her healing remedies had been handed down through generations to ease the suffering of others. Shaken, Bridie had to hurry to keep up with her angry husband, hoping yet to change his mind.

Peter continued to march the complaining Gorran down the street. 'I will not have you, my family or the good Lord insulted, dear wife. They think I am weak. But I will show them that I am as strong as my brother and cousin. Right will always triumph over evil. Now fetch the keys, if you please.'

She respected her husband for his stand but it did not stop her stomach churning with fear as she returned to the church. The village might have appeared deserted, but Gorran's cries of protest would draw a crowd like cockroaches out of the woodwork. When she returned with the keys she was relieved that the street remained empty. David Gorran was sitting slumped over the stocks with his legs stuck through the holes in the wood, and his loud cries had faded to an incomprehensible mumble.

Peter snapped the large lock shut and fastened it. 'Use this time wisely, Gorran, and repent of your sins.'

The old man peered blearily up at him and mouthed a blasphemy.

Peter took Bridie's arm. 'Come, wife, I shall return after evensong to release him.'

Bridie glanced at the overcast sky. 'It looks as though it could rain later. He will be soaked.'

'The better to sober him and bring him to his senses.' Peter had no sympathy with the man.

95

He heard Bridie catch her breath at the harshness of his remark. She bowed her head. It was not her way to condemn his actions, but he knew that her tender heart was troubled that the man might suffer. Her attitude always amazed him. Bridie had taken no offence at the drunkard's cruel words, though there was now a shadow of pain behind her expressive eyes. She would be worried that her past made her unsuitable as his wife.

He watched her as she self-consciously tucked a tendril of hair under her Dutch cap. She had no notion that her beauty shone from both inside and out. Her complexion had been dusted by the sun to bring out a smatter of attractive freckles across her nose but was otherwise smooth and unblemished. Long lashes fringed her berry-brown eyes, which were as large and trusting as those of a young fawn. Her beauty alone could never move him. He had seen too many women famed for their looks who had hearts sealed in ice. It had been her kindness and compassion that had captivated him from the first time they had met. She knew when any parishioner was ill, or if a family was without adequate clothing or food, and always found a way to supply what was needed without them feeling it had been an act of charity. She would visit the sick and the elderly and read to them from books. Though Peter would have preferred that she read from the Bible, he never criticised her in this, for he saw how quickly the women had come to show deference to her and accept them amongst the community.

He reached out to take her hand. 'Your heart is too gentle, my love. To keep the respect of my flock I must never show weakness. It would destroy my authority.'

Bridie was unsettled all afternoon. It had started to rain shortly after they returned to the parsonage and she kept thinking of David Gorran in the stocks. It was not uncommon for them to be used as a punishment for drunkenness and disorderly conduct, fighting in the streets, or the common nuisances of allowing your dog to roam the streets and bite someone or your pig to wander into another's garden.

She kept glancing out of the window, her frown deepening as the rain continued. Peter sat in a chair by the fire holding Michael on his knee and waving a brightly painted rattle. The baby's hands reached out to follow the toy's movements and Peter chuckled.

'Have you ever seen a more contented child?' His handsome, chiselled features had softened with love and pride. This was a side of the strict, pious man few people glimpsed.

Bridie smiled. 'He is a darling, a veritable angel. He rarely cries, but then if I am not here Ma anticipates all his needs.'

'We have been blessed, wife.'

'Truly blessed, husband.' She turned absently to the window and breathed easier when she saw that the rain had lessened. Nevertheless, her anxiety made her say, 'Will anyone accompany you to Polmasryn this evening.'

Peter placed the rattle in his son's hand and sat him on a rug propped up with pillows. 'Why do you ask?'

'Because of the villagers. No one attended the services today. I am concerned how they will react when they discover Gorran in the stocks.'

'He was drunk. He has spent many days in the stocks.'

Bridie chewed her lower lip. 'But the villagers have been acting strangely all week. I do not think they actually hate us, but . . .' She covered her cheeks with her hands and fought to overcome her fears. 'They do not want us here. I thought I had begun to win the women over, but after what Gorran said today, about myself and Senara, it is obvious they do not trust us. And that reflects on you and Adam.'

He came to her side and took her into his arms, his lips warm against her brow. 'No one speaks out against my cousin. It is I who have to prove myself. Not just as a preacher but as a man who will stand up for what he believes is right, even if it means fighting for it. They are testing me. I shall go alone to Polmasryn. I do not fear them, and it would take a foolish man indeed to strike an appointed preacher.'

'But they tried to kill you last year.' The memory filled her with dread and she clutched at her husband's arm for support.

'Mordecai Nance was responsible for that. He paid the price for his evil deeds.' He kissed her lips to halt her protests and his dark eyes were gently mocking. 'And did I not escape and later fight him?'

'Japhet could not have acted more bravely,' she praised, stamping down her fears. 'But tonight I will come with you. I would not have your flock think that I am intimidated by their censure.'

She would not be persuaded otherwise, though Peter was clearly reluctant for her to accompany him. He must then expect some trouble.

A light drizzle was falling as they made their way to the service at Polmasryn. Bridie drove the dogcart and Peter rode his horse beside her. As they entered the village, two men were standing at the stocks. Bridie hoped they would not cause a scene. Apart from them, the village was again eerily quiet; the doors of the houses were closed, and there was no sound of children at play.

'Good evening.' Peter addressed the pair cordially.

The brothers Ethan and Mose Dunn turned to eye them sourly. Bushy beards covered their faces and upper chests and their beefy arms hung at their sides. They were shepherds who lived in a hut on the edge of the moor, and Peter suspected that they worked for Sawle, hiding his cache of contraband in isolated places until it was safe to take it further inland. They were also accomplished poachers, and Mose had two dead rabbits tied to his belt. A skinny sheepdog sat at their heels.

'What gives you the right to put Gorran in the stocks without some kind of hearing?' Ethan challenged. The brothers had never been known to attend church, and when Peter had been a lay preacher they had often heckled him if they passed when he was giving a sermon in a hamlet.

He took exception to Ethan's tone. 'The man was drunk and blaspheming. I but did my duty.'

'Then happen you take your duty a mite too seriously.' Ethan stepped aside to reveal the prisoner in the stocks.

Bridie could not contain a shocked gasp. Gorran was lying unmoving on the ground with vomit over his clothing. There were rotten vegetables around the stocks, showing that someone had been here during the day taunting him.

Peter dismounted from his horse and bent over the man. Gorran's face was grotesquely twisted, mouth gaping and his tongue lolling on his chin. He was clearly dead.

'He must have choked on his vomit.' Peter took the key from his pocket and unlocked the stocks. 'Take him back to his cottage and have Widow Cooper lay him out, and I will perform the Last Rites after the service.'

'You'll be talking to an empty church, Parson,' Mose Dunn snarled. 'Might as well tend to him now, seeing as how you could be held responsible that he died.'

'And how do you know my church will be empty?' Peter accused.

'They've all gone to Trewenna. I passed a villager on the way who said you'd been taken ill. He'd bin at Polruggan this morning and found the place empty. Happen your father will be pleased to have a full church.'

'But the service was scheduled here for this morning and we did not pass anyone on our journey.'

Ethan shrugged, but Peter detected a smirk pulling at the corners of his mouth. 'If you came by road, it be likely the villagers walked across the fields. That be the shorter way.'

That was true enough, but it was extremely unlikely that no one had mentioned the matter on Peter's return to Polruggan. He was not about to argue in the street, however. He had an uncomfortable feeling that the brothers were mocking him.

'I will lay the man out if you carry him to his cottage,' Bridie suggested. 'He should not be left here and Widow Cooper will not be pleased to perform such a task if she has walked to Trewenna this evening.'

The laying out was unpleasant. Not only did Gorran stink of vomit, but his bowel and bladder had also emptied. Bridie gritted her teeth and performed her Christian duty. The Dunn brothers had disappeared as soon as they had laid Gorran on his unkempt bed. The sackcloth sheets had not been washed in months, or the blanket. Bridie stripped these from the bed and found a cleaner blanket in the second bedroom to spread under the body.

Her task finally finished, she stood at the foot of the bed as Peter intoned the Last Rites. He had been to the church whilst she had been working and no one had attended the service. He had left a note at the churchwarden's cottage that Gorran's funeral would be at noon tomorrow and for him to procure a coffin and inform the villagers.

'He always had money for drink. There must be some in the house to provide for a coffin. As he has no relatives the rest will be given to the parish for the benefit of the poor.' He spoke another prayer over the body, and then said almost apologetically, 'It was a tragedy that he died whilst in the stocks.'

'Did he die or was he murdered?' Bridie stunned him by announcing.

A candle had been lit by the head of the bed. Gorran was in his best trousers and a clean shirt. A strip of linen circled his head from his crown and was tied under his chin to keep his jaw from dropping open. Two pennies rested on his eyes. Bridie lifted back the collar of his shirt to reveal bruises on his neck, and added, 'Perhaps Sir Henry Traherne should be informed of this. The Dunn brothers should be questioned.'

'It makes no sense that he was murdered,' Peter replied.

'It would be another way to discredit you.'

Sir Henry Traherne heard Peter's account of the incident when the young parson called at Traherne Hall the following morning before the funeral. The Hall was a square redbrick mansion with carved pediments over the casement windows and had been built in the time of William and Mary. The gardens were formal, with low box hedges all neatly trimmed and regimented. There was not a sign of a weed on the gravel drive; Lady Traherne would dismiss any gardener who was so lax in his duty. Peter did not care for such formality or the grandeur of the gilded plasterwork in every room. It had been lavishly redecorated since Sir Henry's marriage but was too ornate to make the house appear welcoming or homely.

The baronet was a friend of all the Loveday men and had been the magistrate who issued the warrant for Harry Sawle's arrest.

A portly and portentous major-domo appeared to announce in a high-pitched whine: 'I regret that Lady Traherne and Lady Anne Druce are indisposed and are not receiving visitors.'

'It is Sir Henry I wish to conduct business with,' Peter returned officiously. He was relieved he had no need to spend a polite half-hour in the company of the two women, who never lost an opportunity to deride Japhet as a rakehell and Gwendolyn a love-struck fool who had lost all sense of propriety.

The major-domo led him to Sir Henry's study. The room smelled faintly of cigar smoke, and Peter guessed that it often served as his friend's retreat from the company of the womenfolk. Sir Henry's wife Roslyn had a shrewish tongue.

Sir Henry arrived within a few minutes. He was dressed in riding boots and breeches and a cutaway jacket with long tails in the latest mode. But the baronet was no fop. The once carroty redness of his hair was now shot through with threads of silver and thinning at the temples. It was cut short to the collar without artificial curls or oil.

He greeted Peter warmly. 'It has been too long since you called upon us. Is your good wife not with you? I trust she is well.'

Sir Henry had never condemned either Bridie or Senara for their lowly birth and had accepted that both Peter and Adam had married for love. Not so his wife and mother-in-law, who frequently found excuses not to receive the sisters. Sir Henry had even been kind enough to loan Bridie the money to buy spinning wheels and bodkins to set up the village lace-making industry.

'My wife has her duties in the schoolroom at Trevowan Hard this morning. She is very well indeed, Sir Henry.' He did not hold back in informing the justice of the peace of the subversive tactics of his parishioners in the last two weeks, which he suspected were intended to undermine his authority, and concluded by expressing his regret at Gorran's demise.

'No blame will be attached to you for this death.' Sir Henry was sympathetic and his expression concerned. 'You but performed your duty. Do you think I should question the Dunn brothers about the marks on Gorran's neck?'

Peter gave a resigned shrug. 'I fear the scoundrels will deny all knowledge and there were no witnesses to any incident. I was too angry with Gorran to notice any bruises. Anyone could have attacked him that afternoon. I fear it was a warning to me.'

'His death will be investigated. It will show that the law cannot be flouted. Though I suspect I will find no proof. These are lawless times, my friend.' Sir Henry regarded the stubborn set of Peter's jaw and feared that he could be in danger. 'I will arrange for some of my men to be in the church.'

'Thank you, but that will not be necessary. I will face my flock alone. I am not afraid. The Lord is with me.'

Sir Henry nodded. 'I did not expect otherwise.' He wondered if Peter was being brave, foolish or plain obstinate, but he had stood up to his attackers last year and won their regard. It was the only language men like Sawle and his gangs of smugglers understood. He was surprised that the villagers were seeking to humiliate their parson now.

Sir Henry decided that there would be a discreet guard of his own men placed in the churchyard in case there was any unpleasantness. But he suspected that the villagers had only been acting on orders – the orders of someone they feared more than the heavy arm of the law. To flout the laws of the Sabbath was still a punishable crime, and heavy fines could be imposed on those who did not attend church.

Later that morning Peter showed no apprehension as he performed the funeral service. To his surprise the church was full, and many of the men had taken two hours from work to attend. Yet Gorran had not been particularly liked. The women were also present, and throughout the service and burial the congregation were reverential. Peter was on his guard when Walter Stone, from a family of known troublemakers in Harry Sawle's pay, approached him after the final prayers.

'That were a fine service, Parson.'

'No more than any of God's creatures deserves. Though Gorran often strayed from the path of righteousness.'

'Happen if some of us had been here that afternoon, he would'na have died.' Stone sucked in his breath through several missing teeth. He appeared to be having trouble saying what was on his mind.

Peter tensed, suspecting some censure that he was in some way responsible for the drunkard's death. But when Stone did not hold his gaze, he guessed that this was an apology.

'There was some mix-up with the times and places of the services, I believe,' he said graciously. 'I will ensure that the churchwarden announces in the village square of a Saturday the hour and place of each service I will conduct on a Sunday. I would not have my flock obliged to traipse several miles to attend the wrong church through a misunderstanding.'

Stone made a choking sound that could have been an acceptance and walked away. As they filed away from the grave, most members of the congregation stopped to speak with Peter and enquire of his family. Many had difficulty meeting his gaze. He had heard the whispers amongst the mourners that bruises had been found on Gorran's neck and the speculation that he had been strangled. To miss a few church services might have seemed a jape to teach their parson not to be so harsh in his sermons on smuggling, but for Gorran to be murdered as a further means of discrediting him had been unacceptable. It had shown them that Sawle would stop at nothing in his bid for revenge, and an unspoken pact had been formed between many of the villagers that the smuggler would not so manipulate them again. That could have been any one of them, murdered for no reason other than Sawle's contempt for the law and hatred of the Lovedays.

Peter was polite and appeared not to judge them. If they had been told to discredit and humiliate him, they clearly now regretted it.

Chapter Fourteen

June had proved to be a temperamental month, in which all the seasons could be experienced in the space of a morning. The day would start with a sea mist, then the wind would cut sharp as a finely honed knife chasing it away and the sun would break through so that the workers in the yard stripped off their coats and jerkins and rolled up their sleeves; then within an hour a sudden downpour would bring a halt to the work.

It had been a difficult month for Adam. The Admiralty had been slow to make their payment for the repair of *Sea Mist* and it had finally arrived last week, but no money had been received for work to continue on the half-built cutter. Within two weeks *Sea Mist* would be ready to sail, and Adam had notified the Admiralty. He wanted the ship out of the yard as soon as possible. He felt its presence had brought bad luck. There had been further delays when some wrong fitments had been sent from the chandler in Fowey, and a spate of careless accidents on the damaged cutter had made the men reluctant to work on her.

Today there was a problem with the new rigging, and two of the wooden blocks that the rope passed through to raise and lower the sails kept snagging and had to be replaced. Adam's temper was on a short fuse, and he was on the quarterdeck threatening to dock a man's wages for incompetence when a lugger on the river hailed the yard. He glanced across to the approaching vessel, which was lowering its sail, and caught sight of a naval uniform. His irritation increased, as he assumed that Lieutenant Shaver had come to inspect the repairs.

'Get the deck cleared of tools. I don't want that old busybody falling over a hammer or box of nails.' He dragged his fingers through his hair, conscious that as he had spent the morning in the carpentry sheds he was dishevelled and there were wood shavings clinging to his breeches.

Shaver was a stickler for appearances, and Adam was annoyed that this surprise visit had caught him at a disadvantage.

He pulled down the shirtsleeves he had rolled up over his tanned arms and yelled for an apprentice to bring him his jacket from the office.

There was a laugh from the lugger and a cheeky voice piped up: 'There is no need to attend on ceremony for me, Captain Loveday.'

Adam did not immediately know the deep voice, neither did he at first recognise the tall, clean-shaven midshipman with the shock of wheat-coloured hair tied back with a black ribbon. The young man held his bicorn under his arm and grinned as he saluted.

'Have I changed that much, sir?'

'Good Lord, it can't be Richard!' Adam voiced his disbelief as he took in the four extra inches of height and broadened shoulders of his stepbrother.'

'Aye, aye, sir.' Richard grinned broadly and stepped on to the jetty,

'You've become a man.' Adam laughed and slapped him on the shoulder. 'You were still a skinny runt on your last leave.'

Richard winced at the heartiness of Adam's touch. The older man paused as he noticed the dark circles around Richard's eyes and the stoop of pain to his shoulders.

'Have you been wounded? Was it in battle?'

'A minor skirmish with two French frigates. We were escorting a supply ship. I received a musket wound. Nothing too serious. I do not want Mama to worry.' Richard dropped his bravado, and on closer inspection Adam was concerned to discover his stepbrother's pallor. There was also a slight tremor to his body.

'We'll go into the office. Your safe return calls for a celebratory brandy. Shall I send to Trevowan for the coach if your wound pains you?'

'No, after a short rest I will ride.'

They fell into step as they walked to the office and Adam enquired, 'When did your ship get in?'

'I docked at Plymouth yesterday and hired the lugger to speed my journey here. There was no time to send word to Mama. She is at Trevowan, I trust, and not in London.'

'Yes, Amelia spends less time in the capital now,' Adam quickly reassured him. 'She will be thrilled you are home. Whenever we learned of another sea battle, your mother worked herself into a rare taking that you had been harmed.' He was overcome at this unexpected reunion. It was the best thing to have happened to the family for months. 'I hope your leave will be a long one to give you time to fully recuperate.'

Richard Allbright nodded, but there was weariness in his movements. The young lad had been two years at sea; that alone took a toll on body and soul, and Adam knew from experience that battle was traumatic. It was never pleasant to witness the bodies of your fellow shipmates blown to pieces by cannon balls, crushed by falling masts and spars, or fatally pierced by splinters the size of spears. But then to be a part of Nelson's fleet and the great victories for England must also have been a thrilling adventure. Adam would have found it exhilarating. The reckless side of his nature envied his stepbrother's lack of responsibilities, which enabled the lad to pursue a life at sea.

'I have been given two months' leave by the naval surgeon.' Richard quickened his step as he regained his land legs. 'Then I am to take my lieutenant's examination at Plymouth.'

Adam gave a low whistle of approval. 'Later I will hear all about your adventures and battles. You must have served bravely and with great competence. You are but seventeen; many midshipmen are in their twenties before they are deemed experienced enough to be put forward for their examination as a lieutenant.'

'There have been many casualties amongst the officers, and I have to pass it first,' Richard said modestly.

'I will help you all I can. Though my own naval law is rather rusty now.' Adam coughed into his hand and his smile was ironic. 'Not forgetting that I was cashiered for duelling with another officer.'

'But that gave you the chance to work as a government agent for England in France. Do you not miss those days?' The note of hero-worship was still in his stepbrother's voice, and Adam was acutely aware that he had been the influence behind Richard's decision to take up a naval career. Amelia had been horrified, for she had planned that her son would take after his father and become a lawyer − a safe, respectable profession. She saw no glory in navy life, regarding even the most courageous of the commanders as little better than pirates. The thought made Adam suppress a smile, for some of them undoubtedly were exactly that. After leaving the navy, he himself had captained *Pegasus* as a privateer on several voyages with letters of marque granted by the government to fire upon and capture enemy ships. It had been a profitable venture but not without its dangers.

He realised he had not answered Richard's question and said lightly,

'Sometimes I miss the sea and the challenges we faced, but only the young and foolhardy thrive on adventure. I am a shipbuilder now and married with four children to provide for.'

'And your last letter spoke of building a merchantman. Is that it over there?' Richard stopped to admire the large ship, its timbers gleaming golden in the sunlight. 'She has good lines and will be a beauty.'

'The future of our yard could depend on her prowess. Now let us have that drink. Perhaps not brandy. Amelia might not approve to smell it on your breath.'

'Mama must accept I am no longer a child,' he snapped.

Adam was shocked. Richard had always been sensitive to his mother's regard. Richard seemed to realise what he had said and rubbed his brow. 'That was ungallant. Mama can be overprotective. I have been drinking rum ever since I joined the navy.'

'Of course,' Adam replied, 'but I would suggest a fine claret.'

After a pause Richard nodded, and as Adam turned away to fill two glasses from a wine flagon, he did not see his stepbrother grip his hands to still their shaking. The colour returned to the young man's cheeks after he had finished the claret and the short rest had revived him.

'The voyage has taken its toll on you,' Adam observed. 'You would not have been given two months' leave if your wound had not been serious. If you do not want Amelia clucking round you like a mother hen, you should not arrive at Trevowan looking tired. Bridie has the dogcart here. I will drive you to Trevowan and return before school is finished for the morning.'

Richard nodded but added: 'A few good nights' sleep and I will be fine.'

Whilst Adam went to the door to shout an order for the dogcart to be hitched for him, Richard took a phial from his pocket, poured several drops into the last of his claret and drank it quickly. His step was firmer as he followed his brother across the yard and acknowledged the well wishes and greetings from the workers who recognised him.

Adam stayed long enough at Trevowan to witness the squeals of surprise and tearful embrace of mother and son. The family had gathered in the winter parlour. The Chinese wallpaper of peacocks remained, but Felicity had replaced the faded curtains with new dark blue velvet hangings at the tall casement windows, and a new blue and gold Persian rug now dominated the space in front of the fireplace. It was a cosy and welcoming room and Adam was pleased that no drastic changes had been made.

Amelia clung to her elder son's hand and her eyes devoured him. Rafe stared at his half-brother in rapt admiration and soon became overexcited requesting stories of battles.

'Later, Rafe,' Amelia laughed. 'You will exhaust Richard with your demands.'

The young boy looked crestfallen and danced from one foot to the other, unable to contain his exuberance. Feeling left out, he glanced at Adam, who winked at him and held out his arms. With a whoop of joy Rafe tore across the floor and Adam scooped him up in a manner that had become their regular greeting. Amelia sighed and shook her head at the boisterous play, but for once did not make a comment that Adam was encouraging Rafe's unruly conduct.

Even Elspeth wiped a tear from her eye and greeted Richard warmly. 'You seem to have done very well for yourself. You went away a youth and have come back a man. You are almost as tall as St John. Welcome home.'

'Thank you. You have not changed at all, dear aunt. You look even younger than I remember you. I expect you are still a demon on the hunting field.'

To Adam's amusement his formidable aunt actually blushed at the effusive words. At Richard's age Adam remembered that he had still been very much in awe of his aunt's corrosive tongue and would not have had the audacity to compliment her so extravagantly.

Richard was all smiles and continued in the same suave manner: 'I have missed Trevowan and of course dear Mama.'

St John was more reserved as he presented Felicity. 'You may not have received word of my marriage. It is with pleasure that I introduce my wife, Felicity, and her daughter Charlotte.'

Richard bowed to Felicity. 'Your servant, madam. I am delighted to meet such a beautiful addition to our family. I look forward to making your acquaintance. And your daughter is charming.' He smiled at Charlotte, who was hiding behind her mother's skirts. 'Does my uniform frighten you, little one? That will not do at all, for you are the prettiest of nieces and it is a pleasure to meet you.'

'The boy has become a charmer,' Elspeth laughed drily.

Rowena flounced forward and stood in front of Richard, her eyes flashing with indignation. 'Am I not your favourite niece? Charlotte can be a ninny at times.'

He held up his hands, feigning amazement. 'This cannot be little

Rowena? This is a veritable fair damsel. Rowena was but a child when I left. This maiden must already be wed and my pining heart will be forever broken.'

'Huh! Your young man has a slick tongue, Amelia,' Elspeth grunted with a withdrawal of approval.

Rowena tossed back her blonde ringlets and regarded Richard's striking features with an echo of her mother's boldness. 'How can I be wed? I am but a girl of ten. Has the sea addled your wits?' She pouted, though she clearly enjoyed his teasing.

'Rowena is a minx,' Amelia responded with unusual tartness. 'She forgets her manners.'

Mutiny flashed in the girl's eyes and she stamped her foot. 'I do not forget my manners. It was cruel of Richard to ignore me.'

Richard laughed. 'A minx indeed, but a delightful one. I will not ignore you in the future, dear niece.'

'Then you will ride with me tomorrow,' Rowena demanded.

'No,' protested Rafe. He had continued to regard Richard as a hero and was clearly impressed at his naval uniform and dashing figure. 'Richard has to see my fort and soldiers.'

'Children, there is time for everyone,' Amelia admonished and stared lovingly into her son's face. 'I have missed you. This hateful war took you away for so long. How long will we have your company before you must rejoin your ship?'

'I must report to the Admiralty in two months to take my lieutenant's examination.'

'That is splendid. You are carrying on the family tradition.' St John could not resist a snide remark as he regarded his twin. 'Unlike Adam, who left the navy under a cloud. He could not take the discipline, and that cost me half my inheritance.'

'St John, you do your brother a disservice.' Elspeth rounded on him, her narrow face flushed with indignation. 'Adam has served his country and proved his bravery in ways you will never match. And it is time that you accepted that it was your ineptitude that cost you the shipyard. Your father—'

St John had flushed, his jaw jutting with belligerence and Adam quickly intervened. 'Aunt Elspeth, I do not need you to defend me. And that is all in the past.' He smiled apologetically at Richard. 'Pay no need to our sibling squabbles. St John and I will always be governed by our wild blood, but we have put our rivalry behind us. It was only adolescent contention, was it not, brother?'

St John continued to glower, and it was Felicity who answered with a light laugh: 'Men and their boyhood feuds. It means nothing. St John has achieved so much.'

Richard bowed to her. 'You are not only beautiful, but also wise and loyal. St John is the most fortunate of men to have won such a bride.'

Amelia had been watching the interchange with a frown shadowing her brow. 'You have indeed become silver-tongued where the ladies are concerned, my son. You also look tired and pale. For you to have been granted so long a leave, I suspect you have been injured.'

'A slight wound, I assure you, Mama. We encountered storms in the Bay of Biscay that blew us days off course. Adam will tell you that all hands are needed during such weather, and the crew become exhausted after battling the elements. A few days' rest and I shall be hale and hearty.'

'Even so, I would have Dr Yeo examine any wound.'

'I have been discharged by the naval surgeon. Please do not fuss so, Mama.'

Amelia regarded him sternly. 'My dear Edward neglected his health and the bullet wound he sustained never properly healed.'

At the mention of Edward, Richard's smile faded. 'It was with great sadness I learned of his death. He was a fine man. I was proud to be his stepson and I hope always to live up to his ideals.'

Amelia brushed a tear from her eye. 'God bless you for that, my dear. We all miss him terribly, but having you here lightens my heart.'

Rafe had squirmed to the ground, and when Adam released him he made a dash for Richard. To avoid being butted in the stomach, Richard had no choice but to catch his brother and hold him as Adam had done. Rafe laughed with pleasure but Richard had lost all the colour from his face as his brother slammed against his chest.

'Confound the child!' he snarled and shoved the boy roughly aside. Rafe burst into tears.

'Richard, was that necessary?' Amelia remonstrated.

Adam saw him turn aside, his face ashen. He suspected Richard's wound pained him and he wanted to hide it from his mother, but his outburst had been out of character. Adam picked up Rafe to calm him. 'You winded Richard. You do not launch yourself at people if they are not expecting it. You are a big boy now for such antics and I am wrong to encourage you.'

'He caught me by surprise.' Richard had regained his composure and the colour was slowly returning to his cheeks.

St John had crossed to the decanter and was pouring Madeira for everyone. As the new master of Trevowan handed the glasses to the women, Richard joined him, surreptitiously adding several more drops from his phial to his own glass. He drank it back in one gulp, and poured himself another. His voice was stronger as he rejoined the company and began to question them about the latest family news.

Chapter Fifteen

The main target for Harry Sawle's retribution remained infuriatingly out of his reach. Both Boscabel and the shipyard were too well protected at night for his men to cause mischief. He could have had the livestock poisoned as he had at Trevowan and Hannah Rabson's farm, but that would have been repeating old patterns and was too predictable. Besides, the Loveday pastures were now too carefully guarded and cattle and sheep kept closer to the main buildings. It was also getting harder for his tubmen to work for him now that there was a price on his head and on any who followed his orders. The death of Gorran should have frightened them into obeying his wishes; instead it had made them more surly and defiant. Harry was losing his hold over the community he had ruled for over a decade. A lesson was needed to bring those tubmen back into line. How dare they defy him?

He would surrender none of his power. He judged his worth by the tyranny he could wield, and with his finances now almost nonexistent he needed that power to restore his fortunes. His devious mind had formed and discarded several plans. To wreak the greatest havoc upon his enemies he needed to remain free from capture and keep his return a secret. If he did anything too obvious, the manhunt for him would be without mercy. So far, apart from to Sal, he had not shown himself in public. Only a trusted few had personally been given orders, and each of them had been paid well for their silence. They were men whose lawless pasts were known to Harry, and if they betrayed him to the authorities he would give evidence so that they met their end on the gallows.

He had been furious when within two weeks his order that no one was to attend Peter Loveday's services had been disregarded. Pious Peter should have been shamed and become a laughing stock as he raged and lectured his fallen flock about returning to the fold. Instead the young hothead had shown a greater restraint and courage than Sawle had expected. He had underestimated the parson. He would not do so again. But Parson Loveday was small fry compared to Adam. Sawle had stayed his hand in dealing with the owner of the shipyard in order to find an appropriate punishment for his enemy. But with the estate and yard guarded, he had been unable to strike in a manner that would bring his adversary to heel.

He had kept his distance when spying on the yard, staying on the far bank of the river inlet as he studied the watchmen patrolling of a night. There were several dogs in the cottages, and these barked at any untoward noise, a shipwright checking any disturbance. He was standing behind a tree now, watching the yard across the river as the last of the shipwrights finished their day's work on *Sea Mist*. The cutter was almost finished. Her new mast was fitted and the rigging replaced, and the damaged lower decks had also been repaired. There remained a section of the ship's rail to be installed and some final fitments replaced on the quarterdeck; then she would be taken by the revenue office and used against smugglers at sea.

The thought was enough to make Harry's blood boil. He wanted that ship back. Twice when the night tide was in their favour he had brought enough men to the riverbank to swim across and sail her. Each time the dogs had been alerted and too many shipwrights had appeared to investigate. He knew it would not be easy. He had already made one attempt, when the ship was first built, to steal her from the yard without paying the final instalment, and his men had been hopelessly defeated.

The cutter was his only way to recoup his fortunes, but even if he managed to steal her from under Adam's nose, he still had to sail her into the river and through the estuary at Fowey. That would be nigh impossible. At night a chain was raised from the riverbed across the harbour mouth to stop the danger of invasion. With the war with France continuing, the guns on the castle ramparts guarded the port closely.

'It would be madness to try and take her, Harry,' Vince Lilycrap wheezed toothlessly, breaking the silence. He had been Reuban Sawle's partner and Harry trusted his advice. 'She be marked as a revenue ship now. Even if we got away from here, we'd be blown out of the water at Fowey.'

'You be getting old, Vince.' Harry did not even glance at him, his eyes riveted on the ship he prized above all his possessions. 'I can't lose her.'

'It bain't possible to take her. Not here at least. Not just to get back at Loveday. It may be possible at another quay when a less vigilant watch can be overpowered.'

Harry did not want to admit that the old man was right. Finally he turned to regard him. Lilycrap's bushy beard was white and he still had a shock of thick white hair. His face and ears were gouged and scarred from a hundred street fights. The single gold ring in his ear glinted in the fading sun and his eyes were sharp and hard as flint. Despite his venerable years, he stood upright and walked as sprightly as any man half his age. Last summer he had wrestled four men at the summer fair and beaten them all. He had worked for Reuban for thirty, years, running the tubmen.

Vince was reputedly the bastard son of a Bristol slave-trader; his mother, the daughter of a disgraced bishop, had died in the poorhouse giving birth to him. In Reuban's day, Vince had been the wits behind any raid on a customs house to steal back confiscated cargo. Had he been educated, he would have made a brilliant lawyer. He had taught Harry every underhand scheme he knew, enabling the younger man to be successful in the smuggling trade.

'There bain't no point in scowling, Harry,' Lilycrap snapped. 'You wanted my advice and I gave it to you. Try and take that ship and your men will be killed.'

No one else would stand up to Harry so fearlessly. Most of his men toadied to him in fear that he would kill them if they disobeyed. Vince Lilycrap was the one man Harry respected. 'It don't sit right with me to have Loveday prosper in this deal with the preventive office. Every shipwright who worked on her is my enemy.'

'That be a lot of men,' the old man mocked. 'You can't take on the world, Harry. And the men don't like acting against their own kind.'

'None of the shipwrights has worked for me.' He spat out his contempt. 'There be no conflict of loyalty.'

'They be Cornish bred and have kinfolk here.'

Harry scowled. 'They will pay. All of them.' His pale eyes were without mercy. 'And this job I shall do myself.'

By mid-morning the following day, Bridie had sent several children to their homes after they complained of stomach pains and three were sick in the classroom. Before allowing them into the yard for their break, she noted that four more children looked hot and uncomfortable.

She sent the elder of the two Wakeley boys to ask Senara to come

113

at once. The boy's sister was being sick as Senara entered the school-room.

'I hoped the children would be spared,' Senara announced as she stooped to put her hand on the head of the girl, who was crying in her distress. 'I have a roomful of men complaining of sickness and the bloody flux. I have no more remedies made up to give them.'

'I've sent three of the class home already. But so many seem feverish,' Bridie groaned. 'What can I do for them, Senara?'

'Close the school for today and possibly the rest of the week. Those who are sick should go to their beds.'

'What can I do to help you?' Bridie offered.

Immediately Senara was concerned for the health of her young nephew. 'I think you should go home, sister. This could be a morbid fever. You cannot place yourself in danger. You must think of Michael. He must be kept away from all forms of infection.'

Bridie paled. Michael was small for his age and Senara had always been worried he would fall prey to infection, which would leave him weakened. 'But I could already be infected.'

'Then do not go near your son for a few days. Ma will tend to him.'

As she returned to the room where she dealt with patients, Senara was shocked to see several men groaning as they jumped from the scaffolding around the merchantman and ran into the wood to be sick or relieve themselves. Her healing room also had more patients than when she had left. Some were doubled up in agony. Many of their faces were now mottled from a rash.

'Dear God, it bain't the plague, be it, Mrs Loveday?' Charity Mumford wailed.

'No, Charity.' She did not wish to spread alarm through the yard, but she suspected that this fever could be just as deadly. Even as she tended the children, more men stumbled into the waiting room and could be heard retching into bowls.

'What ails them, Mrs Loveday?' The overseer's wife was ashen with fear.

'They all have fevers and the bloody flux.' Senara was puzzled by the violence and speed with which the illness had spread. 'Perhaps the school-house should be closed and an infirmary set up there for the sick. If they go back to their cottages the whole yard could be infected within hours. I will need three or four women who are well enough to help to tend them. I have sent for Dr Yeo and would welcome his opinion. I have seen disease like this in towns where sanitation is poor. But the cottage privies are emptied regularly and the midden cart was here last week.'

Another two men came into the waiting room. 'You've got to give me something for this pain, Mrs Loveday. I can't work the way I be.' One of the senior shipwrights, a strong, muscular man, was deathly pale and his hands shook.

'This is very serious,' Senara confided to Charity. 'Do what you can to make them comfortable. I must speak with Adam.'

She found her husband walking back from the direction of the double row of cottages in the yard. He was with Ben Mumford and both men looked grim. A woman ran out of a cottage, sobbing. 'Mrs Loveday, please have a look at my Susie, she be right poorly. She can't keep nothing down her and now she be barely breathing.'

'I'll come as soon as I can, Mrs Bowen.' Senara knew Susie was consumptive and would need extra care. She turned a frantic gaze upon Adam. 'There are so many sick. I sent for Dr Yeo, but it's like some dreadful marsh fever. The entire yard could succumb to it by night-fall.'

'Should the stricken be isolated?' Adam asked. 'Half the men are unable to work and several women and children are also ill.'

'It would be a sensible precaution to isolate the sick from the healthy. But until we know the cause . . .' She broke off, troubled. 'I have a feeling it is no ordinary fever.'

To her relief, at that moment she saw the dark-haired Dr Yeo ride into the yard. His round face was flushed from the fast pace of his journey. He rode a grey hunter that carried his stocky body without effort. He had a no-nonsense approach to his patients, his arms and shoulders as broad as any Cornish tin miner's.

As she moved to greet the physician, Adam held her arm, his voice thick with worry. 'You must take care you do not become infected, Senara.'

'I will not abandon the sick.' Her tone was sharp, but seeing the fear so stark in his eyes she understood his wish to protect her and added, 'I would not expect you to abandon the yard while your men are ill. I also have my duty to help our people.'

He nodded, and their gazes held in a brief moment of love and understanding. It was that fierce exchange that sustained them both in the exhausting hours ahead.

Adam paused to watch his wife greet Dr Yeo and waved a hand in acknowledgement to the physician, then he gestured to Ben to follow him. 'I have seen fevers like this abroad and in the poor quarters of cities. We must check the well.'

Three women were drawing water from the well that had been dug between the kiddley and the cottages. Adam shouted to them to leave their buckets where they were. 'That water may be contaminated. Have any of you drunk it today?'

White-faced with alarm, the three women shook their heads.

'I last came here yesterday afternoon,' replied Mrs Dyer, a portly woman who took in washing for some of the unmarried shipwrights

'Are any of your family sick?' Adam asked.

'Not that I know of.' She glanced towards the schoolhouse, from where the children were emerging. Her expression cleared to see her only child running and laughing. Some of the others progressed slowly and their faces were flushed.

Adam wound down the bucket on the windlass. The shaft was deep and it took several moments before he heard it plop into the water below. He drew it up and over the side and sniffed it cautiously. It seemed to him that it had a faint taint to it, but that could have been his imagination. He tipped the water on to the ground but could not be certain if anything was amiss. He was not about to take any risk.

He leaned over the side to peer down into the dark depths. The sunlight glinted feebly on a small patch of water far below him. He stared hard, uncertain if he could see anything floating, but the shadows were deceptive. Yet there was a whiff of tainted air. Wells could be musty and there was moss growing on the inside of the bricks, but this smell was sour.

'Get four men to rig up a pulley around the well and I will go down and investigate. I can see nothing from here.' He spoke first to Mumford, then addressed Mrs Dyer. 'No one is to drink the water until I have made this inspection.'

His gaze swept over the other two women. 'Inform everyone in the cottages of my order. No water drawn today must be drunk until I say so.'

The well water was usually pure, fed by an underground spring. His stare hardened as he stared about the yard. Half the workers seemed to be affected in some way. Most of them would have drunk small beer in the morning. A few of the cottages had goats to supply milk for the children, but many of them would have had only water.

He strode to the carpentry sheds and orders were given that any man taken sick was to return to his cottage to prevent the contagion spreading. He fretted while the pulley was being erected. He feared some form of typhoid fever that could decimate his workforce and their families.

Senara also had the same suspicion and she waited in a state of anguish whilst Dr Yeo examined several patients.

'How many are ill?' he questioned.

'Half the workers and some of their wives, but the children seem to have less resistance. Mrs Bowen says her daughter is hardly breathing. Would you look at her next?'

Dr Yeo spent two hours examining every patient. In one of the cottages the elderly mother of Philip Acre, a carpenter, was lying on a trestle bed in the corner of the single downstairs room. The carpenter's wife was scrubbing the floorboards where her mother-in-law had been sick. The small rag rug that had been the only floor covering was soaking in a washtub outside the front door and there was a pile of soiled sheets beside it. The smell of sweat and vomit was so powerful that Dr Yeo pressed a nosegay to his face as he bent over the woman. He had advised Senara to do the same as they approached the patients, trusting that the perfumed herbs would give them some protection from infection.

The old woman's face was slick with sweat and twisted with pain as she defecated on to her bed. Her whimper of distress was pitiful to hear.

The younger woman wailed in frustration. 'That be the third time this morning, and the children are the same. What am I to do?' She was sweating herself and Senara noticed a rash on her arms and neck. Suddenly she retched into her wooden pail and collapsed on to the floor, clutching her stomach.

Dr Yeo drew Senara to one side. 'For so many to be ill in so short a time is most disturbing.'

A youth was hailing the doctor from outside, and emerging out of the darkness Dr Yeo squinted in the sunlight.

'Mr Loveday has found a dead sheep in the well.'

Dr Yeo saw a large oilcloth-wrapped bundle being heaved over the side of the well, and orders were shouted at the curious group of children to keep away. Then Adam's head appeared as he climbed up the rope tied to the pulley and his long legs swung over the wall of the well. He had a kerchief tied over his nose and mouth but his clothing was saturated. He pulled off the mask and leaned back against the stonework, breathing heavily.

'Get that carcass burned. The well must be drained and cleaned before it can be used again.'

Dr Yeo stared at the leg sticking out of the oilcloth. 'How the devil did that get into the well?'

Adam knew it had been a malicious warning. Only one man was capable of trying to poison an entire workforce out of spite. 'It did not drown of its own accord.'

'Has it been dead long?' Dr Yeo held a kerchief to his nose and his eyes were dark with foreboding.

Adam let out a harsh breath. 'Long enough to be riddled with maggots.'

'Then we must hope that the water has not been too badly infected and the effects on those stricken will clear up in a day or so. I will advise your wife on preparing a purge and a restorative. If any can afford chicken broth it will aid their recovery. But who would throw a dead animal in a well?'

Adam regarded *Sea Mist* as she rode the swell of the tide and rued the day he had agreed to build her. Once she had saved the shipyard from bankruptcy. Now it seemed she would destroy all his family had worked for.

'At least knowing the cause of the sickness it can be treated.' Dr Yeo looked less harassed. 'But it is possible the weakest may not survive.'

Adam closed his eyes against his anger and pain. He blamed himself for this catastrophe that had struck the yard, and condemned Harry Sawle to the deepest pit of Hell. Only he could be behind this. But still no sight of the smuggler had been seen in the district.

Dr Yeo drew Adam aside. 'I would advise that as a precaution you put the yard into quarantine until we know the severity of the contagion. Once such a fever takes hold it could spread by other means. And you should change those sodden clothes. They may be infected in some way. Though if you did not actually drink any of the water, you may have escaped contagion. I cannot say for certain how these pernicious diseases pass from one to another. But I think you and your good wife should remain at the yard and not risk it spreading.'

Adam nodded. He did not like the thought of Senara risking her life by tending the sick, but he did not attempt to dissuade her, knowing it would be pointless. Her skill was needed and her care and remedies would save many lives that would be lost if they were left to suffer unattended.

Adam had the inlet of the underground stream at the bottom of the well blocked with granite boulders. The water was then drained so that the well could be cleaned. In the meantime he ordered casks of fresh water to be drawn from the well at Boscabel and brought into the yard. For purposes other than drinking or cooking, river water could be used.

Adam took a room in the Ship kiddley for himself and Senara. He paid Pru Jansen to slaughter all but a few of her laying hens to make broth for the workers. With half the workforce affected, he stopped work on the merchant ship and concentrated on completing the repairs to *Sea Mist*. He wanted her out of the yard for good. She had brought nothing but bad luck.

Chapter Sixteen

Senara commandeered half a dozen shipwrights' daughters between the ages of nine and twelve who were so far unaffected by the illness to help her in brewing the herbs needed to combat the vomiting and dysentery. From her collection of dried herbs hanging from hooks on the beams of her workroom she gave four of them samples of the leaves and roots to be collected and told them where they grew in abundance.

'If you meet anyone in your work, tell them there is sickness here and to keep their distance. Return as quickly as you can.'

The other two girls were sent to help Pru Jansen pluck the chickens for the broth that would be fed to all those afflicted.

Senara then took a large cauldron and partly filled it with the fresh water that had been brought from Boscabel and put it on the trivet over the fire in the hearth. It was the start of three days of unremitting work. She visited each cottage and assessed how many were sick and who was capable of nursing them. To these she gave instructions on how often the infusions she had brewed must be given, and that any fluids dispelled from the body within the home must be immediately cleared away to prevent any noxious humours re-entering the body.

Hours were spent preparing the remedies, which needed to be boiled and then reduced in quantity to concentrate their efficacy. She slept little, and on the second night was called upon to attend the wife of a shipwright who had gone into premature labour. The six-month baby was stillborn and the mother, weakened from her ordeal and the sickness, needed all Senara's care to pull through the night. But her tortured body could hold down no sustenance, the fever stripped her of the last of her vitality, and she died as dawn was lighting the sky. Sadly in the next three days she was not the only casualty. Philip Acre's elderly mother also succumbed, and so did an old man whose lungs were rotted with mining dust. Also Susie Bowen died.

By the end of the week the sickness had passed. The dead had been buried at Trewenna within a day of their passing but without mourners as the yard remained in quarantine. A week later a special service for all those who had perished and a thanksgiving for the survivors was attended by everyone.

Senara mourned the losses. Dr Yeo had attended the service and saw the weariness in her step.

'It is now time for you to take care of yourself,' he advised. 'I recommend at least three days of rest.'

She pressed a hand to her temple. The grief that had fallen on the community of workers pressed like a lodestone upon her heart. 'I should have done more.'

'No one could have saved those who were taken. The old and vulnerable are always at risk when such pestilence strikes. Your diligence saved the lives of many. No more sickened after the first day. Without Adam so quickly detecting the source of the infection and your skill in making purges and restoratives, many more would have died. You must take comfort in that.'

His words brought little consolation to her.

Adam was equally preoccupied. Short of able-bodied carpenters, he had worked with the men who were fit enough to continue the repairs on *Sea Mist*. A week after the funerals, the cutter was again seaworthy. Adam had been ordered to sail her to Falmouth, where he would be paid. He did not like the arrangement, as it had been agreed originally that the money would be paid before delivery. But neither did he want *Sea Mist* in the yard for a day longer than was necessary. She had brought a curse with her.

He undertook the short voyage to Falmouth with half a dozen men. It was the first time he had been at sea in months, and normally he would have relished the feel of the helm beneath his hands and the wind on his face as it filled the canvas. Shortly after they sailed out of the estuary at Fowey, a thick sea mist wrapped them in a smothering embrace. It clung to the tendrils of Adam's hair and droplets of water ran down his face. The weather echoed the heaviness of his mood. Would Senara have seen it as a portent of danger? Yet he rather welcomed the fog. It tested his seamanship even in these waters he knew so well. Lanterns were lit fore and aft and the ship's bell was rung at regular intervals as a warning to other ships in the area. All but a single sail was furled, making their passage slow and laborious.

Sounds were muffled in the eerie atmosphere. A sailor ran out a line and called out the depth of the sea bed. Another was on watch to ensure they did not pass near to outlying rocks or headlands. This close to the shore they could encounter slower-moving fishing sloops returning to harbour. In a collision the cutter would crush them. To sail further out could mean them chancing upon a merchant ship en route to either Plymouth or Falmouth. An impact would cause severe damage to *Sea Mist*, for which Adam would be responsible. This was also ideal weather for any smuggling agent anchored off the coast to put his rowing boats to sea to land a cargo. The irony of *Sea Mist*'s past and present ownership did not escape Adam. This would be the last time any smuggler would trade safely in these waters once the vessel became a preventive ship.

An hour later the mist showed no sign of lifting. Then a shout was heard ahead of them. Fearing an imminent collision, Adam peered into the mist, his body tensing with trepidation. The voice was louder, more frantic.

'Ahoy! Help!'

'Man in the water! Three points to starboard, Cap'n,' shouted Abe Tonkin. He was originally from Mevagissey and was a cousin of the Tonkin family who lived in a tied cottage at Trevowan.

A broken lobster pot, several shattered planks and other debris from a fishing sloop bobbed into view.

'Lower the longboat and get a line out to the man,' Adam shouted. 'There is no time to waste. If we overshoot him, when we bring the ship around we may never locate him.'

Adam leapt into the longboat as it was lowered. Abe and another man pulled on the oars. The voice in the water was indistinct as the current carried the man away.

'Hail there! Keep shouting,' Adam ordered.

'Ahoy!'

'Over there, Cap'n,' yelled Abe as the mist thinned enough to reveal a figure holding on to a broken mast.

They hauled the longboat closer and Adam threw the rope so that it landed near the man.

'I can't swim.' The pale face was bug-eyed with terror.

'Loop the rope around yourself and we will pull you in,' Adam instructed.

The seaman clung to the mast, too terrified to move. Adam yanked off his boots and dived over the side of the boat. The shock of the cold water momentarily took the breath from his lungs, and then he struck out towards the seaman. He put his arm around the frozen body.

'Let go the mast. You are safe.'

'Can't move.'

Adam prised the man's arms from the wood and his weight dragged them both under the water. The fisherman panicked, kicking out and flailing wildly with his arms, putting both their lives in danger. Adam kept his hold on the man and surfaced, but the struggling fisherman was gulping and spluttering, having swallowed a great deal of sea water. The waves were choppy and he slipped back under. With water splashing over his head, Adam grabbed the man's collar and managed to keep him afloat until the longboat edged alongside him. Abe Tonkin hauled the fisherman over the side with Adam pushing at the man's legs, and then he heaved himself into the boat.

The fisherman lay unconscious and not breathing. Adam rolled him on to his chest and pushed down on the man's shoulders several times until the prone figure shuddered and coughed up the sea water in his lungs.

'Thought he were a dead 'un there, Cap'n,' said Abe.

The prow of *Sea Mist* loomed before them, her name bringing another start of fear from the recovering man. He was younger than Adam had expected, and clearly inexperienced. 'The devil's ship. God help me.' Then, realising what his statement implied, he hastily amended: 'No disrespect to Mr Sawle or the men who work for him.'

'You have nothing to fear from your comment. The ship is now in the possession of the preventive men,' Adam explained.

The fisherman was visibly relieved. 'I thought I'd gone from the frying pan into the fire for a time there. Two of me cousins be in gaol for working for Sawle. And Grandfather do reckon an uncle died because of that smuggler.'

'Where are you from?' Adam asked.

'Polperro, Cap'n.'

Adam did not answer immediately. Men from Polperro, like those from so many of the small fishing villages, would have taken a night's work from Sawle at some time in their lives. The fisherman was little more than a youth and had yet to learn caution in speaking of such matters. 'You are way off course from Polperro.'

'I got caught in a current, then the fog came down. That were why I tried to stay close to land. It were me undoing. I hit the headland rocks and the lugger was smashed to pieces. I've bin in the water for hours. I could'na have lasted much longer. I'd lost the feeling in me arms.'

'You are safe now. This ship was taken from Sawle's men last month and damaged when *Challenger* fired upon her. She was repaired in my shipyard and I am sailing her to Falmouth to resume her service.'

The young man's mouth gaped open despite his chattering teeth and shivering figure. 'Me wits have gone begging. I remember hearing of her capture. You be Cap'n Loveday. I owe you my life. Cuthbert Freake at your service, Cap'n.'

'If we don't get some rum inside you and those wet clothes off you soon, you'll be at death's door with the ague,' Adam said as they climbed the rope ladder over the side of the cutter. He led the man to his cabin, but there were no spare clothes aboard so Freake was swathed in blankets.

'I assume you are a fisherman.'

'Me grandfather be the fisherman. He'll have my hide. It were his boat. He broke his arm and I took to sea alone. We needed the money from a catch. It be three days since we've eaten. Now how will we earn a living?' He dropped his head into his hands.

'You are alive. You look strong enough. If you cannot fish then you must find other work on the land.'

'But the lugger. It were all Grandfather had. How can I feed him, me ma and two sisters?'

Adam sympathised with the young man. 'The loss of the boat is a hardship, but you have your life. Your family will be grateful for that. We are sailing in the opposite direction to Polperro but you can travel back with us. I intend to hire a lugger to get us from Falmouth to Fowey. It will take you on to Polperro.'

Freake struggled to control his emotions. 'It were an ill day when me dad were taken by the pressgang. I were never good at sea. Me grandfather were teaching me but I kept getting it wrong. I'll never make a fisherman.'

'The sea is not in everyone's blood. And a word of warning about Sawle. Be careful to whom you mention his name and dealings. Hours in the water and being close to death may have cast your wits away with the wind, but such comments could cost you your life if they were overheard by the wrong person. I am no friend to Harry Sawle and would see him behind bars.'

'Then I be doubly obliged to you, Cap'n Loveday. If there be any way I can repay you . . .'

Adam waved his gratitude aside. 'Get yourself work on the land if that suits you better and you will provide for your family. It is good to hear that you will have no dealings with Sawle. Most of his gang are in prison, and if there is any justice he will soon join them.'

By the time Adam returned to the quarterdeck, the fog had lifted and they were passing the headland guarded by the circular castle at St Mawes. A wide stretch of water known as Carrick Reach cut inland for several miles, and on the headland opposite St Mawes lay Falmouth, with its own castle high on the cliff.

Once moored, Adam ordered his men to stay on board and went in search of Lieutenant Shaver, who was supposed to meet him with his money. It took two hours to track the officer down, and the man's manner was far from welcoming.

A money pouch was tossed across the table. Adam did not need to open it to know that it contained much less than the full payment.

'That's half,' Shaver barked without apology. 'The rest will be settled at the end of the quarter. There is little money in the Treasury's coffers. They are overburdened with paying for new ships of the line to protect our country from its enemies.'

In any other circumstances Adam would have sailed the cutter back to the yard and refused to allow the revenue office to take possession of her, but he wanted shot of her and her malign presence. He swallowed an angry retort. He could not risk insulting the Admiralty for breaking the terms of their contract, for he needed the money to complete the other work in the yard.

'I was also to receive another instalment for the partly built cutter,' he reminded the officer curtly.

'There has been some delay. I have not received details. Payment should be delivered to your shipyard at the end of the month.'

With that Adam had to be satisfied, but it left him with a nagging sickness in the pit of his gut. He had a notion that the revenue service was prevaricating. If funds were so short and they had *Sea Mist* in their possession, there was no urgency for another cutter. Especially as Sawle had not been working in the district recently.

The day following Adam's return to Trevowan Hard, a letter from the Admiralty arrived. He broke the seal and was not surprised at the terse information within. He was ordered to stop work on the half-built cutter they had commissioned. All Admiralty money was to be spent to repair ships of the line to maintain the fleet in the war with France.

Adam tossed the letter on to his desk in disgust. His fears were realised. Without the money, he would be hard pushed to pay the next quarter-day wages, and it was unlikely that another customer for the cutter would quickly be found. He flicked open the order book, but he knew its contents by heart. A fishing lugger was currently in the dry dock and a merchant ship was due to be overhauled next month.

Pride of the Sea was the only ship being constructed, and his share of the merchant investment had been to pay the cost of her himself. Her sea trials were planned for ten weeks' time.

Before then he had to settle the chandler's bill for the fitments, and there was also the cost of four cannon to be met. Not only was there the danger of her encountering French warships, but the southern seas were the haunt of pirates. The cannon were a vast expense but a necessary one. The group of investors wanted the ship ready to load at Falmouth by the beginning of September, in preparation for sailing to Australia a few weeks later. A warehouse was filled with goods waiting to be loaded, and Adam had heard from the shipping agent that ten families had paid passage as settlers to the new colony. He had yet to negotiate whether she would carry convicts from the Plymouth prison hulks.

That was the side of the New South Wales venture he had little taste for. There was no way that so many convicts could be transported without them suffering to some degree. Whilst in the navy he had witnessed the horrors and misery suffered by the slaves chained in a slave ship. He abhorred the slave trade and all it stood for. But it continued to survive despite the diligent work of the abolitionists. The pressgang created another form of slavery. Was the transport of convicts any less an evil?

It was a moral dilemma he anguished over. He had concluded that with England's gaols overflowing, transportation was a kinder sentence than hanging. At least if he was paid for their passage he could refuse to cram them into the hold like so many cattle, and provide adequate food for their voyage. That was how he had salved his conscience when transporting them in *Pegasus*.

Chapter Seventeen

Gwendolyn stared into the looking glass hung on a nail in her bedroom. She scarcely recognised the thin oval face, with its dusky sun-browned complexion and rosy cheeks. Her brown hair was lighter, tinted with red and gold highlights from the sun. She ran through her daily duties in her mind. There were many – work was endless as Japhet strove to establish the farm and sawmill. The store in Parramatta also took up much of her time, for Meg and Jim Duffy, the emancipated couple who worked there, could not be entirely trusted, as both had originally been transported for theft. Gwen visited the store twice a week to check the ledgers for stock and goods sold. So far the couple had been grateful for the opportunity to live above the shop and earn a wage. It was the cash wages that seemed to keep the ex-convicts honest. Most work in the colony was paid for in the general currency of rum, which led to greater drunkenness and disorder.

In the isolated haven at Trewenna Place, Gwendolyn could almost believe that this beautiful land was civilised. It was different when they journeyed to Parramatta or Sydney Cove. Even the ticket-of-leave prisoners were jealous of those who had come willingly to this land. Few convicts who had served their sentence had the money to pay for passage back to England. To escape the resentment and drudgery, many drank themselves senseless, and on gaining their freedom sold their land and squandered the money on more drink before a ship would take them home. The men could work their passage as seamen but the women were forced to return to servitude or die paupers.

Gwen's maid, Biddy, sauntered into the room. She had taken so long to answer her mistress's summons that Gwen had to think for a moment why she had rung for her. This was the third lady's maid she had employed since her arrival. The first, Maria, who had come with her from England, had cried incessantly when she learned her mistress was to stay on, and Gwen had paid for her passage home. The second was drunk most of the time. Biddy had been maid to one of the officers' wives who had died of a fever a month after her arrival. She was good at caring for Gwen's needs and loved the children, but resented any menial work, considering it beneath her.

'You are to work with Eadie today. The first crop of onions have been picked and they need stringing together and hanging in the outhouse.'

The woman's face crumpled. Apart from a beakish nose, she was pretty enough when she did not scowl. 'I can't be doing that, Mrs Loveday. I never thought that by taking work with an English gentlewoman I would be expected to perform such lowly tasks.'

Gwendolyn was weary of her maid's whining. 'Life is different here, Biddy. We all have to work or we will starve. I do not complain.'

Biddy twitched her skirts as she walked away, her feathers clearly ruffled. 'I wish I had never come to this God-forsaken country. My life is not much better than that ragamuffin Eadie. But I weren't a thief. I did nothing wrong to live in exile with the lowest of mankind.'

'We are settlers, Biddy.' Gwendolyn lost patience. 'I have said you may take employment with any of the soldiers' wives who are returning to England with their husbands.'

'Most of them are no better than doxies. My late mistress was an exception. Few of the officers have brought their women here.'

Gwen let her mutterings pass. There was a hierarchy amongst servants, and in England a lady's maid was one of the highest. She understood Biddy's unhappiness. There were days when she too found life here difficult, but she had Japhet's love to sustain her and that made everything worthwhile. Her previous life seemed almost unreal now. In England she had been waited on by a dozen servants: a lady's maid dressing her hair and caring for her clothes; footmen cleaning her shoes and running her errands. Two nursery maids had been employed to tend and watch over Japhet Edward. There had been upstairs maids, downstairs maids, laundresses, seamstresses, cooks, gardeners and grooms, to name but a few. Here there was only Biddy and the young convict woman Eadie to help with the heavier tasks in the house.

Biddy had been devoted to her late mistress. She had had a difficult childhood, helping her widowed mother run a lodging house for retired officers near St James's Barracks. When her mother had married a gout-ridden major whose infirmity did not stop him trying to get into Biddy's bed of a night after her mother was asleep, she had left the house and found work with the captain's wife, who had trained her as a lady's maid before deciding to accompany her husband to New South Wales.

Biddy had been shocked on her arrival when she witnessed the depravity of the convicts and their women in Sydney Cove. When her mistress died within a month, she had been terrified of what would happen to her. Gwen had known her from the maid's visits to their store in Parramatta, and finding her in tears one day had engaged her.

Gwendolyn had hidden her own shock at the degeneracy and brutality of life in the penal settlement. She had been spared the worst sights by staying at the governor's mansion until Japhet had been freed from his servitude. They had left Sydney for their land beyond Parramatta on the Hawkesbury River. There the beauty of the new country had moved her. She did not mind the simplistic life; she believed in Japhet's vision for their future. And she understood that he wanted to return to England a wealthy man in his own right and not build their future on her inheritance.

She heard Eadie singing as she worked. The young convict woman had been a rare find and was a diligent worker. Unlike Biddy, she never complained. Yet she had suffered unimaginable horrors and tribulations. When she was fourteen, she had been found guilty of stealing a pair of gloves from a woman in the market. She had seen the woman drop them and had picked them up intending to return them. At that moment her younger sister, who she was in charge of, had been knocked into the gutter, screaming inconsolably when she cut her knee. The woman by then had discovered that the gloves were missing and declared that they had been stolen. Eadie was found holding the gloves as she tended to her sister. No one believed her story, and she had been arrested and found guilty at Exeter Assizes. She had been taken to the prison hulks in Plymouth to await transportation and on her first night had been raped by two gaolers.

By the time she was put on board ship for Sydney Cove, she was already big with child. The baby was born on the voyage but had not survived longer than a month in the dreadful conditions within the hold. She had arrived in the colony half starved and with a dullness in her eyes from the constant abuse she had suffered on board. Japhet had taken pity on her when he had seen her fighting off the unwanted attentions of a marine and gone to her rescue. The greater tragedy was that her story was not uncommon; most of the female prisoners were regarded as prostitutes, although few of them had followed that profession before their transportation. Some had willingly become the concubines of sailors or marines to ensure their protection from being used by a dozen other men; others like Eadie had been raped as easy game.

Gwen had nurtured the convict girl back to health and Eadie had repaid her with gratitude and loyalty. As for Japhet, he was strict with the men who worked for them. None of them had committed violent crimes, and like Eadie they had all been weak from starvation when they arrived. Gwendolyn had fed them as generously as they were able, and soon their health and strength returned.

They respected Japhet because he did not ask them to do any job he would not have tackled himself, and they had heard of his reputation that he knew how to take care of himself in a fight.

Gwendolyn tidied the bed that Japhet had built for them. Ropes supported the dried-bracken-filled mattress. Japhet had promised her that a grand bed with hangings and a swansdown mattress would arrive on Adam's next merchant ship from England. As she worked, Gwendolyn swatted at the flies buzzing around her head. They were a constant irritation. Even in winter they plagued them. Her months here had brought out hidden strengths Gwendolyn had not thought she possessed. She had learned to be wary of some of the black-skinned male natives. She had tried to win the confidence of the groups of women she found searching for grubs, but in the past outlying farms had been robbed and the settlers and convicts murdered. Testament to this was the discovery of the skeletons of escaped convicts who had been killed by the natives' spears. The men, with their painted bodies, did not trust the people who had come uninvited to plunder and steal their land. And in that Gwendolyn sympathised with them. Apart from the threat of the natives, there were also the river floods to contend with that drowned the crops, and the flash floods from violent and sudden thunderstorms that in minutes changed the arid red earth to churning lakes. And if danger of drowning was not enough, forest fires could consume vast acres in minutes. The blackened trunks of trees bore testimony to their force and destruction.

Until she had fallen in love with Japhet, Gwendolyn had been timid by nature, her personality overshadowed by her overbearing mother and sister. Her family had not approved of her attraction to the black sheep of the Loveday family. They regarded Japhet as a fortune-hunter. Gwendolyn had shocked them by emerging from her meek shell to become a resilient and determined woman. Especially when she had sailed to follow her husband across the seas and deliver his pardon. That voyage had taken nine gruelling months. It had toughened her to unexpected hardships, but nothing had prepared her for the suffering, cruelty and deprivation she had found at her destination.

The harsh screech of a sulphur-crested kookaburra brought her back to the present. The sun was rising above the trees and the heat was increasing. Most work outside was done in the morning and late afternoon. She stepped on to the veranda, which provided a cool palisade around their house. The scent of eucalyptus hung in the hot air. Japhet spoke of the house as a temporary structure that would be replaced by brick, but Gwen did not plan that far ahead. Each month she stayed here, her homesickness for Cornwall became sharper. If she was honest, she missed the more genteel side to her previous life. Japhet had promised her that they would return to England within five years, his fortune made. He would not break his word to her.

Though life had been difficult, there were times when she found it rewarding. She was proud of her husband. She had always seen qualities in him where others saw only his womanising and wild blood. This new country had fired his imagination and his sense of purpose. She stared at the acres of land cleared of trees. Japhet had worked as hard as any of the convicts to provide pasture for the cattle he had purchased, and a field of wheat had been planted. Though Gwendolyn had not intended to remain here, she had brought with her a small chest of silver to provide for any eventuality during the voyage. It had enabled them to buy livestock and build the store in Parramatta.

Her husband was striding across the fields, accompanied by two convicts with scythes over their shoulders. The first crop of hay was being harvested today, and the labourers, who had been born in London, needed to be taught by her husband how to cut it correctly and not take a leg off with the long, unwieldy blade. Japhet saw Gwendolyn watching him and lifted a browned arm in a wave. A rush of love for him made her place a hand over her heart, which had tightened with pride. Japhet thrived in this wild community and faced each new challenge with enthusiasm, passion and an amazing amount of skill.

Japhet Edward appeared at the corner of the veranda, chasing a lizard across the sun-baked earth. Gwen had discarded the long skirts he would have worn in England and fashioned him a pair of breeches. At two he liked to climb and run, and the skirts hampered him. In his excitement he tripped and grazed his knee. Gwendolyn ran to him but he pushed her away, wriggling from her grasp, and let out a howl of disappointment that the lizard had vanished. She laughed. He was so like Japhet, always on the lookout for some new adventure.

A voice hailed her and she turned to see an officer approaching on horseback. Her son's loud protests had masked the sound of his arrival. It was Captain Haughton. Her heart sank. She did not particularly like or trust Japhet's partner in many of their new ventures. She glanced in the direction in which her husband had disappeared. He was on the far side of a group of trees and would not be aware of the officer's arrival. Biddy had headed off in another direction in pursuit of Japhet Edward, and Eadie was at the back of the house finishing the week's washing and hanging it on the lines before she began threading the onions.

Gwendolyn removed her apron that protected her gown as Captain Haughton dismounted and tethered his mare to a hitching post in the shade of a tree.

'Your servant, Mrs Loveday.' There was a sheen of sweat on his face from the exertion of his ride and a fine dusting of red earth covered his scarlet uniform. He brushed it distractedly from his sleeves before performing a courtly bow.

'The cursed sun burns ever more ferociously, though its brightness is dimmed by your radiance, dear lady.'

'Captain Haughton, what brings you to our farmstead on such a hot day?'

His smile broadened. 'Do I need an excuse to visit a beautiful woman?'

'A married woman,' she was quick to remind him.

There was a cry from Druce, who had just woken from his morning sleep. 'Your pardon, Captain, I must attend to my son. The servants are busy with other tasks. Please be seated and I will ring for one of the women to bring you a refreshing lemonade. My husband will join you shortly. He is supervising work in the hayfield. Eadie will summon him.'

'I would not take him from his work. I have an hour before I return to my unit. They are guarding convicts who are clearing a road north of here.'

She hurried away to retrieve Druce, whose cries were rising to a climax. She lifted him and found his linens soiled and wet. She stripped them off and changed him, and his cries stopped, but he was sucking noisily at his thumb, a sign that he would soon demand feeding. Gwendolyn had not engaged a wetnurse for him and hoped the baby would remain content until after Captain Haughton had left. She could not leave her guest unattended, but neither was she prepared to feed her child whilst he could come upon her.

Neither Eadie nor Biddy had answered the bell she had rung, and carrying Druce she found the servant struggling to hang the last of the sheets on the line. There was no sign of Biddy, who had gone off in a sulk on the pretext of keeping Japhet Edward occupied.

'Leave the sheets, Eadie. Captain Haughton has called. Please bring us a jug of lemonade and some of the scones baked this morning. Then summon the master from the hayfield.'

She returned to the house to find Haughton standing by Japhet's

132

desk in the parlour, leafing though a pile of papers. His spying angered her.

'Those papers are private, sir.'

He raised a mocking brow as he turned to regard her. 'They tell me that the profits from the store have exceeded our expectations.'

'My husband would already have notified you of your share. He is honest in all his dealings.'

'It is reassuring to have confirmation.'

Eadie arrived with the tray of lemonade. Druce had been biting on the gold locket Gwen wore around her neck and now he started to cry. There was a bright red patch on his cheek showing that he was cutting his third tooth. Haughton frowned and looked displeased at the noise the baby was making. Gwendolyn held the child to her shoulder and deftly poured two glasses of lemonade, handing one to her guest. She had taken exception to his tone, which had held an accusing note. He now stood too close to her for comfort, his manner intimidating. Japhet's partnership with the man was one of convenience. He needed the military on his side while the officers still had so much power in the new colony, and he fed Haughton's greed. He certainly did not trust him.

'Do you doubt my husband's integrity, Captain Haughton?' Gwen challenged.

He sneered. 'How quickly you defend him. Loveday may have been pardoned of the charges against him, but in London he had a reputation of a rogue. He thinks that because he has the ear of the governor, he has the upper hand. Many of my fellow officers believe he is taking profits from imported goods that are rightly theirs. You should warn him to have a care of offending them, madam. If he puts one foot out of line they intend to use it to strip him of all he has achieved. In fact they would take pleasure in breaking his arrogant spirit.'

She gasped. Hatred blazed in the soldier's eyes and she was fearful for Japhet's life.

'Is that a threat, Haughton?'

Gwen had not heard Japhet enter the room, and neither had Haughton from the way his face bleached of all colour.

As the officer faced his partner, his lips stretched into a false smile. 'No threat, my good fellow, but a friendly warning. I have beneficial news. You are about to be even busier. Most of the goods from the ship of Kilmarthen's investors have been sold in your store. And this morning, a month before she was expected, your cousin's ship *Pegasus* was seen approaching the harbour. She should be anchored by now. Though I have to say some of the officers are far from pleased, as she has arrived so close behind the other ship. I would suggest you have a contingent of your own men to guard the goods as they are unloaded and a watch put on the store. I can only do so much to placate the officers.'

Druce continued to cry and Gwendolyn paced the floor, patting his back to pacify him. 'Druce is teething and fractious. Please excuse me. I will take him into the bedroom and tend to him. He will not settle.' She hurried out. The tension between Japhet and Haughton sparked in the room and the child's cries would add to it.

Japhet watched her leave, and when he turned back to the officer, his expression had hardened. 'I did not like your manner towards my wife. Any man who seeks to intimidate her will answer to me. I will not warn you again. Next time we will cross swords.'

'Lay a hand on me, Loveday, and you will be thrown in gaol for attacking an officer of the Crown.'

Japhet grabbed Haughton's stock and pushed him up against the wall. 'I would be upholding a gentlewoman's honour. It will be you who will be disgraced, not I; that is if you survive the duel.'

Haughton was sweating profusely. 'You mistook the situation,' he blustered. 'I was warning your good wife that you need to act with more caution in your business dealings.'

Japhet released him, though he was tempted to teach the knave a lesson he would not forget in a hurry. He would now have to spend some days in Parramatta whilst Adam's goods were brought ashore and there was no point in antagonising the officer. 'Just as long as we understand each other, Haughton. There is much to be done once *Pegasus* is unloaded. As a gesture of goodwill to your fellow officers, I will present them with a gift from the cargo. Kindly convey my compliments to them.'

'It may take more than that.'

'I do not pay protection money.' Japhet's expression hardened. 'If you cannot uphold your side of our agreement by keeping the officers from interfering in my business, then you are no use to me as a partner.' To emphasise his words, he stepped closer, his body taut with suppressed menace. 'I have rights granted to me by the governor to trade those goods. I can use your share of the profits to pay for armed guards to protect the shop, or you can earn your share.'

'The army rules here, Loveday,' Haughton sneered. 'You would do well to remember it.'

'The freed convicts are beginning to outnumber the soldiers, and they have long memories of the cruelties inflicted upon them by the military while they served their time. I can order *Pegasus* to turn back with her cargo on board once the new convicts are put ashore. There are many countries in the East who would trade spices for her cargo.'

'A risky venture, as well you know, Loveday.'

Japhet found Haughton's manner difficult to stomach. His voice was laced with warning. 'The profiteering of the army will not be condoned in London. Such action would soon reach the ears of investors there. Supplies will dry up. The militia will suffer as much deprivation as the settlers and convicts. It may even cause an uprising. Are your officers willing to risk that? *Pegasus* is one ship. Hundreds will follow in future years.'

Panic flared in the officer's eyes. He had been ostracised by several of the other officers for his partnership with Japhet. He was weak and afraid.

'No one gets rich without risk.' Japhet pursued his attack. 'Where's your backbone, man? Two years and you could be wealthier than your wildest dreams. Or do you intend to live off your army pay until a bullet, dysentery or sheer incompetence kills you? Your next posting could be Europe. There our brave army is cannon fodder in the bid to bring that upstart Corsican general to his knees.'

Haughton's eyes bulged with horror. 'I am one officer amongst many. I can only do so much.'

'I will speak with the governor.' Japhet curbed his anger, taking control to ensure there would be no problems. 'I shall request that you be in charge of unloading *Pegasus* as the only officer I deem trustworthy. It will be noted in his dispatches to England. Any officer who then acts against you will be shown to be in breach of Governor Hunter's orders and could be court-martialled and recalled to England in disgrace.'

'Hunter has shown he has no such power over the New South Wales Corps.'

'Power is given to those who are not afraid to use it,' Japhet fired back. 'Tell the other officers that the British government has been appraised of their shameful conduct.'

'Is that truly the case?' Haughton was visibly shaken.

Japhet grinned. 'My friend Sir Gregory Kilmarthen would certainly have given his report to Mr Pitt's government. It is simply a matter of time before steps are taken by them.'

'That could take years.'

'Or months.' Japhet shrugged. 'That is the risk. I'm prepared to gamble and buy time so that the militia stay out of my business for the next two years. Are you prepared to do the same?'

The challenge was thrown down like a gauntlet. Haughton hesitated, his eyes narrowed as he studied Japhet. 'What if they are not persuaded? They resent our partnership.'

'I shall call at the barracks tomorrow.' It was a confrontation that Japhet had hoped to avoid. But Haughton was incompetent and too easily swayed.

Japhet had talked his way out of many difficult situations in the past. He had faith he would succeed this time. If he failed, he could say goodbye to the fortune he intended to make in this country. Failure, therefore, was not an option.

Chapter Eighteen

Although the sickness in the shipyard had passed, the mood of the workers remained anxious. This was a summer of uncertainty and uneasy speculation. With no money to continue work on the revenue cutter, Adam was forced to lay off a quarter of his workers. Those who rented houses in the yard were allowed to stay if they took casual work in the area. It had not been an easy decision for him to make. The small local yards were fully manned, and to find work the skilled shipwrights would have to travel far afield. At least the families of the workers would not be homeless.

Although there had been no sightings of Harry Sawle or further incidents for a month, Adam doubted that they had been wrong in assuming that the smuggler had been involved in poisoning the well and the livestock. The militia had been informed that Sawle could again be in the area and a reward of a hundred pounds was offered for information that would lead to his arrest. It was as though the smuggler had scuttled back into an invisible midden he inhabited. Only the bad taste and smell of his evil remained to taint the atmosphere.

Talk of revenge was never far from the conversation of any Loveday man, but with no information coming to light of Sawle's whereabouts, there could be no action. Yet the fear generated by the mention of the smuggler's name continued to hang over the village of Penruan, and the families who worked for the Lovedays. To lighten the mood, Adam suggested a cricket match between the workers at Trevowan and those at the yard, with St John and Adam as the captains.

St John was insistent that as Trevowan was the main family home it should take place there. Adam agreed. Felicity was revelling in her new role as hostess, even though it was to be a modest event. A whole ham, cheese, cakes and cider were provided, and a fiddler was engaged for country dances in the evening. Bridie had organised a treasure hunt and games for the children.

Peter was to play on Adam's side and Uncle Joshua on St John's. Richard, despite his protests, had been ordered by Amelia not to participate because she feared it would be detrimental to his recovery. He was given the role of ensuring that the two scorers notching the runs on a stick kept an accurate tally of the score. Sir Henry when he learned of the event insisted on being the umpire.

'Someone neutral must keep the peace,' he had joked. 'Your family is too competitive. There will be no rivalry between the teams.'

In the spirit of reconciliation, Lady Traherne and the Lady Anne Druce would also attend, although they had still not graciously accepted Gwen's marriage to Japhet. It was an uncomfortable truce insisted upon by Sir Henry, who was adamant that the two families remain friends. Another unsettling guest was Sophia Quinton, Felicity's mother. Adam could not explain why he did not like her. Her voice was penetratingly loud and she often had unpalatable opinions, but then so did Aunt Elspeth. Was it her fawning need to please, or something more sinister: a predatory nature that Senara had hinted the woman possessed? Aunt Cecily, a friend of hers since childhood, was often less than welcoming of her company, her usual patience discarded at Sophia's vanity and outrageous flirting with any man present. Adam had also noticed how Uncle Joshua made excuses to be elsewhere when she joined them. Amelia certainly had no time for St John's mother-in-law, and referred to her as 'that ghastly creature who has forgotten her breeding'.

But the family was large, and its dynamics could be complex in the need to keep the peace. Somehow Sophia, with her overbearing bonhomie, seemed to compound the underlying tensions of the family. Adam and St John skated on thin ice around each other, the unspoken anger in their eyes conveying that the rivalry was far from buried. Though Rowena was four years older than Charlotte, she showed many of her mother's traits and ensured that she was the centre of attention. Charlotte adored her stepsister and followed slavishly in her shadow. Also after such a long absence Richard was a virtual stranger. His experiences at sea and of war had toughened him from a boy to a man, but Adam sensed secretiveness about his manner now. He had been an open, ebullient youth, questing for adventure, likeable and endearing. Since his return he was often sullen, short-tempered and self-centred.

Adam and St John set up the wickets on the lawn behind the orangery. These consisted of two stumps with a bail along the top very similar to the narrow hurdle entrance to a sheep pen, also called a wicket. The servants carried chairs and tables for the family to sit in the afternoon shade created by the house. The workers and their families were spread on the grass around the trees on the edge of the orchard. All the children had already set off on the treasure trail, supervised by three of the women from the yard.

Sir Henry arrived and had brought with him a fashionably dressed stranger, whom he introduced as Phillip Nankervis of St Austell.

'Phillip has recently returned from his Grand Tour, and with so much upheaval in Europe he spent much of his time in the Holy Land and Egypt.'

'Are you related to Sir Sidney Nankervis?' enquired Amelia.

'I am his third son.' He was good-looking, above medium height, with short curly brown hair and dark brown eyes.

'Sir Sidney owns one of the larger clay pits in the vicinity of St Austell, does he not?' Amelia persisted, eager to learn all she could about their guest.

'That is correct, Mrs Loveday.' Mr Nankervis bowed to the ladies and his eyes crinkled with interest when he was introduced to Hannah. 'My condolences on your sad loss, Mrs Rabson. I met your husband several times through acquaintances in St Austell.'

'Oswald passed away over eighteen months ago, Mr Nankervis,' Amelia noted. 'How long have you been abroad?'

'Ten years.' His gaze remained fixed on Hannah and she replied politely: 'There must have been much to occupy you.'

'I visited many ancient sites. I am a keen archaeologist and spent some years on an excavation in Mesopotamia.'

Hannah's eyes widened in surprise. 'How fascinating. You must have many interesting tales of your travels.'

'Which I would take great pleasure in regaling you with.'

Hannah blushed, realising Mr Nankervis had thought she had been flirting with him. 'That is most kind, sir, but I am sure your time is precious if you have but recently returned to your homeland.'

'I have many old acquaintances to visit, but it is an equal pleasure to meet new people.' Mr Nankervis was admiring in his regard. 'Especially if they are intelligent, beautiful and with a reputation for courage.'

At that moment he was called by Sir Henry, who introduced him to Adam, Peter and Joshua. Amelia turned to Hannah and smiled with pleasure. 'You have made a conquest, my dear. Mr Nankervis is handsome and his family is a prestigious one. He can be no more than five or six years older than yourself.'

Hannah was quick to reply. 'I pray you, do not set your mind upon matchmaking. I have no interest in attracting a husband.'

'Then you are foolish. Oswald would not want you to live alone. Your children need a father.'

Hannah stood up and shook out her sprigged muslin dress. 'I promised to help Bridie with the treasure hunt.'

Amelia sighed and exchanged a look with Cecily as Hannah walked away. 'Mr Nankervis was most personable. Do you not agree?'

'I would not presume to influence Hannah in her choice of a husband, even if she was ready to consider remarriage. It will only make her cling to her independence more stubbornly.'

The game was to start at noon, and St John went into the house to collect a couple of spare cricket balls from the gun room in case one became lost. During the practice sessions a great deal of time had been wasted hunting for lost balls. Since the game had been decided upon two weeks ago, both teams had spent three evenings a week practising bowling underarm in a straight line and hitting the ball. It was the first time some of the workers had played, and their efforts had caused a great deal of hilarity and also arguments.

As St John entered the house by the side door near the servants' entrance, he heard a giggle in the corridor and a man's persuasive laugh. Annoyed that the servants were not attending to their duties when there was so much to be done, he rounded a corner and saw Richard with his hand against the wall hemming in the governess, Ruth Shaw. She was a shy, rather timid woman in her early twenties, of moderate beauty, with a slim, shapely figure, and came from a good but impoverished family with five marriageable daughters.

Ruth had her head bent and her face was flushed as Richard ran a finger along her cheek. St John summed up the situation at a glance. His stepbrother was demanding a kiss: not a serious matter in his opinion, especially as the woman found his attention pleasing. However, with the children occupied she was supposed to help with the other work needed for the day to be a success.

'Have you not work to attend upon, Ruth?' St John said sternly.

She jumped guiltily and side-stepped around Richard to hurry away. His stepbrother turned a bland expression upon St John. 'I only delayed her a moment or two.'

'Just remember that she comes from a good family.' St John felt it was his duty as master of the house to remind him of the fact. 'And if your mother or Aunt Elspeth had come upon you, Miss Shaw would have been dismissed for wanton behaviour. It would be too vexing to have to look for another governess who can handle Rowena.'

'Are you sure you have not an eye on her yourself?' Richard mocked.

'She is a pretty creature, lonely and eager to please.' He sauntered away whistling a jaunty tune.

St John glared after him. He had smelled spirits of some kind on Richard's breath. It was early to be drinking. He hoped that his step-brother could hold his liquor and would not cause a scene later in the day. His moods were unpredictable. More than that, he resented the young man's remark about the governess. Had it come from one of his friends he would have replied with a suitably bawdy answer, but from Richard he found the comment unsettling.

Nearby, a clock struck the half-hour, reminding him that the match was soon to start and he had yet to retrieve the spare cricket balls.

The weather was perfect for the occasion. It was sunny but with a sea breeze that took the sting out of the heat of the sun. St John's team won the toss and chose to bat first. Their score at the end of their innings was seventy-five runs, with St John scoring twenty-three of them, his last ball caught by Peter. Uncle Joshua had managed sixteen before, red-faced and panting, he was run out. Two hours later Adam's team were all out for sixty-eight runs. Peter had made nineteen runs when Dick Nance bowled him, and Dick also bowled out Adam after he had made thirty. St John was disgruntled that Adam had beaten his score but enjoyed the acclaim as captain of the winning team. Amelia had purchased a silver chalice and named it the Edward Loveday cup, and it was to be awarded annually to the winning team.

'The best team won,' St John could not resist crowing.

Adam shrugged off the rivalry and returned with a grin, 'We will get our revenge next year. Then we intend to score a century. But I'll have to entice Dick Nance away from Trevowan to be the gamekeeper at Boscabel. He not only bowled Peter and myself out, he made a dozen runs. The highest score of any of the workers.'

St John, who joked as he presented it, awarded Dick a bottle of brandy. 'That's to keep you on my side, Nance. I cannot have my best player and gamekeeper going over to the opposing team.'

Felicity was fanning her face rapidly. 'I suggest the ladies take tea in the orangery where it is cooler.'

Joshua slapped Dick on the back, proclaiming, 'Enjoy your brandy. You played well.' He fanned his own hot face with a copy of the *Gentleman's Magazine*, which contained an article he had been discussing with Sir Henry.

The estate workers loudly cheered the embarrassed gamekeeper when he joined them. Joshua was tired from his exertions, feeling his age as he leaned back against a tree. A giggling Sophia thrust a tankard of cider into his hand.

'You look exhausted,' she cooed, and fluttered her eyes in a grotesque parody of coyness. 'You always were a fine figure of a man, a superb athlete. It was a splendid show you gave us. You had such passion for the game that I was quite breathless. You proved to your nephews that there is life in the old dog yet. But then experience always outweighs youthful enthusiasm, do you not think?'

He suppressed a shudder at her forwardness. He was weary of her innuendo. Her low-cut jonquil muslin gown was stretched tight over her large breasts, which she brought attention to by constantly dabbing with her lace handkerchief.

'You flatter me. I am out of practice. It is many years since I last played.'

She winked brazenly and dropped her voice to a seductive purr. 'You always excelled at sport. Your passion was unmatched.'

He glanced across to where Cecily was entering the orangery. Hannah accompanied her, with an attentive Mr Nankervis hovering close by. Hannah walked briskly inside, leaving the disappointed gentleman staring after her. Cecily had paused to look back at Joshua, and he was jolted by the glare of disapproval. His wife had been offhand in her manner towards her old friend since Felicity's marriage to St John. Her condemnation made Joshua's heart squeeze with pain. Could she have guessed his guilty secret? His brief affair with Sophia had been so many years ago, and her reappearance in his life had brought him nothing but remorse. Sophia was determined to flirt in the most inappropriate manner as though they were young lovers. He did not want Cecily hurt, and he had no intention of encouraging Sophia.

He decided that the best approach was to be forthright with the insufferable woman. 'Have you no care for decency, madam? Your reference to the past passion between us is an insult to my dear wife and your friend. To betray her was unforgivable of us both. This play-acting of yours must stop. It is a foolish game that will only cause hurt.'

'How disappointingly staid you have become,' she said with a thinning of her lips. 'A little light-hearted flirting is acceptable between old friends.'

'Not if it can cause pain to a dear woman who does not deserve it. I must ask you to stop this nonsense.'

Her eyes were cold and calculating. 'It was not nonsense when you declared your passion for me. As I remember, you could not have enough of me.'

The woman's lack of decorum shocked him. It made him regret even more the rash impetuousness of his early manhood. He was no hypocrite and believed himself to be broad-minded for a cleric. The indiscretion of youth was one thing; maturity should bring dignity, responsibility and consideration for others. 'Do not make me say something I will regret, madam. The door to anything that passed between us was locked many years ago. I pray you do not sully your friendship with my wife by this new mischief.' He bowed curtly. 'Your servant, madam.'

He did not trust himself to be courteous to her a moment longer. How could a time of innocent fun before he had wed Cecily turn into this nightmare? Unhappy in her own marriage, Sophia had briefly been his mistress, then disastrously they had met by chance at an inn after his wedding. Cecily had been away from the rectory for two months, tending a sick aunt. Sophia had come to his room naked beneath her cloak. His flesh had been weak and to his shame he had succumbed to her seduction. It was the only time he had been unfaithful to his wife, and he never wanted her to know about it.

Sophia stifled her pain at the humiliation of Joshua's rejection. She had convinced herself that her flirting was harmless fun. But the memories of their lovemaking were too strong to maintain that illusion. She had loved him for years. He had come into her life and stolen her heart at the point when she had realised her marriage was a disaster. Her husband was a drunkard, abusive, and a womaniser who found her unattractive and boring. He had married her for her money. His conduct had almost destroyed her, and as her looks faded she became more desperate. She needed men to adore her to prove that she was worthy of a man's love. Over the years there had been many lovers, who had bedded her then abandoned her without a second thought. No matter how hard she tried to please them, they never stayed with her for long. Only Joshua had been kind to her and during their first time together had made her feel unsullied, a woman of charm and interest. She had fallen hopelessly in love with him and had been devastated when she learned that he had married. To her mind Cecily was so homely and good, she would never hold the fidelity of a man of Joshua's passion. She did not see his marriage to her friend as a barrier, and it did not stop her loving him, or dreaming of what could have been.

How she envied Cecily the love of such a good and passionate man. How different her own life would have been had she met Joshua before her first marriage.

She blinked rapidly to dispel the sting of tears. She knew people thought her too loud, too opinionated, too frivolous to take seriously.

But how else could she hide her pain and loneliness? She might be a silly ageing woman who dreamed of romance and happiness, but she had created a role that had flattered and enticed many an older man into her bed, though the triumph of her conquest was always fleeting, leaving her discontent. The years had hardened her; to achieve her goal of perceived happiness, she would be completely ruthless.

Shaking off her moment of weakness, she saw Richard Allbright emerge from the walled rose garden. There was a swagger to his step. For a moment she feared that he might have witnessed her exchange with Joshua. Richard swayed slightly, apparently unaware of her presence in the shade of the elm. There was a flash of light in his hand as he raised a silver hip flask to his lips and drank before replacing it in his pocket and moving on to the house.

Sophia was about to follow him when another figure caught her attention. The governess appeared in the arch of the garden entrance. She paused to glance nervously from side to side, then ran towards the servants' door to the house. The woman's cheeks were flushed and her hair, usually twisted neatly into a chignon, was in disarray. As was the crumpled skirt of her gown. Sophia smiled at discovering the lovers' tryst. She was not the only one bent upon seduction, it seemed.

Chapter Nineteen

Market day in Launceston was proving a bitter disappointment. Early in the morning Hannah had collected Bridie and Maura Keppel, who had taught them lace-making, and driven them in her farm cart to the town. To her irritation Bridie had been eager to discover more of the interest Mr Nankervis had paid her at the cricket match.

'You mama told Peter that Mr Nankervis called at the farm two days after the match before he left Traherne Hall.'

'His visit was inconvenient as I was making cheese at the time,' Hannah replied.

'What did he have to say?' Bridie grinned.

'That he was returning to St Austell.'

'Oh, you are being evasive. Did you not find him handsome?'

'What does it matter how I find him?'

'Well, when a man comes calling . . .' Bridie shrugged.

'There is no romance brewing, if that is what you are thinking.' Hannah spoke sharply. 'I told him I did not usually receive visitors during farm working hours of a weekday.'

Bridie's eyes were wide with astonishment. 'Hannah, what a thing to say!'

Hannah stared straight ahead, watching the mare's bobbing head as she drove the cart. Her body was tense. 'He vexed me. I was in an old gown and helping Lillith. I was up to my arms in curds when he walked into the buttery after Jeannie told him where I was working.'

'Then you were interested enough in him to be upset at appearing less than at your best,' Bridie giggled.

Hannah shook her head in exasperation. 'I was busy and in no mood to make idle talk with a virtual stranger.'

'That is not like you.'

'I suppose I was offhand with him, but I have no wish to encourage would-be suitors.' She regretted that her irritation at his visit had provoked her to forget her manners. It had been a difficult morning. The new overseer had less initiative than Sam Deacon. If she was not vigilant, some important repair job or task did not get done. Mr Nankervis's visit coincided with the discovery that a fox had killed half the chickens because they had not been shut in their coop properly. Also two long-handled scythes had not been put away after they had been used to cut back poisonous weeds in a meadow, and a calf had cut its leg on one.

Jeannie Sawle, who was with them, looked crestfallen. She had accompanied them as Hannah had a dozen large cheeses, butter, cream and several dozen eggs to sell.

'I be truly sorry, Mrs Rabson, for not sending him away. I will not make the same mistake again.'

'I think you made your lack of interest plain,' Bridie said. 'But if you did not scare him off for good and he comes calling again, then you will know you have an avid suitor on your hands. That would not be so bad, would it? He is charming, and has visited many exotic places in his travels. I thought you would have found him fascinating.'

Hannah guided the horse around a young goose-girl on her way to market with a dozen geese spread across the King's highway. She had not been entirely truthful with Bridie and was deliberately evasive when answering her questions. Her sharpness toward Mr Nankervis had indeed stemmed from being caught at a disadvantage. Her hair had been tied back and hidden under a plain linen kerchief. Lillith had been working beside her, and she was conscious of the overseer's wife's interest in the conversation whenever Mr Nankervis paid her a compliment. He apologised gallantly for not warning her of his visit, and was intrigued by the cheese-making, plying her with questions on the procedure.

He had disregarded her terse manner and insisted that she proceed with her work. He had then spoken of various of the countries he had visited, which had captivated her imagination. Though he had stayed less than half an hour, she had found herself enjoying their conversation. When he made to leave, there had been a teasing light in his eyes. 'I presume you have a day when you are at home to visitors. May I call upon you then?'

'I thought you were leaving Traherne Hall on the morrow. You spoke of visiting friends in Camelford.'

'For a day or two, no more. Sir Henry has invited me to return for a musical evening next week. He hoped that I could convince you also to attend. Lady Traherne spoke of your love of Mozart.'

Hannah had hidden her surprise at the invitation. She did not believe that either Roslyn or her mother would wish for her company. 'There is too much to do at the farm.'

'The Lady Anne Druce mentioned that you would refuse. That you were ashamed that your brother had been transported and now shunned polite society. Japhet was pardoned, was he not? Your cousin Adam praised the enterprises he has set up in New South Wales and the success he has achieved.'

Anger spiked her at the Lady Anne's spite. How dare she intimate that she was in any way ashamed of her brother? 'I have not shunned society. I am proud of my brother's courage when he was wrongly accused. His friends have always been loyal to him. The Lady Anne seems to have forgotten that I have been in mourning.'

'Then you will attend,' he had persisted. 'You must miss Japhet keenly. I liked him immensely.'

The unexpected compliment, when those who did not know the whole story behind his arrest often reviled her brother, touched her deeply. She had realised with a pang how long it had been since she had spent a night away from her home, free from the cares of running the farm. For a moment she was tempted. She adored Mozart, but to accept might wrongly encourage Mr Nankervis that he could be other than an acquaintance.

Seeing her hesitation, Mr Nankervis lowered his voice to a confidential whisper. 'I gained the impression from Sir Henry that he hoped your attendance would lessen the antagonism his mother-in-law has to your brother's marriage to her daughter.'

In such circumstances it would be difficult to refuse. 'Then I shall be happy to attend.'

His smile had been dazzling and she had been flattered at the bold appraisal in the handsome man's eyes. Again it was a shock to acknowledge how much she had missed the attention of a man other than those of her family. Her heart still ached at the loss of Oswald, but the pain was lessening.

A laugh from Bridie jolted her from her reverie. 'You are woolgathering, Hannah. Could it be Mr Nankervis has made a greater impression on you than you admit?'

Hannah refused to be drawn. 'I was thinking of the tasks I must accomplish in Launceston. I hope the rain holds off. How much lace do you have to sell?' She closed the subject, her expression unreadable.

Bridie sighed. Cecily had confided in her that the family had hopes for a romance between the knight's son and Hannah. But with her husband's sister refusing to talk, Bridie turned her attention to the day ahead. She and Maura had a large basket of lace to be sold for the women of Polruggan, Polmasryn, Trewenna and Trevowan Hard. It was not the women's best work, for that was sold at a higher price to a fashionable haberdasher's in Bodmin. More women had taken up lace-making in the little free time they could find, and Bridie was anxious that they make a decent wage from their work. It had begun raining as they approached the town, which rose steeply from the surrounding plain.

Hannah had first gone to pay into the bank the money from the sale of Lisette's piece of jewellery, which would be used to meet that year's taxes and replace the poisoned heifers. Then she intended to call on a friend who had given birth to her third child two weeks ago. Her friend's husband was a major in the marines and was serving with the British fleet under Lord Nelson.

Now, two hours after setting up a trestle table in the market, little of the work had been sold, and Bridie was despondent.

The church towers were stark silhouettes against the low dark clouds. Rain puddles spread into larger pools as the townspeople hurried about their business with their heads bent and hats and shawls pulled over their hair. Wooden pattens protected shoes as passing carts and animals splashed the dirty rainwater over women's skirts. No one was of a mind to linger.

Bridie groaned, pulling the hood of her cloak further over her Dutch cap. 'How can I face the women? We have taken but a few shillings. I have let them down.'

'You cannot help the weather,' Maura advised. She put aside her own misgivings about the women's dissatisfaction. It had been a hard winter and spring, with more tin mines closing and poor fishing. 'You take too much upon yourself. Some markets are good, some bad. There is little money for fripperies. Today there are more women selling goods than buying non-essential items. The eggs and chickens have sold. The lace will sell another day.'

'But I have instructions that the women gave me to use their money to purchase vegetable seeds. One even hoped there would be enough for a piglet to raise for next winter.' She stared despondently at the unsold lace. Jeannie had rigged up an oilskin sheet to protect them and the goods from the worst of the rain, and a constant stream of water dripped from it on to the side of Bridie's skirt. The parson's wife kept fussing that the lace would discolour if it became wet. 'They are depending on me.'

'You have done your best,' Maura comforted.

The two friends huddled closer under the oilcloth. With most of the dairy produce sold, Jeannie had been given an errand by Hannah to use the money to buy a large kettle from an ironmonger's, as her old one had burned dry, its worn base forming into several holes. It had been Oswald's grandmother's, and had been mended so many times it was now past repair.

Bridie looked so downcast that Maura put a motherly arm around her thin shoulders. She owed much to the parson's wife, who had become her friend. When she had first met Bridie, she had been living in a cave on the moor with her two daughters. They had been there for two months after her husband had been taken by a pressgang in Fowey and, unable to pay the rent, they had been evicted from their lodgings. A proud woman, Maura had sold a few pieces of lace to buy them food but had been unable to find work that would also give her a home to her young daughters. Bridie had found her a cottage to share with a childless widow in Polruggan and given her the opportunity to teach the women how to make lace.

'All the traders are faring badly,' Maura continued. 'Next week the weather will be better. We will come again then. The gentlewomen of the town will not venture out in this.'

Bridie stared up at the sky. There was no sign of it brightening. She was beginning despondently to put the lace away when two young women accompanied by two sergeants in uniform paused by their wares.

One picked up a lace collar and declared: 'This would be simply perfect to pretty up my dress for our wedding. I canna get wed without something new. 'Twould be bad luck.' The woman had barely put her girlhood behind her and was heavily pregnant. The sergeant was at least twenty years her senior, with the complexion of a hard drinker and lecher.

'Bin enough spent on this fool wedding if you ask me,' he growled.

The young bride burst into tears. 'Don't you want me to look pretty? My godfather, Captain Hinny, would expect no less. He and his good wife will be at the church. He were most insistent on that.'

The sergeant scowled and handed over the money for the collar. Bridie felt sorry for the girl. Whatever the circumstances of her pregnancy, this was no love match and she looked to have a miserable life ahead of her. But what choice did she have? An unmarried woman with a bastard child would never be accepted into decent society, and she was no woman of the streets. By her dress and manner, Bridie guessed her to be a yeoman farmer's daughter.

There was a commotion ahead of them. Several lads in patched and worn clothing were jostling each other and shouting names at any unaccompanied passer-by. Maura tutted her disapproval. 'Those gangs of prentices are a plague on decent folk. They're not so brave on their own. Their masters should have more control over them.'

'Their masters often use them little better than slaves. They work for a pittance with barely enough food to keep them alive and a bed in a dingy attic or cellar. But these youths look more like beggars than apprentices. Their clothes are rags and they are barefoot.'

Bridie's sympathy faded as they continued to jeer at the people in the market. Without provocation they pushed to the ground an old woman carrying a heavy bundle of faggots on her shoulders.

Bridie cried out in protest, and seeing blood on the old woman's face went to her aid. The youths had run off. The woman cursed with the vengeance of a crone as she struggled to her knees, weighted down by the sticks tied to her back. 'Devil's spawn, a pox on the lot of them.'

'Are you hurt?' Bridie put a hand under her elbow and helped her to her feet.

The woman shrugged her off roughly. 'What be it to you? Decent folk bain't safe on the streets.'

Bridie ignored her rudeness. 'Your face is cut and you are badly shaken. Sit by our stall and I will fetch you some water from the well.'

'Water!' She spat on the ground. 'I wouldna mind a glass of gin.' She held out her gnarled and grubby palm. One eye was covered in a white film, blinding her sight; the other was dark and menacing as that of a viper. 'Got a penny or two for a tot of gin? That will see me right.'

'I have no money for gin for you,' Bridie said primly.

'Then bugger off with 'ee,' she screeched, and there followed a torrent of invective that would have made a trooper blush.

There was laughter from behind Bridie, and she assumed the urchins were still making mischief. The change in their voices made her blood run cold.

Maura cried out: 'No. Stop that!'

A crash followed, and as Bridie swung round she saw that the beggars had toppled the oilskin and the trestle table that held the lace. The delicate handwork was tossed on the cobbles and kicked into a dirty heap before the youths ran off down a side street clutching a stolen cheese. The table containing the farm produce was also tipped over. The eggs were smashed and the remaining round cheeses rolled along the ground. A ragged man snatched one up and sprinted away. Maura was struggling to rescue the others, but another two were stolen and the rest were covered in mud.

Horrified, Bridie ran to inspect the work that had taken the women months to produce. It was ruined.

Maura had piled the rescued cheeses into a tower, and putting her hands to her face, she wept. Fortunately, she had not been hurt. 'Those monsters . . . they took the money,' she wailed. 'The senselessness of it. They need putting in the stocks for this mindless destruction.'

Heedless of the puddles soaking her skirt, Bridie scooped up the lace. Many of the pieces were torn and all were covered with filth, ground into the intricate patterns. 'How could they? How can I make this up to the women? I have failed them abysmally. And what of Hannah's money from the dairy goods?'

'Jeannie took some with her, but the rest has been stolen.'

'The authorities must be informed. For the good of the town the market should be a safe place to trade.' Bridie glared in the direction she had seen the children scattering. 'I could take a stick to those tykes myself. They've stolen the livelihood of the lace-workers. Is that not a crime? They are no better than a cut-purse.'

'They are probably adept at that also. And of disappearing into thin air,' Maura advised. Calmer now, she comforted Bridie. 'I will rinse the lace under the market pump. That will get rid of most of the dirt. At home I will wash and repair what I can. There will be enough to save for the next market. Not all is lost.'

Bridie checked that no lace had been left on the ground, and Maura wrapped it in a cloth to take to the pump.

'I should not have been so stubborn; I should have allowed Peter to accompany us,' said Bridie. 'He wanted to, but I cannot expect him to abandon his parish duties every time I travel. Hannah also would not hear of him escorting us. I suppose that since nothing has been heard of Sawle recently, we cannot blame the smuggler for this, despite the fact that he has caused so much trouble in the past.'

Chapter Twenty

Hannah's visit to her friend Geraldine McCurdie had been distressing. Geraldine lived in a steep street close by the castle walls. The new mother was confined to her bed after a difficult labour, with only a single maid to tend her and her other two children. Another servant had been dismissed before the birth for sneaking men into her basement room of a night. The moment she saw Hannah, Geraldine burst into tears.

'You are a godsend. I have been at my wits' end. I have never been so miserable.'

'You have yet to recover from the birth,' Hannah consoled. 'It cannot be easy without Major McCurdie to comfort you. You must also be worried about him fighting this war. Your tears are natural.'

Geraldine dabbed at her eyes. 'When we first wed, George intended to leave the army. Then came the war with France and it would not have been honourable. That was when he was promoted to major. I was so proud of him.'

'And rightly so.'

Geraldine clutched Hannah's hand and lay back exhausted on the pillows, her voice shaky. 'I dread to imagine the dangers he faces. I cannot sleep at night fearing he will be killed.'

'He has much to live for and much to come home to. How delighted he will be to hear you have been safely delivered of a son.'

'It could be months before he returns. Every day his life is at risk.'

'You must not think that way.' Hannah's voice sharpened to bring her friend to her senses. 'Major McCurdie's duty is to his country and yours is to support him and raise three beautiful children.'

Geraldine dabbed at her eyes. She looked mournful and helpless. 'I am so weak and foolish. You are right. But then you are so brave. For my other confinements Mama was here to support me. Her death has been difficult to bear.'

'I only do what must be done. As will you. You have more strength and courage than you give yourself credit for. Once you have rested, these doubts will pass. It is natural for you to miss your mama.'

Hannah fussed over the baby, bringing a smile back to her friend's face. 'That is better,' she encouraged. 'I will do all I can, Geraldine. I will find a servant for you from the hiring in the market.'

'But it is so late, and in this weather there will be no one suitable,' Geraldine groaned.

'I will find someone. I promise. I shall return in an hour.'

As Hannah walked through the streets, she was worried about her friend and concerned that it would be difficult to find an available servant. She paid little mind to the passers-by hurrying about their business, until she was brought up short by something about the figure crossing the road not far in front of her. The man was wrapped in a caped greatcoat, and a wide-brimmed beaver hat was pulled low over the eyes. But she would know that arrogant strut and scarred face anywhere.

She glanced left and right hoping she could call upon the help of the dragoons she had seen earlier in the town. None were in sight. Without another thought for her own safety, she lifted her skirts to run nimbly after the smuggler, avoiding the worst of the puddles. The rain had stopped and late shoppers had crowded into the road, and she had difficulty keeping her prey in sight. A sedan chair obstructed her passage, and when she finally overtook it, she was dismayed to find that Harry Sawle was no longer ahead of her. She doubled back to check the side streets with their closely packed overhanging houses. Instinct told her he had gone this way. There were some shops, and several painted signs hung from the upper windows of inns and taverns.

There were enough people on the street to show her it was a respectable quarter. A carter was delivering furniture, his vehicle blocking the road, and a pulley had been erected to raise a spinet to the second storey of a house where the window had been removed. A large table and lacquered cabinet remained on the cart to be hauled aloft in the same manner, as the door was too narrow for the furniture to be carried through. A bewigged man with a florid face waved his arms out of the window in a state of agitation.

'Have a care! Those are my wife's most precious possessions. The rain was an ill omen for our move. Have a care, I say!'

Several onlookers gawped as the spinet bumped against the wooden frame of the overhang. Hannah pressed on, forced to push through the spectators. Her frustration mounted. Where the devil was Sawle? He could be in any one of those taprooms, and they were not places she cared to venture alone. He had gone to ground like the rat he was.

Her eyes narrowed as she touched the dagger she now always wore at her waist. Her hatred for the smuggler was so intense it burned her throat. This was the first sighting and proof that he had returned. She had hoped to find his lair and call on the justice of the peace to arrest him. In that she had failed. She could, however, alert the authorities that Sawle was in the town, and a search could be made for him, but she suspected it would be a waste of time. He could be long gone before any search could be effected.

At least we know he is here. Adam must be informed, she reasoned. She scanned the street again. There was a shout from the carter as the spinet swinging on the rope was hauled through the window to an accompanying crash inside the room.

'Fools! Dolts! Imbeciles!' the owner shrieked. 'You'll pay for any damage.'

A younger man, probably the son of the house, dashed into the street and grabbed hold of the jerkin of one of the carter's men. 'I'll have your hide for your clumsiness.' He threw a punch, but the man's fellow workers came to his aid and three of them piled on to the young hothead, knocking him to the ground.

Hannah was sickened by such unnecessary violence, though the young man had brought it upon himself by his unprovoked attack. The crowd jostled for a better view of the fight, shouting and laying wagers on the outcome, and Hannah was pushed against a wall, the breath knocked from her lungs.

'Get out of my way,' she fumed. She gave the man in front of her a shove with all her strength and managed to squeeze past. The incident had added to her anger at losing Sawle, and she paused a moment to draw a steadying breath. Had she not done so, she would not have heard the plaintive sob from the gloomy alley leading away from the street.

A woman's figure was slumped against the wall, clutching her cloak about her neck, her hair in straggles around her face. It took a moment for Hannah's eyes to adjust to the murky light. Then, shocked, she ran forward.

'Sweet heaven, Jeannie! What has happened to you?'

The girl launched herself into Hannah's arms, weeping uncontrollably. 'He said such vile things. The dirty bastard mauled me like I were a common doxy. He . . . he . . . grabbed me, dragged me down here. His vile hands . . .' Her sobs were wrenched from a throat husky from screams drowned by the noise of the fight. Her teeth chattered and she was trembling violently.

'Shush, my dear. You are safe now. Did this man just maul you, or did he do more?'

Jeannie twisted her head aside and vomited into the runnel in the centre of the cobbles. When she straightened, her eyes were wild and staring with horror. 'He tried to rape me. I fought him, but he were too strong. He ripped my dress, gloating as he told me what he would do to me. Saying that no one would want me when he had finished with me. I prayed he would kill me rather than defile me in such a way.'

Jeannie broke down again, and Hannah held her tight, outraged at this attack. She was certain it had been Harry Sawle. He wanted to strike at Mark by attacking his wife. He hated his brother for working for Hannah, seeing all the Lovedays as his foe, and any who sided with them as his enemy too. No woman deserved such a fate, especially Jeannie, who was so sweet and gentle. The young woman was in danger of becoming hysterical and Hannah hated pressing her further.

'But he did not rape you, did he?'

Jeannie shook her head, unable to speak through her sobs.

'Thank God for that.'

'But I could die of shame,' Jeannie wailed. 'He said I deserved it.'

'That is nonsense. The filthy lecher should be tarred and feathered. You are safe now. Try and calm yourself or we will attract a crowd. You do not want that, do you?'

'The crowd saved me,' Jeannie gasped on a shuddering breath. 'I heard you shout for someone to get out of the way. He cursed and spat your name and shoved me to the ground and ran off.'

'You have had a lucky escape, Jeannie.'

Red-rimmed eyes regarded Hannah with deepening terror. 'The things he said . . . they were vile. He knew who I was. But how? He laughed when he said he would show me how a real man took a woman, not like my milksop of a husband. He sounded like he hated me. Why?'

'It could only have been Mark's brother, Harry. I saw him in the street and was following him to find where he was lodging. I lost him at the crossroads.'

Fortunately the alley remained deserted and the commotion in the street was occupying the pedestrians, so no one paid heed to them. The assault sickened Hannah. Had she not seen Sawle and followed him, he could have killed Jeannie. When that fiend met his maker, the world would be a better place to live. For Jeannie's sake she had to control her anger and remain calm.

'Thank God it was not any worse. He could have killed you, Jeannie.

155

This is my fault for being stubborn. Mark and Peter wanted to escort us.'

'I knew Harry was evil after the way he beat Mark and left him for dead.'

Jeannie clawed at her clothes as though she now found them and her flesh unclean. Hannah grabbed her hands to stop her hurting herself.

Jeannie wailed: 'He said he'd be waiting for my husband if I told him what happened. You saved me from that monster, Mrs Rabson. He ran off when he heard your voice.'

'It was fear of the authorities being alerted that saved you. He will go to ground now and disappear.'

'How can I tell Mark what happened? Yet he will know.' Jeannie would not be pacified. She wrenched her hands free and opened her cloak. Her bodice and chemise had been ripped and her breasts were exposed. Bruises already darkened them and there were bloody trails where his nails had gouged her.

'Sawle will pay for this outrage,' Hannah vowed.

'No, Mrs Rabson. Mark must never know. He'll go after his brother and be killed. I love him so much. I could'na risk that.' Jeannie gulped for breath. Although she continued to shake violently, she tried valiantly to calm her sobs. 'I gotta be strong, Mrs Rabson. I daren't tell Mark. It will be the death of him. Yet how can I stop him finding out? And I don't want this to become gossip. It would shame me so. Yet I canna hide these marks.'

Sobs again made her incoherent and Hannah folded her in her arms, pulling the hood of the woman's cloak over her hair and face. Hannah also feared for Mark. She did not doubt his courage in hunting down his brother, but he was no match for the older man's vicious cunning and strength. The solution had already been given to her.

'Take deep breaths, Jeannie. You must listen to me. There could be a way to spare Mark. My friend Mrs McCurdie is desperate for another servant to help with the children while she is recovering from the birth of her son.' She went on to give the reasons for the last woman's dismissal and explained that the young mother's husband was a marine fighting at sea. 'I promised to engage a servant in the market but I doubt anyone suitable would be left by now. Would you work for her until I can find someone?'

As Hannah spoke, Jeannie had stifled her tears. Hope now replaced the fear in her eyes. 'Won't Mark think that strange?'

'I shall explain that Mrs McCurdie was in dire need of help. You will of course keep the extra money she will pay you, as well as your wages from me. That will appease him. He has a caring nature, and it will only be for a couple of weeks, until your bruises heal. I shall ensure that another servant is engaged by then.'

'Oh, that be so good of you, Mrs Rabson.' The dread lifted from the young woman's face. She wiped her eyes and attempted a brave smile. 'Mark will understand, and I will not fail your friend.'

'Then this attack will remain our secret to save Mark from danger. But I vow that my family will make that villain pay for his attack upon you.'

Jeannie looked down at her torn bodice. 'How can I present myself to Mrs McCurdie like this?'

Hannah examined the younger woman's dress. 'There is a shop of second-hand clothes in the next street. I shall purchase another skirt and bodice for you. This one can be mended later. You have the skill.'

'I will never forget this, Mrs Rabson.' Jeannie dashed the last of her tears from her eyes. 'I don't like lying to Mark, but I would not put him in danger.'

'At least some good has come out of this evil. Mrs McCurdie does need your help. I would not have been able to leave her to cope alone. But I want to see that you are settled and have no lingering effects from the ordeal you have suffered. You are a strong woman, Jeannie, and a brave one.'

'If I know Mark will not hear of this, then I shall not let that monster frighten me. I got away with a few bruises and scratches. I were lucky.'

Jeannie's resilience was heartening, and Hannah was confident that she would have no lasting malady. Caring for Geraldine and the children would keep her busy and stop her dwelling upon the incident.

An hour later Jeannie was settled at Geraldine McCurdie's house, the young mother taking an instant liking to her. Hannah returned to the market, satisfied that Bridie and Maura would accept without query her reason for Jeannie staying in Launceston. She was shocked to find Bridie so upset by the assault on the stall by the urchins. She sympathised and made light of it but was certain that if Harry had been in the town he was also behind this. It was another way of striking at her family.

Chapter Twenty-one

The next day Hannah visited Adam at the yard. The weather had changed drastically. The rain had cleared and there was not a cloud in the sky. The heat from the sun was relentless as a furnace, and after yesterday's downpour the air was oppressive and difficult to breathe. A heat haze shimmered over the land, and the cows, sheep and horses loose in the fields found whatever shade was available. Apart from the song of a skylark that hovered high in the sky, there was no other bird-song. The workers in the fields had also fallen silent, their backs bent against the sun as they either hoed out weeds within the lines of crops or filled sacks with early peas. The thin muslin of Hannah's gown stuck to her shoulders and her cheeks were flushed from the high temperature.

Usually in the week the noise in the yard would have been deafening; today there was only the sound of a few hammers and saws. Though she was troubled by the events at Launceston, Hannah was disturbed to see that work on the cutter had been abandoned. A canvas had been erected on one side of the merchant vessel so that the shipwrights could continue to work efficiently and not be drained of energy. Yet only a dozen men were working on her. Six other men were scraping the hull of a fishing lugger free of barnacles in the dry dock. The carpentry sheds too were quieter than of late.

Her frown intensified. She knew the shipwrights and their families had recovered from the sickness, and she now suspected that Adam had been forced to lay off many of his men. That would have hit him hard, and he must be worried about the future of the yard. He had enough problems to deal with and she felt bad about adding to them. However, she knew her cousin would not thank her for keeping to herself the incident in Launceston.

Adam was in the forge, in discussion with the blacksmith, who was shaping glowing hot metal into a ploughshare. There were a dozen other new ones stacked in one corner, along with the metal shapes of scythes and spades. The yard carpenters would make the wooden handles of the tools, which were part of the merchandise that would be sent out to Australia. The cost of all these iron goods came out of Adam's pocket, and though his profits would be substantial, it must be stretching his finances to the limit.

When he saw Hannah standing inside the door, he waved a hand in greeting. The forge was even hotter than outside and she dabbed at her neck and brow with her handkerchief. Giving a final instruction to the blacksmith, Adam joined her. His handsome face was tense, dark smudges of tiredness circling his eyes, and lines of worry evident around his mouth. As he greeted her, the muscles relaxed into a warm smile.

'What has brought you here in this heat, Cousin? You are looking far too serious.' He was teasing her, but there was concern in his eyes. 'I am as ever your servant. What is amiss?'

'I should not burden you with new problems.' Her reluctance weighted her voice. 'From the look of the yard you have enough of your own. How many men did you have to lay off?'

'Nothing escapes your observation.' He grimaced. 'Twenty men. I cannot pay their wages when there is no work. Some have stayed on in their cottages and have taken up casual work on the surrounding farms.'

'I wish I was in a position to engage some, but apart from the haymaking, I have servants enough for the milking and dairy goods.'

'You are wise to keep the running of the farm simple. There are often difficulties with the migrant workers.'

Even with his own troubles, it was typical of Adam to support and encourage her. This further confrontation with Sawle had come at a bad time for him and he would be relentless in pursuit of their enemy. It made Hannah hesitant to speak.

'I am to visit several of the ports with plans of the cutter to try and win new customers.' He sought to reassure her that matters were not as bleak as they appeared. 'Someone may take the gamble that I have a cutter already half built. Unfortunately, this war makes it more difficult. Few are willing to invest and risk their ships being taken by the French.'

'Have not the excise office paid for the work to date on their vessel?'

They paused in their walking to regard the cutter. The wood of her skeleton was already darkening from the time she had been exposed to the elements, and her hull remained unpainted.

'They have broken their contract and money is still owed to me for the work already done. I am entitled to make good my losses. I have consulted a lawyer. The last instalment was due to be paid over two months ago. He advised me that providing I inform the excise office that unless the money is received by the end of the month their contract is void, I shall then be within my rights to find another customer for the vessel. Should a customer be found, the excise office might take the matter to a court of law for return of their money. But I shall worry about that only if such a case should occur. I have it in writing that they will not pay for work to continue.'

'I wish you success.'

He nodded his appreciation and his stare became sharp and assessing as he opened the door to his office and stood back for her to enter. Hannah fidgeted with her reticule; she could never keep her hands still when she had something difficult to say. Adam frowned, watching her restless hands.

'Whatever is wrong, you had better tell me or I shall think the worst.'

She did not take the chair he offered and rested her hip against his desk. 'You will hear something of it when you speak with Senara on your return home. Bridie would have visited her today. There was an incident at Launceston yesterday. Actually two incidents, which I am sure are related. Some urchins pushed over Bridie and Maura's stall at the market and the lace was trampled into the ground. Most of it was filthy and torn and they were obviously unable to sell it for the other women. Also some cheese and money were stolen. That was upsetting enough . . .' Her face flushed with anger and she pushed away from the desk to stand in front of him. 'This I tell you in confidence. Jeannie was attacked. I had sent her on an errand. By good fortune I was returning from visiting Geraldine McCurdie and heard a woman cry out in terror from an alley. There was a distraction in the street and no one else appeared to have heard. Jeannie had been dragged into the alley and assaulted by Harry Sawle.'

'You wait until now to tell me.' Fury tightened Adam's features. 'I should have been informed yesterday on your return, whatever the time. I would have gone to Launceston and searched every cur-infested inn until I found Sawle.'

'He will be miles from Launceston now. I did not return until noon today. It is a long journey and we stayed overnight at the coaching inn. Besides, you could not have achieved anything.' She sought to calm him, fearful that he would do something rash. 'His attack on Jeannie was all part of his warning to us.' She went on to explain all that had happened whilst Adam paced the small office, his broad shoulders rigid with tension, and ended by saying, 'That is why Mark must not know what happened to Jeannie. His brother left him for dead last time they fought.'

Adam picked up a hammer lying on his desk and slapped it against his palm. 'We now have evidence that he is in the district. The militia will hunt him down.'

'Sawle is too wily for them. He'll now go to ground for a while.'

'I'm not allowing him to get away with this. The whole county will be scoured for him. And what of Jeannie? And Mark? He can't go after his brother alone.'

Hannah held up her hands to halt his tirade. His anger alarmed her. He wielded the hammer as though he wanted to smash it against the smuggler's skull. 'Any vengeance against Sawle must be carefully planned. Jeannie was bruised and scratched but not badly hurt. She does not want Mark involved. Mark is a good man but he is no match for Harry. Jeannie is terrified he will be killed if he goes after his brother. We must respect her wishes.'

'That blackguard must pay for this outrage! Sawle has mocked us for too long.'

'He must also have been behind the hooligans wrecking Bridie's stall,' Hannah reasoned, needing to defuse his anger. 'We will use that and my identification of him in Launceston when we notify the authorities.'

Adam stared at her with murder in his eyes. She wished now she had not spoken. Honour, pride and loyalty raged through his blood.

He rapped out: 'Sawle will be gloating that he has got away with this. He must be stopped before he strikes again.' His tone proclaimed the smuggler's death sentence. Hannah's fears were all for this brave but headstrong man. His blood was up and he would retaliate with no heed to the danger he would face. She was desperate to calm him.

'Sawle will have gone to ground after this outrage. Your priority should be the yard. You cannot allow your anger and desire for revenge to destroy everything your father worked for. Our time will come.'

For a moment she dreaded that he would storm out of the office to search for the smuggler. The fury remained in his eyes as he stared unseeing ahead, and she clutched his arm, praying that common sense would prevail. It was one thing to bring Sawle to justice using the law, but revenge could have far more sinister consequences. The wildness and fiery nature of the Loveday blood had nearly destroyed Japhet. It must not wreck Adam's life.

'Adam, you must put your hatred aside.'

'I'll not let him get away with the atrocities he has committed.'

'That is not what I said. The family are united in wanting to bring Sawle down. He is playing cat and mouse with us. He wants you to go chasing after him; that way he will always be one step ahead of you. If we neglect our farms or the yard to pursue him at this time, our crops and livelihoods will suffer. That would delight him. We destroyed his income from the smuggling and he wants to destroy ours by any means. We shall defeat him by carrying on as normal and by being ever alert to what he would throw at us. He will overstep the mark, become too confident, and then we will have him.'

Adam drew a shuddering breath. 'You are right, of course. But such inactivity galls me.'

'You will spite Sawle most by prospering. Attend to the yard and find new orders. The excise office might not want the cutter, but Sawle did not lead the only smuggling band in these parts.'

Adam regarded her solemnly, and although the battle remained in his eyes, his voice had lost its lethal edge. 'You always had more sense than the rest of us cousins put together. Sawle will spit blood if I sell her to a rival gang, and it will show the revenue that they cannot treat us in this inconsequential manner. There is a customer in Falmouth who uses tubmen on the north coast between St Ives and Ilfracombe in Devon. I turned him down because he could not afford the full price. He deals with the Guernsey agent who purchased another cutter from the yard. *Challenger* and *Sea Mist* will make it difficult for them to trade in these waters unless they have ships to match their speed.'

'The revenue will be furious. They will make trouble for you.' She already regretted her part in his making this decision.

Adam saw her distress and kissed her brow. 'You worry too much. I am entitled to recoup my losses on the cutter. If I sell her ostensibly to a respectable merchant, how can I be responsible if she then carries contraband? I will leave for Falmouth tomorrow. This deal would solve my financial problems and give more shipwrights work.'

Hannah hoped that it would not also bring repercussions in its wake. But Adam was optimistic and she allowed herself to be persuaded that it was a sound decision. At least it had stopped him pursuing Sawle on some wild goose chase.

Hannah had driven the farm cart to the yard. Her children no longer attended the school here, but were at Trevowan sharing the governess St John had engaged for Rowena and Charlotte. Their lessons would finish in another hour, and she had decided before leaving the farm that she would collect them from Trevowan herself instead of sending Mark. Her stockman had understood about Jeannie staying in Launceston, but she had seen from his expression that he was far from happy. At least she had been able to give him a task he would enjoy. Two of

Japhet's mares were ready to be serviced by Lord Fetherington's Arab stallion. Mark would be away at Lord Fetherington's estate for a few days.

When she arrived at Trevowan, she discovered that Elspeth and Amelia were calling upon Squire Penwithick and his wife Dorothy. Felicity, who was suffering from the heat, was reclining on a chaise-longue in the cool of the morning room. Her face was shiny with perspiration and her blonde hair clung in dark tendrils under her brow and cheeks. She was lethargically cooling herself with a lace fan.

'Are you all alone, my dear?' enquired Hannah. 'This heat must be difficult to bear. I carried Davey all through a hot summer. It was exhausting in the latter weeks.'

Felicity smiled wanly. 'I am better for your company. I have been abandoned.'

Hannah laughed, thinking she was being flippant, but when Felicity's brows drew together she realised that she was annoyed.

'Then it is fortunate that I have an hour before the children finish their lessons. With a house full of family, it is rare that we have time together alone when I call. Is St John not here?'

'He had business in Fowey, or so he said. Basil Bracewaite called this morning and they disappeared together. That man is a wastrel, a bad influence. I would have thought that marriage and a young child would have taught him responsibility. He boasted that he had won fifty guineas at hazard last week. I do not approve of gambling. Richard accompanied them eagerly.'

'It has led many a young blood to ruin,' Hannah agreed, but she was eager to change the subject. She did not want to listen to a stream of criticism of St John and his friends. 'How do you find Richard? I have seen little of him since his return. Amelia must be delighted that he is home.'

Felicity shrugged. 'I heard them arguing this morning. Amelia likes to keep him close to her, but the young man will have none of it.'

'That is understandable. The navy has turned him from a youth into a man.'

'I do not trust the lad.'

Hannah was taken aback by such harsh judgement. 'He was a well-behaved youth and has charming manners.'

'A man with a silver tongue is not to be trusted. They have an answer to everything. Have you noticed how he never quite looks you in the eye?'

'I remember Richard as being shy and in awe of his stepbrothers and

163

cousins.' Hannah laughed. 'He adored his mother, and was especially kind to Rowena.'

'Oh, he certainly has a way with the ladies. Even Elspeth is charmed by him.'

'Then he cannot be so bad. Elspeth is a shrewd judge of character. Nothing gets past her sharp eyes. We have all quaked when she has found us wanting in her estimation.'

'Perhaps she is mellowing with age.' Felicity remained acerbic.

Tears of mirth stung Hannah's eyes, although she knew St John's wife had not intended her remark to be amusing. 'Elspeth will never mellow. The heat has stolen your good humour, Felicity. Let me brighten your mood. What morsel of gossip will bring a smile to your lips?'

Felicity sighed and rubbed a hand across her eyes. 'I am quite out of sorts. Your pardon. I fear that I lived with only Charlotte for company for too long. The Lovedays seem to fill every room with their head-strong views and their way of taking the bull by the horns whenever it suits them. It quite bemuses me at times.'

Hannah stifled a laugh. 'We are a boisterous and passionate brood to be sure. And I have invaded your rare moment of privacy. I shall wait in the garden for the children's lessons to end and take no offence that you wish to be alone.'

'No, I pray you do nothing of the sort. I am mortified. I did not mean . . .' Felicity fanned her face more vigorously and stared at Hannah. Then she saw the difficulty her companion was having in keeping her expression from smiling. 'Oh, you Lovedays! You are dreadful teases. Your humour is droll.'

'But now you are smiling,' Hannah said with a grin.

Felicity laughed. 'You are better than a tonic, my friend. Pray, tell me of yourself. You are always cheerful and it cannot be easy coping with so much on your own. You are a remarkable woman, Hannah.'

'Thank you, but I am not so unusual. I have been fortunate to be blessed with my family and friends.'

'You loved your husband very much. I did not know Oswald well. When I first met your family he seemed rather aloof at any social gath-erings. Many people were surprised at your choice, for you were so full of life.'

'Oswald was shy. He had a quick wit and loved poetry. He was the kindest man I have known.' She paused, startled that grief no longer assailed her at these memories. Instead she smiled, wanting to speak of him. 'He loved the farm and had a gentle understanding of the needs of the animals. He was proud of his heritage and adored his family. He would have moved mountains for me if I had asked him. He was my life and my passion.'

'He must have been exceptional for you to love him so ardently. You must miss him dreadfully.'

Hannah nodded. 'I am not whole without him. But that is often the way with an abiding love. He lives on through his children. Davey is very like him in looks. Abigail and Luke have his way with animals. Florence has his quiet thoughtfulness. The evenings and the nights are the worst. Memories fill every room.'

'I came to despise my first husband,' Felicity confessed. 'He was a drunkard and a wastrel. I did not mourn him. Even so, widowhood was not easy. A widow is less acceptable in society than a married woman. Many who think that we are desperate for a husband and security for our children view us with suspicion. After one disastrous marriage I was loath to risk another. Then there are the fortune-hunters looking for easy pickings, or the philanderers bent upon seduction.' Felicity shuddered. 'But I have found happiness. I am sure you will do the same, my dear. You are too pretty to stay unmarried for long. Indeed, I am surprised there is not a line of beaux queuing at your door.'

'A few have tried and been sent on their way. I am not ready to accept another man to take Oswald's place.'

'Then a certain Mr Nankervis will be mortified. It was obvious to everyone at the cricket match that you had caught his eye. He is handsome and charming. He would make a good catch.'

'You make him sound like some kind of ailment. You catch a cold or a fish.' Hannah laughed.

'Sir Henry called briefly this morning. He said he had invited you to a musical evening next week and that Mr Nankervis will also be attending.' Felicity would not be diverted from her speculation.

'I may not be able to go,' Hannah hedged.

'That would be a shame. St John and I have been invited. We could take you in the coach, and there would be no need for you to be away from the farm overnight.'

Hannah frowned. Since the incidents in Launceston, she had forgotten the invitation to Traherne Hall. It seems so trivial in comparison.

'I think we should not snub Sir Henry.' Felicity fanned herself more vigorously. 'St John tells me it is the first invitation we have received from him since Japhet and Gwendolyn's marriage. If the couple intend to return to England, everything must be done to ensure that there is no longer any bad feeling between our families.'

'You are right.' Hannah had no enthusiasm now for the visit.

Felicity continued to study her. 'Perhaps it is not Mr Nankervis you pine to be reunited with. There was talk of another man who seemed to have found favour in your eyes. I saw it myself when St John was paying court to me.'

'There is no one in my life now,' Hannah replied with a stiffening of her body.

Felicity gave a tinkling laugh, convinced that she had found the source of Hannah's affection. 'Do you not miss him since he left? Mr Deacon had the bearing of a lord for all he worked as your overseer. He was a wonderful father to that young boy of his, and something of an enigma. He never spoke of his past, did he?'

'He was always honest with me.'

Felicity's eyes widened. She swung her legs off the chaise-longue and leaned forward, inviting confidences. 'Be truthful, you were not entirely immune to him. He was handsome and brave when dealing with the smugglers who caused you so much trouble. I was shocked to learn that he had left the farm so abruptly. Did he propose and you refuse him? Of course, such a match would have been frowned upon. You are from a revered family and he was a—'

'You know nothing of Sam. The social standing of his family was higher than ours.' This was a subject Hannah did not wish to discuss. She did not allow her thoughts to dwell upon Sam Deacon. She dared not. They were too confusing and dangerous for her peace of mind.

'Then he was a black sheep,' Felicity persisted. 'Like your brother Japhet. Is that why you defend him so ardently? No one could dispute that your brother is an adorable rogue, yet the Lovedays always stood by him. Did Mr Deacon's family disinherit him?'

'With respect, Felicity, that is not your concern.'

'Again you defend him most heatedly.' Felicity wagged a finger and looked insufferably pleased with her conjecture. 'It shows you care more than you are telling.'

'There is nothing to tell.' Exasperation sharpened Hannah's tone. 'Sam became a good friend. He was loyal and dealt with difficult matters that could have ruined the farm. I am greatly in his debt. Of course I miss him.'

She stood up, mortified by her outburst. A flood of memories overwhelmed her. Sam Deacon, or Captain Charles Samuel Deighton to give him his correct title, had been a friend, no more, a rock and a confidant during her bereavement. Though too often for comfort his image had become imposed over that of Oswald as she went about her work on the farm.

'I can hear the children have been dismissed from their lessons. I have much to attend to on the farm. Good day to you, Cousin.'

On the drive home Hannah wondered if indeed she was not being entirely truthful with herself. She could never have coped with the first months of her widowhood and the challenges that had faced the farm had Sam not been there to encourage and support her. She had received no word from him since he had left, and that was as it should be. Sam had his own difficult family issues to contend with. They could take years to resolve. He had been a loyal friend, and that was all. Yet if she looked deep into her heart, there was a special place for that vagabond overseer who had departed so abruptly from her life.

Chapter Twenty-two

'I will not have this matter discussed further,' Colonel Sir Hugo Deighton raged at his younger son. 'My decision was made years ago. I will not change my mind. I will not acknowledge that bastard child as part of our family. Now get out!'

Sam Deighton had known that persuading his father to accept the past would be difficult. So far it was proving impossible. This was his third time of calling upon his father at Merle. Today he had challenged him whilst he breakfasted alone in the dining room. The irascible colonel had chewed on a mouthful of devilled kidneys, ignoring his son. His stubbornness had made Sam's blood boil and his own temper erupted.

'You cannot mean that. You brought us up to uphold family honour. Charles is your grandson. Does that mean nothing to you?'

'His mother should have thought of honour when she ran off and fornicated with that knave.' Forty years ago that ear-splitting voice had rallied the English army as it fought against the American colonists who sought independence from their sovereign country. Age and a debilitating head wound received at the Battle of Lexington that had ended his army career could not wither the colonel's outraged bellow.

It did not impress Sam. 'You drove Catherine away when you forbade—'

The rest of Sam's protest was drowned out by his father's fury. 'Insolent whelp!' The glass of the overhead chandelier shook at the violence of the outburst, and one of the crystal pendants fell to the floor. 'I will not have that trollop's name mentioned. And you have equally displeased me. I forbade you to search for her. Now you return with her brat and would shame us all. I order you gone from here. I never want to set eyes on you again. You are no longer my son.'

'Is refusing to acknowledge your blood your answer to everything?' Sam raged. 'Are you so blinded by your bigotry that you have lost all sense of family loyalty? If you do not want Charlie as a grandson, there is someone else who does. His other grandfather. His lordship would adopt him as his heir. That would disinherit you and my brother.'

'A bastard cannot inherit,' Sir Hugo sneered, refusing to look in his direction.

'Lord Eastley says that his son and your daughter were married.'

'Utter poppycock! The cur seduced her, then abandoned her. At least you had the decency to call him out and run the blackguard through.'

'He deserved to die. He was weak, and so terrified of his lordship's wrath that he abandoned Catherine.'

Still the old man would not face him. It had been five years since Catherine's death, and the colonel had no forgiveness in his heart. A muscle pumped under the furrowed indent of the bullet wound on his brow and his Grecian profile was stained red by his anger. That wound had changed a charming, charismatic man into a bad-tempered tyrant. His thick white hair, cut fashionably short, needed no powder to enhance it, and his sweeping military moustache touched broad side-whiskers. There was a chilling arrogance and set to his square jaw that brooked no insubordination as he pronounced his judgement.

'That is proof that she was not wed. It would have been better for us if the brat had been stillborn.' He speared another kidney with his fork in an infuriating and dismissive manner.

Such venom disgusted Sam. He had loved his sister, who had been young, innocent and trusting until her cousin had cast his lecherous eye upon her. The marriage certificate that Eastley declared was in his possession must have been forged. His lordship was capable of that. Eastley hated his brother for marrying the woman he had once loved. They had quarrelled twenty years ago over some inconsequential matter and never spoken since. Yet after Eastley's son's death, Hugo was heir to the palatial family home. At Reginald's funeral, his lordship had vowed that he would burn the ancestral home to the ground before Hugo or his sons could inherit. It had been a hot-headed rejoinder intended to provoke the colonel. Sam cursed the stubbornness of the brothers, which had torn the family apart long before Catherine and Reginald had become lovers. Had there been no feud, the cousins would have married for love, or if seduction alone had been Reginald's plan, they would have been forced to marry to protect the reputation of the family. Either way Catherine would still be alive and Charlie would have a secure future. Sam had little love or liking for his autocratic uncle, and he disliked the same traits in his father.

To calm his anger, he stared over his father's head across the spread of land that was bordered in the distance on the west by the River

Tamar. On the far side of the river was Lord Eastley's property, Highcroft Manor. Merle had been the Lady Isabella's home when she married Hugo. The redbrick house had been built in the time of William and Mary, and was not as large as Highcroft. When he first arrived, Sam had taken lodgings in Merle village with a woman whose husband was serving in the army. He had not visited Highcroft Manor, hoping first to resolve his father's prejudice against his grandson. All the communication between him and his uncle had been through the lawyer who had tracked him down at Hannah Rabson's farm.

The Loveday family had shown him the power of loyalty and honour to keep a family united against their enemies. Even when rivalry and jealousy had come perilously close to destroying the family, the men had pulled back from the brink of their enmity to unite and triumph over adversity and those who would bring them to ruin. Why must his own family remain so stubborn? He needed to convince his father that such a course was the only solution now, but the set of that rigid jaw warned him he would be wasting his breath. Nevertheless, he had to try. He could do with Hannah Rabson's wisdom and common sense to give him the right words to say. It had been her gentle understanding and urging that had made him determine to protect Sam by all the means in his power from Eastley's manipulation.

'Who was at fault that Reginald was not brought to account for seducing your daughter?' Sam challenged. 'They should have been pursued when they eloped.'

'She defied me. I ordered her to stop seeing the knave. If she had been a soldier under my command she would have been court-martialled.'

Sam sighed. 'She was not a soldier, Papa. She was a young, idealistic girl very much in love.'

Merciless pale eyes turned to pierce him. They were bright with anger and loathing. 'Treacherous dog! Do I need to ring for the servants to forcibly remove you?' He would never listen to reason or admit that he had ever been wrong in his judgement.

Sam's contempt matched the older man's. 'Did not Mama defy her parents by choosing you as her husband? You were the younger son, a poorly paid captain in the army. Had she married your brother, who had asked for her hand first, Lady Isabella's dowry would have united the two lands as their parents had always intended. Her father did not disown her for choosing the lover of her choice.'

'My intentions towards your mother were always honourable,' the colonel exploded. 'Unlike that blackguard Reginald . . .'

'How do you know whether his intentions were honourable? You

170

would not allow him in the house, and you locked Catherine in her room until she refused to have anything to do with him.'

'By her disobedience she brought her own fate on her head. The knave was only playing with her affection.'

Sam threw up his hands in exasperation. 'What proof have you of that? Lord Eastley is as pig-headed as you. He disowned his son. Reginald would have been penniless. He was weak and betrayed Catherine by bowing to his father's will.'

Colonel Sir Hugo Deighton rose from the table, his body ramrod straight. His hand shot out to strike Sam's face. Sam was faster, gripping his father's wrist. For a tense moment their eyes locked in mutual fury and contempt, then Sam flung the older man's arm away. 'Brutality was always your way. It will not work now, sir.'

He spun on his heel and marched from the room. He had lost count of the number of times his father had beaten him into submission as a child. There was still a scar on his shoulder from where the colonel had taken a horsewhip to him when he was ten. He walked through the hall of Merle House for what could be the last time. Even through his anger his throat cramped with a sense of loss. His powerful stride froze and he paused to look up at the line of ancestral portraits on the oak staircase. His gaze focused on the painting of his mother as a young bride. The Lady Isabella wore a cream silk ballgown and a lace fichu, her blonde hair piled high and powdered. Her smile was serene, welcoming everyone who entered her home. Even her love and compassion had been unable to curtail the wrath of her husband upon their daughter. Catherine's death had broken the gentle woman's heart and she had fallen into a decline. Sam stared into the soft honey-coloured eyes – the same eyes as Charlie and Catherine.

His mother would never have condemned her grandchild to hardship and insecurity. The boy's future was worth fighting for, no matter the pain or the consequences. To deny Charlie his heritage would be to deny all that was fine in his mother and grandmother. It could not be achieved without a battle. Sam valued family loyalty. There was no denying that his father was Eastley's rightful heir. All Sam wanted was for Charlie to be acknowledged and given a good education and security for his future.

A galloping horse startled a flock of grey and pink galahs into noisy flight. The scarlet and white of the New South Wales Corps was clearly visible through the trees. The breakneck speed at which the horse was being ridden did not bode well. A trail of red dust from the arid earth followed in its wake.

Japhet was working at the sawmill, supervising the final stages of the building. The soldier shouted to him on his approach and the horse skidded to a halt amidst a cloud of dust and flying stones. The rider's face was wet with sweat and dark patches spread across his jacket. Breathless from his ride, he was also swaying in the saddle from exhaustion, and at first his words were incoherent. He was not a man Japhet recognised, and from the unfaded red of his jacket he had probably only recently arrived in the colony.

'Take a deep breath and tell us again,' Japhet commanded.

The man nodded and took several gulps.

'Have the natives attacked another homestead?' Japhet prompted.

'No. Convicts!' He finally got his breath enough to gasp. 'Several of them got drunk. They'd smuggled some spirits with them when they were taken into the bush to clear a road. They killed two guards.'

The incompetence of the militia stunned Japhet, and his anger erupted. Those convicts would be desperate men and a danger to the settlers. His fears for his family rose. 'There would have been more than two guards. Why did the others not apprehend them?'

'They'd also been drinking and had fallen asleep. They'll be court-martialled.'

'So these men are still at large?'

The soldier nodded. He had finally regained his breath. 'They've murdered an entire family and stolen their horse and food.' He sawed on the reins to turn his mount. 'I've got to warn others.'

Japhet grabbed the bridle, one hand automatically calming the sweating, snorting animal. His stare was harsh with tension. There had been several false alarms about such escapes, but he knew it would be foolish to ignore the warning.

'Where was this attack?'

'One of the outlying homesteads.' The man's fear was stark on his face. 'North. Three miles. The Browns' place. Six murdered. Two were women convicts. They'd also been raped.'

Japhet's blood turned to ice. His farm was isolated. The convicts would be desperate for supplies and would try and escape into the mountains.

'These convicts are armed, I take it.'

The soldier nodded. 'They stole muskets and ammunition belts.'

This was worse than any other incident, and uncomfortably close to home. Japhet's fears were immediately for Gwen and the children. 'Are they headed this way?'

'No way of telling. They are desperate men.' The soldier jerked on the reins and the horse reared, its hooves perilously close to Japhet's head. 'I have to warn others and summon the garrison.'

'How many firearms do they have?' Japhet held on to the bridle, bringing the horse down on to all four hooves. His shirt stuck damply to his powerful shoulders as his muscles strained to control the beast.

'Brown had two guns, the guards another two.' The soldier lowered his voice. 'There must be a score or more convicts with them now. Others joined them from a neighbouring farm. The settlers of that farm were in Parramatta, so escaped harm. But they took another three guns, pickaxes and axes. You'd be wise to take refuge in Parramatta.'

'I'm not running away from those thugs.'

He released the bridle and the soldier galloped away. This was no false alarm but a very real danger. Japhet would fight the convicts without hesitation, but he could not risk the lives of his wife and sons. He'd hitch up the wagon and take them and the women servants to Parramatta.

He ordered the mill workers to get back to the farm. Two of the convicts hesitated, their faces belligerent at the news of an insurrection. Japhet was already mounted and drew his pistol from the saddle holster. He aimed it at the stronger of the two, a man known as Slit-Nose Burns, a convicted cattle thief who'd had his nose slit in a fight in a brothel. He had been frequently flogged as a troublemaker until Japhet had brought him to work in the sawmill and put him in charge of the other convicts. Slit-Nose had reformed with the responsibility but had an uncertain temper. 'Burns, you'd be a fool to throw your lot in with those men. You've only two years left of your sentence. They'll eventually be caught and hanged. There's no way through the mountains, and if the militia don't kill them, the natives will.'

Rebellion sparked in Burns's eyes, but Japhet would kill him rather than risk his treachery, and his own glare showed his resolve. Whilst Slit-Nose wrestled with the temptation, his companion edged away from him saying, 'I ain't gonna join no rebels. They'll be dead meat in a month.'

'You with me or against me, Burns?' Japhet challenged.

The murderous light faded from the older man's eyes and he held up his hands. 'You be right, Mr Loveday, the risks ain't worth it. I ain't heard of no one escaping and surviving on land. You treat us right. I'm with you.'

Japhet holstered the pistol and gave a nod of appreciation. 'Get back to Trewenna Place as fast as you can. There's enough of us to make a stand if we are attacked.'

He veered his horse to gallop towards his home, praying that the escaped convicts had gone into the bush and would not attack them. There was no sign of any rebels on his ride and the farm looked peaceful on his arrival. He ran into the house and found Gwen feeding Druce.

'We're leaving, Gwen. Grab what you need. I'll harness the horses. There's been another convict attack on settlers. This one was serious and only three miles away. I'm taking you to Parramatta.'

'No, Japhet. We cannot just drag the children into town. If the convicts are that close they could attack our wagon. It is better to stay here and defend our property.'

He admired her courage but his fear remained. 'I will not risk your life or those of the children. If we go at once, the road to Parramatta will be clear.'

Gwendolyn battled against her own fears. 'We have to stay and face this crisis. The convicts are part of this life. To make our life here work we have to fight for our rights. I travelled halfway round the world to make my home with you. I will not be driven from it by some drunken guttersnipes.'

'Gwen, I will not risk—'

Her voice thickened with emotion. 'I will defend my home if I have to. We chose this land knowing it would not be easy to make a life here. We are in this together. No more partings. There have been too many. You taught me to use a gun. If any convict dares to endanger my children, I will shoot him.'

Japhet was about to protest, but the defiance in her eyes stopped him. He forced a reassuring smile. 'They may not come in this direction. Our own convicts are loyal. I chose only those who had a short term of their sentence left to serve and who wanted to learn farming or carpentry skills. They will not be so foolish as to risk re-offending. We will show these convicts that we are a force to be reckoned with.'

Chapter Twenty-three

Tension at Trevowan had increased since Richard's arrival. St John had thought his presence would have ended the women's bickering, which had tested his nerves in recent weeks. But Richard was certainly not the complacent and accommodating youth he had been on his last leave from the navy. There was a chilling arrogance about his manner now, and his mood could change from affable to truculent from hour to hour.

St John had returned from inspecting his crops after another downpour in the night, and was in a dour mood. A quarter of the wheat field had been flattened and was ruined. It was a loss he could ill afford. As he walked past the orangery, he saw Felicity dozing on a chaise-longue. His wife was constantly lethargic from her pregnancy and spoke of little but the forthcoming child and the exploits of Charlotte and Rowena. She complained that Rowena was leading the younger girl astray and that Charlotte was becoming defiant. Such conversations bored him.

He tiptoed past the door, unwilling to wake her. From an upstairs room he could hear Amelia and Richard's raised voices and groaned inwardly. He was in no mood for Amelia to demand that he speak with Richard about some matter of her son's behaviour. Could she not understand that all young men needed to kick up their heels on occasion and cut the bonds of their mother's apron strings? He had enough troubles of his own without having to play father and counsellor to his wayward stepbrother.

He contemplated riding to visit his friend the Honourable Percy Fetherington, and then remembered that two days ago Percy and his wife had gone to their town house in Truro for a month. Whilst there he would attend the horse-racing, and a host of gaming parties and entertainments. A flash of envy surfaced. Percy, as the heir to the ailing Lord Fetherington, had no financial worries and he had married a wealthy heiress. Lucky devil. Why hadn't St John found such good fortune as the young nobleman?

A door banged on the first floor and the rapid pace of a man's footsteps on the stairs was accompanied by a sharp command from Amelia. 'Richard! Do not storm out when I am talking to you.'

St John shut the door of his study to avoid becoming drawn into the argument between mother and son.

Another raised voice blasted the stairwell. 'Where are your manners, Richard Allbright?' Elspeth berated. 'How dare you speak to your mama with such disrespect! You are an insolent and ungrateful wretch.'

'I am not a child. I will not be treated as one.' There was petulance in every syllable.

'From the outburst I just overheard, you have the manners of a child,' Elspeth responded. 'If you wish to be treated as a man, then act like one.'

'Is not fighting a war and seeing men blown to pieces before your eyes man enough for you?'

St John was spurred into action by this diatribe. A gentleman did not talk of such distressing matters before a woman. The lad had gone too far. He flung open the study door. Richard had paused in the hall and was drinking from a hip flask.

Elspeth was stamping down the stairs, her face white with rage. St John halted her. 'Aunt, I will deal with this.'

'The ingrate . . .' Elspeth continued.

'Such censure will make matters worse.' St John glared at the slender figure quivering with rage.

His aunt clamped her lips shut but remained on the stairs, waiting for St John to address the matter. He ignored her and turned to the young man. 'Richard, you disgrace yourself by this conduct. You will apologise to your mama and Aunt Elspeth for this outburst. And is it not rather early in the day for you to be drinking?'

'They do not understand.' Richard took a second swig and some of the tension left his body. With a guilty gesture he pocketed the flask. There seemed to be an inner battle within him and he drew several deep breaths. When he spoke again, his voice was calmer but still condemning. 'Neither would you understand. You have never faced the enemy in battle, or suffered the nightmares—'

A harsh tut from Elspeth earned her a warning glare from St John. Richard's comment had flicked at St John's pride. Adam had won glory and been acclaimed a hero for fighting French ships when he captained *Pegasus* in the early days of the war with France. St John had had no inclination to face the rigours and squalor of army or naval life, but he had hated his twin for the hero-worship given to him by the family on his bold escapades.

'Insolent whelp! My duties as Trevowan's heir kept me at home,' he snapped. 'I did not seek glory in action.'

Richard scowled. 'There is no glory. I defy any man to say he is not terrified.'

'By all that's holy!' Elspeth uttered an unladylike oath. 'Is the knave craven? The Lovedays have served the navy with pride.'

For a moment it looked as though Richard would retaliate. St John bit back his own retort. Amelia had appeared at the top of the stairs, her face drawn with worry. Richard's eyes narrowed as they settled upon his mother. Then his mouth stretched into a hearty smile and he sighed. 'I ask your pardon, dearest Mama. I am forever your servant.' He bowed to Elspeth. 'My pardon, Aunt Elspeth. My behaviour was unforgivable.'

The sudden change of mood was as disconcerting as his uncharacteristic outburst. His eyes were strangely dark, and though St John was not the most perceptive of men where another's emotions were concerned, those eyes held both fear and vulnerability. The emotion passed quickly, and the slick charm Richard used so effortlessly returned. When he turned to Amelia, his smile was bright. 'I am your adoring servant, Mama. As you so fervently desire, I shall be honoured to escort you to visit Lady Anne Druce and Lady Traherne. I know you wish to maintain the social proprieties and show a united front over Japhet and Gwendolyn's marriage.'

St John was relieved. He found the company of the Lady Anne and Lady Traherne onerous, and with the quarter sessions sitting Sir Henry would be in court as justice of the peace. Richard would relieve him of the duty of accompanying the women on their visit. His gratitude made him add, 'Your mother finds it hard to accept that you have become a man so quickly. It is four years before you come of age. You must be patient with each other. But I would be failing in my duties as master of this house if I did not remind you that at all times you are expected to act as a gentleman.'

Richard bowed curtly in acknowledgement. 'I am justly reprimanded and will not forget again. I shame Mama by my conduct. She brought me up to abide by the rules of etiquette.' His smile did not waver, but St John did not trust the honeyed apology. He knew insincerity when he heard it. Had he not been a master of it when he was Richard's age?

He returned to the sanctuary of his study. The incident had added to his morose state of mind. There was something decidedly odd about Richard's behaviour, but for the life of him he could not fathom what it was. Seventeen was not an easy age for a man. He remembered his own hot blood and frustration when he felt his desires were being curbed. He soon forgot Richard, however, as his own financial problems returned to trouble him. His greatest concern was that the harvest would be poor unless the weather soon changed for the better. He needed a good harvest to replenish his coffers. Fortunately, the money he had inherited from Uncle William had paid off the outstanding loans on the estate, but the quarterly running expenses were high, and with so many family members dependent upon him, he had been forced to curb his gaming. It made him resent the lack of riches that Felicity had brought to their marriage. The shortage of money did not trouble his wife. She was content with a homely life and did not miss the entertainments that had been so important to St John. Then he would see her swollen figure and be heartened. Felicity carried his son; for he was certain that the child would be a boy. For that he could forgive her the ennui that persecuted his days.

But he remained discontented. Ill luck had dogged him in recent years. It went back to the disastrous days of his marriage to Meriel Sawle. He scowled. Even with Meriel dead, the curse of his association with the strumpet had not lifted, and much of his present-day crisis he laid at the door of Harry Sawle. Still the smuggler eluded justice. He was like a vengeful phantom striking and disappearing at will. Every day that the cur walked free to enjoy the triumph of his recent persecutions of his family, St John's hatred festered. Sawle must be laughing at the ineptitude of the military to arrest him and the ineffectiveness of the Lovedays to uphold their vow to bring him down.

Harry Sawle was far from laughing. He had seized the opportunity to attack his brother's wife in Launceston on impulse. Trust a Loveday to stop him getting his full revenge on the wench. He wished it had been the uppity bitch Hannah herself he could have humiliated instead of her servant. He wanted to crush her proud spirit and hear her beg for his mercy. In all their recent encounters she had defied him with a courage and resilience few men had dared. It had earned his reluctant admiration, but that did not mean that he would spare her from his retribution. Apart from her costing him a cargo of contraband last year, today she had raised a hue and cry that had almost resulted in his capture.

The inn where his mare was stabled had an armed guard outside, and anyone entering was stopped and questioned. These men meant business. Had the landlord betrayed him for the reward money? He would not put it past him. The man had been surly on his arrival, telling him to stay hidden as he did not want to be arrested for aiding a wanted man. Harry had kept out of sight for a week, and when he ventured out today, someone must have alerted the authorities for them to be waiting for his return.

He backed away from the inn. He resented leaving an expensive mare behind, but it would be too risky to return there. He pulled his hat down over his eyes; his scarred face was too easily recognisable. The militia were swarming in the streets, and there were guards outside all his old haunts. That could not be coincidence; someone had certainly peached on him. Fear clutched his black heart. Once no man would have denied him refuge or turned King's justice against him. His power was waning, and with it the terror that had kept him a force beyond the law.

He cut through the narrow streets cluttered with farm carts returning home at the end of another market day. The vehicles were being stopped and searched. He scowled with displeasure. He could not escape by hiding in one of them as he had planned. From under the brim of his hat he surveyed the streets. Nearby on the closed shutters of a shop a square of paper flapped in the breeze. Some of the lettering caught his attention. Harry had little reading except a few words and numbers, but he knew enough to recognise his own name in large bold letters and the sum of one hundred pounds printed below. A reward that would keep a family in comfort for many a year. It would tempt the loyalty of any but the most stalwart friend. And Harry had few of those. For years he had prided himself on being feared and hated, and relished the fact that women pointed to his figure in the street to frighten their children into obedience. The notice had been freshly printed, and as he scanned the street around him, he saw that more had been posted on trees and windows.

His first instinct was to run. But that would draw attention to him. Fortunately, the street remained crowded and he ducked down an alley. A sleepy whore loitered in a doorway. She was tall, with aspirations of attracting a better class of customer, as her dress was moderately clean and she wore a yellow wig and mobcap. She must once have been pretty until the gin had bloated her looks and her body. Her eyes were bleary with drink.

'How about a good time, my lovely?' she mumbled and drained the dregs of a gin bottle. Then her eyes widened with shock as she recognised him.

As her mouth opened to cry out, Harry shoved her back into the doorway and slammed his fist into her jaw. Her head snapped back and she crashed to the floor, out cold. That saved her life, for he would have killed her to stop her squealing. He yanked off her dress and petticoat and pulled them on under his greatcoat. Beneath her wig her hair was shaved, and there were fresh scars visible on her back. Within the last few months she had been shorn of her locks as a sign of her shame and publicly whipped through the streets. A common punishment for a doxy.

He plonked the wig and mobcap on his head and wrapped his own muffler around the lower part of his face to hide his beard and scars. Inside the house there was a battered old basket. Looping this over his arm to complete his disguise, he joined the thinning crowd leaving the town. He might present an incongruous sight, but it was no less strange than many of the poor, who wore a strange assortment of clothing to protect them from the elements. With each step he planned a fitting revenge on all who had brought this about. This was another indignity he had been forced to suffer at the hands of the Lovedays. He had been merely taunting them so far. Now they would truly feel his wrath.

Chapter Twenty-four

Hannah was nervous as she awaited the arrival of the coach from Trevowan. After another storm the previous evening, the cattle had churned the sodden earth leading from the fields to the milking sheds. Wooden planks had been laid from the door of the farmhouse to protect Hannah's shoes and gown from the mud, and the carriage would halt further away from the house to avoid its wheels turning the yard into a quagmire. Mark Sawle was in the yard, ready to hold the horses, and Hannah's nervousness was heightened at seeing the tension in St John's expression as he stepped down from the vehicle to assist her to enter.

The reason for his displeasure was immediately obvious. Sophia Quinton was in the carriage, chattering witlessly to a bored-looking Richard about a ball she had attended at Traherne Hall when Sir Henry's parents were alive.

The moment Hannah was seated, Sophia harangued her. 'My dear daughter cannot bear the jostling of the coach in her delicate condition. The roads are quite appalling after the storm.'

'I am sorry Felicity must miss the entertainment.' Hannah addressed her stony-faced cousin, who was now seated beside her. 'Are Elspeth and Amelia not attending?'

'Amelia has a headache and Aunt Elspeth would not leave one of her mares which was off its food,' St John replied.

Hannah smiled at him, trying to lighten his mood. She could guess why he was brooding. With Amelia and Felicity staying at home, he would have hoped to spend an hour or two at the card tables. She had thought Sophia had returned to her own home after the cricket match. The bad weather must have delayed her departure and she would have seized upon the opportunity to visit a house as grand as Traherne Hall. 'I appreciate that you have come out of your way to collect me. I would have had to decline the invitation otherwise.'

Before St John could reply, Richard cut across the beginnings of another speech from Sophia. 'You are looking lovely, Hannah. Mama says this is the first time you have attended a social gathering outside the family since your widowhood. With your permission I shall be enchanted to be your escort for the evening.'

'That is most kind of you, Richard, but there will be other young women with whom I am sure you would rather spend your time.'

Sophia gave Hannah a knowing wink. 'A pretty young widow does not want a callow youth spoiling her chances of attracting an eligible beau.'

'I am flattered by Richard's offer.' She quelled her irritation at the woman's insensitive remarks. 'I would be honoured for him to escort me. He is very dashing in his naval uniform.'

'The estimable Mr Nankervis will not approve,' Felicity's mother added slyly. 'Richard, are you willing to face pistols at dawn for the privilege of escorting your beautiful cousin?'

'Mrs Quinton, it is comments like that which have kept me from accepting invitations from my friends.' Hannah could no longer contain her anger. 'I am in no hurry to replace Oswald in my life. My love for him has not faded since his death. Few men have the qualities that made him so special. I am content to bring my children up alone. I do not need a husband to make my life complete.'

'I meant no offence to be sure.' The older woman fidgeted with the rows of pearls around her neck. She wore a low-cut crimson taffeta gown; the accompanying georgette fichu did nothing to conceal her ample cleavage. Her cheeks were heavily rouged, which served to emphasise the lines around her eyes and mouth. 'What a singular woman you are. A widow is often viewed as an outcast amongst society.'

'I have never cared for the views of society. I lead my life as my conscience sees fit and not as convention dictates.' Hannah had seen many predatory widows desperate to replace a lost husband and better their station in life. It stung her pride that people would suspect her motives were the same as those of such creatures.

'In all my born days I have never heard such brazenness,' Sophia expounded, looking most disconcerted.

'Is it brazen to be content to live in seclusion and celibacy?'

There was a strangled snort from St John, who was struggling to contain his amusement at the exchange. The barb had struck the older woman, who had visibly paled. Hannah remembered her manners to a guest. 'I have taken no offence at your opinions, Mrs Quinton. I love to hear Mozart played. It was at such a concert that I first met Oswald. My thoughts will be with him this evening.'

St John squeezed her hand as the coach bumped along the rutted track into the drive of Traherne Hall, and opposite her Richard bowed his head to conceal a grin.

'There is the house!' Sophia gushed as she struggled to recover her composure. 'It is as fine as I remember. So elegant, with its red brick. Cornish stone can be so dour and oppressive at times.' She was completely oblivious of the insult to her host, for Trevowan was built of local stone.

'There is nothing oppressive about Trevowan.' Richard did not trouble to curb his outrage. 'When I first saw it, set back from the cliffs, I thought it was as enchanting as a castle. After the smog and claustrophobia of London, I thought it truly splendid. I loved the estate farm and its animals, and the cove where I learned to sail the dinghy and played pirates. There is no finer place in all Cornwall. Perhaps you mistook the word oppressive and intended to say prepossessing, which means attractive.'

'I did not mean to imply that Trevowan was unattractive,' Sophia blustered at realising her blunder. 'It is a lovely house. Indeed, it is most splendid.'

'And I trust that our family has always made you welcome,' St John added with an underlying edge to his voice.

Their guest finally had the grace to flush. 'I am a silly, foolish woman at times and speak without thinking. I adore Trevowan. Felicity is proud to be its mistress. You have made her very happy, St John. Second marriages can bring great comfort.' She glanced sidelong at Hannah. 'I know your mama would be delighted to see you happily wed again and the burdens of running the farm taken from your shoulders.'

Hannah turned away to look out of the opposite window. She dared not reply or she would say something she would regret. Mrs Quinton was the most vexing woman she had ever met. Even her gentle Mama had lately found a plethora of parish duties to keep her occupied if her old friend called unannounced, and her father had a habit of disappearing whenever she paid a visit to the rectory.

To her relief the carriage halted at the front of Traherne Hall. Visitors had already disembarked from several other conveyances. With pleasure she saw her mother and father walking up the stone steps with Squire Penwithick and his wife, who had brought them in their carriage.

Sophia blocked the doorway as she waved and called before alighting. 'Yoo-hoo! Cecily, Joshua.' She clambered down without waiting for St John to assist her and pushed past a liveried footman to hurry after them.

St John sighed as he helped Hannah to descend. 'If that woman was not such a trial, she would be amusing.'

'How a sweet creature like Felicity could have such a harridan as a mother . . .' Richard cut off his comment with a chuckle. 'Look, Cousin, to avoid Mrs Quinton your father has positively sprinted up the steps to waylay the Reverend Mr Snell and his wife.'

Hannah frowned. Her mother had no welcoming smile for her old friend, not that her coolness halted the gusto of Mrs Quinton's greeting. There was something very wrong between her parents and this woman.

It was not a matter she could dwell upon. They were swept into a flurry of greetings and chatter as the footmen handed round glasses of Madeira on silver salvers. Thirty or more guests were present. All the rooms at the Hall had been renovated since Sir Henry's marriage to Roslyn. There was ornate gilded plasterwork on all the ceilings and walls, and the very latest designs in furniture seemed fragile and insubstantial compared with the Queen Anne and early Georgian pieces in the Loveday houses.

St John had disappeared as soon as he spotted a group of his friends. Hannah's father was engaged in a serious conversation with the Reverend Mr Snell, and her mother was ensconced with Sir Henry's elderly aunt Lydia. Their talk of parish duties clearly bored Sophia, who soon drifted away to join three widows who were casting covetous glances at two widowed gentlemen. Her high-pitched laugh carried above the conversations of everyone present, causing many to turn and glance at her. She waved and giggled to any who caught her eye. The woman was an insatiable social climber and Hannah pitied St John that she was such a frequent visitor to Trevowan. She doubted Elspeth would tolerate her flighty ways for long.

To Hannah's relief, she noticed that Mr Nankervis had been cornered by a matron intent upon foisting her unmarried daughter into his company. Fortunately Richard proved a diligent escort and seemed happy to remain at her side.

She greeted Roslyn and the Lady Anne warmly and was shocked at the extravagance of Richard's compliments upon their hostess and her mother.

'Lady Traherne, your grace and beauty outshine us all.' He bowed reverently and raised Lady Anne's hand to a hair's breadth from his lips. 'And if I did not know better, I would say this charming creature was your sister, not your mother.'

Roslyn had a long horse face and protruding teeth and strongly resembled her mother. Gwendolyn was the attractive one of the family, inheriting the classical bone structure of her handsome father. Richard's audacity had gone too far and Hannah braced herself for one of Lady Anne's scathing set-downs.

Instead the older woman beamed at him. 'Such a delightful young man. Amelia has raised you to have impeccable manners. Welcome to our home. I hope we shall see a great deal more of you during your leave. It is an honour to have the company of a man wounded in defence of our glorious country.' She glanced at Hannah and the sting was back in her voice. 'Unlike others who spent their youth indulging every decadent whim.'

Hannah bit her lip to stop a sharp reply. Lady Anne was obviously referring to Japhet. Her head tilted stubbornly. 'We are all proud of Richard for following the tradition of our family and serving in His Majesty's navy.'

She pulled Richard away before she said something she regretted and endangered the fragile truce between the two families. 'Your compliments were rather excessive, Richard. Was that wise? It would not do to have those two think we were ridiculing them.'

'I intended no ridicule. Do women not like compliments?'

'No woman is averse to them, but they should be sincere.'

'But is there not an inner beauty in all women if you look deeply enough?'

From the point of view of Christian love and acceptance, preached by her father, Hannah could not dispute that. But she could not abide insincerity and she suspected that Richard's charm had ulterior motives. 'A heartfelt and truthful compliment can be uplifting, but they should never be tools to ingratiate oneself with another. A wise woman would know the difference and despise the falseness of honeyed words.'

He was unabashed. 'Your wisdom is as humbling as your beauty, dear cousin. And before you protest, that is not a compliment. It is a statement of fact.'

'Which I take with a pinch of salt,' she parried with a smile. 'Is there any young lady here to whom you would like to be introduced?'

'Spare me the machinations of the matchmaking matrons.' She gave a mock shudder. 'I have no wish to pay court to anyone. It is four years to my majority. Time enough then to consider marriage. Though I consider that age questionably young. I would prefer not to wed and be tied down to a domestic life until I am thirty.'

Hannah approved of his decision. Although his midshipman's pay was poor, when he became of age at twenty-one Richard would inherit the income from a score of properties in London. They would always provide him with a comfortable income to support a wife and family. However, Hannah suspected that Amelia would be furious if she encouraged him not to seek a wife until then.

'Japhet felt much as you. If marriage is regarded lightly, then inevitably unhappiness follows.' A teasing sparkle lit her eyes. 'But Cupid's arrow strikes when the heart least expects it, and has brought many a young blood to an eager marriage.'

'I am sure you are right, Cousin, but I intend my head to rule my heart for some years to come.'

He turned aside to smile at Rachel Oakes, a buxom wife whose husband was a gambler and always abandoned her at these gatherings. Rachel returned the smile with an inviting fluttering of her lashes. Hannah had seen that response too often at Japhet's interest shown to a discontented wife, and she suppressed a sigh. She hoped that Richard would be discreet if he indulged in any romantic liaisons. Much as she had adored Japhet, his womanising had almost been his downfall.

An announcement was made for the guests to take their seats in the music room. Hannah saw Mr Nankervis bearing down upon them and kept her arm firmly linked through Richard's. Mr Nankervis was not so easily deterred. He halted in front of them.

'Mrs Rabson, I had hoped to escort you into the recital,' he declared.

'I have already agreed for my stepcousin to do so.'

'I am sure he will stand aside on this occasion.'

She felt Richard stiffen and was annoyed that Mr Nankervis had dismissed him so arbitrarily. 'Once I give my word, I would never break it. Come, Richard, Mama has saved us two seats and is eager that we join her.'

Mr Nankervis did not move aside. 'Then I ask for the honour of accompanying you to the refreshments laid on for us after the music.'

They were holding up the progress of the other guests, and Hannah was uncomfortable at the curious glances they had attracted. 'My cousin St John is to attend me.'

'I overheard him accepting an invitation from Mr Bracewaite to join some friends at the card tables. It sounds as though he will be engaged elsewhere. If your cousin fails in his duty, permit me to step into the breach.'

If St John was engaged at cards, he would forget all about his obligations to Hannah. She nodded grudgingly, and was irked to see the smile of pleasure on the face of her mother, who had witnessed the exchange.

'Mr Nankervis is such a charming man,' Cecily said effusively as Hannah sat beside her. 'You have made a conquest, my dear.'

Hannah did not reply. She had no wish to encourage her mother's speculation. Richard had gone to the aid of a woman who had spilled the contents of her drawstring bag when it fell from her wrist. From her fawning expression, he was also lavishing her with compliments. It made Hannah frown. Richard did seem to flatter the ladies with more diligence than was necessary.

Then a deep laugh to the right of her caught her attention, and she turned to see a man of medium height with short blond hair. His back was to her and he was chatting to four women with rapt expressions on their faces. As though sensing her regard, he turned. His gaze locked with hers and a broad grin lit his handsome face. Hannah felt a stab of pleasure. It was three years since she had last seen Japhet's old friend Nicholas Trescoe. He raised a hand in greeting to her, but one of his companions was speaking animatedly, reclaiming his attention.

'Hannah, did you not hear what I said?' Cecily said with impatience.

'I am looking forward to the recital, Mama. And I have just seen Nick Trescoe. I had not realised he had returned.'

'At the end of last month, I believe. He's been in London and at his uncle's estate in Wiltshire. He never stays in one place for long. His mother despairs of him.' She gathered her thoughts to return to her reprimand. 'I was speaking of Mr Nankervis, my dear.'

'And I would prefer not to discuss him. I hate the gossip that is generated every time a woman speaks more than a cursory greeting to a man of her acquaintance.' Hannah found herself smiling as the four women around Nick laughed at an anecdote. There had been a time in their youths when he and Japhet had been inseparable, and Nick, the older by one year, encouraged her brother in their wilder scrapes. He had spent little time in Cornwall in recent years.

Nick escorted the four women to their seats, and as he passed the row where Hannah and her mother were seated he paused briefly to bow to them. As he moved on, Cecily whispered, 'He has not changed. Still a ladies' man. Still cavorting about the country. There were rumours last year that he was to wed Captain Ivey's daughter from Truro. Nothing came of it and they say the girl was heartbroken. She died of a fever two months later.'

'Mama, gossip like that made Japhet notorious, and half of it was never even close to the truth.'

Cecily looked contrite. 'Your pardon. I am not myself tonight. I miss Japhet so. Seeing Nicholas is a painful reminder of the price your brother paid for his reckless life. I fear sometimes that he will not return from that God-forsaken place.'

'He will come home,' Hannah protested. 'And his letters are much in praise of the beauty of the new land and the opportunities for anyone bold enough to seize them.'

There was a spate of giggling behind them and both women frowned at recognising the high-pitched tone.

'That woman constantly draws attention to herself,' Cecily snapped.

'I do hope Mrs Quinton will not whisper and giggle all through the music. I have never known such a chatterbox.'

Cecily sniffed her disapproval. 'I thought she would have left Trevowan by now. Amelia cannot stand the woman.'

'But you used to be close friends, Mama.'

'That was many years ago. Before I saw her true colours.' A shadow crossed Cecily's usually serene face and her voice became harsh. 'St John would be wise not to allow her to get her feet too firmly under his table, or he will rue the day.'

The opening strains of the violin halted any further questions. The music was uplifting, and Hannah lost herself in its magic, despite the constant whispering several rows behind them. Sophia was seated next to Norman Liddicoat, a cousin of Squire Penwithick, and was leaning towards the gentleman and giggling behind her fan. Mr Liddicoat's wife looked furious and kept digging her errant husband in the ribs to get his attention. Cecily rolled her eyes heavenwards and gave an exasperated shake of her head.

'That woman has lost all decorum.'

When the music ended, Hannah was not surprised to discover that St John had forgotten her. Richard in his naval uniform had attracted the attention of several men eager to hear of his experiences at sea. She had wondered briefly if Nick Trescoe would join them, but he was occupied with the four women whom she now recognised as the Liddicoat cousins. Then her heart sank as Mr Nankervis approached.

'Oh Mama, that man is persistent. I am not interested in furthering our acquaintance.'

'Then you are foolish. What is there not to like about him? Is he not pleasing of eye and manner, from an impeccable family, and will one day inherit a fortune from the clay mines?'

Hannah studied his good looks. There was nothing to fault in them or his conduct, but then neither did she feel any spark of attraction. 'He would make a poor farmer.'

Cecily tutted in annoyance. 'That farm should not stop you from taking a suitable husband. Tenants can easily be found until Davey is of age.'

The thought horrified her. 'The children love the farm.'

'Mr Loveday appears to have abandoned you, Mrs Rabson.' Mr Nankervis bowed to her, interrupting any further reply to her mother.

'For that I am eternally indebted to him. I am delighted at the chance to become better acquainted with you.'

Hannah was disconcerted at her mother's words and suddenly saw her escort as an intruder who could disrupt her world. Yet without being rude and snubbing him she could not refuse his offer. She had expected Cecily to accompany them to the grand salon where the refreshments were awaiting them, but she was heading determinedly towards a group of her friends. Her mother had deliberately left them alone. Hannah's usual vivacity deserted her. Mr Nankervis did not appear to notice as he took two glasses of wine from the salver of a passing footman. He spoke animatedly of his recent travels on the continent and of the Italian marble statues and urns he had shipped back to grace the gardens of his father's estate. He was a good raconteur, and despite Hannah's unwillingness to encourage his attentions, her interest in the places he had visited and the great treasures he had seen soon had her challenging him for more information.

They were interrupted when Lady Traherne tapped him sharply on the arm with her fan. 'Mr Nankervis, you cannot monopolise dear Hannah; Mrs Bohun has been dying to hear of your travels. Her sister met you in Gibraltar. She is eager for news of her.' Roslyn's eyes were dark with anger as they flickered disparagingly over Hannah. 'It was wrong of you to keep Mr Nankervis all to yourself and it is against all the proprieties. I have a care for your reputation, Hannah, even if you do not.'

Used to Roslyn's sharp tongue, Hannah paid no heed to her comment as Mr Nankervis was steered towards Mrs Bohun. But when she heard the French gilded clock on the mantel chime the hour, she was shocked to realise that she had been talking to Mr Nankervis for some considerable time. The gossips were bound to make much of it, and that had been the last thing she had intended.

People were beginning to take their leave and she scanned the room for sight of her family. There was no sign of St John or Richard. Her mother was speaking with her father and Joshua departed in the direction of the gaming room, no doubt to remind his nephew that he had promised to take Hannah and themselves home. At that moment Richard reappeared, entering the room from the door leading to the terrace. His face was flushed and he was adjusting his stock and straightening the line of his naval jacket. As he merged with the guests, Hannah saw Rachel Oakes, the young wife Richard had been paying attention to earlier, also returning from the terrace. She was equally flushed and the front of her gown was creased. It was obvious that the pair had been together and that they had been taking more than the air on the terrace.

When Cecily joined Hannah, her eyes were twinkling with antici-pation. 'You have certainly made an impression on Mr Nankervis and put quite a few matrons' noses out of joint. They see him as a suitor for their daughters. He is the most eligible bachelor in the county. It is time to end your mourning. He is not the only man who has eyes for you. Nicholas Trescoe was asking after you. Not that I am sure that I approve of his wild ways, but he was very supportive of Japhet during his trial. There was no truth in the gossip about him and Captain Ivey's daughter. Apparently he has been staying in Wiltshire to help his uncle run his estate. The poor man suffered a riding accident that laid him up in his bed for four months. Oh look, there's Richard. I wondered where he had been. Amelia would never forgive me if he had joined St John at the gaming.'

Hannah was not about to enlighten her mother upon Richard's disap-pearance, and Cecily's interest in Mr Nankervis and Nick Trescoe had taken all the pleasure from the evening. Was this how every invitation away from the farm would be in the future? Even her joy of meeting an old friend was marred by her mother's inclination to matchmake. As the youngest of five brothers, Nick had studied at Oxford and often visited his uncle in Wiltshire. It was galling to remember that as a young maid she had once had a secret infatuation for him and would hang round him and Japhet when he called at the Rectory. That was before Oswald had courted her. It would have been pleasant to reminisce about those halcyon days of innocence and youth, but the speculation in her mother's eyes was a warning that any friendship could soon become the gossip of the county.

There was also no sign of Sophia Quinton. Hannah supposed that she should look for her. If St John had been pulled away from the gaming tables he would be displeased to be kept waiting by his mother-in-law. Lady Anne Druce was coming down a staircase and called to Hannah.

'Mrs Quinton swooned shortly after the recital. Even my smelling salts failed to fully revive her. She has a headache. I have put her in a guest room and she will stay the night. Sir Henry will have her driven back to Trevowan tomorrow.'

'That is most generous of you, Lady Anne. I shall drop in on her before we leave. Felicity will be worried about her mother.'

'I should not disturb her. She has finally fallen asleep.' Lady Anne moved on to attend to another guest who was complaining that his carriage had been blocked in by another.

Hannah found her mother, who was waiting in the hall with her father and St John. Her cousin was looking pleased and was telling Joshua that he had won a hundred guineas.

'There you are, Hannah,' Cecily remarked. 'A footman has gone to collect our cloaks. But Richard and Sophia have disappeared.'

'Sophia has been taken ill,' Hannah replied. 'Lady Anne has put her in a guest room and she will be driven back to Trevowan tomorrow.'

'She disgraced herself by drinking too much Madeira,' Cecily said waspishly. 'She constantly had a glass in her hand and she was sticking like a burr to Norman Liddicoat. There is nothing wrong with Sophia other than that she has her eye on someone else's husband. It is a habit of hers.'

Joshua choked and spluttered, causing St John to strike him on the back. 'Careful, Uncle.'

'I had a pheasant tart earlier. It has been repeating on me all evening.' He looked white and shaken and was staring at his wife in a strange manner.

'Where's that stepbrother of yours, St John? I told him we were leaving,' remarked Cecily, ignoring her husband's discomfort.

Richard sauntered into the hall. 'It has been a most pleasant occasion.'

Hannah had reservations about the evening. It had certainly put a different perspective on her future, and Richard's behaviour was disturbing. St John had returned to his gambling after promising Felicity that he had stopped. He might have won tonight, but that could give him false optimism and could lead to heavy losses if he continued. Why could her family not learn from the lessons of the past?

Chapter Twenty-five

Adam was experiencing the same restlessness as his twin, though for very different reasons. There were so many problems besetting the family at the moment that there did not seem enough hours in the day. He had been unable to find a purchaser for the half-built cutter, despite having spent three weeks sailing to all the ports from Dartmouth to Bristol. The self-styled Captain Marsh, the Falmouth smuggler whom he had hoped would purchase it, had been grievously wounded in a recent attack on his ship by *Challenger*. He had escaped arrest but it would be many months before he was strong enough to go to sea again. Adam found him slumped in a chair by the fire of an inn in Penzance. The bearded, heavy-built smuggler looked surly and dispirited.

'You've got a nerve coming here. That damned cutter of yours were near the death of me. She be a curse to these waters, destroying the free trade and imprisoning hardworking Cornishmen.'

'Then the new cutter is your means to outwit them. You know the waters and landing sites better than any revenue man.' He had tried to rally the smuggler's fighting spirit. 'What of your sons? Do they not want to triumph over the authorities?'

'They be tired of the trade. Those revenue cutters do their work too well. My sons have scattered to find work elsewhere.'

'There is scant work for untrained men,' Adam counselled. 'I came to offer you a deal on the cutter. A cheap price to get her finished and out of my yard quickly. She could be ready in four months.'

Captain Marsh turned his head away. 'Without my boys there be no point in a new ship, and faint hope of raising your price.'

Adam became more disheartened at every port. No one was prepared to invest while the war was at its height and shipping was in danger from enemy attack. The Guernsey smuggling agent had also declined. The vigilance of the revenue ships had resulted in many lost cargoes.

He was also worried about his hay and cereal crops, which were slow to ripen. At least the home farm kept the family provided with vegetables, and Eli Rudge was an excellent gamekeeper, snaring or shooting rabbits, hares, eels and wild fowl so that his family never went hungry. Times were harder for the labourers. Many of the children were taken out of lessons at Trevowan Hard to scour the moor for berries and edible roots. Poaching was a hanging offence, and with little money to pay the shipwrights, Adam used the game on his land as part of their wages. Even that did not solve his financial problems. He needed *Pegasus* to return with a full hold of spices and goods from the East. But that would not be for many months and he had no idea how much profit would be made from the voyage. He had suffered many a sleepless night worrying that *Pegasus* had been attacked and captured, and her riches stolen. But worrying solved no problems; action was what was needed. And in that he did not spare himself. He would rise early and work for two hours in the fields at Boscabel before putting in a full day at the shipyard and then returning to his estate to work for another two hours.

Senara found him discussing with Eli Rudge the drainage ditches to be cleared. With so much recent rain, the fields were in danger of flooding if the ditches were not maintained. She brought a jug of ale and half a roasted chicken to Adam's study as the grizzled bailiff was leaving. He had barely touched his evening meal, as there had been a stream of enquiries from Rudge and Billy Brown, their herdsman, to discuss. Adam's figure was thrown into relief by the single candle burning on his desk. His cheeks were hollowed and his eyes sunken from weariness. His hours of labour had made his muscular body hard as iron and his arms were brown as a peasant's from the time he spent on the land and working amongst the shipwrights on the merchantman.

'You cannot keep up this pace, my love,' she admonished gently.

'I have to keep abreast of our debts and ensure the farm can support us this year. The yard is like a sponge where money is concerned. I may have to lay off another half-dozen men.'

'We will survive. I have been making extra remedies to sell at the market, and the lavender soaps and sachets are popular with the town wives. The honey and camomile creams are also much in demand with gentlewomen to soften and whiten their hands.'

'You work as many hours as myself. The children demand much of your time.' He pulled her on to his lap and held her close. 'I should not have spent so much money on renovating Boscabel. It has drained our resources. The situation in the yard has never been so bad. We could lose everything. I cannot afford to pay the men to finish the merchantman.'

'Can another investor not be found?'

Adam shrugged. 'It means I will have to sell my share of the partnership. I cannot cut the profits to the original investors. Yet it may be the only solution left to us. I will then receive only the cost of the ship and income from her cargo.'

'Yet it would free you of debt and worry.'

'And end so many of my hopes for the future.'

She could feel his despair and sought to bring him comfort. 'We have enough money for our personal needs. The estate is beginning to show a profit and you have restored Boscabel to a home any family would be proud of.' She had always been apprehensive at his need to make Boscabel a rival in splendour to Trevowan. She had been content living at Mariner's House in the shipyard. But Adam had been ambitious. When he had purchased Boscabel, his father had still been alive and it had seemed it would be many years before the financial obligations of the shipyard would fall on his shoulders. She kissed him before continuing. 'We will weather this as we have other problems. When *Pegasus* returns she will restore our fortunes. In the mean time we can cut back on servants here. I will not go to the yard so often. Charity Mumford can deal with the common ailments I often treat. I shall have more time to run the household here.'

'We need the servants. The house is too large for you to cope with alone.' He rubbed his hand across his eyes. 'I should have listened to you. I wanted too much too soon. I wanted to prove to Papa that I was worthy of my inheritance and show that we could expand the yard and build larger ships. My pride demanded that Boscabel be returned to its former glory. And as for my crackpot idea of investing so much of our money trading in New South Wales . . . again it was pig-headed pride.'

'It was a wonderful dream. And what is the quality of life if we do not have those dreams?' She could not bear his anguish.

'Yet where has it brought us? You work harder than any of the servants. You sold the jewels from Uncle William's legacy to buy more livestock and you have not had a new dress since Tamasine's wedding.'

'I have no vanity that I must be decked with precious gems to show my worth to the world. As for dresses: I have more than sufficient. Frills and furbelows are not practical for everyday wear. I have a good Sunday gown for church, and the dress I wore for Tamasine's wedding suits any grander occasion we attend.' Seeing him about to protest, she put a finger to his lips. 'I did not marry you to be paraded in the latest fashion. I married you because I loved you and you had a grander vision for your life than riches and status. And it was that vision that drove you. Your ships are the finest in their class. Once this war is over, merchants will flock to you to build them vessels like *Pride of the Sea*. You have provided work for many when otherwise their families would have starved. Even now you allow them to live in their houses paying little rent, and Boscabel's game ensures that none of the families are hungry.' Her voice became stronger in her need to reassure him. 'Do not betray your vision, my love. Is it not always darkest before the dawn?'

Senara left him to check that the children were finally asleep. Her reasoning was sound, but Adam could not easily shake his mood. He dropped his head into his hands. Too many things had gone wrong this year and he must face his hardest challenge yet to keep the shipyard solvent. If that was not dire enough, his vow to bring Sawle to justice had come to naught. The smuggler had again gone to ground like the rat he was, and Adam's financial worries meant he could not actively hunt the smuggler down himself.

'You've got yourself a reprieve, Sawle. But not for long. Once the yard and the jobs of my workers are safe, I shall search for you. I will have my revenge for all the suffering you have caused.'

Revenge remained uppermost in Harry Sawle's mind too. The authorities were scouring the countryside for him and he had gone into hiding on Bodmin Moor. He did not believe in a code of honour among thieves. He had disregarded it to further his own ends too often in the past and had made many enemies amongst the smuggling fraternity. He feared discovery. Trusting no one, he had made his home in a cave and had hidden in a crevice a cache of gold coins that would ensure him a safe passage to America, where he had heard an enterprising man could make his fortune. He had considered losing himself in London or one of the other big cities where he was not known. But he had never liked city life, and why the hell should he run? His pride rebelled. If he was going to suffer, so was anyone else who had had a hand in his downfall.

He had stolen a horse that he kept hobbled in a nearby copse. Dangerous bogs surrounded the cave and no one went there. His trips had become nocturnal, and he took secret delight in spying on his enemies. He'd witnessed the sleepless nights as Adam Loveday paced the grounds of his home to find ease from his financial problems. There was Richard Allbright sneaking out of Trevowan to meet a farm girl in the woods, or to visit a bawdy house in Fowey. St John had also made clandestine visits to his old friend Bracewaite to gamble until the small hours of the morning. From the short rein on St John's temper, he was obviously losing. The Rabson farm had been harder to get close to. The gamekeeper who patrolled the grounds of a night was over-ready with his blunderbuss and had turned in two poachers in recent weeks. Both the male and the female servants on the farm were very protective of their mistress. Hannah never went anywhere without one or more of them finding a reason to accompany her.

The Lovedays were not the only ones he spied on. The nights he peered into the lit interior of the Dolphin caused him even greater anger. The inn thrived. It was always packed to capacity with both villagers and soldiers. On two nights *Challenger* had been docked in Penruan harbour and the crew had gone to the inn for food and drink. That had been the ultimate betrayal by his brother, welcoming the men who had been their adversaries. His anger towards the Lovedays took second place as he plotted to destroy Clem, who had become a traitor to the free-traders in his quest for respectability.

One night he had snooped around the inn and went into the stables. There had been evidence of the upturn in his brother's fortunes. He and Keziah now owned two bay mares and there was a pony for their son. On a Sunday they paraded to church in their finery, greeted by the villagers with respect and welcome. It was a far cry from Harry's childhood and the abuse he had suffered at the hands of his violent father. There had been no smart clothes and the only way to get from one village to another was by foot. The only education he had received was from the knocks that life had dealt him. With great concentration he could scrawl the ill-formed initials of his name when he was forced to put his mark to a paper. Keziah had taught Clem his letters and writing in the early years of their marriage. Did Clem think himself better than his illiterate brother? Was that why he had not hesitated to steal the inn from him? Clem had been the brawn in their smuggling days; Harry the brains and cunning. That cunning was working over-time now as his hatred and resentment grew.

Clem and Keziah's world revolved around their son. The boy was a milksop. There were no back-breaking chores for Zach. When the boy was not attending Trevowan Hard school, he played with his friends in the village or was fussed over and cosseted by his doting grandmother. Sal had had little time for her children when she ran the inn, and Harry could never remember her cuddling him.

Sal and Clem lived in luxury compared to the squalor Harry had endured as a child. The inn prospered where he had barely scraped a living from it. Jealousy spiked him. Everything Clem touched seemed to turn to gold. Yet when had he risked life, limb or freedom to create this fortune? Harry discounted the many dangers faced by a fisherman and the years that Clem had also been under Reuban's brutal rule, earning a pittance from the smuggling runs. The villagers clearly liked Clem; they had only ever regarded Harry with fear and resentment. So Clem thought he had got the better of his brother, did he? He would learn how easily his world could crash in ruins.

Chapter Twenty-six

After three weeks of fearing an attack, word arrived at Trewenna Place that the militia had routed the escaped convicts. Most had been killed in the fight, and five who had been caught had hanged. It was rumoured that a few who had escaped and run into the bush had evaded the search party sent to find them.

The mill could not stay idle for long, and Japhet had resumed its running with extra guards posted. However, wary that some of the escaped convicts could become desperate for stores and risk more attacks on homesteads, he insisted that Gwen never venture far from the house without carrying a gun. The convicts and servants had all been ordered to be vigilant and warn of any strangers on their land.

'There is nothing to fear,' Japhet reassured his wife as they prepared for their bed. 'Few convicts make a successful escape. Most are killed by the natives, starve in the bush or fall prey to the poisonous snakes and spiders.' He loved the untouched beauty of this new land; the virgin earth was rich in nutrients and farming would be profitable. But for the convict it was a place of back-breaking labour, scant rations and brutality for any misdeamour. Their years of servitude stretched as unrelenting as eternity, with no reward or respite.

'Desperate men breed insurrection and any man with backbone will plan to escape.' Gwendolyn did not look convinced. She had been brushing her hair and sat on the end of the bed, which was covered in a patchwork quilt.

'As this latest attempt proved.' Japhet sat beside her and held her in his arms. 'It is lunacy and doomed to failure. Many once thought it was possible to walk to China. Others speak of a sea route along the eastern coast, and rather than submit to the horror and tyranny here are reckless enough to face the hazards of such a voyage. None has survived.'

'That is not true. Before your arrest there was much talk in the London news-sheets of a successful escape of convicts from the first fleet. Did not Will Bryant and his convict wife Mary steal a boat and sail the eastern passage? The Bryants hailed originally from Fowey and I was naturally intrigued by their story.'

'It is not spoken of here.' Japhet frowned.

'Reputedly they sailed over a thousand miles to a chain of islands,' Gwendolyn explained. 'Will died there of a fever. Their two children also perished. An English ship arriving at the island arrested Mary and two other male convicts and they were taken back to England and Newgate prison. I marvelled at the woman's bravery, but was shocked that a mother would risk the lives of her children. Having now witnessed the misery that many women convicts endure, and the squalor in which they raise their offspring, I supposed she thought that the children might die quickly from drowning rather than face a lingering death from starvation in the early years of the settlement when food was scarce.'

Japhet's expression cleared. 'I remember the story now. The woman attracted the attention of the lawyer James Boswell, who pleaded her case and eventually won her reprieve. For a short while she was the toast of the town. But her story is an exceptional one and unlikely to be repeated. Any convict taken back to England would be re-transported and on arrival punished as an example to others who dared to flout the laws of the land. What happened to Mary Bryant?'

'She disappeared from London and did not return to Cornwall as far as I know.' Gwendolyn turned in her husband's arms to hold him tight, her voice taut. 'It is a story to inspire the desperate.'

Japhet kissed her with building passion. 'You risked everything to come here. I will not fail you. Do you miss England?'

'You are my England. I have no regrets.'

He kissed away the tension from her brow and her body until her senses caught fire and all fears were obliterated. Locked in each other's arms they slept, and it was not until the next morning after Japhet left for the mill that her unease returned. Her body still glowed from their night of passion, and to take her mind from her fears she put on her oldest gown to work outside.

Gwendolyn had surprised herself at her resilience in coping with her new life. She took pride in the unfamiliar work and the skills she had acquired. She was hoeing a row of Indian corn, and the hem of her cotton dress was dusty and a straw hat protected her head from the sun. Her mother would be appalled to see her working like a peasant, but Hannah would have encouraged her. Hannah had become her inspiration. She was not too proud to work on her land, and Gwendolyn now took satisfaction in seeing a row of seeds she had sown burst through the red earth and grow. She had taken willingly to toil she would never have done in England. With so much work needed to be accomplished each week, and so few servants, every hand was needed to ensure their success.

She opened her fan, which hung on a fine chain at her waist, to cool herself, but even the air was hot. It was only late spring, but the heat was already intense.

Eadie laboured at her side, singing tunelessly as she worked. Suddenly the servant broke off and gasped, 'There be a soldier come a-visiting, Mrs Loveday.'

Gwendolyn stopped her work and sighed at seeing an officer trotting along the track to the house. She was annoyed. She hated visitors arriving unexpectedly and finding her in her work clothes. When he was close enough for her to recognise him, ripples of alarm made her shiver in the humid air. Lieutenant Barty Grosvenor was no friend of her husband, and had openly contested Captain Haughton's partnership with Japhet. He was the most virulent of the officers of the New South Wales Corps who believed that only they should have the monopoly on selling any goods imported to the colony. This was his second visit to the homestead in a month. Last time he had demanded a cut of the profits made on the goods sold in the Loveday store in Parramatta, threatening that he could make life difficult for the family. Japhet had told him in no uncertain terms to go to the devil.

'Send a man to fetch the master from the sawmill, Eadie.' Gwendolyn shook the red dust from her work gown and smoothed a hand over her hair as she anxiously watched the servant run across the fields. Lieutenant Grosvenor had dismounted and stood on the veranda awaiting her. He raised a hand in greeting. It was a friendly enough gesture, but she remained suspicious of the motives behind this visit.

None of her apprehension showed in her cool, polite voice and she smiled graciously. 'Good day to you, Lieutenant. What brings you to Trewenna? You have found us much occupied. My husband is at our sawmill.'

'Loveday has proved most enterprising.' Grosvenor sounded displeased. 'It is at no small inconvenience that I was forced to travel here on a matter of business.'

That he rode unaccompanied by soldiers puzzled her. She remembered her manners. Her lifestyle might be very different here, but common courtesy had been inbred in her. 'You must be thirsty after your ride, Lieutenant. I can offer you buttermilk, fresh this morning, or sweetened

200

barley water or small beer we brewed ourselves. We have no strong spirits at the moment.'

'Small beer would be most acceptable, thank you, Mrs Loveday.'

Gwendolyn nodded to Eadie to fetch the drink. She did not like the way the officer's gaze travelled over her figure, lingering upon her breasts. The heat had moulded the thin cotton of her gown and petticoats to the curves of her body. 'Please be seated, sir.'

He continued to tower over whilst appraising her. 'It is not often I have the chance to speak with a cultured and beautiful woman. And you are universally famous within our colony. Few women would literally follow their husband to the end of the earth.'

'Then few women have the good fortune to be married to such a remarkable man.'

'He was a convict.' Grosvenor still made no move to be seated. His stance was intentionally threatening.

Gwen's eyes flashed with a dangerous light. Too many of the officers thought that the women settlers as well as the convict wenches were fair game. It would take more than his ill-bred arrogance and bullying to intimidate her. Even so, she was relieved to see Patch Evans sitting under a tree near the veranda cleaning Japhet's musket. Biddy and an ex-convict, Talbot, had driven to Parramatta for supplies and she felt more vulnerable than usual. Her voice was harsh as she defended Japhet. 'My husband was innocent of the crime of which he was accused. He had made dangerous enemies in England. A man too cowardly to face him man to man, but dastardly enough to lie and try and bring him to ruin through false evidence at his trial.'

'The trial was the talk of London. Quite scandalous. A beautiful woman deceived by a fortune-hunter was how the news-sheets depicted you. Your husband is a blackguard, a highwayman and a whoremonger. You were greatly wronged, dear lady, yet you stand by him even now.'

Gwendolyn rose abruptly. 'Please leave, Lieutenant Grosvenor. I will not have such talk in my home.'

'I meant no insult. Your heated defence of your husband's character but proves your courage and loyalty.' He stepped closer and dropped his voice to a mocking whisper. 'You deserve so much more than this life. How can a man profess to love you, yet allow you to forgo living in a grand mansion amongst the gentlefolk and society where you belong?'

'More settlers arrive with each ship. Many are genteel. You forget yourself, Lieutenant. I have asked you to leave. Must I summon my servants to have you forcibly removed?'

'No servant can lay a hand on me with impunity. To molest any soldier in the colony would result in their arrest and imprisonment. But I take no affront. I admire your spirit as well as your beauty. You take my words amiss. I meant only to praise your forbearance and courage.'

A volley of gunfire from upriver made Gwen jump violently. Since the attack on the Browns' farm she was nervous of anything that could signal that escaped convicts were in the district.

Grosvenor stepped closer, apparently unaware of the shots. 'Only a woman of passion would follow a rakehell across the sea from England. He does not deserve you.' He grabbed her and pushed her back against the wall, his mouth violating her lips.

Outraged, Gwendolyn struggled, but his arms were like steel bands around her body. She managed to free one hand and slapped his face, then ordered, 'Get out of here!'

He chuckled and tightened his hold on her, his mouth again on hers. She wrenched her head aside, rage scalding her body at this fresh outrage. Her foot came up and she scraped her sole along the length of his shin. The officer yelped in agony, and at the same time there was the click of a musket being cocked. Eadie screamed as she arrived carrying the beer. 'No, master, don't kill him.'

'Give me one reason why I should not blow your brains out, Grosvenor? 'Release my wife,' demanded Japhet, the musket raised to his shoulder. Patch Evans stood behind him, his fists bunched and ready to fight.

Every vestige of colour had drained from the officer's face, and hopping on one foot he released Gwendolyn. 'Only too willingly. She is a damned viper.'

Gwen darted away and her eyes widened with alarm as she regarded the fury in her husband's eyes. She put out a hand to plead with him. 'Japhet, my love. Do not shoot him. I have not come so far to have your life jeopardised by this imbecile's stupidity.'

'You would spare him after what I witnessed?'

Her heart clenched. She knew his temper could be volatile, and Grosvenor deserved to be brought to account, but not this way. If Japhet attacked him it could be seen as an act of insurrection against the government. Two Irish ticket-of-leave farmers had been hanged for ambushing two soldiers and killing them. There was much resentment and unrest amongst the Irish political prisoners who had been sent here, and now that some had served their time, they were proving rebellious against the governor's edicts for law and order.

'Lieutenant Grosvenor's unbecoming conduct is a matter for his commanding officer to decide,' Gwen reasoned.

'A court martial will bring your good name into disrepute,' Japhet retaliated, his hazel eyes resolute. 'Do you think I will tolerate that?'

He lowered the musket. Grosvenor could still not put his full weight on his injured leg, and as he began to relax Japhet's fist smashed into his jaw. 'No one attacks my wife or family without answering to me. Luckily for you, Gwendolyn had already dealt you some punishment.'

The lieutenant reeled backwards, and as Japhet advanced he squeaked, 'Mr Loveday, I meant no disrespect to your good wife. Indeed, I do not know what came over me.'

'You took advantage of what you thought to be a vulnerable woman. You dishonour your name and rank as an officer and a gentleman.' Japhet towered over his adversary, his muscles tensed ready for a second strike.

Grosvenor flinched. 'You mistake the matter.' He turned to Gwendolyn, pleading: 'Mrs Loveday, my profuse apologies. I was overcome by the sun. I have been in this barbaric land too long. A thousand pardons. I hold you in the highest esteem.'

'You cower like a woman,' Japhet blazed.

Lieutenant Grosvenor had revelled in his power over the convict women; he had begun to think himself invincible in claiming their favours. He remembered all the gossip surrounding this man and saw his own death written clearly in Loveday's eyes. Japhet was known as an accomplished duellist with both sword and pistol. It was also rumoured he could fight bare-fisted with the strength and guile of a footpad, giving no quarter. More importantly, he had won the favour of Governor Hunter. If this matter came to his attention, Grosvenor knew that he would not only be cashiered, but would also likely be imprisoned for molesting a gentlewoman.

As Loveday continued to skewer him with his murderous glare, Grosvenor spread his hands in supplication. 'I have apologised to your charming wife. What more can I say to convince you it was all a misunderstanding?'

Another volley of shots drew Japhet's attention to the surrounding trees. He glowered at the officer. 'There is a great deal of shooting today. Too much for someone to be hunting.'

'It must be the convicts!' The officer was sweating profusely. 'Sir, I implore you to accept my apologies.'

Another gunshot sounded closer, making Japhet step back. 'It could well be convicts firing. This matter between us will be settled later. Where are your men?'

'In Parramatta.' Grosvenor raised trembling hands to adjust his stock.

'I came to discuss business with you, Loveday. Now I must ride to warn other settlers.'

'Stay where you are!' Japhet warned. 'So you are alone?'

Grosvenor nodded and swallowed hard. Gwendolyn could almost smell his fear. She still dreaded that Japhet would attack him again. A muscle pumped in her husband's jaw, but he controlled his anger. His expression was unreadable when he finally pronounced: 'Count yourself lucky that every man will be needed to fight these convicts if they come.'

Chapter Twenty-seven

'Here is news to cheer the family.' Senara waved a letter at Adam as he returned from the shipyard in the afternoon. She was in the old hall of the house, crumbling lavender and honeysuckle flowers into a bowl to freshen the room, which smelled musty when it was seldom used. 'Peter collected it from the posting inn when he was in Fowey. It is from Tamasine.'

'How is my sister?'

'Blissfully happy in her married life.' Senara laughed and shuffled the four pages of neat copperplate handwriting. 'The house is divine. Max's friends adore her, as we all knew they would. Even the estimable mother-in-law is rich in praise of her. Tamasine is convinced they have confused her with some other saintly soul. And of course Max worships the ground she walks upon.'

The tension relaxed in Adam's face. 'Max struck me as a tolerant man. I am delighted she is so happy. She deserves to be surrounded by doting family and friends. Her life has not been easy.'

'Tamasine waxes enthusiastic about the coming Season that they will spend in London. And she adds that it would be even more perfect if we could find the time to visit the capital.'

Adam frowned. 'I am delighted that everything has turned out so well for my sister, but how can we leave Cornwall at this time? I am needed at the yard.'

Senara laid the letter on the polished oak table and flicked some broken flower stems into her hand. 'If you read between the lines, I think she is nervous about her first Season as a married woman. Her last visit to London was not a happy one. Max has been a good friend with his investment in *Pegasus*'s cargo. After the strain of the last months it would be good for us all to have a break from the conflict here.'

'I would not leave while Sawle is still at large. He has been behind the disasters that have befallen us. He could try anything in our absence.'

There was a stubborn edge to Adam's voice, but Senara was equally determined in her resolve. She was appalled at the hatred driving her husband.

'Reward notices are in every town and village. He is the most wanted man in Cornwall. He could be caught by then.' She shrugged. 'And if he is not, by refusing this invitation Harry Sawle has won another victory over us. He is dictating how we lead our lives.'

'You twist my words. Sawle is a menace to everyone. He runs rings around the militia. The only way to bring him to justice is to hunt him down ourselves. Until now I have had too many responsibilities at the yard and here. We have allowed him to remain free for too long.'

'This hunger for revenge can bring nothing but further ill fortune to our door. Why can you not let the authorities deal with Sawle?'

'Because he made his attacks on us personal. He makes a mockery of the law and justice.'

Senara shook her head. Adam was becoming obsessed with his vendetta against Sawle. She loathed the smuggler and all he stood for, but she had always abhorred the old adage of an eye for an eye. Revenge could become a vicious spiral of increasingly violent attacks.

'This is no petty family feud,' Adam reminded her. 'While Sawle remains free he threatens the lives of all our community, not just the Lovedays.'

'Then I pray that he has left the district for good.'

'You are too gentle a soul, my love. You are prepared to see good in everyone. Some people are beyond redemption. Harry Sawle is one of them.'

The stubborn set of his jaw warned her it was hopeless to try and convince him otherwise. She tried another route of coercion. 'And for him you are prepared to slight your sister and her husband? This is important to Tamasine or she would not have mentioned it.'

At any other time Adam would have done everything in his power to support his sister, and there was regret in his eyes. 'There are too many problems at the yard. Orders need to be secured. This is not a time to be gallivanting in London. Tamasine will understand. Besides, I thought you had no liking for the place.'

'I am a country girl at heart.' She touched his clean-shaven cheek. 'It is so long since you have been able to relax away from the cares of the estate and yard.'

'Maximillian will keep Tamasine diverted. Time enough next year to visit their home in Dorset and my sister can show me how grand a lady she has become.'

★ ★ ★

At Trevowan the need for diversion was eating at St John. He was bored with the company of so many women in his home.

Felicity had not risen from her bed. Her legs were swollen from her pregnancy and made walking difficult. Dr Chegwidden had insisted that she rest at all times. St John sauntered out of his dressing chamber, patting an emerald pin securely into the folds of his cravat.

'I have a mind to attend the next race meeting at Truro.'

'You would abandon me when I am indisposed with our child?' Felicity was outraged, and tears rolled down her cheeks. 'How could you even consider it? We are but a few months wed. The gossips will make much of it that you would desert me at such a time.'

Her weeping failed to move him. She used tears too often to get her own way. There were times when she acted like a spoilt girl, and it was far from endearing.

For the sake of the child she carried, he kept his voice low and reasonable. 'I will be away for no more than a week. That is hardly desertion.'

'If you loved me you would not leave me.'

'What has this to do with my loving you?' Her possessiveness was cloying. She had become more clinging with each month of their marriage. The euphoria he felt that she was carrying the heir to Trevowan remained, but he wearied of her demands for his attention. 'You will not be alone. And your mama could continue her stay here.'

'I thought you wanted her to leave,' Felicity whined. Her eyes were red and unattractively swollen. 'Mama has been quarrelling with Elspeth and it is obvious that Amelia disapproves of her.'

'She disgraced herself at Traherne Hall. Why can she not be more dignified? She has also upset Cecily, the most amenable of women. My aunt refuses to have anything to do with her, though she will not say why. They used to be friends.'

Felicity burst into fresh tears. 'I do not understand why Mama acts as she does. Or why she has fallen out with Cecily. I know she can be difficult. She does not like living alone.'

'Then she should take more care not to antagonise my family or act so outrageously in public. She was intoxicated at Traherne Hall. Fortunately neither Roslyn nor her mother suspected that that was why she was taken ill.'

'It is mean of you to say such things,' Felicity sobbed, her beauty destroyed by the accusing curl of her lips. 'Mama would not—'

He interrupted sharply: 'My dear, it has been abundantly clear since our marriage that your mother causes trouble wherever she goes.' The need to flee the room and find some peace with his friends was growing more pressing. 'I have said nothing until now. But matters cannot go on as they are.'

Felicity stared at him in despair. Out of loyalty she had defended her mother, but she knew how embarrassing Sophia's behaviour could be at times. She had suspected for a long time that her mother drank immoderately. The signs were uncomfortably familiar from her marriage to a drunkard. Not that Sophia had fallen that far. She also knew that Sophia was desperate to catch herself another husband. Her mother was lonely and unhappy and that made her act unbecomingly. Felicity was determined that she would not cause a rift between St John and herself. 'I will speak with her.'

'She will take less offence if it comes from you.'

His strident tone shocked her. It held no affection. She could sense his underlying anger that she had protested too strongly about his visit to Truro. The thin line of his lips warned her he would go whether she objected or not. It was a sobering acknowledgement. In recent months she had thought that St John truly loved her. She did not want to return to the days of mistrust when he had learned that she had not come to him with the fortune he believed. The child she carried had saved her from a loveless marriage, or so she had thought. Now she saw that she had deluded herself. St John thought only of his own interests. He had returned to his gambling when he visited Traherne Hall. She feared that there would be more if he travelled to Truro.

She could feel his restlessness and resentment. Her pregnancy left her exhausted; she did not have the strength to argue with him. Once the child was born, he would curb his wilder ways for the sake of the future of his son. She swallowed her pain, wiped her eyes and, forcing a smile, held out a hand to him. 'Your pardon, my love. It is wearying that I am so often confined to my bed. Of course you must go to the races. I will rest and be strong again by the time you return. And I promise Mama will be gone by then.'

Instantly his mood changed. He raised her hand to his lips, and then sat on the bed beside her to stroke her cheek. 'My dearest brave Felicity. How wonderful you are. I do not deserve such an understanding wife. I will be at your side and your most devoted servant until I leave in two days.'

His words dispelled her fears. Had she judged him too harshly? Who could blame him for wanting to escape Trevowan at this time? Sophia had caused trouble with his family. Also the arrival of Richard Allbright had not been the happy reunion his mother would have wished. Felicity did not particularly like her husband's stepbrother. She found his charm too slick and he rarely held a person's gaze when he addressed them. That to her spoke of a deceitful nature. The young man needed careful watching.

First, though, she must deal with her mother. Sophia had clearly overstayed her welcome. Her presence had clouded Felicity's chance of getting to know Amelia and Elspeth. She doubted she would ever hold great affection for Elspeth, who was too sharp and condemning with her tongue. But she liked Amelia. She felt an affinity with Edward Loveday's widow, who was a woman of high principles and did not approve of the scandals and wilder nature of the family she had married into. Amelia would prove a good ally in the future in her quest to control St John's wayward conduct. She was not being unreasonable. Had he not agreed to curb his less desirable habits as a condition of their marriage?

Chapter Twenty-eight

'Your convicts should be locked in a storeroom to ensure they do not join the insurgents,' Lieutenant Grosvenor warned Japhet. An hour had passed since their confrontation, and both men were tense in each other's company. 'It is never wise to trust them.'

The gunfire had stopped, but a spiral of smoke in the direction of another homestead warned them that the settlers had been attacked. Patch Evans glared at the officer and started forward to accost him. Japhet blocked his move.

'Our men are too near the end of their sentences to risk joining any rebel convicts,' Japhet stated. 'I would trust Evans with my life.'

'Aye, but will they fire on their own kind?' The officer was checking his pistol after loading the musket Japhet had taken from a locked cabinet set into the wall.

'They will if they are attacked or threatened. I know my men.'

'Since you were once one of them, they may pass your farm by,' the officer taunted. 'They looked upon you as a leader on the transport ship, so I heard. Then you ingratiated yourself with the captain and the settler Silas Hope. You never missed a chance to turn misfortune to your advantage.'

Japhet lifted a dark brow to regard the officer and suppressed his anger at the man's insinuation. 'Every man has a right to seek his own prosperity in the circumstances in which he finds himself.'

Gwendolyn linked her arm briefly through her spouse's to show their solidarity. 'It is a saying my husband often uses, and I agree with him. It has stood us in good stead.'

Another shot, closer this time, tightened Japhet's lips. 'Take Eadie and Japhet Edward into the bedroom and stay away from the windows.'

'This is my home and I will defend it,' Gwendolyn protested. 'Eadie will care for our children.'

The convict Slit-Nose Burns hesitated by the open door before entering. Japhet had left him at the sawmill with their second convict worker Allen. Another man, a stranger, was with him. His shirt and breeches were smeared with dust from the red earth. Japhet held the musket ready to fire if needed.

'Don't shoot, Mr Loveday. I'm Edwin Coulter. I've just taken up land about a mile from here. Half a dozen convicts broke into my tent while I was working in the fields and stole my rations. They were like wild men, dirty and thin as skeletons. I reckon you heard the gunfire.'

'You work your land alone?' Japhet voiced his surprise.

The settler was young and fresh-faced and looked no more than twenty. He explained: 'My wife is in Parramatta staying with her sister until I build a house for her. One of my convicts joined the renegades. The other man was shot. They also shot the servant girl.'

'You did right to come here,' Japhet answered. He turned his attention to Slit-Nose. 'Where's Allen? He should not be at the mill alone.'

The convict hung his head. 'He ran off, sir. Took fright into the bush like a scared rabbit. Said he weren't about to be tarred with the same brush as those runaways.'

Japhet's lips tightened in anger. 'I thought better of the man. He would stand more chance here.'

Lieutenant Grosvenor disliked being overlooked and stepped forward. 'My men warned you of danger when those rogues first escaped, Coulter. If they are back in the district they are probably weak from hunger. They have taken the provisions they need. I should ride to rouse the garrison.'

'With respect, your best course of action would be to stay here and we will confront them.' Japhet rounded on him. 'They may be weakened but they have guns and have proved that they will kill rather than risk a vicious flogging. They are scavenging for food and are no doubt hiding in the woods.'

'I wouldn't be surprised if they are after the horses,' Slit-Nose offered.

'Put the lieutenant's mare and our two horses into the stable, Burns.' Japhet turned to Edwin Coulter. The man had the greyish look of dysentery, which struck many of the settlers unused to the meagre rations and the climate. 'I see you carry a musket. Do you have much ammunition?'

'Just a few shots.'

'Then take a powder flask and musket balls from the boxes on the table. You and Burns stay in the stable and shoot any armed attacker who tries to steal the horses or approaches the house from that direction.'

The stables were built at a right angle to the house. Alongside them was the storehouse. It was that which the convicts would be most interested in. From the front and kitchen windows of the house the outbuildings could be covered by protective fire.

Gwendolyn picked up a musket. 'I will fight beside you.'

Japhet shook his head and took the firearm from her. 'I need you to reload for me. I've only the two muskets, and once they are fired I will be at the convicts' mercy if they storm the house.' He laid a primed pistol on the table.

'What arms do you carry besides your pistol and sword, Lieutenant?' he asked.

'None.'

'I'd give much to have your sword,' Japhet said. 'But I have an axe that will do as well, and my dagger.'

Eadie, who had been ashen-faced and silent until now, gasped: 'Dear God, will they kill us all?'

When his infant son Druce began to cry, it hit Japhet with a jolt how vulnerable his family could be. He had never backed down from a fight in the past, feeling invincible when only his own life was at stake. Now he found that it was far more harrowing to know that his wife and children could be killed if he failed to protect them.

'Tend to the children in the bedroom, Eadie,' he ordered. 'No harm will come to you. We are prepared and will shoot any armed convict who approaches the house.'

'But we are outnumbered,' wailed the servant.

'We have the might and skill of the military,' Japhet offered in an ironic attempt to comfort the frightened woman. 'And the convicts might be armed, but they will be short of ammunition.'

'There's still time for me to return with my troop.' The lieutenant was pale and nervous. For all his bluster he was an officer who had seen no military action and used his power of threatened floggings to keep the convicts in line. Without his men to protect him, his sweating figure showed his fear and inexperience.

Japhet bit back a scathing retort. He was disgusted at how cravenly the officer was acting. 'Even if you did leave, there is no telling which way the convicts are heading. They could skirt this farm and you would run into them on the road.'

'It's dusk. Talbot and Biddy could be in danger returning from the town,' Gwendolyn groaned.

'There is nothing we can do for them. If they heard the musket fire they will be on their guard.' Japhet saw his wife's anguish but was helpless to reassure her. The servants had rowed downriver to Parramatta in a boat he had purchased with the last of the money Gwen had brought with her from England. It was a valuable asset for their store to be able to ferry goods along the river, which was the main highway to the expanding homesteads along its bank. 'The servants should be safe. Coulter's land is further upriver.'

'Will your troop be alerted by the smoke, Lieutenant?' Gwendolyn asked. 'Surely they will come to the aid of any settler knowing that there are dangerous men loose in this area.'

'Two transport ships arrived from England yesterday. Most of them are supervising the unloading of the convicts.'

'Then this matter must be dealt with by us.' Japhet positioned himself by the window and indicated that Grosvenor keep watch in the kitchen.

The light was fading fast. It had been an hour since the last shots were heard. They would be more vulnerable to attack once darkness fell. Japhet glanced at the sky. It was overcast. There would be no moon to give them warning of the convicts creeping up on the house. No one spoke; they were intent on listening for sounds to warn them of an approaching attack.

'Loveday, a boat has pulled up by the riverbank,' Grosvenor shouted. 'Looks like your servants have returned.'

No lights had been lit in the house and Japhet stared out of the window to see the dark forms of a man and a woman walking towards them, talking companionably. The ticket-of-leave servant Talbot had a soft spot for Biddy. The maid had scorned his attentions, thinking herself above an ex-convict who had served time for picking locks and breaking into warehouses. Jamie Talbot was intelligent, with an easy charm, and had an eye for a pretty woman. He had a natural cunning and sense of self-preservation that Japhet had come to admire. He was the son of a locksmith in London and had been apprenticed to his father to carry on the trade, but he had fallen in with a bad crowd at fourteen who had showed him an easier way to make his fortune. Once his first crime had been committed, they had used blackmail to ensure he did what they wanted. He had long since repented of his crimes, and since serving his sentence had worked to save enough money to one day set up his own business as a locksmith in Sydney.

Clearly that charm of his had been working overtime in Parramatta, for Biddy was laughing and at ease in his company. They passed under the shadows of a tree left standing to provide shade in the garden and Talbot pulled Biddy to him and kissed her. Japhet would have grinned at his audacity if he did not feel the couple were in danger.

213

As he opened the door to urge them to make haste, his words were lost in an explosion of gunshot. Biddy screamed and slid sideways. Talbot caught her and hoisted her limp body over his shoulder, then ran for the house. Japhet looked in the direction the shot had come from and saw three stooped figures edging around the stables. He fired, and one pitched to the ground and lay still. Coulter, alerted to the danger, was briefly outlined in the door of the stable as he fired a second shot that brought another man down.

At that moment Talbot stumbled into the house and Japhet kicked the door shut behind him. His second musket was propped by the window and Gwen was shaking a measure of power from the flask into the muzzle of the first weapon.

'Biddy's bin shot,' Talbot declared. He placed her on a chair by the hearth.

Her cloak had fallen back, and even in the gloom Gwendolyn could see the spread of blood on the white sleeve of the chemise that served as a blouse under her laced bodice. She expertly rammed the shot into the musket, then hurried to examine the maid. Biddy groaned as she pulled aside the material. The servant had been lucky. The bullet had passed through the flesh of her upper arm. It was bleeding copiously, which was also a good sign, as it would cleanse the wound. Gwendolyn reached for her sewing basket and took out a strip of linen cut from an old petticoat that she had put aside to make a shirt for Japhet Edward. She folded this into a wad and pressed it against the wound. Biddy cried out in pain.

'You are not seriously hurt,' Gwen told the maid. 'Hold this pad in place and it will stop the bleeding. I know your wound pains you, but we need you to help with reloading.'

'I can see some men making for the river,' Japhet shouted. 'They are after the boat. Talbot, come with me. If they take the boat they will strike at other farmsteads along the river. Patch, stay here and guard my family as you would your own.'

The one-eyed servant carried a machete. Japhet tossed one of the muskets to Talbot and they ran towards the river. A shot was aimed at them from behind the stables, and from within the building Burns opened fire on the convicts. Grosvenor remained at the post he had taken up by the kitchen window. He seemed frozen to the spot in fear, and had not attempted to shoot. Furious at his hesitation, Gwendolyn turned on him.

'For the love of God, where is your backbone, man? My husband is doing your work for you. There is a chance to capture the convicts and make an example of them.' Her autocratic tone was one that had frequently been adopted by her mother when dealing with inferiors.

It shook the officer to his senses. Though ashen-faced, he drew himself to his full height and ran outside. Gwendolyn watched from the window. With no spare gun available, she picked up a meat cleaver, prepared to defend to the death her home and children. Shadowy forms were moving by the stables and river. She could not discern which were the escaped convicts and which her husband and his men.

'Dear God, do not let Japhet be shot by mistake!' Her fear tightened her throat.

Then she heard his voice raised in command. 'You are surrounded. My men are armed. Surrender and your lives will be spared.'

The reply was a musket flaring in the darkness from the paddock by the stable. Then two figures ran forward. A shot brought one of them down. The other threw himself to the ground and rolled into the shadows.

Japhet knew that everything depended on the next few minutes. He was breathing heavily as he rested his shoulder against the trunk of a tree and assessed the situation. By his reckoning they now outnumbered the convicts, but a desperate man often had the cunning and strength of two. Their attackers had nothing to lose but their lives, and they had already forfeited those by running away, for the lashing as punishment often killed them. Japhet, though, had everything to lose.

His sharp mind worked rapidly and was cold and calculating. Talbot was guarding the boat and Coulter edging closer to the stables. Grosvenor appeared from the house and ran towards the river, away from the main fighting, his white breeches and waistcoat clearly visible in the moonlight. Japhet had stripped off his own shirt as he left the shadows of the house and was bare-chested, his black breeches blending with the darkness.

'We fight for freedom.' A gruff voiced hailed from the paddock. 'Fellow convicts, join us. Why serve a master who uses you like a slave?'

'And what can you offer us?' Talbot returned. He had left the river to join Japhet. 'Starvation and the constant threat of the noose: what life is that?'

'Freedom is what I offer.'

'Death is what you will give us.' Talbot had edged closer to the paddock. He had recognised the voice of a man who had bullied many on his transport ship; two convicts had died from his brutality, one of them Talbot's friend. 'If we serve our time we will have land of our own in two years. You'll still be on the run. If you live that long.'

Japhet too recognised the leader's voice. Harold Snape had been at the colony when Japhet arrived and was the most violent troublemaker. He had been flogged twice, but instead of subduing him, the punishment had made him hate everyone in authority or who had earned their freedom.

Several dark shapes appeared out of the trees. There were more of them than Japhet had estimated. Others must have joined them since they attacked Coulter's place. Some figures were moving towards the boat.

'Get back to the river,' Japhet ordered Talbot, but he feared the servant was too far away.

Only Grosvenor stood between the convicts and the boat. A shot from the officer had come too soon to find a target. He would be unarmed for some moments as he reloaded. The convicts nearest the boat seized their chance and ran at a crouch to the river. Japhet fired and brought down one man, but two more were circling the lieutenant in preparation for attacking him. If they had not fired they must be out of ammunition, or else thought he was easy prey. A third convict was untying the boat whilst Japhet was reloading. There was also intermittent firing from the direction of the storehouse, where others were intent on stealing provisions. Slit-Nose and Coulter were firing intermittently from the stables, keeping the convicts at bay.

Japhet leapt from his position of cover. He fired at the man by the boat and the convict fell into the water, floating face down into the current. The two men grappling with Grosvenor had brought the officer down. He was kneeling holding his hands over his head as the convicts struck him with the butts of their muskets. With no time to reload his own weapon, Japhet swung the handle of his pistol down on to the neck of one attacker. The man reeled aside, then whirled to come at him, arms outstretched. Japhet kicked out, his boot landing hard in the man's gut. As he bent double, another kick to his chin laid him out cold.

Lieutenant Grosvenor was curled into a ball on the ground, groaning beneath the vicious blows delivered to his head by Snape. Japhet grabbed the assailant by the scruff of his neck and jabbed two swift punches to his throat and the side of his temple that brought him to his knees. He paused to stuff his pistol into his waistband, then drew the dagger that was always hidden inside his boot and pressed it to the convict's throat.

'I always wondered if you were half the man your reputation foretold,' Snape scoffed.

The bearded face above the point of the blade glistened with sweat in the moonlight. Japhet could smell the man's fear. 'Now you'll find out how I defend my own, Snape. Call your men off, or die!' He increased the pressure of the dagger and a tickle of blood showed dark against the man's skin.

There was a glint of rotting teeth as the convict's mouth stretched into a mocking grin. 'I'm dead meat anyway. So are you as tough as they say, Loveday?'

'Believe it,' Japhet answered. He had survived attacks by villains on the streets of London too many times not to have learned that ruthlessness was the only law they heeded: The weak die – the strong survive. This man would have raped Gwen, then killed her and murdered his sons. To keep his property safe from future attacks Japhet had to enforce the law of the underworld. With the sound of shots and fighting continuing around him, he plunged the dagger into the convict's heart, shouting as the man flopped forward: 'Your leader is dead! Surrender and we will show you mercy.'

Grosvenor had staggered to his feet and was swaying as he shook his head to clear his wits. A volley of shots came from the back of the house. Then silence. The moon had gone behind a cloud. The darkness cloaking the buildings held its secrets. Japhet did not know if his family were alive or dead.

Then a woman's scream turned his blood to ice. As Japhet reached the house Patch Evans came out of the building, the machete he was holding stained with blood.

'That were the last of them. Your family are safe, master.'

Relief flooded Japhet, and his voice was gruff as he issued orders before going to his wife. 'Coulter and Patch, tie up any of the attackers who are still alive. They will be taken back to Sydney to face trial.'

He turned to the officer, who had limped after him. Grosvenor held out Japhet's dagger, which he had drawn from the convict's torso. Japhet took it and wiped the blade on the grass to clean it of blood.

'Their leader would have been tried for the murder of two convicts in a fight at the compound had he not escaped. You obviously knew Snape but did not hesitate to confront him.'

'It was him or me.' Japhet shrugged. 'I am loyal to my friends but do not fear my enemies.' It was a warning to the officer that they still had unfinished business. 'Are you hurt?'

'Some bruises, and my head will be sore for a few days. I owe you my life, Loveday. And a sincere apology for my earlier behaviour. The success of your store has earned the resentment of many of the officers.'

'Do you remain one of them?'

217

Grosvenor shook his head. 'Not now. I would not have us as enemies. They are fools. You have a right to protect your cousin's goods and profit as his agent. Haughton speaks strongly for you, but then he is your partner. If you can accept that I regret my actions towards your wife, I will add my support to his. Though I must warn you that several of the officers envy you for all you have achieved in so short a time.'

Japhet considered this. Grosvenor sounded sincere; he did not appear to be using flattery to save himself from Japhet's anger. His face was battered and his uniform ripped and dirty, showing how bravely he had fought despite his earlier show of cowardice. He did have some backbone. Japhet kept his voice neutral. 'This is a land of great opportunity. I have used the skills I learned in my homeland to advantage. But fortune smiled on me when my cousin and his friends saw the riches to be made in exporting goods here. It is no longer just a penal settlement; it is a new colony for our sovereign, and the settlers will prosper.'

'I admire you your vision, Mr Loveday. I have hated every day of my duty here.'

'In a few years settlers will be arriving in their hundreds. New towns will be built and who knows what riches lie beneath the ground. Copper, tin, gold or diamonds. A man could be wealthy as a maharaja. Consider the wealth acquired by the early settlers in the American colony. Enough to make them fight for their independence.'

'Is it all about faith and speculation, Mr Loveday? Your sawmill will make you a wealthy man. Wood is the cheapest building material and this land is covered in trees. That's what I'd put my money in if I were a settler not a soldier.'

'What stops you investing and acquiring a nest egg for your future? Wood is a plentiful commodity, but the great buildings of the future will be made of brick. If there were a settler or convict who knew how to make bricks, another easy fortune could be made. I'd invest in it myself.'

Grosvenor laughed. 'Indeed you have a grand vision. Are you sure you will stop at nothing short of being governor of this land?'

Japhet shrugged aside the comment as absurd. 'The governor is in the pay of the King and has too many responsibilities to make his fortune. He must abide by the law of the land or will face disgrace. A man willing to gamble can walk a different tightrope when he uses the law to advance his own interest – providing he is discreet. Your fellow officers openly flout the law with their monopoly on spirits and imported goods. It cannot last much longer, and some will pay a high price on their return to England.'

The officer's eyes narrowed, and Japhet tensed, aware that after the exhilaration of beating the rebel convicts he had been less than discreet himself. He did not want Grosvenor poking his nose into his affairs to stir up trouble.

Nevertheless, he refused to concede any point. There was the sound of light footsteps and Gwendolyn was framed in the doorway of the house. Japhet spoke tersely. 'Lieutenant, I believe you have an apology to make to my wife.'

'Of course.' Grosvenor's hesitation was slight. He bowed to Gwendolyn. 'Mrs Loveday, you are a remarkable woman and it is obvious why you followed your husband from England. Few settlers would have faced those men as he did. Those who are wounded will be brought to trial. And I humbly crave your pardon for my earlier conduct. You will always have my highest regard.'

Gwendolyn inclined her head in acceptance. The intensity of the convict attack had made them allies, and the lieutenant appeared genuinely ashamed of his behaviour.

Later that night, when they were finally alone, Japhet took her into his arms. He kissed her with passion and whispered against her hair: 'I could have lost you tonight. How could I risk so much? You and the boys are all that is important.'

She caressed the beloved lines of his cheek. 'We are safe. Is this not our life now? We have achieved so much. No one will drive us away.'

'You deserve better, my love. Unlike most of the settlers here, we do have a good life to return to in England.'

'And we will return, but not yet, not until you have fulfilled the dream you saw in this land.'

That was the spirit that had captured Japhet's heart. It was why he would never fail Gwen's belief in him.

Chapter Twenty-nine

Senara had prepared a restorative for Felicity, which she knew would lift her sister-in-law's spirits. It was not uncommon for a pregnancy to strip a woman of vitality, and lately the atmosphere at Trevowan had been far from peaceful. Felicity had confided in her that the personalities of many of the Lovedays were overwhelming at times. She was a slave to convention, and her sensibilities were often shocked by her new family's lack of regard for how they were viewed by their peers, their passion and enthusiasm for life, and the volatile nature of their temperaments. Though no one could describe Felicity's mother as a pillar of sobriety. The woman's predatory nature and pursuit of pleasure verged upon the undignified. Her conduct must be a further trial for Felicity.

She would have found an ally in Amelia, who had always been rather strait-laced, but Felicity seemed blind to her mother's failings. Any criticism from Amelia and she was instantly defensive, and would retaliate by judging Richard for his inconsiderate behaviour and the violence of his mood swings. Instead of allies, they had become antagonists. It did not help that both Amelia and Elspeth in their time had been in charge of running the household. The two older women were quick to judge any fall in their exacting standards. No household could be run efficiently or amicably with three mistresses, and until Felicity irrevocably staked her claim, there would always be dissension.

Senara could feel the undercurrents of tension the moment she entered the house.

Jenna Biddick, in her long white maid's apron and pristine mobcap, curtseyed to her.

'Mr Loveday be in Truro, Miss Elspeth be giving Miss Rowena and Charlotte riding lessons in the paddock. Mrs Edward Loveday be tending her beehives and Mrs St John Loveday has not yet risen from her bed. Who shall I send word to that you be here?'

'I have already paid my respects to Miss Elspeth in the paddock. I came to see Mrs St John Loveday. I have a restorative for her. There is no need for formality. If she is indisposed, please enquire if she will see me in her bedchamber. I shall wait in the orangery.'

Her step was light as she approached her favourite room in the house. She liked the bright openness created by the large windows, and the great Italian marble urns with their fruit trees. On a cloudless day the sun filtered through the foliage, creating dappled patterns across the floor. The room gave a panoramic view of the estate. She could see Amelia, in her wide-brimmed hat draped with a fine net to protect her face from bee stings, inspecting the hives in the orchard.

A raven swooped low across the lawn leading to the walled rose garden. She watched it land and expected it to strut imperiously across the grass searching for grubs and worms. Instead it flapped its wings in an ungainly way and hopped in a lopsided manner. She frowned. The raven had been injured in some way. Then she saw that it had lost one of its feet and suspected that it had been caught in a snare of some kind. Normally she enjoyed the sight of these majestic birds, but this one saddened her. More than that, its presence brought with it a sense of unease. With her knowledge of portents and omens, she did not usually view ravens as harbingers of ill fortune, although many people did since they fed off carrion. She saw them as messengers from the ancient gods. It was the fact that this one was injured that sent a shiver down her spine. It turned towards her and for a moment the sharp glint of its eye connected with a primeval instinct deep within her. Then with a squawk it flapped its wings and flew away towards the cliffs of Trevowan Cove.

As it disappeared behind the headland, Senara saw a figure appear at the top of the cliff path. It was Richard Allbright, dressed in moleskin breeches and a shirt. He was without a jacket, his waistcoat was unfastened and his stock was untied, the ends flapping like a pennant in the breeze. His gait appeared unsteady. It was halfway through the morning. Surely he had not been drinking to excess this early in the day? Her eyes narrowed. Or was he in pain from the exertion of climbing the steep steps cut into the cliff? He wiped his hand across his brow before pulling something from his waistcoat pocket and raising it to his lips. It was too small to be a hip flask, and when he had finished drinking, he threw it back over the cliff to the sand below.

'Mrs St John Loveday will see you in her bedchamber,' the maid said from the doorway.

'Thank you, Jenna.' Senara pasued and watched Richard as he resumed his walk back to the house. His step was noticeably steadier. Superstition made her question the incident. Had the raven shown her this for a reason? Richard's moods had been uncharacteristic since his return. Was his wound still paining him? He should be well on the way to recovery now.

She could not dismiss her misgivings, and after leaving Felicity she wandered down to the cove to walk along the beach. After an hour, she found a small clay phial that had remained intact when it landed on the soft sand. Her nose wrinkled with distaste at the strong smell of opiate that still clung to its interior. As she returned to the steps she saw a similar phial that had been smashed on a rock and was partially hidden by seaweed from the last high tide.

It confirmed her fears. No wonder Richard had been acting so strangely. He was clearly addicted to these opiates. The ship's surgeon must have administered them to control the pain when he had been at sea. And if she could not break him of their hold, he would become ever more dependent upon them, until his craving wrecked his career and finally took his life.

Although she had half a dozen tasks needing her urgent attention at Boscabel, Senara set out to find Richard. She did not have far to look. He was by a stile that led to the path to Penruan. A giggle had drawn her attention, and she saw Jenna's young cousin, Mary, who lived in the village, balancing a basket of fish on her hip. The pair stood by a tree out of sight of the house. The girl was blushing at something Richard had said, and her gaze was rapt as she stared up into his face. He put a hand around her waist and drew her against him.

'Mary,' Senara called sharply. 'Are those fish meant for the family's meal today? Winnie Fraddon will be waiting to prepare and cook them.'

Guiltily, Mary Biddick jumped back. 'Master Richard was asking if my pa would take him out in a fishing smack.'

'Mr Allbright has my husband's dinghy he can sail at any time.'

The girl's blush deepened at having been caught in a lie. Richard kept his back to Senara, who had fixed Mary with an enquiring stare. The young woman edged sideways and bobbed a nervous curtsey.

'I had better get these fish to Mrs Fraddon.' She hurried away, but cast several glances back at Richard.

Senara suppressed a sigh. Richard's philandering could soon become a problem. When he turned on his heel to face her, his expression was tight with anger. 'Pray spare me a lecture on hindering the servants in their work. Mama has expressed her displeasure in the past. It was but some harmless fun.'

'Your intentions did not look harmless to me. They looked more like seduction.'

'You did very well for yourself winning Adam,' he sneered. 'And your sister Bridie caught herself a parson. Not bad for a bastard. The women servants and villagers now have an eye to emulate your good fortune. You set a precedent for them.'

He was deliberately trying to goad her, and she refused to rise to his baiting. 'I was fortunate in winning the love of an honourable man, as was Bridie. Are your intentions honourable, Richard? I somehow doubt it.'

'My intentions are no different from those of any red-blooded male.' His tone had lost its arrogance and his mood veered to petulance.

'Are you then prepared to face the consequences if any of those women become with child? St John paid a high price for pursuing Meriel Sawle.'

He laughed derisively. 'That was also how you snared Adam, was it not? I am not so gullible. I will not make the same mistakes as my stepbrothers.'

'I left Trevowan before Adam knew I was with child. His father had chosen a bride for him. His love for me made him defy his father and spend several months seeking my whereabouts because he chose to marry me. I was not fearful of bringing a child into the world and supporting it. As part gypsy I had no reputation to lose. And I knew my family would always stand by me. Can you say as much for these young women you pursue?'

'I have never forced a woman against her will. I give them no false promises. They are free to deny me or take the consequences of our pleasure.'

She wanted to slap his selfish face. But she knew most young gentlemen viewed women like Mary as fair game. The girls themselves should be more aware of their place and forget silly romantic dreams. Senara knew Amelia would be too embarrassed to lecture her son on his morals. She doubted that he would take note of St John or Adam since they had been no different in their youth. Edward would not have hesitated to speak his mind. Because Adam's father had forgiven his younger twin for his reckless marriage, and accepted Senara into his family, she felt for his sake that she had to try and make Richard more aware of his responsibilities to his family. 'I do not judge you, but surely you must realise

223

that your false flattery will turn many a maiden's head. Girls like Mary are too naive to know how horrific the consequences could be for her. She was fifteen last month.'

'And from the boldness in her eye she is no innocent.'

There was no point in appealing to his decency or conscience; he was interested only in his own gratification. The two pottery phials she had found on the beach dug into her clenched fingers. She had been side-tracked from her main intent, and having antagonised him, it would be harder for her now to give him her advice.

'Was there anything else you wanted to say?' He did not hide his irritation. 'I suppose you will complain to Mama or Adam that I have not accorded you the respect due as my stepbrother's wife.'

'Your mother taught you the manners of a gentleman. How you use them is upon your conscience. What has happened to the proud young warrior so eager to fight for his country? Since your return you act like a petulant child.'

He rounded on her with fury in his eyes. 'What would you know of war and its horrors? Or of seeing men blown to pieces, or having to serve with the dregs of humanity who hate your guts for being super-ior to them?'

'From Adam's stories I know that naval life can be brutal. He warned you of that before you enlisted. You have likely experienced horrors I could not begin to imagine. Yet I have seen sailors and soldiers, their bodies or spirits crippled by what they have endured. War also produces heroes and great feats of courage. It brings the best or the worst out of a man. No one disputes your courage. You chose what you saw as a life of adventure and glory in the navy instead of becoming a lawyer like your father, and must have faced many dangers. You were wounded in defence of your country. A wound I believe that took a greater toll upon you than you have admitted.'

His lips were white and tense, his pupils dark and dilated. 'I have an appointment in Fowey soon.' He began to walk away.

'And I can guess what this appointment concerns. What mounte-bank do you visit to procure your drugs?'

He paid no heed to her and increased his pace. She ran after him and thrust the two phials into his vision. 'I know what these are, and they were not prescribed by either Dr Yeo or Chegwidden. I will not speak to your mother of your deplorable womanising, but I cannot ignore these. Some fool naval butcher who called himself a surgeon gave you excessive amounts of opiates. You now cannot live without them.'

He tried to snatch the phials from her but she was too quick for him and stepped back. 'Destroying the evidence will do you no good. I know how deadly this drug can be. I want to help you.'

'I do not need help. Occasionally I take a few drops to ease the pain.' He refused to meet her stare and his manner was furtive. 'You are making too much of it.'

'Dr Yeo has told us that your wound is healed and there is no underlying infection. I have seen how destructive an addiction to opiates can be. And I am not the only one in the family who has noticed how rapidly your mood changes from morose or lethargic to an excess of euphoria or energy. I have seen you use a hip flask when you think others do not notice.'

'That contains brandy. I do not need opiates.'

'Then hand over to me all of these drugs you have in your possession.'

'Those were the last, I swear it.' He would not look at her and his brow and upper lips were dewed with sweat.

'Then you will not object if I speak with St John so that a thorough search can be made of your room?'

His lips thinned to a cruel line. 'I shall deny it. Mama will believe me.'

'But will the rest of the family take your word against mine?'

For a long moment he remained defiant. Senara stood her ground and held his gaze. She did not speak and her eyes softened with compassion. Gradually the insolence dissolved from his manner. He shook his head and his stare was now stark with fear.

'I have truly tried to stop,' he confessed reluctantly. 'But you cannot know the pain . . . the sweats and cramps . . . the shaking that grips my body . . .' He shuddered. 'It is impossible. I need those phials.'

'Because you are addicted to the opium.' Her tone was sympathetic. 'I do know how you suffer. I helped someone with the same problem many years ago. It is not easy, but you can rid yourself of this addiction and lead a normal life.'

He rubbed his hands across his face, clearly distraught. 'The pain and spasms start within a few hours of ignoring the craving. I could not hide the sweating and shakes. Mama would call a physician and he would know what ails me and tell her.'

'If you trust me I can help you. You can stay at Boscabel. To spare Amelia you could tell her you are spending a week or two with a friend before you return to your ship.'

He withdrew his hands from his cheeks, his expression haggard. 'She will not countenance that. She is too possessive of my company. And how can I stay at Boscabel and Adam not know?'

'Adam would have to be told, but he will understand. He knows the brutality of an operation at sea and the methods used to sedate a patient. He will not blame you.'

'He will think I am weak. I cannot agree.' Richard groaned and turned away to hide the tears that had sprung to his eyes. For all his bravado, he was young and vulnerable.

Senara put a hand on his arm. 'It will take a great deal of courage to see this through. Adam will respect and support you. I cannot allow you to destroy your mind and body, which is what will happen if you continue.' When he remained silent, she spoke more forcibly. 'If you do not agree, then I will speak with St John on his return from Truro.'

He looked trapped. 'Give me time. A few more days to pacify Mama that I must leave Trevowan. There is the summer fair next week. I will come to Boscabel after that.'

Senara hesitated. It was too long a time for her to be comfortable about. But she knew that to break the vicious hold the drug had upon him, Richard must be ready and willing to relinquish his reliance upon it. 'Then you must promise me that in the mean time you will cut down on the number of doses you take. Too much of this opiate can kill you.'

He flashed her his most charming smile, which did not reach his eyes. 'Dear lady, I will not fail you.'

She sighed, but could not rid herself of the uncomfortable feeling that she could not trust him.

Trust was an issue that Sam Deighton now wrestled with constantly. His uncle's lawyer had again called on him. Lord Eastley had demanded an interview with him. He intended to make Charlie a ward of court, and the boy would be in his power however strongly Sam protested. He did not doubt that the courts would award in favour of his lordship. Power and position were weightier than love. Since Eastley was clearly prepared to make the facts of Charlie's birth public, there must be more behind the case than Sam had first believed.

'Lord Eastley has only the best interests of the boy at heart.' Frederick Simmons, the lawyer, had been extremely patient yet persistent throughout all Sam's protests. He was seated at the polished window table in Sam's landlady's parlour with his papers spread before him. 'That is why he has not forced you to hand over his grandson. The boy has great affection for you.'

'He is not usually so considerate,' Sam returned. 'And why now does he declare that his son and my sister were married? When you first came to me, you said his lordship intended to adopt Charlie.'

His landlady, Mrs Hedges, was looking after Charlie. He could hear him laughing as she played with the boy. Mrs Hedges had made the stay here bearable. She was middle-aged, with a wealth of common sense. Her own son had died of cholera at the age of seven in India, where her husband was serving as an army captain. She had been devastated by the death and it had affected her heart and health. Having always found the heat unendurable, she had returned home with her youngest daughter last year. The three eldest girls had all found husbands in the army during their stay in India.

Mr Simmons pushed back a lock of fine hair from his brow. He was a decade older than Sam, his narrow face etched with deep lines. His eyes were shrewd but in this instance not unkindly. In the past their exchanges had been terse and short. 'His lordship wished to proceed with caution. No illegitimate child could inherit, and he preferred not to have his brother aware of his intentions at that time. I understand your apprehension.' He tapped a tapering finger at a document. 'This marriage certificate is not forged. The parson himself has sworn an affidavit that he performed the ceremony five months before Charles was born.'

'A marriage Eastley never acknowledged. He disowned his son.' Sam paced the small parlour. The information had rocked him. It vindicated his sister but still did not alter the truth. 'The actions of Charlie's grandfather caused the death of both his parents. Reginald was too weak to face his father's censure and abandoned his wife. Because of his cowardice Catherine killed herself. Until now his lordship has wanted nothing to do with the child. How can I condemn Charlie to live with such a tyrant?'

'Because you will want what is best for him. Charles Deighton is the rightful heir to Lord Eastley. In the fullness of time he will be a rich and influential man. Those facts are indisputable. Or would you deny him his birthright?'

Sam sat down opposite the lawyer and sank his head into his hands. 'Riches do not maketh the man. Reginald was proof of that. What life will the child have in a home that is devoid of love?'

Mr Simmons gathered together his papers and put them in a leather document case. He stood up. 'His lordship wishes his grandson to be given the best education to prepare him for his future. He has also requested an interview with you, sir. It is better for all concerned if these matters are settled out of court. There is your own family to consider and the difficulties that they might raise.'

Reluctantly Sam agreed to the meeting. 'Firstly I want to speak to this preacher who says he married Reginald and Catherine. Then I will meet with his lordship.'

Chapter Thirty

Holy days and fair days were always welcomed by all the local community and not to be missed. Today was no exception. The Lammas fair was held on the edge of the moor, and the families travelling on foot left their houses at daybreak to reach there by mid-morning. August was a temperamental month and the weather could never be relied on to be dry and sunny. Today the sky was clear and boded well that it would remain so.

Mark Sawle drove the cart transporting Hannah, her children and the Rabson Farm servants. Adam and Senara rode their horses, with their older children and servants following in the cart. Peter and Bridie had come to Boscabel first with Leah, who would stay behind and care for the two infants Sara and Michael.

The tracks across the fields to the moor were thick with people, and passage was slow, but this did not spoil the holiday atmosphere. Those on foot sang or gossiped with neighbours as they walked, the children running ahead playing tag, their voices high with excitement. Many a bottle of cider was drunk on the way, adding to the festive mood.

The noise from the fair could be heard from a great distance. Hurdy-gurdies, flutes and fiddles proclaimed the merriment already in progress. Hawkers cried out announcing their wares. Wagers were shouted on the wrestling matches and cockfights. Travelling showmen bellowed of the delights of witnessing the bearded lady, the world's fattest and tallest man, the Cornish merman, and the two-headed calf. Quacks proclaimed the efficacy of their cure-all elixirs, and a man on stilts strode through the crowd in the costume of a pirate beckoning all to join him where his fellow actors would perform a play at noon. A tightrope had been erected between two poles, and beneath it a troupe of tumblers and acrobats were giving a display, whilst a family of dwarves jostled each other as they collected the attendance money from the spectators.

The carts and carriages were left in an adjoining field with grooms to attend the horses. St John and Adam's parties arrived within minutes of each other. Amelia had chosen to stay and keep Felicity company at Trevowan; whilst Elspeth, having recently celebrated her sixtieth birthday, declared herself past such flibbertigibbet cavorting and had gone riding instead. St John, Richard, Rafe, Rowena and Charlotte had made an early departure before Sophia took it into her head to join them.

St John was looking forward to a day free from the burdens the womenfolk placed upon him. His week at the races had been a reminder of the carefree life he was missing, and he had returned fifty guineas richer from his wagers.

The Loveday children's eyes were bulging with excitement as they clambered from the carts, demanding to see everything at once.

'Is that man a giant?' Nathan stared in awe at the pirate on stilts.

'Want to go up there,' Joel demanded as he spotted the ladder against the pole of the tightrope.

'We will see everything in time.' Adam smiled at the boys' enthusiasm.

'That man is standing bareback on his pony.' Rowena was wide-eyed with wonder as a dark-skinned rider in yellow turban, red silk pantaloons, and short red silk tunic passed them.

A juggler followed him, tossing five coloured clubs in the air as he announced, 'Come witness the proficiency of Sheik Abdullah as he performs tricks never witnessed before on his Barbary mare Zanoba.'

Rowena gasped. 'We must see him perform, Papa.'

St John murmured an absent reply. The cockpit had caught his attention: a circle of straw bales within a large striped pavilion tent.

'Papa, can we see Sheik Abdullah's performance?' Charlotte lisped, adding her voice to that of her stepsister.

This time he frowned. 'All in good time.'

'Are we stopping you from doing something more important?' Adam flared. 'It is obvious where your mind is. This should be a day for the children. Charlotte has never been to a fair. Felicity will be concerned she does not witness its baser side.'

St John turned on his brother. 'Then you play nursemaid. Richard's leave will soon be over. He wearies of Amelia's constraints and of being surrounded by children. It is time he indulged in some manly pursuits.'

Richard made no protest. His eyes were over-bright and there was an uneasy restlessness about his manner. He was obviously eager to be with St John. 'I am sure Rowena and Charlotte would prefer to be with

230

your children, Adam. Senara is wonderful with them. St John promised Mama that this would be a day I would remember.'

St John drew some silver coins from his pocket and gave them to Rowena. 'Treat yourself and Charlotte to something nice.'

'The girls are welcome to stay with us,' Adam returned. If his twin was selfish enough to desert his daughter, preferring to drink and gamble, then there was no point in a confrontation in front of the children. 'But you have made your own promises to Felicity, St John. And I am sure Rowena would rather have your company than your money.'

His twin grinned infuriatingly, untroubled by his conscience. 'Rowena will enjoy the company of her cousins. She often says she does not see them enough. As to the promises I made to my wife, they are between Felicity and myself. Besides, what the eye does not see . . . Richard and I shall meet up with you all later.'

'Amelia will not relish her son returning in his cups,' Adam cautioned, but the two men were walking out of earshot.

Rowena clutched the coins in her hand with a mutinous glare at her father's disappearing figure. Charlotte burst into tears. 'Your papa does not like me. Richard does not like me. He is mean to take Papa away.'

'St John adores you, my lovely,' Senara pacified her. She was annoyed at her brother-in-law's disregard for the girls' feelings. Charlotte was shy and timid, and she desperately wanted to be accepted by her new family. 'Your papa has things he needs to do with Richard. You know Richard likes you but he must return to sea soon. There is a lot he must do before then and he cannot spend all his time with young girls.'

'He would rather be kissing the serving wenches,' Rowena giggled. 'I've seen him.'

Senara exchanged a bleak look with Adam. She had not yet told him of the phials she had discovered, but his stepbrother's conduct in other ways could not be ignored. She lowered her voice to a whisper so that the girls would not hear. 'I think you should pay more heed to what Richard gets up to, Adam. He will break Amelia's heart if he is not careful.'

Adam's eyes narrowed as he stared after the young man. 'There is something not right about him. I am not imagining it, am I?'

She shrugged. 'Let us not spoil this day by talking of Richard's failings. We have some very impatient children eager to see Sheik Abdullah.'

With so many children clamouring to visit different sights, they would have to keep a sharp eye on them or one of them would get lost. She warned Nan, the nursery maid, 'Keep a tight hold on the youngsters' hands.' Then she turned to her sons. 'And Nathan and Joel, mind you stay close to us. No exploring on your own.'

Bridie took Charlotte's hand and Rafe tried valiantly to curb his impatience when Peter ordered him to stay beside him, but he could not stop squirming and wriggling in his excitement. Rowena considered herself too grown up to be supervised but was happy to walk beside Adam and keep up a steady stream of demands as to the sights they must visit.

Hundreds of people were continuing to approach the fair. Senara, who was wary of crowds, was anxious that they did not get separated from the children. 'If any of you get lost, make for the tightrope and wait there. It is easy to see above the heads of the crowd.'

'You worry too much.' Adam lifted Rhianne on his shoulders. She alone was content to watch the sights with her parents. The boys were drawn by the squeals of the greased pig in a pen full of yelling and diving youths trying to catch the animal. The crowd roared with laughter at the antics and the fights that broke out amongst the lads as the pig kept slipping from their grasp.

'Papa, there is a cup to be won for the best score of the day on the archery butts,' Nathan declared. 'You must enter for it. You too, Uncle Peter.'

'I'm no match for your father, lad,' Peter said without rancour. 'But I might give it a try later.'

'Papa will win the cup,' Joel announced. 'He'll beat Uncle St John and all his friends. Papa is the best.'

'Thank you for your faith in me, son.' Adam grinned. 'But I've never won the cup yet after a dozen years of trying. Japhet won it twice. And so did Uncle Joshua.'

'But you always do better than Uncle St John, don't you?' Nathan did not want to be left out of praising his father. 'I'm going to compete against Rafe in everything I can and I'm going to win.'

'Oh dear, not another generation of rivalry,' Senara groaned. 'It is the taking part that is important, boys – not the winning.'

'Is that right, Papa?' Nathan did not look convinced.

'If your mother says that it is so, then it must be right. She is a very wise woman.'

'But what do women know about fighting?' Joel piped up. 'They are not soldiers or naval commanders. You fought the French, Papa. And you always beat Uncle St John and Uncle Peter.'

'Not always,' Adam replied diplomatically. 'We lost the cricket match, remember.'

There was a shout of recognition as they were joined by Hannah and her children. Joel wriggled to pull his hand from his father's firm grasp. 'Look, everyone. There's a fire-eater. Can I be a fire-eater one day?'

Senara rolled her eyes in exasperation. 'There's enough fiery spirit in you, young man, without adding to it.' She turned to Bridie, who was grinning. 'What am I going to do with Joel? He is not happy unless he is slaying dragons, which is his favourite game at the moment. Scamp usually fits the role of dragon, though the poor dog is getting too old for such games.'

The older children started a game of tag, running off in different directions. Within seconds they were lost amongst the press of the crowd. Senara felt the hairs on her neck prickle and a flush of heat sped through her body.

'Call the children back,' she demanded.

'They will come to no harm,' Hannah responded. 'They will not go far.'

'They must stay within our sight.' She was adamant.

'That's not like you to spoil the children's games.' Hannah studied Senara with concern.

Senara felt the moment of panic subsiding, but she knew better than to disregard it. She could not rid herself of a feeling of emptiness and loss, of a child calling in the darkness afraid and alone.

'Are you ill, Senara?' Hannah frowned. 'You look as though you have seen a ghost.'

'The children must stay close. You must heed me.'

Adam took one look at his wife's ashen face and shouted loudly for the children to come to him. He had witnessed too many of her premonitions to question her fear. The children were given a lecture on keeping with each other and not running off.

'But there is so much to see,' Davey protested. As the eldest he clearly felt he could look after himself and be trusted not to get into mischief.

'And we will see it all, but you could easily get lost amongst so many people, or hurt in some way,' Hannah said sternly.

Caution and good intentions on the part of the children gradually slackened as the day lengthened, but the adults kept a wary eye on their exploits. The festive atmosphere was contagious, and soon even Senara was caught up in the mood of enchantment and relaxed her vigilance. Predictably there were bouts of drunken belligerence from some of the

233

fairgoers, and Senara did her best to steer the children away from the fights that broke out, or the men lurching about too drunk to walk straight.

Sheik Abdullah impressed them all with his riding skills. The tightrope walker and the tumblers enthralled them. However, the strolling players were a disappointment. Their clothes were shoddy and dirty and they forgot many of their lines, the women eyeing up any prospective man with money to spare to take into their tents after the show.

The Lovedays explored the stalls selling everything from tinware and enamelled jewellery to sugary confections made into the shape of animals. The men competed at throwing a horseshoe the furthest. Then Nathan urged his father to enter a competition where the men balanced on a felled tree set some feet above the ground and used a pillow to knock an opponent to the ground. This proved the most entertaining for the children. The crowd roared with laughter every time a man was knocked down. Adam took on five challengers before he was beaten and Peter managed six before he was dislodged from his perch.

'Peter is tenacious as a barnacle,' Adam declared. 'Anyone trying to change his views on certain topics will agree with me.'

Whilst the family were watching Peter's final fight, in which he displayed surprising agility against a much stockier opponent, Clem and Keziah Sawle joined them with their son Zach.

'There be more to the parson than we thought,' Clem remarked good-naturedly.

'Are you having a go, Clem?' Adam said.

Clem rubbed his rugged jaw. 'I dunno. Reckon there be too many men eager to give me a pasting. I don't fight now.'

'Parson be a man of God, Pa.' Zach gave his father an adoring stare. 'This bain't proper fighting. You could beat them all. I'd be so proud of you.'

'He wouldn't beat my papa.' Joel jutted out his jaw in proud defiance.

Adam laughed. 'Clem is a formidable opponent. Let's see how good you are. It will be something to talk about in the Dolphin for many a month.'

Clem peeled off his jacket and handed it to Keziah, then clambered on to the pole. There was a chorus of shouts and wagers as he was recognised. He managed to equal Peter's six challengers before he was finally beaten. Zach was jumping up and down and cheering wildly. He turned to Rowena, grinning. 'I bet my pa could beat your pa, cousin.'

'My papa is not here, so we will never know.' Her voice was light and teasing and she ruffled the younger boy's hair.

Adam watched the scene with astonishment. He had not realised that Rowena had such affection for her Sawle cousin. It was good to see that she showed none of her mother's airs and graces. After Meriel had married St John, she had looked down on her family and the village where she grew up.

'Who is minding the Dolphin?' he asked Clem when the older man returned hot and sweating from his exertions.

'We've given the two barmaids and the potman the day off. Old man Biddick will man the bar if there be any customers. Most of the locals are here and there'll be little trade until this evening. Most of them will already have spent their money anyway. We shall have a lean time until the next catch is sold.' He did not seem unduly perturbed. It was a sign of how much the Dolphin Inn had prospered under his management.

'Enjoy the rest of your day,' Adam said as they followed the cries of the children, who had spotted a dancing bear.

Senara held back. In the past she had seen too many such animals mistreated. The brown bear was on its hind legs, rearing above the chanting crowd that circled it. Through its nose it had a large iron ring, which was fastened to a thick chain and sturdy post. An Elizabethan fluted ruff was round its neck. The bear's owner banged on a drum and jerked the chain to make the bear move from hind leg to hind leg in an ungainly parody of a dance. Senara blinked back tears of anger. There were bald patches amongst its fur from poor food and care, and festering sores on its muzzle and hind legs from being beaten when it refused to perform.

'Call the children away, Adam. I will not have them witness this cruelty. It is barbaric the way the bear is treated. It is not a fitting entertainment.'

'You should not get upset. There is nothing you can do. The owner is not breaking any law.'

'I do not have to watch an animal being tortured and I would teach my children to have greater respect for a noble beast.'

'Bear- and bull-baiting are common events.'

'At least this bear does not have dogs tearing at its flesh in the name of sport,' she raged. 'I wish there was a way to save it from its misery.'

Adam understood her pain and disgust. He had never had a taste for blood sports. 'You cannot save every injured creature you see. It is hardly something we could keep in a barn or a paddock.'

To cheer her, Adam called to Peter to keep an eye on the children

235

and he pulled his wife into the centre of a group of dancers as a fiddler struck up a country reel. Bridie had fallen silent and looked tired but she would never complain that her back or leg was aching. Peter saw an empty bench near a quoits pitch. A man held out a handful of horse-shoes.

'Come try your luck. Throw the shoe over the peg and win a prize for your lady.'

'Sit awhile, wife. I would show the children the art of this game.'

The children clustered around him, vying to go first. Hannah smiled at this more jovial side of her younger brother. He had changed much since his marriage and was less fanatical about his religious beliefs. With the children occupied she mentioned to Bridie that she would look at the horse sales taking place in a nearby paddock. 'I will not be long.'

'Take all the time you need. Peter is enjoying himself and it gives you a break from your brood. But should you go unescorted? Remember Launceston.'

'I can see Mark and Jeannie by the paddock. I will be safe with them.'

Mark turned as she approached. 'None of these can match your brother's mares and foals.'

Hannah nodded as she studied the animals. There were a couple of hunters and ponies that were fit for a gentleman's stable, but most were workhorses whose spirit had gone out of them.

'Japhet's horses were bred for the thoroughbred sales at Tattersalls,' she replied.

'Would you offer them to a private buyer with a discerning eye for horseflesh?' A familiar drawl made her smile. Nicholas Trescoe regarded the horses with a disdainful air. Mark and Jeannie moved discreetly away, though Mark kept an eye on his mistress should she not wish to be troubled by the gentleman.

'Nick, how good to see you.'

'Have you been deserted by your family?'

'My cousins and brother are here.'

'I saw Peter surrounded by a gaggle of children.' He raised a brow in amusement. 'He was teaching them to throw a horseshoe. A very different vision to how I remember him at the last fair I attended here. Then he was preaching and pontificating at the immorality and licen-tiousness of these places of iniquity.'

Hannah did not take offence at the statement, for Nicholas had often teased Peter for his piety. 'He is married and a father now. It has mellowed him. Much to the relief of the family! I should rescue him. My children can be a handful and so can Adam's.'

An auction had begun for the last of the horses and there was a sudden press of men around them. Nicholas took her arm and led her through them. 'How many children do you have?'

'Four. Two boys and two girls. Adam also has four, including twins.'

'There have been so many changes since I left. I was sorry to hear about Oswald. He was a good man.'

'The best.' She felt her throat tighten with emotion and swallowed to control the rush of unexpected pain. She did not want Nicholas to be embarrassed by a show of grief.

A band of drummers and flautists blocked their path, and Nicholas guided her around them, taking them further away from her brother.

He chatted on, seemingly unaware of her inner struggle. He had not released her arm and she gently extricated it from his hold.

'I have heard how well you run the farm and how you raised the mares and foals that belonged to Japhet,' Nick said. 'Sheba was a remarkable mare. Your brother often spoke of running a stud farm.'

'I could not bear to part with Sheba.' It was easier to talk upon a bond they both shared – their affection for Japhet. 'It has been some years since she last ran a race. I have sold none of the foals, and by the time Japhet returns they will be ready for breeding themselves.'

'I would like to see them. Japhet had a remarkable eye for horse-flesh. I have always had a mind to own an Arab. Perhaps I could persuade you to sell one.'

'They are not for sale,' she said firmly. 'Now I must rescue Peter, and if Adam has returned he will worry if he finds I have wandered away. He can be very protective.'

'Perhaps he has a right to be. I saw the attention Mr Nankervis paid to you at Traherne Hall. You must have many beaux queuing at your door.'

'Hardly.' She laughed. 'I am too busy. The farm and children take all my time.'

'Ah, we can put your cousin's mind at rest. There he is. He is dancing with his wife. Shall we join them?'

'I could not. It would not be seemly, and I really should return to Peter and the children.'

'When did you ever care what was seemly?' he challenged. 'Peter was enjoying himself when I saw him. Are you such a staid matron that you would forgo all pleasure?' He again claimed her arm, this time in a more proprietorial manner, and steered her towards the dancers. 'This will put the roses back into your cheeks. The Hannah I remember loved to dance.'

His laughter was infectious and the music made her blood race faster. She yielded to his persistence and laughed as he swung her round, their steps matching perfectly as they stomped and clapped, whirled and circled.

When the dance ended, her cheeks were flushed and she held her side to ease the stabbing stitch. 'I fear I am too old for this. But it was exhilarating. Thank you, Nick.'

'The honour was all mine, and you will never be too old for dancing.'

Adam hailed them. 'Nick. St John mentioned you were back. Life looks to have served you well.'

'And you have not done so badly.' Nicholas regarded the younger man with admiration. 'What is this I hear of a new merchantman you are building?

Adam shrugged off the praise. 'You must call at the yard and dine with us at Boscabel.'

'I would like that.'

'Are you home for long?'

'That depends on Mama's machinations. You know how she can be. I have already been introduced to a dozen prospective brides.'

'Is the thought of marriage so onerous to you?' Hannah enquired.

The laughter faded from his eyes. 'I was betrothed three years ago. My fiancée died of smallpox a month before our wedding.'

'Nick, I did not know. How dreadful of me to tease you.' Hannah was appalled at her levity.

He brushed it aside. 'Time passes and the pain heals.'

Adam changed the subject, quizzing Nick on what he had been up to in recent years. Senara drew Hannah aside. 'He does not seem as black as his reputation painted him. Was he a rakehell?'

'No more so than Japhet. With four older brothers he had no responsibilities at home, and not wanting to join the army or navy and being totally unsuited to the Church, he needed to find a place for himself in the world.'

'Many would not view him so charitably,' Senara observed with a knowing smile. 'Mayhap the death of his fiancée mellowed him. Yet his spirit is not dimmed. It would be difficult not to like him. And he is undoubtedly handsome and charming.'

'Nick has the same irrepressible joy of life as Japhet. And do not think I am impressed with his good looks,' Hannah said rather too emphatically. 'I know him too well.'

'You two would be well suited.'

Hannah shook her head. 'No matchmaking, I pray you. Nick is a friend.'

Senara was not convinced. There was a softness about Hannah's manner in Mr Trescoe's company that went deeper than friendship. But would the stubborn young widow acknowledge it? Somehow Senara doubted it. Hannah first had to admit that she was ready to open her heart to another. Though whether it would be to the charismatic Mr Trescoe or someone else was too soon to tell.

Chapter Thirty-one

Mark and Jeannie Sawle were enjoying one of the most carefree days since their marriage. They had been reunited after Jeannie returned from Launceston and a new maid had been found for Hannah's friend Mrs McCurdie.

Jeannie had been nervous that she would not be able to hide from her husband the effects of Harry Sawle's attack. She slept badly and often woke sweating from a recurring nightmare that Mark had pursued his brother and been killed. This was the first time she had been able to laugh again.

They spent much of the day with Clem and Keziah. The brothers had not been close in recent years, as Mark had been driven away from his home by Harry's brutal behaviour. After their wedding Keziah often invited the couple to Penruan on their day off. Sal had been delighted with the reunion of the brothers, and Mark and Jeannie adored Zach, making a great fuss of their nephew.

Slight of frame and shy by nature, Jeannie was in awe of Keziah's tall, strapping figure, her wild red hair and energetic approach to life. It was not long before she discovered warmth and pleasure in Keziah's company. Although the older woman tolerated no slackness from her servants, she had a soft heart and found nothing too much trouble for those she cared for.

'The fair has brought a return of the sweet girl I remember.' Keziah linked her arm with that of the dairymaid. 'I thought you be sickening with some pestilence last week when you returned from Launceston. Or were you just lovesick at spending so long from Mark?'

Jeannie dared not hold that bold gaze for fear she would blurt out her terror, and stared at her feet. 'Of course I missed Mark.'

'Mrs Rabson should not have expected you to work for her friend.'

'I did'na mind,' Jeannie quickly reassured her. 'Mrs Rabson has been good to us. We have a lovely cottage.'

'It be no less than Mark deserves,' Keziah proclaimed. 'He be a good stockman. I hope she appreciates his work and yours.'

Jeannie nodded. 'Mark be devoted to her. Few employers would have anything to do with Harry Sawle's kin. She never stopped his wages when he were attacked, and paid his doctor's fees.'

'You mean when that brute of his brother had him kicked and beaten almost to death.' Keziah did not mince her words.

Jeannie flinched at the memory, making Keziah regard her with concern.

'Harry has much to answer for,' the older woman fumed. 'It makes me ashamed to bear the same name. If he gives you or Mark further trouble, you are to tell Clem. He bain't afeared to sort that bully out.'

'Clem is a good man,' Jeannie acknowledged. 'Sal says he would have gone the same way as Harry, knowing no better, if you had not taken him from that life.'

'Their father was a brutal man. Yet Mark never took after him. Clem fell into bad ways. That were Harry's doing. Being the eldest, Clem do feel responsible for the way Harry went bad. It don't always sit right with him that we now have the Dolphin.'

'As the eldest, Clem be the natural heir. Harry can't dispute that. It bain't as though he can go to the law.' Jeannie suppressed a shiver of fear. 'Let's not talk of that fiend. I fear he'll return and ruin all our lives.'

'You be right.' Keziah drew a sharp breath and her body relaxed. 'I'd not wish to talk of the devil and find he's appeared.'

Jeannie held up her fingers in the sign to ward off evil. Keziah laughed. 'I were jesting. Harry knows there be nothing for him here. He must be long gone by now, or would be if he had any sense.'

Clem had overheard the women talking and had seen how his brother's face had set with anger.

'Harry bain't in these parts, Mark,' he said. 'I should have driven him off myself after what he did to you.'

'You be wrong. He bain't gone. He'll never leave. Not while there be unfinished business here.' Mark clenched his fists in impotent fury.

'He bain't gonna show his face here. Not with a price on his head. Too many people would recognise him. Enjoy this day, little brother.'

'I hate him but I bain't scared of him,' Mark blustered.

Clem shot him a veiled glare. 'You should be. I've woken at night wondering what evil he plans to befall us next. I could thrash him in a fight, but that bain't Harry's way. He be more devious than Satan. Be ever vigilant, brother. Let down your guard and he'll find a way to destroy you.'

His stare was protective as it fell upon his son. Rowena and Nathan Loveday were talking to Zach. He was proud that they had accepted the boy as a cousin. It would help overcome the tarnish to the name of Sawle that Harry had brought upon them. He did not want Zach to suffer because of his uncle's reputation.

With the crowd milling around her, Senara searched anxiously for sight of the children, who had wandered off. Her sharp stare found Rhianne and Charlotte with Bridie; they were watching a woman string blue and red glass beads into a necklace. Adam and Peter were with Joel by a stall selling songbirds and parrots in cages. The boy was standing with a blue and yellow parrot on his shoulder, eager that the bird be purchased for him.

'I can teach it to talk, Papa.'

'We have enough wild birds that your mama has rescued and tamed. The owl sits on your arm.'

'Owls can't talk. This one talks.'

'Where are Rowena and Nathan?' Senara asked her sister.

Bridie's mouth gaped in alarm. 'They were here a few moments ago.'

'Rowena wanted to find Zach,' Charlotte whined. 'She won't play with me. She said I'm a baby. She got Nathan to go with her.'

Senara called to her husband and they began to search for the children. Rowena, Nathan and Zach giggled as they heard the adults calling to them. They were sitting under the cloth that covered a stall selling sweetmeats, munching on a handful of sugar mice Rowena had bought with her father's money.

'We should go to them.' Nathan began to crawl from under the stall.

'Young Master Goody-Goody,' scoffed Rowena. 'Go and play with the little children. I thought you had more spirit.'

'But Mama is worried,' Nathan protested. 'I'm not a goody-goody.'

'Zach is not running back to his parents,' Rowena continued to taunt.

The older boy was staring adoringly at his cousin. In his eyes Rowena could do no wrong. It made her more reckless.

'Why do we not go and see the freak show again?' Rowena handed out another sugar mouse each to hold the boys' attention. 'Nathan, I dare you to tug the bearded lady's whiskers to see if they are real. Or are you too much of a scaredy-cat?'

'I'm not scared.'

'Then prove it. Or go running back to your mama like a goody-goody.'

'Come on, Nate, I double dare you,' Zach urged.

A double dare was a challenge he could not resist. Three heads popped out from under the cloth and with delight saw no sign of their relatives.

'Last one to the freaks' tent has to tug the beard.' Rowena scrambled up and ran through the crowd, and the boys gave chase.

They never reached the tent.

A man blocked their path. 'Did I hear you say you wanted to see a freak show?' His voice was strangely muffled. He wore a long cloak with a hood shielding his face. 'Forget the bearded lady. It's a man dressed as a woman. Come with me. I can show you an animal that be half-dog and half-goat.' He beckoned with his finger, drawing them away from the press of people, and moved to the side of a covered stall selling copper- and tinware.

'Wow, that be something,' Zach said excitedly as he followed.

Rowena held back. She did not like going with someone whose face was hidden. 'I think we will await until my papa can show us.'

'But Mr Loveday be the one who sent me, Rowena. Said how much you'd be amazed at such a sight.' He continued to beckon. 'Come, there is nothing to fear. You'll be the envy of your friends and family. Quickly, the tent be just over there. A few yards, no more.'

'How come you know my name?' She felt her throat tighten with fear.

'Your pa told me, lass. How else would I know it?'

Zach was hopping from one foot to the other in his eagerness to see the goat-dog. 'C'mon. It will be something special to tell the others. Won't they be mad they missed it?'

'I'm not so sure,' Nathan hedged. 'I can hear Papa calling. We should get back.'

'Perhaps we should.' Rowena backed away.

Nathan made a grab for Zach's arm. 'We can see it later.'

With a speed that caught them all unawares, the cloaked man sprang forward. There was a blur of a short cudgel in his hand as he lashed out at Nathan and Rowena's heads. Both children were knocked to the ground and lay unmoving. Zach opened his mouth to scream, but a blow to his temple cut it off and he was also knocked unconscious. Their attacker picked him up and hid him under his cloak before running off.

Nathan had been momentarily stunned and shook his head to clear his wits. The movement sent spears of pain through his skull. Rowena stirred and cried out as she sat up.

'What happened?' Manfully Nathan tried to halt his tears.

Rowena stood up and staggered. There was a bruise forming on her brow. 'The man in the cloak hit us.' She whirled round. 'Where's Zach?'

Nathan's memory returned as his frantic gaze searched the fairground. His head felt as though it was being pounded by hammers. 'He's gone. Perhaps he went to get Papa.'

Fear brought a rush of nausea to Rowena's stomach. 'The man hit us. He's gone and so has Zach. He's taken him. We must find Uncle Adam.' She grabbed her cousin's hand and pulled him after her. 'I can hear him calling over there.'

Adam saw the children first. Both were sobbing and there was mud on their clothes. At first he assumed that they had got under the feet of the crowd and been knocked over. His initial relief that they were safe turned to anger that their prank at running off could have ended in one of them being harmed.

Both children spoke at once.

'Where's Uncle Clem?' Rowena burst into fresh tears.

'Zach's gone. A man hit us and took him.' Nathan was now shaking from the shock of the attack.

'Which way did the man go?' Adam demanded.

The two children stared at him dumbly. At last Rowena managed to speak through her sobs. 'He knocked us down. We did not see where he went. We were by the stall selling copper warming pans.'

Adam and Peter ran off to search for Zach.

'I'll find Clem,' Bridie offered. 'Perhaps Zach escaped and is safe with them.'

Senara ordered all the children to stay close to her and crouched on the ground to examine her son and niece's bruises. 'This is what comes of not doing as you are told.'

She breathed deeply to stem the rising panic that her premonition had been right. She prayed that the boy would be found unharmed within the precincts of the fair. Her intuition was that he was in very real danger.

Unaware of the peril his daughter had faced, St John had pocketed thirty pounds' winnings from the cockfights and an hour spent playing hazard. Richard had lost ten pounds, and had grown bored and wandered off when the dice went against him. Belatedly St John remembered his responsibilities and went in search of his stepbrother. He found Richard in an ale tent, slumped on a rickety bench. A slatternly wench sat on his lap, and while he fondled her under her skirts she was removing his purse from inside his shirt.

The stupidity of the young man sparked St John's temper. He could not believe that during Richard's time in the navy he had learned nothing of the duplicity of whores who served in taverns. He snatched the purse from her hand and hoisted her from Richard's lap, snarling, 'Go find yourself easy pickings elsewhere. And be grateful I do not have you arrested, as you deserve.'

Richard peered at him blearily. His eyes were half closed and his words slurred. 'Whoa there, my good fellow. The wench was most obliging . . .'

'Obliging enough to lift your purse, you idiot.'

Richard flopped forward listlessly, and losing his temper St John grabbed hold of his collar and jerked him upright. Richard giggled inanely.

'You are disgustingly drunk. It's not three in the afternoon. Have you no sense of propriety?'

'I don't sneak off to gamble when I've vowed not to.' Richard wagged an accusing finger.

St John was affronted. 'I have greater respect for my family than to be seen in my cups during the day. Your mother will be furious. You'll not be sober by the time we return to Trevowan. I would leave you to sleep it off here, but you will likely be robbed by another whore or her accomplice. They'd haul you off somewhere and strip you of your fine boots and clothes and sell them. Did the navy teach you nothing of such pitfalls?'

He hauled Richard to his feet. 'Can you walk? I will get you back to the coach. You can sleep it off there.'

Richard staggered but managed to recover his balance. 'I am not drunk.' He put one foot carefully in front of the other and leaning on St John proceeded to walk from the tent.

Relieved that he would not have to carry Richard back to the coach, St John hoped the fresh air would sober his stepbrother. Their passage through the press of people was erratic, and St John was thankful that they encountered none of their neighbours or friends. On their approach to the carriage, Jasper Fraddon, who had stayed to tend the horses, rose to his feet where he had been sitting under a tree and helped St John get Richard into the conveyance.

Richard sprawled across the seat.

'I am much indebted to you, brother,' he mumbled, his stare glazed.

'Take care you stay here,' St John snapped. 'If you wander off you can walk back to Trevowan.'

'Aye aye, Cap'n.' Richard gave a mock salute, his gaze becoming trancelike when St John had expected him to close his eyes and sleep.

'Say nothing of the young master's condition, Fraddon,' St John ordered. 'I do not want gossip getting back to his mother. It will upset her.'

'I'd not have Mrs Loveday distressed,' the head groom replied. The man's face, wrinkled as a raisin, regarded St John for a long moment before speaking. He was an old and trusted servant. 'With respect, master, this young pup has more than a drinking bout to answer for during his leave.'

'What do you mean by that?' He was about to tell the servant that it was not his place to pass judgement on his betters, but in view of Fraddon's long service he kept silent.

'He's always pestering the maids. Winnie says the governess is often in tears but is tight as a clam as to what upsets her. A young lad will tumble any wench who be willing, but he has been surly and ill-tempered to some of the tenants. Not acting like a gentleman as your father would have expected, if you get my meaning, sir.'

St John knew that Winnie Fraddon was no gossip but would obviously discuss with her husband anything that troubled her. Fraddon was a loyal retainer who knew his place, and would never speak out of turn. To have done so now meant that there was more cause for concern than he had intimated. Clearly Richard was no longer young and malleable and needed to be reminded of the conduct of a gentleman. St John disliked disruption in his life. If Richard were dallying with the governess, the woman would have to be dismissed as unsuitable to be in charge of his daughters. If one of the maids or tenant farmers' daughters became pregnant by him that would cause further dissension in his household. He cursed the selfishness and recklessness of the young. Richard had to be brought to account for his actions, and that was not a responsibility he relished.

'I will inform Mr Allbright that his conduct is unacceptable,' he told Fraddon. 'Has one of the grooms not relieved you of your duties here?'

'I be too old for such gallivanting. The lad will not get drunk or into mischief. He were told to keep an eye out for when the family wished to return to Trevowan.'

St John's conscience stirred that he had abandoned his daughter and stepdaughter for so long. He did not want Charlotte whining to her mother. He would find them and treat them to a gift from his winnings, which should keep them happy.

He found Senara and Bridie heading back to the coaches and carts. Rowena was crying, and when she saw her father she ran into his arms and sobbed against his chest.

'You've got to find him, Papa. Save Zach. I do not want him to be hurt.'

'Whatever is she babbling about?' he demanded, alarmed by the extent of his daughter's distress.

Senara explained what had happened. 'We will keep the children occupied here if you want to join in the search for Zach. It could have been Rowena who was taken.' She dropped her voice to a whisper. 'I believe that it is no chance abduction. Who now sees his brother as an enemy?'

'You think Sawle kidnapped his own nephew?' St John sounded surprised. 'Even he would not stoop so low.'

'Would he not? Clem idolises the boy.' Senara was so outraged by the way the children had been attacked and Zach seized that she forgot her usual need to restrain her family when dealing with Harry Sawle. 'In Harry's eyes his brother stole the Dolphin from him. That and the confiscated cargoes mean he has lost face in the community. He needs to show that he is still a man to be feared.'

'If you are right, he deserves no mercy. But surely he would not strike in so public a place. It would be madness with a price on his head.'

'The madness of revenge drives all reason aside.' Senara was furious. 'Sawle is conceited enough to think he is invincible when it comes to striking at those who have crossed him. I pray the boy is found unharmed.'

Before St John left, he warned the two women that Richard was in a drunken stupor and sleeping it off in the coach. Senara kept her own counsel that Richard was under the influence of opiates and not drink. The priority of this day was to find Zach.

For two hours a search covered the entire fair. Clem's years of respectability and his popularity as the new landlord of the Dolphin had won him many friends who wanted the boy found. Yet Zach had vanished and no one remembered seeing the man in a cloak. But then on a fair day you could become invisible if you kept to yourself whilst everyone else enjoyed the revels. With so many spectacular sights, a man in a hooded cloak was unremarkable.

Keziah was distraught; terrified she would never see her son again. Senara consoled her. 'He cannot have been taken far.'

All pleasure had gone from the day and the children were now subdued and tearful. To cover further afield Adam and St John had unhitched the carriage horses and ridden them bareback, grateful for Elspeth's insistence when she had first taught them to ride that they should not be allowed to use saddles. As the light began to fade they had to acknowledge defeat.

When the men returned, Keziah was sobbing in Senara's arms. A

247

spark of hope that had leapt to her eyes on their arrival was doused by bleak despair when they reported their failure.

'Clem is still searching,' Adam told her. 'Though it is hopeless in the dark. We will take you home.'

'I should be with Clem,' she protested.

'Tomorrow all Penruan and the people of the surrounding villages, our estates and the shipyard will scour the countryside for him. We will not rest until he is found,' Adam insisted. 'Sal may already have heard of her grandson's disappearance. She needs you.'

Chapter Thirty-two

Two further days of searching for Zach Sawle ended in failure. Neither was there sight nor word of his uncle. The fine weather had changed to a perpetual mist that covered farms, woods and the moor for several miles inland.

At the church services on Sunday prayers were said for Zach and his family. Because of the thick mist the search had had to be called off. Most of the Loveday family were dining at Trevowan; Peter, Bridie, Joshua and Cecily were lunching instead with Hannah on the farm. All were in sombre mood.

Richard was absent, and that disturbed Senara. He had promised her that after the Lammas Fair he would come to Boscabel so that she could treat his addiction. Amelia was surprisingly relaxed given that her son was not at the meal. When the women retired to the orangery to leave the men to their port and cigars, Senara could no longer contain her concern.

'Where is Richard? I am surprised he did not join the family today. He is not ill, is he, Amelia?'

'No. He is spending a few days with a naval friend. They served together on his first voyage. Richard learned yesterday that his ship was at Falmouth.'

Senara hid her anger. That was the ruse they had agreed Richard would use when he came to Boscabel for treatment. Not only had he betrayed her trust, but he was also putting his life in danger as he self-ishly pursued him own pleasures.

'You look annoyed, Senara.' Amelia addressed her. 'Why should my son's absence upset you?'

'You mistake me, Amelia,' she replied quickly, though her words were truthful. 'I was thinking of young Zach. My heart goes out to Keziah, and like all of us I fear for his life. I am angry that he has not been found safe and unharmed.'

'It is a shocking thing to have happened,' Elspeth raged. 'A child, a sweet innocent to be taken by some fiend.'

'I have ordered that a servant attend Charlotte and Rowena at all times,' Felicity groaned. 'Any one of our children could be taken in such a manner. It was broad daylight in a public place. Who would do such an evil act?'

'No disrespect to you, Senara, but it could be that the gypsies took him,' Amelia observed. 'Children have sometimes gone missing and never been seen again after they have travelled through a district.'

'And the gypsies are always conveniently blamed as they are mistrusted by everyone,' Senara returned. 'Yet why would they kidnap a child? They have problems feeding their own offspring.'

'One likes to believe that we are living in civilised times,' Felicity contributed. 'But taking a child is the worst form of barbarism. When I think it could so easily have been my dear Charlotte. Thank God she is too well behaved to run off in such a wild manner. Rowena and Nathan had a lucky escape. We must be more vigilant of the safety of our children. Discipline is so important.'

'Children cannot be kept on leading reins.' Senara bridled at the insinuation that the children were wild and unruly. 'Rowena is head-strong but she was wary of the cloaked stranger and warned Zach not to follow him. Nathan can usually be relied upon to do as he is told. And Keziah would have instilled in Zach the need to be cautious of strangers. Though with everyone in Penruan knowing him, it is unlikely he could come to any harm in their village. He was excited with so many new sights to be experienced at the fair.'

'It only takes an unguarded moment for evil to strike,' proclaimed Amelia as she pulled her shawl around her shoulders against the chill in the air. 'An opportunist will always seize their chance.'

Elspeth gripped her walking cane with whitened knuckles. 'I agree with Senara that you cannot cosset children too closely. I never did the twins. The hard knocks of life and how they coped with them made them who they are today: leaders of men, respected by the community.'

'But there have been times when they have placed their lives in parlous danger.' Felicity shuddered. 'There has been much scandal, which I pray never touches our lives again.'

'There is nothing worse than a coward.' Disdainfully Elspeth regarded Felicity over the top of her pince-nez. 'The twins could never be accused of that. One expects a young buck to sow his wild oats.'

Senara rubbed her temple and Elspeth turned her piercing glare on her. 'What do you think of this affray? Will the boy be found? Is that blackguard Sawle involved? You often have a way of knowing these things.'

Senara saw Felicity hastily cross herself and suppressed a spurt of irritation. 'I have a headache and have no premonition of the outcome. But I do not sense that Zach has been harmed.' A frown creased her brow and for some moments she stared into the flame of a candle on the table beside her. 'Yes, he is unharmed, though undoubtedly frightened. That would be expected. And yes, I do suspect Harry Sawle took his nephew to teach his brother a lesson.'

Amelia wiped a tear from her eye. 'Then we must all pray that the knave returns the boy to his parents, before this madness ends in disaster.'

'It is already too late for that,' Senara proclaimed. 'Clem will never forgive his brother for this.'

Elspeth rapped her cane on the marble floor as her anger flared. 'Harry Sawle is condemned by everyone. He will not keep his freedom much longer. What I fear is that he realises he is cornered and will use the boy as a bargaining tool.'

Felicity gasped and cradled her stomach as though protecting her unborn child. 'That is too wicked. He must be stopped at all costs.'

'That is what your husband and mine are planning.' Senara voiced her exasperation at her sister-in-law's naivety. 'They will not hesitate to place their lives once more in parlous danger, as you put it, to avenge this disgrace. No doubt it will cause a scandal. But you should be proud of them and not quake in your shoes at what the gossipmongers will say.'

She excused herself to walk in the grounds and calm down over Felicity and Amelia's prissy considerations. Obviously they had fallen in love with their husbands because of their boldness and courage, which was a large part of their personalities. Why did wives think they could then change those qualities in their men when it was inconvenient to their needs? But if she was honest with herself, so much talk of revenge and retribution upset her as well. In so many cases it became an endless cycle. Why could not people learn compassion and forgiveness, as Uncle Joshua had preached in his sermon this morning? Why must man resort to barbarity to right a perceived wrong? Fear bred hatred. Would the world not be a better place if people could forgive more easily?

Yet after all the ill Harry Sawle had brought upon them, Senara wrestled with her own conscience. She would have to look very deeply into her heart to forgive him. Had it been one of her own

251

children at his mercy, would she feel compassion for their abductor? It would certainly test every particle of her faith. But forgiveness did not mean condoning his conduct. With Adam and St John determined to halt Sawle's reign of terror, she prayed that they would hearken to the voice of reason and allow the courts to pass sentence for his crimes.

In the dining room St John and Adam were for once in agreement. St John sipped his brandy and expounded: 'Harry Sawle has to be stopped in this vendetta. The authorities are ineffectual against him. The way he has struck at his own brother proves that he will be utterly ruthless when he turns his wrath upon us.'

'Until now he has been playing cat and mouse with our family,' Adam agreed. 'He must suspect his days of freedom are numbered. We must be prepared that his revenge will be swift and merciless. Certainly he will strike sooner rather than later.'

'Which is why he must be stopped. Yet we have searched everywhere we can think of.' St John groaned. 'Even Clem has tried every haunt of Harry's known to him. He has vanished.'

'At least he seems to have the boy with him. There has been no sign of a body, and for that we must be grateful.' Adam paced the room and halted by a portrait of his great-grandfather, Arthur St John Loveday. It had been painted when he was in his fifties and he wore the long curling periwig fashionable at the time. The ravages of his harsh seafaring life as a privateer fighting against their ancient enemy the French were carved into his ascetic face. His eyes were impenetrable as a storm-tossed ocean, the nose imperiously aquiline and his mouth compressed in a line that would not be swayed from the path of his judgement. This was the founder of the family shipyard, and by marrying the beautiful heiress Anne Penhaligan, he had established the Loveday name at Trevowan. His son and grandson had built on his success, and Adam was not about to let a vicious thug like Sawle bring to ruin all the Lovedays had achieved.

'What would old Arthur have done?' St John broke into his twin's thoughts.

Adam gave an ironic laugh. 'He'd have hunted him down with dogs and run the blackguard through, and to hell with the consequences.'

'So what is stopping us doing the same?' St John was serious.

'Few dogs are trained to hunt men. Besides, by now his trail would have gone cold.'

'You are not opposed then to running the blackguard through?'

'It is no less than he deserves,' Adam replied. 'However, I would rather not take the law so drastically into my own hands if it can be avoided. Sawle, like all bullies, is a coward at heart. A quick death would be too easy for him. Festering in a cell knowing that he'll dance at the end of a rope will be his greatest nightmare. Also his hanging will be a cause for rejoicing to everyone he has terrorised.'

'But first we have to find him. And he seems to have vanished into thin air,' St John snapped. 'The man mocks us.'

Adam again studied the portrait. Arthur Loveday had always been an inspiration to him. His ancestor had never liked being forced on to the defensive and had always preferred to attack his enemies with surprise and stealth. Sawle for the time being held all the advantages. He could strike at any time without warning. Adam had never felt so impotent when it came to defending the lives of his family. Fury blasted him, but it had to be controlled and channelled into cold logic if he was ever to get the better of Harry Sawle's devious mind.

'He'll surface and then we must be ready for him.' He addressed his twin with lethal calm. 'Clem and many of the villagers of Penruan continue to search the moor and coastal caves to see if he has hidden the boy there.'

St John cracked his knuckles, his expression fierce with his own anger. 'I had hopes that we would find him in the cave where the smugglers held Peter last year, but there was no sign of him when Peter took us to it. I cannot see him sparing the lad. It will be his body they will find. Harry's way was always to toss those who crossed him into the sea.'

Adam shook his head. 'Harry has one chink in his armour and that is Sal. He will not harm her grandson and break her heart.'

'He believes Sal betrayed him by handing the Dolphin over to Clem,' St John scoffed. 'He would have killed Mark because he was jealous that he was Sal's favoured son. He did not care if his mother's heart broke then.' He replenished the brandy in their glasses. 'I've had enough of Sawle and his brutality this year. We have all been affected. I know this battle is Clem's fight and he is as eager to bring his brother to trial as we are, but it goes against the grain to let him triumph and we fail. We should be out there now.'

'Sawle will reveal himself in time and we will be ready for him.' Adam felt the same but could see no logic in pursuing a wild goose chase that would have Sawle laughing at their failure.

Jenna Biddick appeared in the doorway and bobbed a curtsey. 'There be a Cuthbert Freake to speak with Cap'n Loveday. Shall I show him into the library, Mr Loveday.'

Adam frowned. 'I recall no man of that name. Did he state his business?'

'Said you'd rescued him from drowning,' the maid replied. 'That he had some information for you. If you were not available he said Mr Loveday might find his news of interest.'

Adam recalled the man and the incident when he had delivered the repaired *Sea Mist* to the revenue. Freake had run his boat aground and it had smashed on the rocks. He glanced at his brother, who remained seated at the dining table.

St John said, 'If it concerns the family, have him brought here.'

Cuthbert Freake edged nervously into the room, twisting his slouch cap in his hands. He was dressed in black breeches and a brown jacket with frayed cuffs, and wore a clean pressed shirt. 'Begging your pardon for this intrusion, Cap'n Loveday and Mr Loveday.'

'I am glad to see you fully recovered from your ordeal, Freake.' Adam wanted to put the man at ease.

'You not only saved my life, I be a changed man from that day, sir. I reckon when you've looked death in the face and made your peace with your maker, and then been given a second chance, you see things a mite differently.'

'I'm glad to hear it,' Adam replied.

'I reckoned my life weren't so worthless if the good Lord had spared me. I stopped drinking and living in fear. You risked your life to save mine. I be indebted to you for that. I were at the Lammas Fair when the Sawle boy were taken. I saw what happened.'

'Then why the devil did you not come forward sooner?' St John stood up abruptly.

Freake stared at him without flinching, his nervousness gone. He ignored St John and looked at Adam. 'Since my rescue I'd taken an interest in your family. I knew one of the boys was your son and the girl your niece, Cap'n Loveday. I'd seen your wife talking to Clem Sawle and his wife earlier at the fair and the boy were with them. I realised it were Mr Loveday's nephew through your first wife, sir.' He briefly regarded the older twin.

'That is true.' Adam forestalled any further show of temper from his twin. 'Did you see who took Zach Sawle?'

'I did, and that's why I knew there'd be foul play. The man's hood slipped back and there weren't no mistaking the scarred face of Harry

Sawle. A year ago I'd never have risked getting near to him. I'd have been too afeared. But I knew I had to follow him. I took care to keep my distance at first. Then he took a horse and I feared I'd lose him. I bain't never ridden in my life so I could'na take a mount to follow, but I've strong legs and pursued him at a run. I've always been able to run at a steady pace for miles.'

'Yes, yes, man, get to the point,' St John snapped.

'Begging your pardon.' Freake continued to address Adam. 'I thought at one time I'd lose him for sure when he headed deeper into Bodmin Moor. He didn't travel across the open country. Too afraid of being seen, I reckon. So I kept on in the direction I'd seen him head. Then his horse lost a shoe and came up lame and he were forced to go on foot. The boy were struggling by then and his progress were slow.'

Freake broke off in a coughing fit. He was still breathing heavily from having run to the house. Adam pressed his brandy glass into the fisherman's hand, and Freake drank it gratefully before continuing. 'Sawle had his hands full with the boy so he did'na seem too concerned someone might be following him. He probably thought as he'd got so far without a hue and cry being raised that he'd not been noticed. The trail were treacherous. I feared I'd get trapped in the bog and sucked under.'

'Where is he?' St John demanded, his patience at an end.

'On the edge of the moor. One of them old mines that go way back to ancient times. I'll have to guide you. You'll never find the safe track across the moor.'

'Thank you, Freake. You have done well. Our maid will take you to the kitchen and our cook will give you some ale and food. I must summon my uncle and cousin from Trewenna, and Clem Sawle must be told.'

'Too much time will be wasted. We should go now.' St John strode to the door. 'I'll order Fraddon to saddle the horses.'

'We would be foolish to try and tackle him alone,' Adam cautioned. 'Peter will join us, and it is only right Clem is told. The boy will want his father. This is as much Clem's battle as ours.'

Within half an hour, Clem had arrived at the estate with a dozen villagers from Penruan prepared to take on Sawle. The years of tyranny had turned the tide against the smuggler leader. In recent times, when villagers had been forced by him to take unnecessary risks, local families had lost over a dozen relatives, either shot, or arrested by the excise men and transported overseas. Clem was mounted and armed with two pistols in cross-holsters upon his chest. The villagers had followed on foot armed with whatever weapons they had available, mostly cudgels.

'Sawle has gone too far this time, taking the lad,' declared the Penruan blacksmith. He was large-framed, with a black beard, and carried a long-handled scythe.

'Time he got some of his own medicine,' shouted Jon Biddick, who had lost a cousin shot by the revenue men during a landing.

There was a chorus of support.

Adam had misgivings about the mob. Their blood was up and as such they would be unruly and undisciplined. He raised his hands to silence them.

'We all want Harry Sawle brought to account,' he said in a calm voice. 'But he is wily and devious. Only by stealth and surprise can we ensure Zach will be rescued and his uncle captured.'

'That man bain't human. The boy is likely dead.' One of the Rundle men spat on the ground.

Clem, who had been silent until now, turned on the villagers. 'You were all at the inn when the messenger came to tell us Harry's hideout had been found. I thank you for your support, but Adam is right. Harry would not hesitate to harm my son, but he would not kill him while Zach provides a bargaining tool for him. I will not risk my son's life.'

'He bain't just responsible for your son's kidnapping; my brother were murdered by him.'

'So were two of my cousins, Jeth and Johnny,' shouted another.

'And my brother Bill,' added a third man.

The villagers were angry and eager for a fight.

Adam again sought to placate them. 'So many of us crossing the moor will warn Harry of our approach. I suggest you spread out about a half-mile round the old workings to cut off his escape if we fail to capture him. We will travel on horseback and you will be slower on foot. But remember that your voices will carry on the moor, so be as quiet as possible.'

Peter and Joshua joined them, and before they set off Joshua said a brief prayer: 'Dear Lord, we ask for your clemency and guidance in our work today and that your young servant Zach Sawle will be found safe and unharmed.'

There was another arrival riding one of Japhet's mares. Mark Sawle nodded to the gathering. 'I were visiting Ma and she told me you were going to search for Harry. Thank God I am in time. I have suffered more than most at his hands. I want to help bring him to justice.'

Chapter Thirty-three

The mist was thicker on the moor. Cuthbert Freake, who could not ride, was mounted behind Clem. Clem had never been at ease in the saddle. He had come to riding late in life, for according to Keziah, mounted on a thoroughbred mare was the way a gentleman travelled. At the fast pace the Lovedays had set, he clung to the saddle pommel knowing he looked as ungainly as a sack of turnips. On a ship it was a different matter. He could stroll across a storm-tossed deck with the agility of a tightrope walker. It didn't help his pride to acknowledge that the younger of the Loveday twins was equally proficient on a ship and also rode like a centaur, his body moving in lithe unison with his mount.

His pride for once was irrelevant under the weight of his anguish. Clem feared that every wasted minute before they found his brother could result in Zach not surviving this ordeal. He had never felt such absolute terror about anything in his life. To counter his worst fears he buoyed his hope with thoughts that his son was a plucky lad. However, Harry was a vicious, black-hearted bastard with no compassion. If anyone else had kidnapped Zach, his uncle would have hunted the villain down and killed him without remorse, though it would not have been from love or family loyalty; it would have been to save face and to show the world that no one struck at a Sawle with impunity.

The vision of Zach's terrified face filled Clem's mind. He had never felt so impotent or helpless. He had thought that the dark days of his smuggling were behind him, the violence smoothed away by Keziah's love. Yet the veneer of respectability was finer than spindrift thrown up by the sea and vaporised in the heat. The depth of his rage consumed him. His entire being was focused on the vengeance he would mete out to his brother. Nothing would satisfy him but Harry's death.

Mark Sawle, usually so gentle of temperament, also burned with anger. The pursuit had churned up all the grievances of the past. All his life he had been terrified of his bullying brother. Harry would attack him with little provocation and over the years had broken several of Mark's bones out of sheer cussedness. Mark loved his nephew with a fierceness that surprised him. The boy must be saved. Harry must die. Not because of the ills that Mark had suffered at those vicious hands, but because if he had taken Zach, no one was safe from Harry's wrath.

Peter Loveday was wrestling with the demons that fed on the wilder side of his nature. He thought he had learned to suppress them in his work for the Lord. How wrong he had been. Now they mocked him. Sawle stood for all that was evil and ungodly in their community. He was an unrepentant sinner who led decent men to their damnation.

He glanced at the hatred contorting Clem's face and saw the tension in his cousin St John's body. They were bent upon revenge, a far darker and more sinister retribution than justice alone. When he thought of that defenceless child at Harry's mercy, his blood ran cold. His own son was so very precious to him, and to think of another child alone, frightened and in fear of his life was beyond endurance. Peter wanted Sawle to pay for his crimes so badly that he wanted to choke the life from his body. The power of his feelings shocked him. It was for God, not his servant, to judge the evils of man. He prayed for wisdom to govern his actions.

St John was tense, his face set in a stony mask. Too often Harry Sawle had got the better of him. Harry had been the one pointing the blunderbuss at his chest when he and Meriel Sawle had been brought before a preacher in a ruined church. Even now, the memory of that marriage brought a bitter taste to his mouth. It had been the cause of the most difficult years of his life. Meriel was dead, and good riddance to her. Today her brother would join her in Hell, if St John had anything to do with it. He owed it to his father's memory to be avenged upon Sawle − nothing else would satisfy him.

Adam kept his focus on the problems they could encounter ahead and a tight rein on his temper, which threatened to blind him to everything but the need to bring Sawle down. He had waited a long time for this moment; too long, his pride mocked him. He must not, would not, fail now.

The moor stretched for miles around them, bleak and forbidding. The ground was treacherous if they strayed from the path. After two miles Cuthbert Freake and Clem drew level with Adam and St John, who had been leading the troop.

'The old workings are on the other side of that tor.' Freake pointed to a low-lying granite crag, bare of trees or gorse. 'It would serve us better if we circle round to the right. If he be keeping a lookout, he'll not expect us from that direction. Also we must ride single file. The bog hereabouts will suck horse and man under without warning.'

Adam nodded, and indicated for Clem and Freake to take the lead. The trees had thinned and the landscape was bleak, the heather and bracken concealing unstable ground. Too many men had succumbed to the bogs for the moor not to be feared for its secret death traps that awaited the unwary.

Their progress was frustratingly slow. No birds sang or crickets called. The dankness of the peat and gorse was acrid in the air and the dense mist chilled their bones.

'The Lord be with us,' Joshua said quietly as he rode at Adam's side.

'Amen, Uncle.' Adam's voice was devoid of emotion, but his eyes were dark and lethal as a coiled viper.

'Do not let your heart rule your head, Nephew,' Joshua counselled.

A pulse flared along Adam's jaw. 'We will do what must be done.' He would not be drawn further.

Joshua trusted Adam to keep a leash on his desire to run Sawle through; St John, however, was a different matter. Every muscle of the older twin was charged with the need for vengeance. Joshua had witnessed the signs in many of his family when nothing would turn them from their purpose. His nephew's lips were thinned to a sharp slash of outrage and his head was cocked slightly to one side. For a moment Joshua saw the face of his grandfather before him. He had not realised that St John had the strongest resemblance to the old man. In his young buccaneering days, Arthur St John Loveday would have made the Sawles pale into insignificance with his fearless valour and the most ruthless streak imaginable. Harry Sawle would have been no match for the old man. But although St John might resemble Arthur St John and bear his name and hot temper, Joshua knew with a sinking heart that his nephew did not have the cunning that had enabled his grandfather to build a dynasty of wealth and respectability with the plundering ethics of a pirate.

When they reached a broad patch of gorse, Freake dismounted. 'Leave the horses here, else he will hear our approach.'

'No one is to speak,' Joshua cautioned.

The animals were tethered. Adam had brought a long length of rope in case they had to descend into a shaft, and he swung this over his shoulder. He had faced many battles in his time at sea and he had no intention of underestimating his prey this day. Even so, his body grew hot and he could feel sweat coating his shoulder blades. They had reached the crown of the tor and the men flattened themselves on the earth to peer over the edge. Centuries had disguised the old workings and few traces of them remained.

Freake tugged on Adam's sleeve and pointed to a large boulder and outcrop of rock. On closer scrutiny Adam saw that around it the grass had been flattened and he could just make out an indentation. It was the opening of a mine shaft, and someone had been there recently. His ears strained for any sound of habitation. All he could hear was the breathing of his companions.

'Where the devil is he hiding?' St John choked on his anger.

'Keep your voice down,' Joshua returned. 'Some of these shafts are shallow and lead into an underground cave. Others are vertical. It is unlikely he would use such as those. We must be cautious.'

'If we rush the shaft we will snare him like a rat in a trap,' St John urged.

'Fool! He'll kill Zach at the first sound of attack,' Clem warned in a harsh whisper. 'I'll go in. I've some experience of this mine from the old days. The entrance is concealed and drops down gradually, then opens out into a cave. If he's here, Harry will be armed and ready.'

'Then we should wait until he makes an appearance, then ambush him,' Adam suggested.

'That makes sense,' Joshua agreed. 'But someone should warn the others coming on foot. They must approach in silence.'

Adam nodded. 'Freake, you go. It could be a long wait. The villagers need to be guided along the safe track. You have risked your life enough. We will confront Sawle. The others are to stay back and bring him down if he manages to get away.'

Despite his earlier bravado, Cuthbert Freake looked relieved and after only a token protest headed at a run back the way they had come.

'I say we go in,' St John persisted. 'It will be dark in a few hours, and with this mist we will soon be too cold to attack effectively.'

'We have no option but to wait.' Peter added his counsel to that of his father. 'The entrance to the mine is narrow. Sawle will pick us off one by one, and as Clem says, the risk to the boy is too great.'

'We have no proof that he is in there.' St John could not control his impatience. 'This could all be a waste of time.'

'Then the Lord will give us patience,' Joshua stated, and sat with his back against a rock.

Clem cursed roundly. 'I bain't gonna sit round waiting on my brother. In this weather he could be in there for hours. Every minute Zach be in danger. I will go in. It's my son and my fight.'

St John protested: 'It's not just your fight.'

'But it be my son's life at risk. If Harry bain't in there I can rescue Zach. If he be laying in wait then I have to take my chances. He bain't to know you be out here waiting for him.'

Adam wanted to confront Harry himself but he could see the wisdom of Clem's words, though it stuck in his craw to admit it. After an inner struggle he said, 'Clem is right. Yet we should investigate the opening of the shaft to see if two of us could enter unobserved. I'll be close behind you, Clem.'

'You want to steal the thunder as usual,' St John sneered. 'I'm the eldest and I've got more grudges to settle with Sawle than you. Dammit, you were not married to his bitch of a sister.'

Clem crouched, ready to spring at him, his fists clenched. 'She were my sister as well. You got her in the family way. I s'pose you thought yourself too good to wed her.'

'Gentlemen!' Joshua interceded. 'This is exactly why we should wait. Your blood is up and you will act too rashly. If anyone is to go with Clem, it should be me. The twins and Peter have young families to raise, and besides I have more experience at defusing dangerous situations.'

Adam shook his head. 'With respect, sir, in a fight you are no match for Sawle.'

For the first time in his life Adam saw Joshua Loveday's temper in all its fury. 'No match!' he ground out. 'I was a better swordsman than you and your brother in my day, and a dead shot. Who do you think taught Japhet?'

Adam coloured. His uncle had fought many duels as a young blood. It was after he had killed an adversary in a sword fight that he had forsworn his old life and become a preacher. 'There was no disrespect intended, sir. A younger man might find it easier to climb down into the cave.'

The anger faded from his uncle's face and with a grimace he conceded. 'Aye, I'm not as agile as once I was, but neither am I so infirm that I am ready to be put out to grass. If this is not to end in a bloodbath, Sawle must be brought to his senses. He may not regard me as so great a threat as yourselves.'

When neither Adam nor St John looked convinced, Clem spoke. 'Harry has no love for either of you twins. He'd relish an excuse to kill you. How will that help Zach? The Reverend Mr Loveday is not his enemy. If my brother be in the workings, the only way anyone will get out alive is if he believes there is no chance of his capture.'

'Will he not guess we have set a trap?' Adam challenged.

'He will be told that Clem and I came alone,' Joshua advised. 'If Sawle is in there and we fail, he cannot stay holed up there for long. He will have to come out and you will be waiting for him.'

'It is a great risk you take, Uncle.' Adam rubbed the back of his neck, where the coil of rope slung across his shoulder chafed the flesh.

Joshua put his hand on his nephew's shoulder. 'You want to bring this man to justice because among other things you hold him responsible for your father's death. Edward was my brother. He never failed me when I was in need. I could never repay him. I will do so now, for if a Loveday life is to be taken, let it be mine. I have lived my life and place my trust in God. I know you will take care of Cecily and Hannah if the need arises.'

'I cannot agree,' Adam protested.

'Nor I,' St John added.

'I am head of the family and your spiritual counsellor.'

Reluctantly Adam conceded. With a nod to Clem, Joshua marched resolutely towards the workings. St John made to rise and stop him but Adam pulled sharply on his arm, preventing him.

'If we show ourselves, there will be a bloodbath,' Adam cautioned. 'This way there is a chance we can save Zach and still capture Sawle. Uncle Joshua is older and wiser than us. He could succeed where we would fail.'

'And how do we face Aunt Cecily and Hannah if he is killed? They will think us craven.'

'He is a brave and honourable man. They will understand.'

Adam leaned back against a boulder and sank his head into his hands. It took all his willpower not to run and join his uncle, and he knew his twin was fighting the same battle.

Chapter Thirty-four

The mine entrance was deceptive. It sloped down only a few feet and then opened up into a cavern. The sides were narrow from a build-up of loose shale and the floor sloped steeply, but they could walk without the aid of the rope or need of a ladder. Their shoes scrunched on the rock chippings that had accumulated over the centuries, and with each footstep the men tensed, aware that the noise heralded their passage. This would be no surprise attack.

After a score of yards they found themselves in deepening gloom. Little light from the entrance penetrated this far. In another few yards they would be in total darkness. Joshua struck the flint against the steel of his tinderbox and held it to the whale-oil-soaked gauze within. The sparks kindled a tiny flame and he held it aloft, but still they could see little, although the cave was now wider.

'These workings cover hundreds of yards and branch out in other directions,' Clem whispered. 'We need torches to explore them.'

'Ssh,' said Joshua. His head was cocked to one side as he strained to listen into the darkness. There was the muffled sound of movement and whimpering a short way ahead.

It could be a wild animal that had made the cave its home but Clem did not hesitate to run forward, Joshua at his side. In the pale flickering light of the tinderbox, a dark form could be seen huddled on the floor. The flame showed large terrified eyes in a small, pale face.

'Zach, thank God you be alive.' His voice cracking with emotion, Clem clasped the boy to his chest and hugged him close.

A kerchief was tied across the lad's mouth to prevent him calling out and his arms and legs were bound with rope. Clem drew a dagger from a sheath at his waist and cut the cord. His son flung his arms around his father and sobbed, his words of relief incoherent through the waterfall of his tears.

'It be all right, son. I'm here. You be safe.'

'Not that safe.' A harsh voice spoke from the blackness ahead of them.

Hampered by the boy, Clem tried to push his son behind him and rise to face his brother. As he moved to draw his pistol, two shots flared in the darkness, briefly illuminating a scarred face twisted with hatred. Clem fell to the ground holding his side, and Joshua felt the impact of a bullet searing his neck. He lost his balance and fell, the shock of the pain making the tinderbox drop from his hand. The flame extinguished and they were plunged into an obsidian gloom.

Zach was now hysterical, wailing and crying. 'Pa! Pa! Don't die, Pa!'

'I be fine, lad,' Clem reassured him. 'He bain't done for me.' He turned on Harry. 'Bastard! What fiend preys on a child?'

'You took what were mine – the inn. I took the only thing you truly valued. Fair exchange, brother.'

Joshua gritted his teeth against the fiery agony in his neck. He could feel the warm blood pouring from the wound, but the bullet had only nicked him and had not lodged in his flesh. Even so, the pain was excruciating. He had also fallen heavily and was winded. He silently cursed his advancing age. As a young man he would have leapt to his feet and launched himself at their attacker. He could hear scuffling from the direction Clem had fallen, and then the sickening thud of a boot connecting with bone.

'What did you bring the preacher for? You'd not be fool enough to think I'd heed him. How did you learn I were here? And how many others be there?'

'There be just the two of us.' Clem's voice was gritty with pain. 'You were seen on the moor with Zach. The price on your head has doubled. The man went to the reverend, trusting that a parson would not cheat him of his reward, and Mr Loveday sent word to me. He did'na want his nephews involved. He knew if they were there'd be bloodshed.'

'That be true, Loveday?' Harry did not bother with the courtesy of a title.

Joshua was about to reply but thought better of it and clamped his lips shut. Harry Sawle had fired in the dark and did not know whether his bullet had found its mark or how badly Joshua was wounded. His mind worked rapidly as he drew his own pistol from his waistband. Sawle had fired two pistols and had not reloaded. If Clem had not fired back he must be badly wounded. Joshua cursed the darkness that made it difficult to work out what was happening. But he could smell Harry Sawle. The smuggler reeked of stale brandy and sweat.

'Seems like the preacher be dead,' Harry scoffed. 'Bit careless of you to bring an old man.'

'Make a run for it, Zach,' ordered Clem.

There was a scampering of feet and the stench of urine where the boy had constantly wet himself in his fear. Then Zach was past Joshua and heading towards the entrance to the cave.

'So you thought the preacher's presence would spare the lad?' Harry mocked. 'I'll see you all dead.' The smuggler launched into a kicking frenzy, his boots thudding into his brother's head and body. He was too enraged to pay heed to his nephew bolting for freedom.

Joshua raised himself silently to his feet, his pistol firm in one hand and a dagger in the other. He knew that if he did not intercede now, Clem Sawle would be beaten to death. The insults had pricked his pride. He would show the smuggler what an old man could do – no ordinary old man, but a Loveday.

'That's enough, Harry. Stand back or I'll shoot.' He pointed the pistol in the direction of the scuffling, and his eyes, now used to the darkness, made out the shape of Harry bent over his prone brother.

A cruel laugh mocked him.

'So you bain't dead yet, Preacher. But you bain't gonna shoot me. I bain't worth you risking going to Hell for.' His leg lashed out, aimed at Clem's head.

Joshua fired, aiming to bring the smuggler down but not to kill him. The shot caught Sawle in the thigh. It would have brought a lesser man to the ground. But the devil was on the smuggler's side and would not give up his acolyte so easily. Harry Sawle spun round and lumbered towards the man of God. The older man swung out with his dagger but the uneven ground of the cave caught him off balance and the blade sliced harmlessly an inch from Sawle's side. Then an agonising pain gouged deep into Joshua's arm as his flesh was sliced to the bone. Before he could respond, Sawle smashed his pistol butt into the side of his head, knocking him out cold.

Breathing heavily, Sawle peered into the darkness and made out the two men sprawled unmoving on the ground. There was no sign of Zach. He shrugged. The brat had served his purpose. He had got his revenge on Clem. The pain in his thigh made him stumble. Let the lad run off. What did it matter? He would get lost on the moor and die anyway. If the preacher was dead, so much the better. That would be another revenge upon the Lovedays. Pity it wasn't Adam or St John.

He was finding it harder to focus his thoughts, and wiping his hand down his wounded thigh he found his breeches sodden with blood. His survival instincts kicked in. In his hunger for revenge he had taken too many risks. Now he had to get out of Cornwall as fast as he could.

266

He had been drinking heavily for most of the time since he had kidnapped his nephew. He was used to vast quantities of liquor and handled it well, but he had eaten poorly in the last few days and his wits had dulled. There was only the need to escape driving him. A trail of blood from his leg wound followed his exit from the mine. He was light-headed as he made the difficult climb up the sides of the opening, and his eyes stabbed with pain as he emerged into the shrouding mist.

Patience was not a Loveday virtue. From the moment Joshua and Clem disappeared into the mine, each minute strung out like an hour. St John fidgeted constantly; Peter was pale and his lips moved in prayer. He was clearly worried about his father, as was Adam. Adam had learned to calm his restless spirit in the years he had been at sea, but even for him the waiting was torture. Then the distant sound of two shots brought the cousins to their feet.

'We cannot stand here and do nothing,' St John burst out, and without waiting for a reply he headed for the mine.

Adam and Peter drew their pistols and Adam nodded to his cousin to follow him. He hurried to draw level with his brother, concerned that St John would act rashly. They did not know who had fired the shots or what was happening. Harry Sawle could be dead, or Clem or Joshua. Anxiety for his uncle prickled Adam's spine. The cost of bringing Harry Sawle to account for his crimes could be high indeed.

'Stay back from the entrance, St John,' Adam ordered, but he kept his voice low. 'If Harry has escaped the others, he will pick us off one by one if we are silhouetted against the opening. Get down. We could still have surprise on our side.'

'Father could be hurt; we cannot leave him at Sawle's mercy,' Peter flared.

'This is hardest for you, Peter, but we must wait. Uncle Joshua is a crack shot. He'd weigh up every possibility. He is more than a match for Sawle.' Adam needed to defuse the anger in his cousin's eyes. Peter had proved his valour last year when he had taken on the smugglers, but he was inexperienced in fighting an adversary like Harry. Sawle had the ethics of a guttersnipe and would cold-bloodedly murder any who crossed him. Peter had fought in self-defence; however, Adam doubted his cousin's religious ethics would allow him to kill. Even a second's hesitation could allow Harry to take another life.

There was the sound of shale being dislodged underfoot, warning them that someone was close to the mouth of the mine. St John raised his pistol to fire.

'Don't shoot, it's Zach,' Adam warned.

The lad was sobbing as he stumbled out into the light. He was stag-gering from side to side, clearly disorientated and blinded by his tears. He started to head away from them, and Adam, fearing the boy would blunder into the treacherous bogs, sprinted after him and grabbed him close to his chest, putting a hand over his mouth to stop him crying out and alerting Harry of their presence.

'You're safe, Zach. It's Adam Loveday. I will not hurt you. Don't cry out. Do you understand?'

He nodded and Adam withdrew his hand. The small body was trem-bling violently as he gasped between his sobs: 'Pa be shot.'

Adam lifted him and carried him back to Peter and St John, and put him on the ground behind a rock next to where St John was standing. 'I need you to be brave and stay here. You will not be hurt. Your uncle will not get anywhere near you.'

At that moment Harry Sawle emerged from the mine. Zach screamed and threw himself at St John, clinging like a limpet to his legs. 'Don't let him kill me, Uncle St John.'

At first angered that the lad had stopped him firing at Sawle, St John was shocked at the boy's address. He had never thought of himself as Zach's uncle. Though of course he was, through his marriage to Meriel.

'If I die, tell Rowena I be sorry if I got her into trouble at the fair. I never wished my cousin harm. I love her. She always be so kind to me.'

St John disengaged the boy's arms, and as he stared down into his tear-streaked face, he felt a fierce need to protect him. Rowena would be heartbroken if anything happened to her cousin. He put Zach gently behind the boulder, saying sharply, 'Stay there and you will come to no harm.'

The incident had taken only seconds, but as St John turned to face the mine, he knew he had lost his chance to kill Harry Sawle.

Alerted by Zach's scream, the smuggler had turned and hobbled in the opposite direction and was fast being hidden by the mist. A chorus of shouts carried to them from the villagers who had followed on foot.

'There he be!'

'At 'im, lads!'

The mist had swallowed them, and Adam was fleet on Sawle's trail, shouting, 'Someone stay with the lad.'

'Don't move, Zach. You are safe there,' commanded St John. He saw Mark Sawle about to follow his twin. He would not be thwarted in this moment of revenge, and he ran after them. 'Mark, your nephew needs you. Keep an eye on the lad.'

Mark hesitated, clearly determined to pay his brother back for the beating he had been given.

'Uncle Mark, don't go,' Zach sobbed. 'Pa's hurt bad.'

Mark returned to his nephew. 'Are you up to going back into the mine to see how your pa be?'

Zach nodded.

'That's a brave lad. We all be proud of you.'

Peter was worried about his father, who had not reappeared. If Clem was wounded, it was likely Joshua was also. He could even be dead.

'I'll do what I can for the Reverend,' Mark said. 'You get that bastard for me, sir.'

Peter was grateful for Mark's suggestion. He knew his father would expect him to help his cousins, and he called upon the Lord to watch over them all as he sped after the twins.

Adam ran into the midst of the villagers, who were in uproar. Somehow Sawle had managed to give them the slip.

'He can't be far. It looked like he was wounded in the leg,' Adam shouted. 'Spread out.'

Frustration ground through him. To have got so close to capturing Sawle only for him to slip through their net defied all natural justice. The mist muffled sounds. The tramp of heavy feet and grunts or heavy breathing could be anyone. The moor was treacherous here; should he risk the villagers getting sucked into the bog? Yet he could not let Sawle escape.

He was about to call the proceedings to a halt when there was a shriek of alarm far to Adam's right.

'Bundy's trapped in the bog!'

'I'm with him,' another yelled. 'Give us a hand.'

A few tense moments passed, then another voice was raised. 'He's out. Bundy's safe.'

'It's too dangerous to progress.' Adam addressed the shadowy forms. 'If you can trace your steps back to the mine, wait there until the weather clears.'

There were many cries of protest. St John's voice could be heard the loudest. 'Abandon the chase if you will. Sawle is too close to let him escape now.'

There was another shot and a scream as someone went down.

'Tonkin's been hit.' It was Peter who informed them.

Adam could not let his brother and cousin continue their pursuit alone, and he prayed there would be no more casualties. The voices were to his left and he headed in that direction. Then a sound to his right caught his attention. The mist had thickened to a dense fog, distorting all sound and sense of direction. Its dampness clutched at Adam's lungs, making his breathing laboured, so that he soon felt as though he had been running hard. His companions' voices were scarcely audible and he realised that he was isolated by the fog.

At the sound of a boot scraping on stone, he froze, gauging the direction. It was close. But was it friend or foe? The hackles on his neck rose as he strained to hear and see in the encompassing shroud that covered the moor. The sense of danger prickled every pore of his body. If Sawle was close, Adam knew he could be the hunted as well as the hunter. An outcrop of rocks, as tall as a man, was a dark shadow ahead of him. It was a place to hide or to lie in ambush. All noise had ceased, muffled by the fog, but his instincts told him that his prey was close by.

He shivered, recalling the dream that had woken him earlier in the year. Then he had been chasing Sawle in a mist and had emerged the victor, but that could all change now. Sawle was not an adversary to underestimate. He put his hand on the rock and it came away sticky with fresh blood. Sawle had indeed passed this way.

Adam drew his pistol, advancing slowly. To call for back-up would alert the smuggler, and he would scurry away like a rat down a sewer.

The fog was disorientating and eerily unnerving. The only sound was the thudding of Adam's own heart, like a hammer pounding an anvil. Then, without warning, a figure launched itself from the top of the rock on to Adam's back, knocking him to the ground. He rolled to break the impact of the fall and found himself staring into Sawle's hate-crazed face. The pistol had been jarred from his fingers when his arm was smashed against the side of the rock. Sawle raised a hand holding a dagger to plunge into Adam's throat. Adam threw up his hands to grab his assailant's wrists. All of Sawle's weight was bearing down on him, giving the smuggler the advantage, and the blade was halted only an inch from its target. With every muscle straining, Adam tried to push the dagger aside, but it remained perilously close. Sawle was heavier and stronger than him and in the past their fights had been won by Adam's greater agility and speed.

'Your friends can't help you now, Loveday. You're a dead man,' Sawle snarled. His exertions caused sweat to drip from his face on to Adam's.

Adam felt a quiver pass through the arms he was resisting. The blade wavered only slightly, but it was enough. Drawing on his last reserves of strength, he managed to heave his shoulders far enough off the ground to throw Sawle off balance. As the weight lifted from his torso, Adam shoved harder and rolled. Sawle was pitched sideways and Adam swung his weight so that he straddled his enemy. The dagger was still pointing ominously close to his chest, but with each second Sawle was weakening. He had lost a great deal of blood. They were up hard against the side of the rock, and two jerks of Adam's wrist slammed Sawle's knuckles against the stone. The blade fell from his fingers. The pistol Adam had dropped was solid against his knee and he snatched it up, pressing it to the smuggler's temple. The temptation to shoot glittered in his eyes.

'Go on, kill me, Loveday. This is your chance,' Sawle goaded.

As Adam's finger tightened on the trigger, he heard his name being shouted. Again the echo of the dream flashed through his mind, when his father had counselled, 'There is no honour in murder.'

With the pistol trained on Sawle, Adam rose to his feet. 'Get up. You will face trial.'

He was dimly aware of shouts in the distance and raised his voice. 'Over here! Sawle is captured.'

He did not see the large jagged stone Sawle gripped as he appeared to stumble to his feet. It struck him above the eye, the pain temporarily blinding him. He shook his head to clear it as blood poured from the cut. When his vision cleared, Sawle had disappeared, but he could hear him running over the rough ground.

'He's got away,' he yelled, warning the others as he tore after the smuggler. He had covered less than two-score yards when he heard the slurping, sucking sound of someone floundering in mud. He advanced more cautiously and the ground became less firm. The mist parted in front of him and he saw Sawle. Both his legs were stuck in the mud past his knees, and the more he struggled, the deeper he sank.

'Damn you, Loveday!' Sawle spat, defiant in his earthy trap.

The mud was creeping up his thighs. In another minute he would be too deep to ever be free and he would be buried alive. There would be no reprieve for him as there had been for Bundy.

'To me, men!' Adam shouted. 'Sawle is here.'

St John arrived first. 'The bastard has got his just deserts.'

'If we had the rope I could get him out, but I left it at the mine.' Adam was searching the ground for a stout branch that would be long enough for Sawle to grab hold of. He found one as Peter arrived.

'Let him die,' St John raged when he realised what his twin intended.

Sawle flailed his arms wildly. 'Don't let the bog take me.'

'Not so brave now, are you, Sawle?' St John sneered. 'How many victims have you killed without mercy? You'd not save us.'

'So you would put us on a level with him,' Adam asked coldly. 'Father would be ashamed of you.'

'Father could be ruthless when he had to be.'

Some of the villagers had gathered closer. One picked up a rock and hurled it at Sawle's head. Blood poured from the cut. 'That be for Jeth and Johnny.'

Others stooped to collect stones, one of the Tonkin men shouting, 'Kill the bastard now.'

Outraged, Adam rounded on them and twisted Tonkin's arm up behind his back. 'Would you make murderers of us all? He will face trial.'

'Adam is right.' Peter added his voice. 'God is his judge, not us.'

'Seems to me God has made his judgement.' Another Tonkin cousin hawked in his throat and spat in the smuggler's direction. 'Let him rot where he be.' He walked away, and after some muttering the others followed him.

Sawle had now sunk deeper into the vice-like hold of the mud. Adam edged forward until the branch was within Sawle's reach. 'Hang on to that. I'll pull you out.'

St John stepped back, scowling. 'You're a fool. The others are right. Let him rot.'

Peter was beside Adam. Sawle had grabbed the branch, blood pouring from the cut on his cheek. Adam braced himself to haul his enemy out of the grip of the bog. The smuggler did not move. The mud held him in a deathly embrace and would not release its prey. Peter also held the upper part of the branch, and he and Adam braced their legs and heaved with all their might. Sawle edged forward a few inches, then, as they paused before another pull, slid back again.

'St John, you cannot turn your back on us,' Peter fumed. Both his face and Adam's were contorted with the effort it was costing them. 'Do you not fear that God will judge you?'

'Confound your stubbornness,' St John groaned. If Adam had ordered him he would have refused out of cussedness. But his cousin had shamed him. He might hate Sawle but he was not a murderer. Sawle would dance at the end of a rope. That would be victory enough. And from the look of fear on the smuggler's face, his weeks in gaol awaiting sentence would be recompense for the time St John had suffered the same fears when he had awaited trial for a murder Harry Sawle had committed.

He put his arms around his cousin's waist.

'On the count of two, we all pull together,' said Adam.

'One . . . two.'

The three men used all their strength, and this time Sawle's body was drawn over the mud. The cousins toppled over as the smuggler came free and was pulled on to firm ground. Sawle rolled on to his knees, breathing heavily. When he tried to rise, St John pulled the pistol from his belt and pressed the muzzle to his temple.

'One false move and you're dead.'

'Someone bring the rope from the mine,' Adam shouted. He had also drawn his pistol and aimed it at the smuggler.

Mark Sawle appeared, carrying the rope. 'You should have let him die. He's shot Clem and given him a kicking. He be hurt bad. The Reverend were also shot and has a wound in his neck and arm. He is now doing what he can for Clem. Zach is with them.'

'We could still shoot him now.' St John kept his pistol trained on the smuggler, his expression murderous.

'His trial will show others that we will not tolerate such evil on our shores. Tie him up, Mark,' Adam ordered.

'With pleasure.'

'My little brother is brave, confronting me with two pistols trained on me,' jeered Harry.

The rope was looped around Harry's wrists and Mark jerked it tight, clamping them together. 'Like you were brave when you got your henchmen to do your dirty work.' He threw the rope over his brother's shoulder and wound it four times round his body. Harry's arms were bound close to his sides and he was unable to move them.

Then madness seized Mark, and he lashed out at his brother several times with his bare knuckles. Both Harry's eyes were blackened and closed and his nose broken before Adam hauled Mark away. The young man struggled in his hold, his fists still trying to find their target.

'No more, Mark. He had that beating coming to him after all you had suffered, but enough is enough now.'

The fight died from the stockman and he allowed Harry to be led back to where the horses were tethered.

Peter had gone into the mine and now came out with Joshua. Adam was alarmed to see the blood staining his Geneva bands. He cradled one arm in the other.

'How badly are you hurt, sir?' Adam asked.

'You good wife will put it right. It is a nick from a bullet and a slight dagger wound. I shall stop at Boscabel on the way home.'

Two of the Rundle brothers from Penruan were carrying Clem, and Zach was weeping as he walked by his father's side. Joshua added heavily, 'The lad is badly shaken. Clem will live, though has a nasty wound. It seems to have missed any vital organs, but it is deep, and Chegwidden will need to attend him. It will be some while before he is back working in the inn.'

Harry did not even glance at his brothers or nephew as the rope around his body was tied so that he had to walk behind St John's horse. He was limping from the shot Joshua had fired, but he was shown no further mercy. It was a small satisfaction to humiliate the smuggler as he stumbled across the moor to the prison at Bodmin.

Wherever Sawle was recognised there was a cheer from the local people. 'Well done, sirs. 'Tis time this villain paid for the fear he brought to this land.'

Chapter Thirty-five

When Peter told Hannah that Harry Sawle was in custody, she gave a heartfelt sigh of relief.

'Thank God. Sawle deserves all that is coming to him.' She found herself inexplicably shaking. They were in the farmhouse kitchen and she was washing Luke and Nathan's faces after they had been eating blackberries she had sent them to collect. Nathan had stayed for two nights at Luke's request, and now free of their chores the two boys ran into the yard, yelling at the top of their voices as they played at pirates.

Peter studied his sister closely. She appeared distracted as she watched the boys through the kitchen window. 'Hannah, what did that monster do to you? I know you confronted him on several occasions, especially when he used Japhet's farm to store his contraband.'

To her consternation she found herself crying. Peter rather awkwardly took her into his arms; he had always been uncomfortable showing his emotions.

'This is not like you. Was there more you did not tell us?'

She clung to him and gathered strength from his compassion. 'It is so good to know that he is behind bars. I had not realised how great had been the strain of not knowing when he could strike. He once threatened that my children would suffer if I did not agree to him storing contraband on my land. When Zach disappeared I was terrified he would carry out his threat. After the fair, Adam sent two men to sleep in the barn at nights.' Even now she would not speak of her encounters with Sawle when he had tried to force his attentions upon her and failed, or his attack on Jeannie.

'I am being foolish.' She took the handkerchief Peter offered and wiped her eyes. 'You said his capture was not without violence, and that Papa was hurt and it will be some weeks before Clem will be able to work. How is Papa?'

'A bullet gashed his neck and he was wounded in the arm and lost a lot of blood. He needed several stitches, and both Senara and Dr Yeo insist that he rests. I am taking his services this week. Papa does not want any undue fuss, though I think he is weaker than he is saying. He says he survived worse wounds from scrapes in his youth.'

'Like most men he will not admit that he is getting older. It was very courageous of him to face Sawle. I will visit them both later.' She hugged her brother, causing Peter to blush. 'I am proud of my family. You were all so brave.'

As Peter was leaving, a servant arrived with a note for Hannah from Nicholas Trescoe. Hannah read it and smiled, saying, 'Tell your master I look forward to his visit this afternoon.'

'Who is calling on you in such a formal manner?' Peter was almost accusing in his manner.

'Nick Trescoe. It was thoughtful of him to enquire if I am receiving guests this afternoon. He knows I am much occupied with my duties on the farm.'

'He is not a man to encourage, sister. He is a reprobate.'

'Do not be so judgemental,' she teased. 'He is an old friend. He was Japhet's best friend.'

'Precisely, and they led each other astray for years. Their reputation with women was far from exemplary. I cannot approve of Trescoe paying court to my sister.'

She laughed at the lunacy of such a suggestion. 'Nick is not paying court to me.'

'Then his intentions are dishonourable. I shall call the knave to account.'

'Now you are being too protective, and not a little absurd. Nick is a friend.' Her brother's attitude spoiled her pleasure at the thought of Nick's company.

Peter was equally incensed. 'Then what of your reputation? Receiving a man like Trescoe will cause gossip. There was enough of that after Oswald died and that Sam fellow was in charge here. You claimed that he was also a friend. It looked more than that to me. I saw the way he watched you. Trescoe is the same. You spent a lot of time in his company at the Lammas Fair.'

'Now you are being ridiculous, Peter.' Her anger sparked. 'I danced with Nicholas twice, and before that our conversation was short and mostly about horses. He is interested in the foals bred from Japhet's mares.'

'I am not being ridiculous.' Peter flushed scarlet in his affront. 'Many would consider you wanton to encourage such a man.'

'Then those people do not know me, and I expect more respect from you, Peter.' She rounded on him but kept her voice lowered, unwilling that any of the servants should overhear. She did not want them speculating that Nicholas was interested in her as a wife.

'I will not have my sister become the cause of gossip,' Peter continued at his most pompous. 'Since you have seen fit to say you will receive him, I will send Bridie to be here when he calls.'

Hannah advanced purposefully towards him and her finger jabbed hard into his chest as she replied. 'Bridie has her own duties. I am in no danger from Nick and I resent your manner. I have enough house and farm servants to safeguard my reputation.'

He took an indignant step back at her attack on his person. 'You cannot be too careful. You are too trusting and headstrong, sister.'

Exasperated, Hannah threw up her arms, her eyes flashing with a dangerous light. 'And you, my pious brother, should have more clemency towards an old friend of the family. You had better go, Peter, before I lose my temper. And do not send Bridie. I am sure she has better things to do with her time.'

'I have not only the family name to consider but the safeguard of your soul—' he began, his words cut short by a well-aimed towel thrown at his head.

'Save your piety and preaching for your parishioners,' she fumed.

He stormed out of the farmhouse and it took some minutes for Hannah to regain control of her anger. Then she felt remorse. Peter had proved many times in recent years that he had only her welfare at heart. She had never liked his pious streak but she had been unreasonable to lose her temper. Tomorrow she would visit him and apologise.

She shook her head to clear the last of her anger. Yet she remained unaccountably ruffled at her brother's manner. Would it be so terrible if she enjoyed some light-hearted flirtation with Nick? And why did Peter assume that if her friend had any intentions towards her they would be dishonourable? Nick was unattached after all.

What surprised her most was how virulently she had defended her friend, and how fast her heart had beaten at the thought of his visit.

She glanced in the wall mirror. She had lost none of her looks and was still only thirty. Did she really want to spend the rest of her life as a widow? Oswald would never have wanted that.

Fleetingly, she thought of Sam. She had still been mourning Oswald when he had left. There had been a strong attraction between them during the last months he worked for her. Sam had supported her in her determination to prevent Sawle using Loveday land to store his contraband. She could not have succeeded without him. He had risked his life and their fight had formed a bond between them. Yet it had been too soon after Oswald's death for her to open her heart to another, even though she suspected that Sam could become someone very special in her life if she allowed it. But he had left nearly a year ago and there had been no word from him.

She had been a widow for two years. Perhaps it was time to start to live again and reconsider her future.

This was the day that Sam had been dreading. He was on his way to meet his uncle. The vicar had confirmed the lawyer's statement and Sam had been shown the parish register that indisputably listed Catherine and Reginald's wedding. There had been no corrections to the page and the entry was clearly written. Charlie was Lord Eastley's legal heir. With so much at stake, how could Sam consider disputing his nephew's birthright? Yet his heart went out to the boy whom he loved so dearly. It would be like having his own son taken from him to be brought up by strangers. And could he trust his lordship not to corrupt or ruin the lad? Charlie was a plucky, intelligent child but he was only five, and all the good and decent values Sam had instilled in him could so easily be destroyed by anyone intent on manipulating him into his own image. It did not bear contemplation.

At Lord Eastley's request, Charlie was to accompany Sam on his visit. As they entered the long drive of Highcroft Manor, Charlie sat on the saddle in front of his uncle. He was excited at the prospect of visiting his grandfather, but Sam had told him nothing of the family feud or what it could involve. It would be too great a responsibility to lie on such young shoulders.

The Palladian house came into view. It had been modernised in recent years and extended to over thirty rooms. A portico had been added, also a large dome behind the sweeping steps of the main entrance, and symmetrical wings ended in pedimented pavilions. The old stables had been knocked down and rebuilt together with an impressive carriage house. Wild fallow deer roamed its park and an ornate Italian-style covered bridge spanned an ornamental lake on the approach to the house. There was also a gazebo built like a Greek temple on an incline overlooking the river. Highcroft Manor was an impressive sight.

'Is that just one family house?' Charlie said in awe. 'It's bigger than a whole row of tenements in some towns.'

'Lord Eastley is a man of great importance, Charlie.'

'More important than Squire Penwithick and Sir Henry Traherne? Their houses were much smaller.'

'He has a position at court and serves His Majesty's government.'

'So he can cut off people's heads?'

'Only the King can order that and then only in cases of treason.' Sam kept his amusement from his voice. Charlie had an enquiring mind and he was often startled by his questions.

'What is Grandpapa like?'

'You must address him as my lord, Lord Eastley or your lordship.'

'But is he not your father's brother? Would he not be Lord Deighton?' Charlie scratched his newly trimmed hair and his face screwed up with puzzlement.

'His lordship takes his title from lands bequeathed to the family by Charles the Second. You need not trouble yourself over the whys and wherefores of the title at the moment. Your grandfather may appear stern, but you must be respectful at all times.'

'So I do not call him Grandpapa?' Sam asked in some puzzlement.

'It must be Lord Eastley.'

'It will not be like having a grandpapa at all. Do neither of my grand-fathers like me? Your father is my grandpapa too, is he not? I have never met him either.'

The sadness in his nephew's voice impaled Sam's heart. 'My father is cross with me, not you.' He hoped to lessen the boy's sense of rejection.

'Then I do not want to meet him,' Charlie declared. 'I've got you, Pa. I do not need anyone else.'

Sam winced inwardly. He had not found the courage to tell Charlie the truth of his parentage, believing he was too young to understand. He hoped that would not backfire on him. He would do anything to stop his nephew from being hurt.

As they approached the house, a groom appeared, so quickly that it was clear he had been instructed to wait for them. Sam's horse was led away to the stables. Close to, the house was even more prepossessing and Charlie's hand crept into Sam's as they mounted the steps to the entrance. A footman in green and gold livery and a powdered wig awaited them in the hall.

'His lordship is expecting you.' The footman led the way to an ante-room towards the back of the residence.

Charlie craned his neck to stare up at the tall dome above them. Sunbeams slanted through the narrow windows around its perimeter.

'It's like a church,' he whispered. 'Who are all the statues? They have strange eyes.'

There were half a dozen scantily clad Italian marble gods and goddesses. Charlie did not wait for an answer, and pointed to a marble bust of Charles II on a pedestal. 'Is that my grandpapa? He's very ugly.'

'No more questions, Charlie.' Sam breathed deeply to quell the nervous tightening of his stomach.

The footman knocked on a closed door and was bid enter.

'I need a wee.' The boy hopped on one foot.

Sam groaned under his breath. Why did children always have such bad timing? Charlie had relieved himself before leaving the lodgings less than half an hour ago. 'You must wait until after this meeting. Remember your manners and all I told you.'

The footman announced them: 'Captain Deighton and Master Charles Deighton.' He stood aside for them to enter.

Sam squeezed his nephew's hand before releasing it and they walked confidently into the antechamber. Sam had prepared himself for a harsh tirade similar to the one he had received from his father. Instead he found himself shocked at the sight that greeted him. Lord Eastley was seated by a blazing fire with a blanket around his shoulders and another over his legs. The sharp features looked a score of years older than his sixty years.

Sam bowed stiffly and Charlie did the same as he had practised all morning. Sam hid his shock and said, 'Your servant, my lord.'

'I doubt it.' The voice was frail and grouchy. 'You've given me nothing but grief in recent years.'

Lord Eastley eyed Charlie with chilling calculation. 'So this is the boy. Step forward, Charles.'

'My name is Charlie, your lordship,' he declared proudly and with no hint of nervousness.

'Charles is more fitting for my heir. You will henceforth be addressed as Master Charles.' The old man continued to appraise him and added, 'I like not his impudence.'

'Some would see it as a strong spirit,' Sam defended. 'It is something to be prized, not broken.'

'He looks well enough and has the makings of good manners.' His lordship focused his accusing glare upon Sam. 'Tell me why I should not have you flogged and arrested for murdering my son.'

Sam was not surprised by the attack. 'He died in a duel of honour, my lord. He had brought disgrace to my sister.'

'And to me by running off and marrying the baggage.'

'Had you acknowledged the union, your son would still be alive.' Sam refused to be browbeaten by his uncle.

A spasm of pain pinched his lordship's features. Whether it was physical or mental was difficult to discern, but it brought no halt to the old man's venom. 'He defied me in a base and cowardly way. He had no backbone. Not like you. You knew honour must be restored, though it cost me my heir.'

'My father became your heir on your son's death.'

'I will not have his name mentioned in this house.' Lord Eastley recovered the fire in his temper that had caused so much dissension in the family. 'He betrayed me. Stole the woman I loved.'

'If we are to discuss past grievances, they are not a subject for young ears.' Sam put his hand protectively on his nephew's shoulder. 'The boy will wait outside.'

'He stays,' his lordship snapped. 'The time for bickering is past. Until the proof was given to me that the marriage had taken place between my son and your sister, I never believed Reginald had the impudence to defy me. He abandoned her fast enough when I cut off his allowance and they were penniless. He denied the marriage to win back his allowance and took himself off to London. I had him followed to make sure he did not return to her.'

'You profess to have loved my mother, yet you would allow her daughter to be dishonoured.' Sam could no longer control his temper.

'I never expected the girl to hang herself,' his lordship flung back. 'Or you to call my son out. It was some months later I discovered that there was a child. Even then he was nothing to me. Not until I learned I had little time left myself. My heart is not what it was. I did not want the estate to go to your father – at least not without a fight.'

'With respect, where is the honour in that? And you expect me to allow Charlie into your care. To quote your own words, my lord: "not without a fight".' He was aware of Charlie's hand sliding into his during the heated discussion.

'From what I have learned of you, that is as I expected,' Lord Eastley replied. 'Your career in the army was distinguished. You have been mentioned in dispatches more than once. Yet you threw it all away to become the boy's guardian.'

Sam had heard enough. He was not prepared to allow this conversation to continue in Charlie's hearing.

'Wait outside, Charlie. You wanted to relieve yourself. A footman will tend to you. Then wait on the chair in the hall until I fetch you. I need to speak with Lord Eastley alone.'

281

'The boy stays,' his lordship repeated.

'He needs to be relieved. Go on, Charlie.' Sam opened the door and smiled encouragement at his nephew. Charlie looked miserable at the angry exchange and the grandeur of the surroundings. Sam promised him, 'I will not be long. You have done nothing wrong.'

He returned to stand in front of Lord Eastley. His lordship glared at him. 'Even now you defy me.'

'The conversation was not fitting for the boy's ears. He is too young to understand it and it will upset him. There has been enough upheaval in his life.' Sam strove to keep his tone reasonable. 'I believe in family loyalty. Catherine's child deserved better than to live in an orphanage on the charity of the parish. I was made his legal guardian by a magistrate before I took him from the orphanage.'

'Then you changed your name and became little better than a vagabond, taking work where you could find it.'

'I wanted no association with the family who had disowned both Charlie and his mother.' Sam tilted his head and there was a stubborn jut to his jaw. 'I thought it best for Charlie if we both disappeared. That's why I moved from place to place.'

'And damnably hard you were to find,' his lordship grunted. 'When Simmons first sought you out, it was a ruse to get back at Hugo. I wanted the boy to taunt him. His lawyers have been very active in informaing me that no bastard can inherit an entailed estate and title. I knew that, of course. It was amusing how easily Hugo rose to my baiting. Then I discovered the truth. That put a very different light on the matter. The boy is Reginald's legitimate child and my grandson. Highcroft is his birthright. As my heir he will attend the best school and will be taught how to manage his property and tenants.'

Mixed emotions ground through Sam. He was delighted that his nephew would have the social position that was his due. Yet at what cost did all these riches come?

'I rejoice that my sister was truly wed, and also for Charlie's future security. But I am his guardian and I will contest my rights in court. I will not have him manipulated to your vindictive will. He will remain in my charge until his majority and receive a fitting education to prepare him for his responsibilities.'

There was a long silence; the only sound in the room was the old man's laboured breathing. 'My heir will be brought up as I command.' Lord Eastley had lost none of his authority. 'Would you have the boy lose everything because of your pride?'

'I want only what is best for Charlie. Pitching him into a legal battle does not seem to me to be in the best interests of so young a child. I will not condemn him to a loveless household to be used as your pawn.'

His lordship's gaze was sharp and assessing. Sam held it with equal determination.

'I will not live out the year,' Eastley announced.

Sam was too stunned to reply.

The old man nodded, and then coughed until he wheezed and slumped back exhausted in his chair. His voice was more frail but still resolute. 'My grandson has need of a worthy guardian. Since you robbed his father of life, it is only right that you make whatever sacrifice is necessary to ensure the boy comes into his full inheritance. But it will be done under my terms. This is his home. He will reside here unless he is at school. As his guardian you will safeguard his inheritance and ensure that the estate prospers until his majority. You proved in Cornwall that you have that capability. Are you prepared to fight your own father for the boy's rights?'

It was not Charlie his lordship had chosen to manipulate; it was Sam, in punishment for killing Eastley's son. For Charlie's future to be secured, Sam's personal happiness would be forfeited. Every fibre of his pride rebelled. He did not want to be tied to Highcroft Manor for twenty years. Yet did he have a choice?

Chapter Thirty-six

Her brother's words stayed with Hannah when Nicholas Trescoe called that afternoon. At first they made her uncomfortable in his company, which was absurd. Nicholas was a friend and she would not allow Peter's judgement to spoil that relationship. But gradually she relaxed. Nicholas was amusing and charming and there was nothing in his manner that was too familiar or disrespectful. Since much of their conversation focused upon Japhet and the amusing side of his escapades, it was preposterous even to consider that he had any romantic intentions towards her.

'Cornwall is a dull place without Japhet.' Nick grimaced. 'For all his daring I never saw him as the pioneering type. The new colony must be a remarkable country to keep him from his family.'

'His wife and two children are with him. He adores Gwen and his letters speak of making up for the pain she suffered when he was arrested. I think he wants to prove to the world that Gwen's faith in him was justified, and that he married her for love and not for her wealth. That is why he will not return until he has earned a fortune by his own endeavours. He was deeply shamed by his conviction.'

'Of which he was pardoned,' Nick protested. 'He has nothing to prove to anyone.'

His heated defence cut through the last of her reservations against him. Too many people had condemned Japhet without knowing the full story behind his arrest. The King's pardon had exonerated him. Why should Japhet need to validate his worth? It was his self-esteem that drove him, and Japhet never did things by half.

'He needs to prove to himself that he can carry the Loveday name with pride. And I respect him for that. Though I do miss him.' They were standing by the paddock where Japhet's mares grazed. With the offspring she had kept from previous years, another four mares and two colts had been born this year. One of the colts, a dappled grey with a pure white mane and tail, was showing signs of taking after his Arabian father. In the past, she had sold the colts. This one she would keep, and she had named him Mercury after the first horse Japhet had owned.

Sheba, Japhet's favourite Arabian mare, had ambled over to them and was nuzzling Hannah's shoulder. Her coat was showing the first flecks of grey around her muzzle and haunches. Nicholas stroked her head. 'She is still a fine animal, though she is getting on in years.'

'She is fourteen. Japhet told me to sell her, as she is too old to breed. But I could not. I want her to end her days well cared for and loved. I still ride her.'

'Such sentiments will never make a good businesswoman,' Nicholas teased.

'The horses' upkeep is paid for by the tenant who rents the farm Japhet purchased before he wed.'

'Are any of the mares for sale? To build the reputation of a stud farm, the horses have to win races.'

It was a problem that had often worried Hannah. 'They need special training. Mark, my head groom and stockman, exercises them, but he has no experience in training racehorses.'

'I could give him some advice.'

'But why would you want to? And in recent years you have never been in Cornwall for longer than a month or so.'

He considered her words for a long moment, and in that time Hannah found herself holding her breath in anticipation. His offer was the perfect solution. It would also mean she would see more of him. The prospect excited her and made her realise how isolated she had become from old friends.

'It is time my life became more settled,' he finally said. 'I would be interested in buying two or three of the three-year-olds and training them ready for next year's race season. Though I would need somewhere to stable them. Would you agree to me renting the stables and I could work with your head groom to train the others at the same time?'

'That is a big commitment, Nick.' Caution governed her remark. She did not want to build up her hopes at the prospect, only to be disappointed if his restless spirit engaged in another venture elsewhere.

'Do you have so little faith in me that you think I would not honour it?' His stare was fervent as he regarded her. 'Or do you not wish for such an arrangement between us?'

He was teasing her, but she also felt that he was testing her in some way. His eyes now crinkled with amusement and something deeper that sent a shiver of pleasure down her spine. The old spell of his charisma was again taking hold and in defence she became more guarded.

'You place me in an awkward position, Nick. It would be wonderful to have Japhet's horses properly trained, but that would mean you visiting the farm on a daily basis. That is bound to cause gossip of another nature. Your reputation with the ladies will bring my own honour into disrepute.'

'Perhaps you fear that Mr Nankervis will cry off from his attentions.'

'I have no interest in that fop.'

'But he will inherit a vast fortune and land. You would become a grand lady if he asked for your hand.'

'Now you insult my integrity.' She cursed the ease with which he could get under her skin and provoke her. 'I want no marriage of convenience. I married Oswald for love. The farm provides for all the needs of my children and myself. I need no man to support me.'

'How beautiful your eyes are when you lose your temper.' The teasing note was delivered with a husky seduction that had sent countless women's hearts fluttering 'You were always a woman of fire.'

The comments Peter had made earlier again mocked Hannah. Nicholas was a libertine – dare she trust him? She turned away from the paddock and walked back towards the farmhouse. Two of the dairymaids were peering out of the window of the buttery, watching Hannah and her handsome visitor when they should have been making cheese. They shot out of sight at realising their mistress had caught them spying on her.

'Compliments roll off your tongue like melted butter, Nick. How often are they sincere? I know you too well to be impressed by them.'

He overtook her and stopped in front of her to halt her rapid pace. 'There is talk that Nankervis would court you.'

'Last week I dissuaded him from calling upon me. I have no wish to leave the farm and he would never make a farmer. And if you kept your horses here, there would be talk about us. For that reason I must refuse your kind offer.' She resorted to defence as protection against the temptation to accept his plan. It offered so many exciting possibilities and so many pitfalls.

'You did not answer my question,' he said smoothly. 'Are the mares for sale?'

'They could be to the right buyer. You are right. Japhet's horses need to win races for him to establish his reputation as a racehorse breeder.'

'Then will you not trust me as Gwendolyn trusted Japhet?'

'Gwendolyn had been in love with Japhet for years.'

'Though it is ungentlemanly of me to say, you once looked with favour upon me.'

His eyes were again alive with mischief. When she felt her cheeks heat from a blush, her temper flared. 'Oh, you are impossible! I was fourteen.'

He grinned broadly. He had always teased her until she lost her temper, and he had done it again now. He put his hand to his heart and looked theatrically stricken. 'And I never thought then you could be so fickle. Besotted with me one minute, then I go away for a month or so and you give your heart to Oswald Rabson.'

'You were away for two years, and in the mean time I grew up.' Her exasperation increased the fire racing through her blood. 'I was never more than a mild irritation to you, following you and Japhet round like a lost puppy. It is too vexing to recall and you are no gentleman to remind me.'

'You had grown to the most beautiful and spirited woman in those two years. Oswald Rabson was a fortunate man.' His expression sobered. 'I was the fool to think such an exceptional woman would wait for this scapegrace to return. You grew up too quickly, Hannah.'

Her heart did a treacherous somersault and she forced herself to remember that he was a constant tease. He made her feel young and carefree again, and as she held his handsome gaze she could feel the old attraction of this fascinating rogue.

In that moment of weakness he took her hand and raised it to his lips, his voice smooth and seductive as velvet. 'Dare I hope that you will come to look favourably upon me again? I am your most devoted servant.' He turned her hand to press his mouth to her wrist, his eyes dark with passion. 'I needed to know that Nankervis is not important to you. Say you will be mine, Hannah. I have waited a lifetime to find a woman I revere and can love with all my heart.'

Her pulse raced. He was so handsome, and for years in her youth she had dreamed that he would utter such words of devotion.

'Yet you were betrothed to a woman you professed to love and were devastated by her death.'

'That is true. Only now do I realise that I never felt for her the passion I feel for you. I thought you were lost to me.'

'I have been widowed for two years. You have not been in Cornwall in that time.' She continued to test him.

'Were you ready to give your heart before this? Knowing you, I think not. I adore you, Hannah. There is no one to match your spirit and beauty.'

She did not doubt the sincerity in his eyes. 'This is so unexpected, Nicholas. I do not know what to say.'

They had reached the house. He pulled her inside and, after ascertaining that they were alone, swung her round so that her back was against the wall and kissed her with a thoroughness that stole the breath from her body. He drew back, leaving her senses reeling. When she recovered her breath to protest at his forwardness, his grin was unrepentant.

'Your lips do not lie, Hannah. Listen to your heart.'

She wished the organ in question were not beating so uncomfortably fast. His nearness did stir her blood, but then a year ago so had another. A man who had his own destiny to fulfil and whom she had sent away. A man who had returned in her dreams on too many lonely nights to set her heart aching with longing. But Nicholas was no dream. He was real and solid and the answer to her maiden's prayer.

It would be so easy to fall in love with this handsome suitor – and a romantic, idealistic part of her had been in love with him since a girl.

When he would again draw her into his arms she put her hands on his chest and said sternly, 'You were always too ready to steal a kiss from the unwary. I will not be so easily coerced.'

'We were meant for each other, Hannah. We are the same, you and I. There is wildness is our blood.'

'I am the mother of four children, and with all the responsibilities of the farm I have long learned to curb the wildness of my youth.'

'But the right man would rekindle it. Does that not excite you?'

She shook her head slowly, trying to clear her mind of the madness he was weaving. 'This is all happening too fast. The haymaking starts next week. It is the busiest time for me. We are no longer the same people we were all those years ago.'

His smile was bewitching and she lowered her gaze lest she fall under his compelling spell. She moved away, and with the distance between them, sanity returned.

At her frown he plunged on. 'Your pardon. You are right. I saw how Nankervis wanted you and feared to lose you a second time. I was ever impetuous. I am used to seeing what I want and taking it. I go too fast. I meant what I said about teaching your head groom to train the mares. At least allow me to serve you in this manner. There will be no improprieties between us. Like your brother with Gwendolyn, I will prove I am worthy of your devotion. By your leave I would help train the mares and dare to hope to lay siege to your heart.'

They were words that would stir any woman's heart, and Hannah was not unaffected by them. Her spirits lifted at the prospect of being courted by Nicholas. Yet she was not so enamoured that she was blinded by his faults. He would make a captivating and exciting lover, but were those the qualities she wanted in a husband and father to her children? He had a great deal to prove before she opened her heart to his persuasion.

There were few patients awaiting Senara at Trevowan Hard and she dealt with them quickly. She glanced towards Adam's office, where he had spent the morning with Ben Mumford discussing the work to be carried out in the yard while he was occupied at Boscabel with the harvest. The door was shut, and as there was no sign of Mumford directing the men, her husband was obviously still engaged with his overseer. She surveyed the yard, aware how worried Adam was as to its future. The merchantman would be launched a few days before the harvest started and would be ready for her first voyage in another two months. He also planned to sail her to the major south-western ports and invite the merchant adventurers to inspect her. Once the war with France was over, there would be rich trade in the East and the new colony. Such merchants needed to plan ahead to speculate on these riches, and a fast ship brought a higher return for their capital. First, though, a crew had to be found and the cargo stored at Fowey made ready to be loaded. With no further work coming into the yard apart from minor repairs, the finances had become precarious. Throughout the summer tenders for new ships had been scarce. Some of them had to be chased and Adam planned to visit all their old customers and contacts in the autumn.

With her husband occupied and Bridie in the middle of her morning lessons, Senara decided to visit Joshua and Cecily. The wound in Joshua's arm had become infected and he had developed a fever. Dr Yeo had confined him to his bed. Senara had prepared a blood tonic for him this morning after tending her patients and now she returned to her herb room to collect it. Before she entered, a woman in a cloak with the hood pulled low over her face hailed her.

'Mrs Loveday, I have urgent need of your services.' The woman kept her face covered, hiding her identity. The cloak was of good quality and the little of the gown visible beneath was of blue silk.

'How may I help you?

'A young man has spent some time at my establishment in Fowey and he has been taken ill.'

'Why did you not call a physician?' It was obvious that the woman could afford one. 'And you have not told me your name.'

'Mrs Flowerdew. Carlotta Flowerdew. I wished to spare the family embarrassment. My establishment is not one some would have their young gentlemen visit.'

'Is it then, and forgive my indelicacy, Mrs Flowerdew, a bordello?'

The woman held her forthright gaze with a steely glint of defiance. 'I run a gaming house on the outskirts of the port. My customers are the sons of local gentry or naval officers. They enjoy the company of the young women I employ and privacy is afforded to them if they so desire.'

'This young man is then a member of my family?'

'I regret to tell you that he is, Mrs Loveday.'

Senara was dismayed but not surprised. She had already seen the eagerness with which Richard pursued any woman susceptible to looks and charm. At least he had had the sense to frequent a more respectable establishment of this kind, if any of them could be deemed respectable.

'Then I thank you for your discretion. I will come at once. How ill is he?'

'I did not expect you to call upon my establishment personally.' The woman was genuinely shocked. 'Could I not take him some physic that would speed his recovery so that we could get him safely to his home?'

'I wish it was as simple as that, Mrs Flowerdew. Even without examining the young man, I suspect the cause of his indisposition. Is he conscious?'

In her agitation the woman's hood slid back from her hair, revealing thick reddish curls. Although her features were thickly powdered, she wore no more rouge than many a fashionable lady. Her face was pretty and unlined. 'He was delirious and kept vomiting. He has been acting oddly the last few occasions he visited us. But this time he did not seem to know what was going on around him. I thought him ill then and tried to persuade him to return to his home, but he would have none of it. He collapsed within minutes of his arrival. I could not throw him out into the street, not being who he is.'

'How long has he been like this?' Senara controlled a rush of fear that Richard had taken too much of the opiates and they had sent him into a coma. She should have been stricter with him and insisted that he allow her to treat him immediately. She had trusted him to keep to his word. Obviously he was more addicted to the drugs than she had realised.

'Two nights. At first I thought he was drunk and needed to sleep it off.' As Senara had not judged Mrs Flowerdew for her profession, the older woman was less nervous in her company and her tone was confiding. 'He scared me last night when he started shaking and sweating, and then he became so violent my servant locked him in the room for his own safety. This morning he is raving and demanding to be set free. From the sound of it he has smashed every piece of furniture in the room. He is like a man possessed, Mrs Loveday.'

'You will be compensated for any damage he has caused.'

'That was not my reason for approaching you. The young bloods who visit my establishment are often drunk and fights break out. It is a hazard I accept. He is young and has faced much in the navy, being wounded as he was. He can be very charming. My women are very fond of him. I knew something was terribly wrong when he began groaning this morning. When I ventured into the room, he was rolling in agony on the floor. I thought he was dying, he was shaking so badly.' She hesitated and her expression was again anxious as she went on: 'I do not want him to die on my premises and the family would not wish for such a scandal. It is why I came to you myself.'

'You have been extremely kind, Mrs Flowerdew. My family is in your debt. The young man's mother would be distressed to learn where he has spent his time. I will come at once, but I think my husband should also accompany me. Especially if the young man is violent. It would be best if we can get him in a closed coach to Boscabel. We will speak to my husband now.'

Mrs Flowerdew drew her hood more closely across her face as they entered Adam's office. Ben Mumford stood up. Her husband's desk was full of papers, his interview with his overseer far from over.

'I am sorry to disturb you, my dear,' Senara said. 'But I have news that cannot wait.'

Ben Mumford left them and Adam looked askance at the presence of Mrs Flowerdew. Without fuss Senara explained the situation. Anger darkened his handsome features.

'The young idiot! Yet why did you not mention his problem before?'

'He promised he would cut back on the medication and asked me to wait until after the Lammas Fair, when he would come to Boscabel and I could treat him. We would devise an excuse for him to be absent from Trevowan for some time. With so much else happening, he broke his word and disappeared. I intended to tell you when he came back.'

'You are not at fault,' Adam returned. His body was held stiffly as he contained his anger at his stepbrother's weakness and stupidity. 'I have seen men succumb to the evils of opium. Recovery must come from their wish to be free of the addiction, or temptation will always take hold. The cure is not pleasant, as you seem to be aware.'

He addressed Mrs Flowerdew. 'We are grateful to you for all you have done. It cannot have been easy for you to come here. I do not like the idea of my wife attending Mr Allbright in your establishment.'

'There is no other choice,' Senara interrupted. 'I am not offended at their profession and I will not be in danger.'

'Indeed you will not, because I shall be with you,' he snapped. 'I knew there was something not right with Richard. I assumed it was because of his experiences of battle. They can change a man.'

He turned to the woman. 'How did you get here? I assume you did not walk.'

'My closed coach is the other side of the wood and I walked the remaining distance. It would have caused too much speculation. The coach is at your service if you have no objection to returning with me to Fowey. And it will be placed at your disposal if you wish to convey your stepbrother to your home.'

Much of the stiffness left Adam's figure. 'You are indeed generous, Mrs Flowerdew. Your offer is most welcome.'

Half an hour later they found Richard unconscious on the floor of the bedroom in the bordello. His clothes were saturated in sweat and his body twitched uncontrollably. Adam lifted him on to the bed for Senara to examine. His pulse was erratic and he flung his arms about wildly, catching her shoulder with his fist.

'We should get him to Boscabel as soon as possible. I doubt that Dr Yeo would have dealt with such a case, but if there is any chance that he has, I would welcome his advice.'

Adam stared helplessly at his stepbrother, his anger gone at the sight of his suffering. 'You saved my life when everyone despaired that I would die, Senara. I will summon Dr Yeo, but I trust you to bring Richard through this, my love.'

'I will give him a sedative that will enable him to travel. His condition must be more stable before he can be moved. If he is taken off the opiates all at once his body could go into shock. The dose needs to be reduced gradually.'

'Shall I send for Dr Yeo?' Mrs Flowerdew had remained within the room. 'I pay him well to attend to the welfare of my ladies. Ours is a hazardous life and some have been attacked by their clients.'

Adam nodded. 'We are greatly in your debt, Mrs Flowerdew.'

She waved his gratitude aside. 'I have the reputation of this place to consider. Discretion is valued by my customers. You have treated me with respect and I value that a great deal. No word of what has passed here will reach the outside world.'

Chapter Thirty-seven

It was not until they were in the closed coach lent to them by Mrs Flowerdew that Adam revealed his exasperation towards his wife. Richard lay across the opposite seat, sedated and sleeping. Dr Yeo had attended him and supported Senara in her proposed treatment. He agreed to call on the patient every three days at Boscabel to check his progress.

'Why did you not tell me of his addiction?'

'I have seen little of you since I learned of it. You rarely return from the yard until it is dark, and then you are closeted with Eli Rudge and Billy Brown discussing the estate. Richard promised me that after the fair he would come here of his own accord so that I could treat him. By then the hunt for Sawle had intensified and you had enough worries without me adding to them.'

'I am never too busy to take care of the needs of my family. You should have told me.' Adam was rarely angry with her, and the fact that he showed his irritation now revealed the weight of the burdens he carried.

'Then I apologise. But I was not to know that Richard would break his word.'

Adam rubbed his temple, clearly perturbed, then laid his head back against the seat of the coach and closed his eyes. 'I had hoped that with Sawle behind bars our luck would change. The harvest starts next week, and with so much rain this summer I fear it will be a poor one. And I am still without a buyer for the cutter at the yard. Boscabel is mortgaged to the hilt and I already have a loan to repay to Cousin Thomas. Our finances have never been so bad.'

'*Pegasus* should have reached New South Wales by now, and it will not be long before *Pride of the Sea* sails. The cutter will sell eventually. She is a fast, reliable vessel. I doubt the harvest will be a complete disaster. You have two fields of hay that will save on food costs for the livestock, and there will be enough corn for our use, with surplus to sell at the kiddley for our workers' families. Have we not grown vegetables enough in the garden plot not only to feed us but also to sell some at market? No one is going to starve. Next year will be a profitable one and should free us from debt.'

He clasped her hand. 'You are always so optimistic.'

'I can never see the point of worrying about something that might never happen. It seems to be that if you fear the worst, you attract disaster to you. Think only of success and success smiles on you. It certainly makes the waiting less stressful.'

'There's no arguing with your philosophy at times. But what of Richard?' He frowned across at his stepbrother. 'This will break Amelia's heart if she learns of it. It is an addiction I've heard that never fully leaves the afflicted.'

'If a man has strong willpower he can overcome it. The first weeks are the worst. We can wean the body from the craving, but if the mind is weak it will seek the solace it has now lost. I hope for Amelia's sake that Richard has both a strong constitution and willpower. He must be cured before he returns to his ship. It will not be easy.'

'How long before he gets over the shaking and sweating?'

'Two to three weeks and the worst should be over, but it will leave him weak, and ideally he will need watching for some time to ensure that he does not succumb to temptation.'

'We cannot keep his presence at Boscabel secret for so long.'

'I shall tend him through the harvest. He will then be strong enough to return to Trevowan. I dislike deceit, but if we are to spare Amelia, some tale must be concocted.'

'Of course.' Adam continued to frown. 'As soon as Richard is able, he must write a letter saying that he is staying with friends for another week or so. I will say Rudge collected it from the posthouse with other family mail.'

'That will at least stop her worrying,' Senara agreed. 'In the mean time, Dr Yeo will write to the Admiralty declaring him unfit to return to his ship. I know of a woman in Warleggan who will nurse him and take no nonsense or fall for his trickery. She worked for many years in an asylum for the insane and knows how these drugs can distort a decent man's perception of reality. For a gold sovereign she will also keep her own counsel about his illness.'

Richard was taken into an attic bedroom where his ranting would not disturb the children and tied to the bed for his own safety. Senara ordered Eli Rudge to drive a cart to Warleggan hamlet to fetch Betsy Nepean. The woman arrived within the hour and stood at the bottom of the bed surveying her patient, who was beginning to stir. She was wide as a wine vat, with arms thick and strong as a mastiff's neck. Her round face topped four chins that wobbled when she spoke, and she had a thick greying moustache.

'He be just a slip of a lad. He won't give me no trouble, Mrs Loveday,' Betsy lisped through toothless gums. 'I'll have two quarts of ale a day on top of my fee if that be all the same to 'ee. It dinna affect my work and eases me aches and pains.' The floorboards creaked as she lumbered over to the sturdy trestle bed that had been placed in a corner and tested it for comfort. She nodded in satisfaction. ''Ee can lock the door on the outside if 'ee dinna trust me to keep him confined.'

'I know your work, Betsy. That will not be necessary,' Senara replied. 'I shall check on him every hour during the day and every three hours through the first nights. He must be given plenty of liquids while he is sweating so much, and you are to allow no one into the room but myself, my husband, and Dr Yeo when he calls. Until we are certain he will not become violent or try to escape from the room, he will be kept bound. You are to summon me at once if his condition deteriorates.'

Betsy laid her meaty fingers upon Richard's sweating brow. There was gentleness in her actions, and when she brushed his wet hair from his forehead it was with the tenderness of a mother tending her own child. Senara also knew that there was steel in those hands. Richard had a rough time ahead of him until the drug was completely out of his body. Betsy would take no nonsense from her patient, yet she would also treat him with compassion and kindness.

'It do break my heart to see so fine a man brought so low,' Betsy said softly. 'He'll be conscious shortly, then all hell will break loose. He'll fight every waking moment to be free of his bonds, and use cunning and guile. His charm will have no power over what I know be best for him, Mrs Loveday. You may have no fear on that account.'

'I trust you implicitly, Betsy, and I am sure I will learn from your skills as a nurse.'

'There's not much anyone can teach you. Your grandmother had a knowledge that far outweighed my own as a wise woman.'

'I have little experience of the sickness that affects the mind when it is obsessed with destroying all that is good in a man,' Senara replied.

Betsy waddled to the padded armchair that had been placed by the bed and folded her arms across her vast chest. She closed her eyes, appearing to doze, but Senara knew that she remained alert to every sound and movement.

As predicted, within half an hour Richard became violent and abusive, and the next few days tested both Senara and Betsy's skills and patience to the limit.

Richard Allbright was not the only reluctant convalescent in the Loveday family. Though his neck and arm wounds were not life-threatening, Joshua had lost a great deal of blood and his recovery was slow. He could not shake off the fatigue that dogged his return to health. Peter had insisted on taking on his father's parish duties as well as his own. It was the first time that Joshua had been ill, and he was a poor patient, frustration at his lack of strength making him quick-tempered. Even the mild-mannered Cecily was sorely tested to remain calm at his waspish ill humour. After a petty quarrel when Joshua had refused to rest and was wandering around the rectory orchard collecting the apple wind-falls and demanding to make cider, Sophia Quinton called unexpect-edly.

When Cecily opened the door to her, Sophia pushed past her without waiting for an invitation to enter.

'I thought you were in Falmouth,' Cecily snapped.

'Where is the dear invalid?' Sophia cooed dramatically. 'How very courageous he was in bringing that arch-criminal to justice. It is the talk of the county. I had to come at once to pay my respects to St John and of course the hero of the hour. My heart bleeds at his indisposi-tion. I have brought him bottles of the finest claret and brandy that he adores. They will revitalise his blood, and I also have his favourite comfits to restore his spirits.'

'You presume much to know my husband's preferences.' Cecily was fast losing control of her temper at the way this woman had barged into her home. Her old friend was heavily rouged and her crimson gown was inappropriately low-cut for an afternoon visit.

Sophia fixed an ingratiating smile on her hostess. 'Cecily, you take the oddest notions. Naturally I asked St John what would please Joshua most. Where is our hero?'

'Will you stop calling him a hero? Anyone would think he captured the smuggler alone.' Cecily had been proud of her husband's role that day, yet was also dismayed that he had risked his life. But the way Sophia was praising and gushing over his exploits grated on her nerves.

'But he was so fearless, so dashing. How can you think he is not a hero?' Sophia peered through the open doors of the downstairs rooms in her search for Joshua.

'I did not say that he was not brave,' Cecily fumed. 'But it is no less than I expected of him. He is embarrassed by such extravagant praise.'

'All men like flattery. Really, Cecily, you take that valiant man too much for granted.'

The fragile hold on her anger was abandoned. Ever since Sophia had come back into their lives, Cecily had kept a check on her contempt for the woman. With each meeting she had witnessed Sophia's blatant pursuit of her husband's attention, and on several occasions had come close to confronting her. She had resisted as they had always been in public.

'How dare you come here and tell me how I treat my husband! How you have the gall to show your face at all and claim a false friendship these past months is beyond decency. For the sake of your daughter and family harmony I have kept my silence.' She stepped closer, scorn lacing every syllable. 'I know your whore's tricks. I will not have you pursuing my husband in my own home. You betrayed me once. You will not do so again. You are not welcome here.'

'I-I do not understand,' Sophia blustered. 'You are my dearest, oldest friend. I was concerned for your husband. Is that not natural?'

'Yes, you are concerned about my husband. Concerned that he will now have nothing to do with you after you seduced him into your bed. Do you think I am so stupid I did not know what happened all those years ago? Joshua could not hide his guilt from me. I knew a woman was involved, and when I learned it was you, the betrayal was twice as sharp. It proved what a self-centred harpy you are. You care for nothing but your own gratification.'

'Cecily, my dear, this is all fabrication on your part.' Sophia covered her face with her fingers.

Unconcerned by this show of distress, Cecily continued: 'Do not compound your sin by calling me a liar. Get out of my home and do not grace these walls again.'

'This is foolish.' Sophia lowered her hands. She had paled beneath her rouge. 'You are my dearest friend. We are family now.'

'No friend would act as you did. You did not trouble to hide your interest in Joshua, even though it was obvious that he wanted none of you. You were not even discreet. He is a respected clergyman. Your conduct jeopardised his living.'

Sophia recovered her composure and her lips twisted with spite. 'If Joshua turned to me, then there was clearly something lacking in your marriage.'

Cecily took a purposeful pace forward, and Sophia hastily side-stepped to find herself wedged against the wall between a table and a chair. 'Any man can succumb to the temptations of the flesh when they are so freely offered. He has loved me for forty years and has been loyal and devoted except for that one error of judgement. Look to your own life before you accuse another of what is lacking. We all reap what we sow. It was not just my husband you pursued, but any available man. As you do to others so will be done to you. But your disgraceful conduct will end now. I will not have my family held up to ridicule.'

'You would threaten me. How the worm has turned in her vengeance!' Sophia jeered.

'It is not revenge I want. In your vanity you cannot see that I pity you. Your conduct has been commented on by acquaintances and mocked. Have you no thought for your daughter's embarrassment at your behaviour? It is causing a rift between her and her husband. St John does not want you constantly visiting Trevowan, any more than I welcome you here.'

'Does he not?' Sophia spat. 'I shall see what Felicity says about that. She is mistress of Trevowan now.' She stared over Cecily's shoulder, her expression starkly malicious. 'Joshua, what have you to say? Your wife forbids me to visit you.'

'Are you surprised? I will not have her feelings disregarded. I too must ask you to leave.'

Sophia's eyes filled with tears and her lower lip trembled. 'Well, really, I expected better from a gentleman.'

As she flounced out of the rectory, Cecily released a ragged breath. Joshua stood in the kitchen doorway, his shoulders slumped and his expression sorrowful. His injured arm was in a sling fashioned from a black silk square. 'I never suspected that you knew. I wronged you and crave your pardon. I have ever been your devoted and loving servant, most beloved of women.'

'I forgave you long ago, husband. And though in my Christian heart I have fought to forgive her, it was not easy. I will not, however, suffer her company.'

He drew her into his arms and kissed her with a passion that had never died between them. 'I am the most fortunate of men and there was nothing lacking in our marriage. My flesh was weak in a moment of madness.'

Cecily smoothed the furrowed lines from his brow. 'We will not mention it again. I should not have lost my temper, but the woman was insufferable. She needed to be put in her place.' She stood on tiptoe to kiss his lips. 'You are my hero. You always have been. You risked your life to bring Sawle to justice.'

★   ★   ★

On her return to Trevowan, Sophia could not contain her outrage at the way she had been treated.

'In all my born days I have never been so insulted,' she declared when she burst into Felicity's dressing room and found her reclining on a day bed.

She had been in a deep sleep and awoke with a start. 'Mama, what is amiss?'

'The Lovedays are not all I expected them to be. Out of the kindness of my heart for the husband of an old friend, I took a few comforts to the Reverend Mr Loveday. His wife was quite the termagant and told me I was not welcome.'

'Oh, Mama, what have you been up to?' Felicity groaned. 'It has been remarked upon how often you visit the rectory.'

'To call upon an old friend.'

'You have called on the days when it is common knowledge that Aunt Cecily visits the elderly or infirm of the parish. St John has mentioned that his uncle finds it awkward when you call unannounced. He has many duties to perform.'

'I never intended . . .'

'Mama, you make many demands upon Uncle Joshua's company when the family call. If I did not know better, I would say that you were flirting with him.'

'Is that how politeness is viewed these days?' Sophia picked up the afternoon gown that had been laid out for her daughter to change into and smoothed the lace on the short puffed sleeves.

'You know very well that such conduct distresses me. Mama, this is very difficult for me to say, but I must ask you not to visit us unless by St John's invitation. You have been away less than a fortnight this time. You have your own friends in Falmouth. I do not want to have to face a recurrence of some of your past exploits.'

'You are a cruel, ungrateful wretch to turn your own mother from your home.' Sophia threw the afternoon gown on the floor in a crumpled heap. 'I suppose that harridan Elspeth and the prudish Amelia have also whined in your ear.'

'Elspeth would confront you to your face if she had anything to say. Amelia did mention that some of her friends preferred that you did not accompany her when you stayed here and she called upon them.'

'I will not stay where I am not wanted. My maid can pack my trunks and I will leave this very day.'

Felicity sighed, too weary to deal with her mother's histrionics. 'It is too late to reach Falmouth by nightfall. The house will be shut up and damp. I am not asking you to leave at once.'

'No, I shall go. I am not wanted here. My own daughter has turned her back on me again.' Sophia marched from the dressing room, slamming the door behind her.

Amelia was coming out of her bedroom, and shot a disapproving look at their guest.

'You need not look down your haughty nose at me, madam,' Sophia ranted. 'My daughter informs me that your high-and-mighty friends and family do not wish for my company. Am I too loud? Too immodest in my speech? Let me tell you, no one here is perfect. Especially your son. He has tumbled half a dozen of the local wenches that I have noticed. He has also been sniffing round your governess. And where pray has he been since the Lammas Fair? Not with an old friend as he will no doubt tell you. He will be in some bordello, drinking and debauching.'

'Richard would never . . . He is too young.'

'I know his type. He has a roving eye for the women. They are never too young.'

When Sophia had left, Amelia clung to the banister rail for support. It had been her greatest dread that Richard would have the wayward morals of his father. His disappearance without word now confirmed those fears. His father had often gone missing for several days and nights and returned dishevelled and smelling of drink and cheap perfume. It had been her greatest shame.

If the harvesting had not already begun and St John been busy with estate work, she would have asked him to search for Richard. Unfortunately that was not possible, and the wait for his return would be torture. She still had some power over her son. His allowance would be cut until he came of age. That might curb his debauchery. She would not be so shamed again.

During the next ten days Amelia was not the only one in torment. Richard suffered greatly as his body craved the opiates it had been denied. In that time he lost a great deal of weight. He was able to keep down little of the food given to him, but Betsy was patient and persistent. The smell of vomit, sweat and defecation made Senara's eyes sting when she entered the room. Even scented herbs and dried flowers placed in bowls could not counteract it. While he continued to rant and scream abuse at every opportunity as his pain-racked body combated the withdrawal of the opiates, the window was kept closed. The haymaking had started, and by the end of the following week Richard seemed over the worst. Though the room remained locked, he was no longer bound. Twice Betsy had overpowered him when he made an attempt to escape.

Senara was relieved to find him sitting in a chair by the window when she brought a nourishing broth for his lunch. His complexion was pale, his cheekbones painfully prominent, and purple smudges ringed his eyes. His hand trembled when he tried to eat and Senara fed him with the spoon. He did not look at her, still angry at the treatment he had received. With only half the bowl consumed, he turned his head away and clamped his lips shut.

'You need to build up your strength, Richard. In a few more days you could return to Trevowan. Betsy will accompany you until you are fully recovered.'

'Do I then replace one prison with another?'

'You were confined for your own safety and welfare. The slightest lapse now will undo all we have achieved.'

'My body is still cramped with pain, yet you give me nothing.' He scowled, obviously feeling he had been victimised.

Senara remained unruffled. 'I know it has been difficult for you. You have done so well. You are now weaned off the opiates and are past the worst. You must be strong. Your mother is worried by your absence. It is difficult to see her anguish and not tell her the truth.'

'What will you tell her?' He held his head in his hands now and stared at the floor.

'I have no liking for lying to a member of our family. The letter you wrote last week has eased her mind. To explain your illness it may be best to say that you contacted a fever whilst at your friend's, and unable to shake the last of its effects you sought my advice before returning home. Your horse is here. You will be able to ride as far as Trevowan in a few days. It may not even be necessary for Betsy to accompany you. That will make it easier for Amelia to accept your story.'

'Mama will not rest until she has every detail of my absence.' He groaned.

'Your tongue has been slick enough over other matters during your leave. You will think of something.'

He glared at her, his manner resentful. Senara did not let it trouble her. 'I do not expect your gratitude. I would merely spare your mother from the worst of the excesses that you have indulged in. She deserves that much respect from you.'

'The sooner I get back to my ship, the better. I can be my own man again there. You all treat me as though I am a child.'

'Which is exactly how you are behaving.' His ordeal had not been

302

easy and it roused her compassion. 'There is so much that is good in you, Richard. Be worthy of your father's name, Edward Loveday's faith in you, and your mother's love and devotion. But the main person you will bring dishonour to if you do not heed the warning this summer has given you is yourself.'

Chapter Thirty-eight

Word spread of Japhet Loveday's success in arresting the escaped convicts. He was summoned to the governor, who received him in the presence of several officers, Grosvenor and Haughton included.

'You have served us all well, Mr Loveday,' John Hunter declared. He looked older and more haggard since Japhet had last met him. The strain of his office was telling on his health. 'The transportees still outnumber the settlers. They cannot be allowed to escape and terrorise our colonists. You are an example to us all. A man must defend his land and family from insurgents.'

'It is the duty of the New South Wales Corps to maintain order,' snarled a bull-necked major.

'And you do an excellent job,' the governor pacified. 'You cannot be everywhere. There must be more liaisons between the settlers and your men, Major. As was proved by Lieutenant Grosvenor being present at Trewenna Place.'

In his report to the governor, Japhet had not mentioned the earlier confrontation between himself and Grosvenor, or the lieutenant's conduct towards Gwendolyn. He did not believe in making unnecessary enemies, but even after Grosvenor's apology he still had his reservations about the officer's loyalty. He would remain wary until the man's actions proved he could trust him.

John Hunter pulled himself up to his full height. 'That is not the reason why you have been summoned here. There has been contention between the corps and Mr Loveday over his handling of imported goods. It had been previously agreed that he would trade with the investors in his cousin's partnership. When Mr Adam Loveday's ship *Pegasus* returned to England, news of the profits of her voyage was greeted with excitement. To the extent that we now have three ships moored in Sydney Cove whose captains have been ordered to deal only with Mr Loveday. I suspect that in the future more will arrive with the same request.'

'We have the right to sell all imported goods.' Two officers stepped forward, their manner threatening towards Japhet.

He held his ground. 'My dealings are with three ships out of the five I saw moored in that convoy. There is profit enough for us all.'

'The new settlers will not deal with any system they see as corrupt.' Captain Haughton spoke out. At his side were Lieutenant Hope and Captain Pyke, who had been friends of Japhet since his arrival in the colony. By protecting Japhet's interests, Haughton ensured his own profits were secured. It was enough to satisfy Japhet of his loyalty. To his surprise, Lieutenant Grosvenor also came to stand beside the officers who supported him.

Grosvenor cleared his throat. 'Mr Loveday has the welfare and the future of this country at heart. It will rise in greatness as more settlers flock here. There is scope for all of us if we have integrity and the vision to become rich. The army has been my life and I have no family in England. When my army days are over I intend to live out my days here and see this colony flourish and grow in prosperity.'

'A population of the dregs of England's gaols will never amount to anything,' the major sneered.

'Yes it will.' Japhet took up the anthem. 'Once their sentence is served, the convicts are given a second chance to make something of their lives. They have survived the prison hulks, the transportation and hard labour. They are capable of building Utopia on these shores.'

The dissenting officers muttered sullenly. John Hunter rapped on his desk to silence them. 'Mr Loveday will be granted the right to trade with any ship that requests his services. Any move by the militia to suppress or hinder his activities will be dealt with in the severest manner and the officers sent home in disgrace.'

'Thank you, Governor.' Japhet inclined his head in acknowledgement.

Haughton, Pyke and Hope shook his hand. 'Congratulations. Law and order will prevail here.'

Grosvenor addressed him. 'Loveday, I am indebted to you in many ways. You deserve the success you have achieved. The corruption amongst the militia brings dishonour to us all.'

Japhet nodded graciously and took his hand. Grosvenor would face the censure of his fellow officers by supporting him. He conceded that the man's inexperience of command had led him to follow the leadership of the strongest. His fight against the convicts had revealed the true strength of his character and he had emerged a better man.

Once they left the governor's residence, the officers outside of Japhet's circle retreated to their barracks. Haughton puffed out his chest. As Japhet's partner he stood to gain the most from this interview.

Captain Pyke rubbed his chin and sighed. 'I should have invested some of my wages in you, Loveday, rather than squandering them in the tavern.'

'That's true.' Lieutenant Hope grimaced.

'There is nothing to stop you forming a partnership,' Japhet advised. 'There is much to invest in. The towns are expanding. Build a decent hotel or houses for rent or sale. In a year or so such property will be in demand as more settlers who do not intend to work the land arrive.'

'I would not know where to start,' Pyke groaned.

'Visit me at Trewenna Place and we can discuss it,' Japhet suggested. 'I need another shop in Sydney as well as Parramatta. I've a mind to build a street of them and sell the others to new merchants. Or join me as an investor and we can share the profits.'

'Loveday Road. How very grand,' Haughton laughed. 'How many more schemes have you?'

'Enough to fulfil my dream. In truth it will happen faster if I do not have to put all the capital into it myself.'

'Will these shops and houses be wooden or built from brick?' asked Grosvenor.

'Either. Though a brick-built hotel will command a higher price and draw in a better class of customer. But bricks are expensive unless they can be made locally.'

'All this talk is making me thirsty,' Haughton interrupted. 'Loveday, I'll arrange for men to be placed at your disposal to bring the cargo ashore.'

'I'll borrow some wagons to convey the goods to Parramatta,' Japhet replied absently, his head now filled with new ideas to build his fortune.

Haughton, Pyke and Hope left him, but Grosvenor lingered. Japhet held out his hand to the lieutenant. 'Thank you for your support today. It is appreciated.'

'Are you serious about the street of shops and hotels, Loveday?'

'It could be built in a year. Think of the profit in selling them. Though I suppose they will have to be wooden frames with wattle and daub. It is a pity, for brick buildings would truly make a fortune.'

'What would you say if I told you I've found a brick-maker who had his own yard in London until he fell into debt through gambling?' Grosvenor said with a grin. 'He has one year left of his sentence. He would build a kiln on the site and knows a bricklayer who can teach others the trade. You could have your hotel, Mr Loveday. But I'd want a share. I've saved most of my pay in the five years I've been stationed here. It's enough to build half a dozen houses on Loveday Road. Once they are sold, I'd have enough money to invest in a road built and named in my honour.'

'I had never intended Loveday Road as its name,' Japhet laughed. 'But I would like to speak to this brick-maker.'

As he rode back to Trewenna, his chest tightened at all he had agreed to. Grosvenor had spoken with other investors and they wanted Japhet behind their building plans. He had protested at first. Then one of the men had stated, 'You have the governor on your side and a section of the officers will support you. By trouncing the convicts when they attacked your land you have shown them that you are not a man to be crossed. They respect that and will give us no trouble. Also your family is a respected name in England and investors there already know you. It brings credibility to our scheme when we sell the property to new settlers.'

Fortune had blessed him in this land, but he missed his family with each passing season. Every day when he returned to Trewenna Place, although Gwen was always bright and cheerful, he was aware of the lines of tiredness in her face. Although she never complained, he knew she found it hard to cope with the excessive heat of the summers. Guilt smote him. He had never thought that love for a woman could consume him like this. He adored Gwen and wanted to give her the life of luxury she deserved. She had been born to a life of ease, not one of servitude, and it was time he honoured his promise to her. He had ploughed back into this country every penny he had earned and he was certain that the plans he had for the next year would mean he could return to England with his head held high. No one would be able to accuse him of living on his wife's income. How sweet that would feel, and what better revenge upon the enemies who had lied and cheated to bring him down and send him to the far ends of the world. He would return triumphant and richer than his wildest dreams.

Another three days showed a vast improvement in Richard's health, and his manner was also more agreeable. Dr Yeo had examined him and declared him fit to travel, and had stated that he had already sent a letter to the Admiralty declaring that his wound had become infected and it would be some weeks before he was able to return to duty. It would give him time to rebuild his strength.

Senara entered the bedchamber to find Richard fully dressed and standing by the window. He was watching the migrant workers, who

307

had finished the harvest, moving on to the next farm. He still looked far from well, but his shoulders were no longer hunched in pain or his body shaking and sweating.

'Dr Yeo says I can leave for Trevowan,' he announced.

'I have done all I can for you. You have a strong constitution. Can I trust you to keep your promise that you will never take those drugs again?'

He nodded. 'I do not know what I shall say to Mama. I have been a beast to her since my return. I was so angry at the world, but I should never have taken it out on her.'

'Amelia has a forgiving heart, especially where you are concerned.' She considered him for several moments before adding, 'Betsy can be dismissed if you keep your word to me, Richard.'

'I am ashamed that I betrayed your trust. But I did not know what I was doing. I was obsessed with the need to obtain more of the opiates. The craving was like a dark demon lurking forever in my mind. I could think of nothing else. I never want to experience that again.'

'It turned you from a gentleman to a knave.' Adam, his clothes dusty from working in the hayfield, entered the room to regard his step-brother.

Shamefaced, Richard bowed his head. 'I crave your pardon, the pardon of both of you, for the trouble I have caused.'

'You were not entirely to blame,' Adam said more kindly at his show of contrition. 'That ship's surgeon was incompetent to give you such a powerful drug. I have seen it happen too often when they have many casualties to deal with and the ship is far from port.'

'I cannot express how relieved I am to be free of that insidious succubus that drained all decency and willpower from my soul . . .' He wiped a tear from his cheek. 'Senara, you have saved my sanity. I am forever your devoted servant. I cannot thank you enough.'

'I need no thanks. Just remember how easy it was to fall beneath its spell and how difficult to rid the body of its evil.' He had lost so much weight and he looked so young and fragile that she could not resist putting her arm around his shoulder and kissing his cheek. After suffering so many days of pain and terror, he needed understanding and encouragement. 'It took a great deal of courage to beat its hold upon you. I am very proud of you, Richard.'

'You were fortunate that when you were taken ill it was in Mrs Flowerdew's establishment,' Adam remonstrated. 'Many such places would have left you to die, then robbed and stripped you before tossing your body into the gutter.'

Richard nodded and swallowed several times as he fought against the emotion that threatened to overwhelm him. 'I got into bad company.'

Adam inclined his head to his wife, who knew that he intended to talk to Richard more severely.

'It is good to have the old Richard back. You are a fine man.' She touched his cheek and smiled encouragement before she left the room.

'Now we will talk, Richard,' Adam clipped out. 'Your conduct has been unbecoming of a gentleman. It will not be tolerated or allowed to continue.'

'I have promised not to take the drug. It was that which made me short-tempered with Mama, which I greatly regret. I was rude, surly and unappreciative of all your family has done for me.'

'It was not only the drug that was to blame and caused us concern. I am not one to preach morals to a young man, but you are earning an unsavoury reputation. I expect more discretion when you seek the companionship of women. It is never wise to press your attentions upon servants of the household, especially a governess. Felicity dismissed the lady in question when she discovered your interest in her. She was deemed of unsuitable character to teach Charlotte and Rowena. St John is furious that he has the inconvenience of engaging another tutor and insists it will be a man this time. There have also been reports of other women. As I said, you must be more discreet.'

'Yes, sir.' Richard refused to hold Adam's stare.

'Look at me when I am talking to you,' he snapped. 'If you want us to trust you, you have to earn that right again. St John will be informed of what has happened here. He has the right to know as you reside under his roof, and he will be the judge of whether your future conduct is in need of greater supervision.'

Rebellion sparked in Richard's eyes. Adam would also have resented curtailment of his pleasure at that age, and added, 'You are not forbidden to visit Mrs Flowerdew's establishment, but I ask that you have consideration of your mother's sensibilities and our family name. Is that too much to expect from you?'

'No, sir,' he readily agreed.

'Very well, I hope that this will be the end of this regrettable episode. I will accompany you to Trevowan and speak with my brother whilst you are reunited with your mother. Dr Yeo says you should be fit enough to return to naval duty in a month. Now that the harvest is in, there will be more entertainments for you to enjoy, as well as hunting, shooting and the races at Truro.'

★   ★   ★

309

There was an emotional greeting from Amelia when they arrived at Trevowan. Adam refused to be drawn into Richard's excuses for his absence and closeted himself with St John for an hour.

'Let us hope that Richard has learned his lesson,' St John said when Adam had finished explaining. 'I have problems enough without playing nursemaid to him. There's a new tutor to engage, and a man will cost more than a governess. The harvest was not as I had hoped. It was a poor crop compared to last year.'

'It was the same at Boscabel. There will be little surplus to sell.'

'There was also the loss of the calves thanks to Sawle's vendetta. I have been harder hit financially than you.' St John scowled.

'He at least will cause no further suffering or hardship to others. His trial is at the next assizes.'

'His death will be a cause for celebration for many.' St John regarded his twin archly. 'You could become a free-trader and use the cutter for a run or two. That should solve your financial problems. You could always claim she was undergoing sea trials if a revenue ship intercepts her.'

'It has crossed my mind.' Adam gave a wry laugh. 'But I know how fast those revenue ships are and I have too much invested in the cutter to have her confiscated. It is just a question of time before there is a customer for her, and in the mean time she is collateral for a loan. It will be a lean winter for all of us, and with no new orders on the books I may have to lay off half the shipwrights.'

'It's as bad as that, is it?' St John for once was sympathetic. 'You have your investment in the voyages to New South Wales. That new merchantman has sailed to Falmouth.'

'And it will be at least eighteen months before she returns. All my money is tied up in her. But I will not allow the yard to go under. Not whilst there is breath in my body.'

Chapter Thirty-nine

The trial of Harry Sawle brought the crowds flocking to Bodmin. Adam and St John had ridden there the previous day in time to see the ceremonial arrival of the judge accompanied by a troop of the local militia. The mood of the town was festive as they anticipated the trial and the smuggler's hanging. The mayor in his chain of office and other important officials and dignitaries greeted the judge in his scarlet cloak and long curled and powdered wig.

St John shuddered as they passed the high grey walls of the prison where he had spent some weeks before his own trial. Now Harry Sawle would know how it felt to be incarcerated, living in a dank cell and every hour in fear of losing one's life. There would be no acquittal for the smuggler and no last-minute witness forthcoming to win him a reprieve: too many people had been outraged by his abduction of his nephew and the shooting of Joshua Loveday. Those incidents alone were enough to hang him, without the years of terror he had inflicted upon the district.

St John slept badly. The town was overflowing and the twins had been forced to share an inn room in a less salubrious quarter than they would have wished. He was haunted by the memories of his own trial, which he had thought long behind him. Though he had been arrested for the killing of Thadeous Lanyon, few doubted that Sawle was the true murderer. Finally justice would be served.

Yet when he entered the old Franciscan refectory, with its vaulted ceiling and stained-glass windows, that served as the assize court, his gut churned at the memories it evoked. Sawle's was the first trial of the day. The room was full of self-important court officers. Bewigged barristers paraded with judicial pomposity and solemnity as they addressed their clerks. The jury in their Sunday clothes had been drawn from the merchants and respectable citizens of the county. They were tense and pale, some no doubt anxious that reprisals could be made against them.

Sawle had associates who would murder their own father for a shilling.

The twins squeezed on to a bench in the crammed public gallery. There was not a good word to be heard about Sawle's character, and some of his more lurid exploits were repeated with gusto. Only three people remained quiet, and they were seated at the back in the darkest corner. Clem and Mark Sawle were grim-faced, while Sal sobbed silently into her handkerchief.

A hush fell over the gathering as a gavel was banged loudly and the judge took his place on the bench. Then jeers erupted as Harry Sawle was led into the dock. He dragged the leg where his wound had not healed properly, and his hands and feet were manacled. His figure was bent and he shuffled like an old man. That was not the only change in him. His scarred face was battered and beaten; his eye was cut and his lip torn and bleeding. No change of clothes had been sent in for him and his jacket and waistcoat were ripped and greasy with grime.

St John chuckled under his breath. 'Not such a braggart now, is he? It's true what they say about bullies; they are craven when there is no one to do their dirty work for them. Sawle met his match in prison and from the looks of it got the beating he has long deserved. There's many a family member been forced to work for him who has ended in gaol. When a prisoner has lost everything he cherishes in life, fear no longer has a hold over him. Sawle lost his power when the gaol's doors closed behind him, and without his henchmen to protect him, he would be sport for any with a grudge.'

The list of crimes levied against Sawle took several minutes to be read out. After every one was stated there were further outbreaks of abuse directed at the prisoner. Throughout, not a flicker of emotion was displayed on Harry Sawle's face.

The prosecution directed a long diatribe at the jury about the evils of smuggling and the crimes committed by the prisoner. Again Sawle could have been carved in marble and did not react.

When the defence lawyer rose to call his first witness, his voice was drowned by boos and catcalls.

'I will have order.' The judge banged his gavel with great energy. 'Another outburst like that and the court will be cleared.'

There were angry murmurings but the protests subsided. Of the first three witnesses who were called, not one appeared, and sniggers broke out.

'Bain't no one prepared to speak for 'ee, Sawle. Can 'ee feel the rope tightening about thy neck?' shouted a man from the public gallery.

Sawle did not respond, but he had begun to sweat profusely. Two more names were called and again no one appeared. The judge ground out with impatience: 'We will adjourn for lunch, and in that time the honourable lawyer for the defence will ensure that witnesses are indeed present and that no further of the court's time is wasted.'

'Bain't no one gonna speak for him,' jeered another voice from the public gallery. The man stood up and waved a fist at the prisoner. 'He be guilty as hell. What you gotta say for yerself, Sawle?'

Harry Sawle turned his cold, malignant stare upon his accuser. The man paled and sat down with undue haste. Then Sawle allowed his gaze to sweep over all those in the public gallery, his bleeding lips twisting into a sneer and revealing several missing teeth. He drew himself to his full height as though drawing energy from the man's fear. Yet still he did not speak.

'Got nothing to say, have 'ee, Sawle? Guilty on all charges,' another cried out, but he remained seated and it was difficult to discern who had spoken amongst the press of people.

After the adjournment, Sawle was led back to the dock to further hoots of derision.

'How the mighty has fallen,' St John said with relish.

The defence lawyer shuffled his papers in embarrassment. Even his glare was contemptuous as it rested upon his client. From the outset he had not been happy defending so notorious a criminal. 'There are no witnesses for the defence, your honour.'

'Then the jury may retire and consider their verdict.'

The foreman of the jury rose to his feet. 'There be no need for consideration. My fellow jurors came to a verdict during the adjournment. No further evidence has been given. Harry Sawle is guilty as charged on all counts.'

The judged turned to face the jury. 'Are you indeed unanimous?'

They all nodded.

The judge reached for a square of black cloth and placed it over his periwig. With that simple but theatrical action he had pronounced the death sentence upon the smuggler.

'Harry Sawle, you will be returned to your cell. Before God and this King's court you have been found guilty of the most heinous crimes of kidnap, grievous assault, smuggling, fencing of stolen goods and murder. At noon tomorrow you will be hanged by the neck until you are dead and your body displayed in a gibbet at the crossroads on the moor as a warning to others.'

Amid the cheers following the sentence, Sal Sawle wept silently on her eldest son's shoulder. 'The shame of it. How can I face the people of Penruan again? The Sawle name be forever tainted by that devil.'

'You have nothing to be ashamed of. Neither has Mark nor myself,' Clem said gruffly. 'Harry knew the noose awaited him if he continued to flout the law. He deserved no mercy for what he did to Mark and Zach. The world will be a better place without him.'

'Take me home,' Sal pleaded. 'I could'na bear to be in this place tomorrow at noon.'

'Mark will take you home. I will stay to the end. I want to know that our life is now free of that devil and all the pain he has caused us.'

'Will they let me see him?' Sal asked.

'Not now he's been condemned. He bain't worth your tears, Ma.' Mark put his arm around her shoulders.

'I brought him into the world. How did I fail him?'

'Reuban's blood were always thickest in him,' Clem comforted. 'Mark had your goodness. And I suppose I must have that too. Harry and Pa's cruelty always sickened me.'

Sal regarded Clem and said heavily, 'You bain't Reuban's son. Your pa were a soldier and I were three months with child when I wed Reuban Sawle. Mark be the image of my pa; a gentler man you could never meet, and I give praise to the Lord every day for that blessing. Does that shock you, my son? I bain't much of a mother. I paid for my sin a hundred times being wed to that monster.'

Clem did not show surprise. 'I've always known I weren't Reuban's. He used to call you names when he beat you when I were a child. I hated him.'

Sal put a hand on each of her sons' chests. 'You be good boys. Sons I be proud of. You will restore the good name of Sawle, and for that I shall be thankful.'

By the next morning the gallows had been built on the edge of Bodmin Moor, the crossbeam rising high above the crowd and the noose swinging like a pendulum in the wind. The overcast sky was heavy with the smell of smoke from the fires of a travelling fair and the people who had camped overnight. Spectators eager for a good place had been there since first light and hundreds more had gathered throughout the morning. A festive air prevailed. Pamphleteers sold the penny broadsheet purporting to be Harry Sawle's confession of his misdeeds, elaborating on the murders of the men who had been found washed up on beaches with their throats cut, and the various terrors he had inflicted on the community with his brutality. No crime was too dark for him to be involved in and related in lurid detail.

314

Apprentices escaped the vigilance of their masters to jeer and mock the elderly or afflicted. Beggars sat on boulders displaying scabrous or twisted limbs as they scratched at their lice-laden clothes and whined for alms from the townspeople filing down from the hill on to the moor. Piemen and orange-sellers did a profitable trade as the morning advanced and the crowd grew restless. An enterprising brewer rolled a barrel of ale to the front of the gallows and was instantly surrounded by a horde brandishing cups and jugs. A balladeer and a troupe of tumblers entertained the bystanders, passing caps round to collect their pennies. Cut-purses and pickpockets glided like spectres through the throng, robbing the unwary. Women huddled together gossiping about Sawle's womanising, forcing himself on victims, for no decent woman would look into his scarred face and not be revolted. Old scandals were revived and mulled over.

Adam and St John were aware of the speculative glances thrown in their direction, and Meriel's name and St John's trial inevitably were resurrected. St John had spent the morning in a tavern drinking heavily and it took all Adam's persuasion to restrain him from starting a fight.

'Still I bear the stigma of my association with that family,' St John fumed, and raised his silver hip flask to his mouth.

'It will all blow over in a week or so and some new scandal will occupy them. Brawling or getting drunk will only feed the gossip,' Adam reasoned.

St John scowled. 'I should have killed the cur to avenge Father's death.'

'It would have been too easy a death for Sawle. You saw the state of him at the trial. He was no longer cock of the roost. His presence had lost its power. He was a broken man, suffering as he made many suffer. There is revenge in that.'

The twins, being taller than most men, had a good view of the gallows. A bell tolled within the prison and a black flag was hoisted. Then a cheer was raised from the town as a tumbrel appeared with Harry Sawle standing on its boards. A dozen militia accompanied it.

Sawle appeared indifferent to the catcalls and abuse being shouted. He stared straight ahead, his arms tied behind his back, body braced against the jolting of the cart on the uneven track. It halted beneath the noose. Sawle raised his eyes to the rope. Then, as though emerging from the torpors of a drug, he shook his head and tried to butt the hooded hangman who had stepped on to the cart behind him. A guard slammed his musket into Sawle's gut and he doubled over. The hangman grabbed his hair and hauled him upright.

315

'Repent of your sins!' A preacher stood by the cart's wheel, his open Bible in his hands.

Sawle hawked and spat in his face. 'I repent of nothing. My name will never be forgotten. I were master of this moor. And there be not one person here who bain't supped brandy or tea from my illicit cargoes. May it choke you in the future.'

The noose was put around his neck. And then the smuggler began to struggle in earnest. A whip cracked down on the rump of the horse pulling the cart, and it shot forward with a start, leaving Sawle's body dangling and jerking in mid-air.

Death did not come quickly. With each laboured breath Sawle uttered blood-curdling curses on his executioners and all who had betrayed him. It was many minutes before the cries were silenced and the body ceased to twitch.

There was a brief moment of silence as the noose continued to swing from the impetus of the corpse's death throes. It was as though the spectators did not believe that they had finally been delivered from Sawle's evil. Then as all movement stilled on the gallows a cry of relief exploded from the gathering. Men flung their caps into the air and women grabbed a partner to swing them in an impromptu dance as someone played a jig on a mouth organ. There was no reverence or respect for the dead; just celebration that they were finally freed from a tyranny that had blighted their lives.

Chapter Forty

A month passed and the Lovedays enjoyed a time of relative tranquillity. Yet it did not bring peace of mind. *Pride of the Sea* had sailed with a full cargo to New South Wales. While loading at Falmouth an interest had been shown in her, for her size made her ideal for longer voyages, but until she proved her speed and capability customers were reluctant to risk commissioning another of her class. The work on the cutter was finished, but there was still no buyer for her. The only work for the yard was for two fishing sloops to have their hulls scraped in the dry dock. The order books had never been so sparse.

Adam feared he had overcome Sawle only to face ruin as the yard floundered. He had failed his father's trust in him. Edward Loveday had broken with family tradition that the eldest son inherited both the yard and the estate of Trevowan. By making Adam heir to the yard he had caused the rift between the twins and many of the problems the family had faced. Adam prized his father's trust dearly. To have broken it mocked everything he believed honourable. Somehow he had to get more orders. Before the winter storms came he planned a voyage to as many ports as possible in the cutter to attract new customers. He was to leave the following week.

The day before he was due to sail, a brigantine with her top spars and quarterdeck shot away limped up the Fowey inlet with a shot-peppered single bowsprit sail. A French privateer had attacked the vessel, and the Looe-based captain and owner was desperate for her repairs to begin at once. Grateful that as yet no shipwrights had been dismissed, Adam delayed his voyage to draw up plans and costing for the repairs. He was working late one afternoon and it was almost dark when he heard a commotion by the wooden dockside. Someone was hailing the yard.

Leaving Mumford to deal with the matter, Adam lit a candle as he continued to calculate the size and shape of the timber to be cut for the work on the brigantine. The damage to the lower decks had been more extensive than he had first thought and it would take eight to ten weeks to get her seaworthy.

Outside the office Adam heard Mumford state, 'I'll inform Cap'n Loveday you be here.'

'I'll announce myself.'

The door banged open and a large silhouette filled the open portal. Adam pushed back his chair from his desk, startled by the brusqueness of the man's entrance. With his mind full of the calculations he had been making, he did not immediately recognise his visitor.

'I thought my arrival might surprise you, Loveday.' The bearded man lumbered to the chair by the hearth and threw himself down on it.

Adam recovered his wits and stared at the Falmouth smuggler he had visited several months ago. 'Captain Marsh! This is indeed unexpected. How may I be of service to you?'

'By quoting a reasonable price for that cutter lying idle in your yard. With my health improved and Sawle out of the way, I've a mind to take over his runs. Those revenue cutters of yours have been patrolling east of Plymouth. I'll be landing my cargo on the north coast. I should get in a few trips before they are back in those waters. And if she is as fast as you say, I'll give the Frenchies a run for their money and trade with Spain.'

The unforeseen turn of events stunned Adam. 'I thought you were also short of cash. I told you the cost of the cutter. You'll not find another ship to match her in size and speed for that price.'

'I've got a partner who came into a windfall some weeks ago. Cuthbert Freake be putting up the money from the bounty paid for Sawle's arrest. And since my sons bain't found work elsewhere, they be eager to return to the sea and what we knows best. Seems like we'll all be benefiting from that cur's demise.'

'I cannot improve on the price I quoted. You know she is worth the money to take on the revenue cutters.'

'You drive a hard bargain, Loveday. I accept your price. Is she ready to sail now?'

'She is. When do you want delivery?'

'Tonight. Tomorrow. Yesterday.' Marsh laughed. 'I were never meant to be a landlubber. My son is outside with a chest containing half the cost. The rest will be paid when the crew arrive in two days. I don't want my connection with her known in Falmouth. We will sail the same night to Guernsey.'

'What about a name? The revenue had not settled on one.'

Marsh rubbed his beard and there was an ironic twinkle in his eye. 'Oh, I think *Revenge* will do very nicely. I had my share of rivalry with Sawle, and twice his men set upon mine and stole my cargo. It be fitting that the price on his head helped pay for her.'

Delighted though Adam was at the sale, it had not solved his problem of gaining further orders for the yard. Had he acted too rashly? Should he have kept to his decision to visit other ports? When he discussed his concern with Senara, she was confident that their luck had changed.

'The sale of the cutter proves that you reap what you sow. Who could have predicted that Freake and Marsh would become partners? Through you saving Freake's life he was instrumental in Sawle being captured. The reward on Sawle's head provided the means for Marsh to recover the losses inflicted on him and for both men to make a new future for themselves. It would not surprise me if even more good came out of Sawle being brought to justice. Many people are grateful for the freedom from his tyranny.'

Adam was not so optimistic. The sale of the cutter had freed him from his immediate financial burdens and he now hoped that the performance of *Revenge*, if she were fast enough to outrun French privateers, would attract new orders. As usual Senara was proved right in her philosophy. He was astounded when a week later a letter arrived from a lawyer in Dartmouth requesting that a contract be drawn up for the building of a merchant ship the same as *Pride of the Sea*, to be completed in a year. A quarter of the price of the vessel would be paid into Adam's bank on signing of the contract, another quarter on completion of her hull, another quarter when she was launched before the masts and fitments were added, and the rest on completion. No individual customer's name was given; only that of a company – Dartmouth Associates. It was not a name Adam was familiar with and it appeared that cost was not an issue. All correspondence and dealings were to pass through the Dartmouth lawyer.

It was too much of a godsend for him to enquire into the mystery of the owner, and he surmised that it must be one of the customers he had visited earlier in the year. As long as they paid on time, the work would progress as normal. His own lawyers were notified of the terms and conditions and the dates stipulated for the payments to be made. Work would start immediately the first payment was received, which meant that none of the shipwrights or carpenters would be laid off over the winter. Notification from Adam's bank that the money had been paid arrived in three days, and a letter from the lawyer notified him that the merchantman was to be named *Good Fortune*.

'Good fortune indeed,' Adam observed to Ben Mumford. The massive tree trunk for the keel had been carefully selected and drawn into place by the yard's horses, the shipwrights were already at work shaping the base, and the first of the ribs were being cut and planed. 'Whoever has commissioned her has changed the fortune of this yard and I trust they will be similarly blessed in their new venture.'

'Does it not worry you that you do not know the customer's identity?' Ben looked uneasy. 'What if they are another like Sawle?'

'The merchantman will sail the high seas. She would be too slow and cumbersome for free-trading. It has secured the yard's finances. That is enough. The customer will reveal themselves in time. They have saved the shipwrights from a lean winter. Are you not grateful for that?'

'Aye, Cap'n, but I don't like mysteries. They usually spell trouble.'

To mark the change in their fortunes, Adam planned a celebration meal at Boscabel for all the family. In two weeks Richard was to return to duty, another occasion to be feasted. With both Richard and Joshua restored to full health, the family were in high spirits. They dined in the old hall, warmed by a roaring fire. As they sipped their mulled wine, the wind outside blew the falling leaves across the lawns and meadows in russet and gold swathes. The children all ate in the nursery, but Bridie, concerned for Michael, who was teething and had a cold, checked on him frequently.

When she returned for the third time, Peter looked anxiously at his wife. Senara smiled at them both. 'You fret too much. All babies get colds when they are teething.'

'I know I worry too much, but your little ones were crawling at his age. He still seems so small.'

'All children are different. Michael is a happy, bright, contented child,' Hannah reassured her. 'Florence did not crawl at all and at a year she just picked herself up and took her first steps.'

'Michael is nearly a year old.'

'He will walk soon enough,' Cecily replied. 'Then he will be into every mischief imaginable.'

'The seasons are turning,' Elspeth remarked. 'I propose a toast to a good winter of hunting.'

'I will drink to a speedy resolution of our war with France.' Amelia gazed worriedly at her son. 'It takes those who are precious to us far from their homes.'

'That upstart Bonaparte is gaining power by the day,' Joshua declared. 'Our heroic Admiral Lord Nelson may well have trounced his navy at the Battle of the Nile, but the French army are far from cowed or beaten. They are still in Egypt and Italy.'

'Let us not mar this day with talk of war,' Felicity gasped. 'There are too many wounded veterans begging in the streets.' She had picked at her food and was heavily pregnant with her child, which was due in a week or so.

'Each one of them is a hero,' Adam proclaimed. 'There is no shame in fighting and giving your all for your country.'

'But there is no glory either for the poor wounded veterans.' Amelia shuddered. 'The streets are full of those blinded or with limbs missing. Your naval days are behind you, Adam. Please, let us change the subject. My dear brave boy has suffered for his country.'

'And as an officer he will be rewarded for his bravery,' Adam reminded her. 'What tales you will have to tell your children and grandchildren, Richard. Mine are pale by comparison. And you are to be considered for promotion to lieutenant when you return to Plymouth. I will help you all I can with the questions they will put to you. It is a rigorous test. Your must be adept at all the skills of seamanship and navigation. It is an honour to be chosen so young. You should be very proud of him, Amelia.'

'We all are,' Senara replied. She was pleased with the change in Richard's behaviour in recent weeks. He drank only moderately and had escorted his mother on all her visits to her friends. Although his roving eye lingered on any pretty maid or female acquaintance, at least he was more circumspect in his interest. There were evenings when he made excuses to spend the night in Fowey with friends. Amelia was not entirely happy with the arrangement, but no one else judged him, for it was the way of most young men.

Hannah had been more vivacious than usual throughout the meal. When the women adjourned to the winter parlour and Bridie again excused herself, she went with her to check that her own children had not become unruly. She could hear Joel's high-pitched voice egging Luke on as they played a noisy game of pirates.

Felicity leaned on Amelia's arm, walking slowly as she cradled her swollen stomach.

'The last few weeks are the worst,' Cecily observed to Senara. 'I carried Peter for almost ten months. I thought he would never be born. Unlike Hannah, who came before her time.'

'Hannah looks radiant and happy. It is time she put her mourning aside and enjoyed life,' Senara said to Cecily.

She had expected Cecily to agree; instead she looked displeased. 'Nick

Trescoe spends too much time at the farm. Supposedly he is training the horses for next year's races. I fear he is turning Hannah's head.'

'What is wrong with that? She has been a widow for two years.' Elspeth joined them and they slowed their pace. The older woman was leaning heavily on her cane, but she would never admit that her leg was paining her.

'Can you honestly see Nicholas settling down to life on a farm?' Cecily said crossly. 'A new venture will appeal to him and he will be off seeking his fortune elsewhere. I would hate to see Hannah hurt.'

'Yet it is wonderful to see her so happy. Is that not important?' Senara replied.

Elspeth was more forceful. 'The farm is a huge responsibility. She cannot be expected to deal with it and the care of Japhet's horses alone.'

'She is aware of Mr Trescoe's nature,' Senara added. 'He has taken some of the burden from her.'

'When did any of our family let their head rule their heart?' Cecily sighed. 'He is too like Japhet, and Hannah idolises him; she never saw his faults. A leopard cannot change his spots. Nick is a born woman-iser.'

'And so was Japhet,' Senara reminded her. 'Do you think that he will break Gwen's heart?'

'Japhet paid for his wildness in a way that brought pain and suffering to us all. He was never all bad; Gwendolyn's love redeemed him.'

Senara raised a brow and said lightly, 'As his mother, you would of course not be biased.'

Cecily chewed her lip. 'I know my son's faults. But I would never question his loyalty. Gwen understands him.'

'And you would accord Hannah less discernment. If anyone can keep a husband under rein, it would be her.'

'But at what cost?' Cecily, who rarely had a bad word for anyone, was clearly distressed. 'That is what I fear. How can I not worry for her? She is too independent and will not listen to me. Nothing would please me more than to see the responsibility of the farm taken from her shoulders and her happily married – but to the right man who will not break her heart.'

'Mr Trescoe was at the farm when I called in the week,' Elspeth observed. 'He was very attentive to the children and had worked hard with the horses. They are in excellent condition and showing great promise. There was no mistaking the adoration in his eyes when he gazed at Hannah. Is he not what Hannah needs at this moment?'

'Nicholas is a charming rogue, I give him that,' Cecily replied. 'I hope

322

then that if he captures Hannah's affection he proves a worthy husband. I thought she should have given Mr Nankervis more of a chance. He was steadfast, wealthy and a man of position.'

'Of one thing you can be sure,' Senara said with a smile. 'If Hannah remarries, it will be for love, not for wealth and position.'

When they entered the winter parlour, Amelia was fussing over Felicity, who had slumped on a chaise-longue away from the fire. Amelia was waving a fan over the younger woman and holding her smelling salts to her nose.

Immediately Senara was concerned. 'How careless of me not to notice that you are unwell. Shall I have the day bed brought in for you to lie upon? Perhaps a restorative would be in order? I have some freshly prepared.'

'Some restorative would be of benefit,' Felicity answered, and then grimaced as she moved her body to be more comfortable in the chair. 'I slept badly and felt a little faint with the heat, and the goose we had for lunch seems to have disagreed with me.'

She cried out and her hands whitened on the arm of the chair. 'I was wrong to blame the goose. The child is starting to come. It is too early.'

'You must not fret. Michael was premature. He thrives,' Bridie reassured her.

'We must get you upstairs. You cannot drive back to Trevowan.' Senara took charge, ordering the servants to fetch the birthing stool from the storeroom and prepare the chamber as she helped Felicity to her feet. Another pain gripped the pregnant woman as they reached the foot of the stairs, and she clung to the banisters for support.

Elspeth had informed the men, and St John appeared in the hall. Hearing Felicity's groan of pain, he picked her up and carried her to the chamber, where a maid was making up the bed and another lighting the fire.

Senara gestured for him to place his wife in a chair. Another pain seized Felicity and her face was dewed with sweat. 'Leave us now. We must get your wife out of her clothes. This baby is impatient to be born.'

'I shall summon Dr Yeo in case his services are needed. Felicity must have every care.' Only Senara's sharp ears heard him add under his breath, 'This time the boy will live.'

She did not take offence that her skills were in question. Adam and St John's mother had died in childbirth and Meriel had borne St John a stillborn son. He would take no chances. It was his aside that troubled her. Throughout the pregnancy St John had referred to the child as a son. It was tempting fate and she hoped he would not be disappointed. A healthy child was what was important, not its sex. But with the estate entailed, only a son could inherit, and that was the passion that governed her brother-in-law's words.

Chapter Forty-one

Although childbirth could be hazardous, Felicity was in the prime of her childbearing years and had the best care in attendance upon her. Hannah returned to the farm confident that there would be no problems with the confinement. A birth was always a good omen for new beginnings, and she felt that the family's problems were behind them. Elspeth had travelled with her, declaring that she wanted to see Japhet's foals as she had not visited the farm all week.

It was years since Hannah had felt so carefree. The farm was running efficiently, and Toby and Lillith Keswick had proved their reliability. Mark needed no supervision with the livestock, and he had doubled the milk deliveries and was still back at the farm by mid-morning. He had also followed all Nicholas Trescoe's advice in training the two- and three-year-old horses and had worked with him to get the younger ones used to the bridle and saddle. Nick visited the farm most days, and she saw his horse in the paddock now.

'I see Trescoe is here again.' Elspeth sounded disapproving. 'I thought on a Sunday he would be with his family.'

'He enjoys working with the horses.'

'It is not good for your reputation that he is here so often,' Elspeth tutted. 'I admit he seems to know what he is doing, but you have Mark Sawle to work with them. Perhaps you should make Sawle head groom and employ another to do his farm duties. Japhet will be proud of his mares and their foals, but they create a lot of work and responsibility.'

'I have been considering that. Gwen was generous in her allowance for the care of the horses, and Mark has a natural talent with them. It would be a shame to waste it. Even so, the expense must be justified.'

'And Trescoe? Does he charge for his work here?'

'It is done in exchange for stabling the two mares he bought and is training for himself.'

'It gives him an excuse to visit every day. Many are beginning to speculate about the two of you. Cecily is even hinting at the prospect of a match.'

Hannah checked a groan. She halted the farm wagon outside the house and waited for the children to jump out and run inside to change out of their best clothes. She did not drive the horse to the stable, as Mark would use the wagon to take Elspeth back to Trevowan. Instead she climbed down and held out a hand to help her aunt to the ground before replying. 'Nick is a friend. A good friend.'

'What man puts himself to so much trouble if there is not more than friendship involved?' Elspeth moved towards the paddock and drew some diced cone sugar from her pocket as the horses approached the fence.

'He needs to stable his horses somewhere. This is the perfect solution.' Hannah defended Nick, but it had been troubling her that he called so often and how much she enjoyed his company.

'His father's estate has adequate stables, Hannah. This charade fools no one.' Elspeth regarded her sternly. 'The family have not objected because he is seen as a worthy suitor. Though to my mind his escapades in the past leave much to be desired. You need someone reliable who is prepared to work all hours as a farmer for Davey to reap the benefits. Your father has already dissuaded Peter once from confronting Trescoe as to his intentions. Your brother is not a patient man. He fears Trescoe is toying with your affection.'

Hannah leaned against the fence, unable to meet Elspeth's challenging stare. 'The fault is not with Nick but with me.'

'What do you mean by that remark?'

Elspeth would be like a terrier with a bone until Hannah answered her truthfully, but how could she if she did not know what she wanted from a relationship with Nick? He made her feel carefree and young again. He also made her feel vibrant and alive and aware of her needs as a passionate woman.

'Out with it, Hannah. Is Peter right in his fears?' Elspeth snapped. The sharpness of her voice startled the foal who had been licking her hand, and it backed away only to be replaced by another seeking more sugar.

Hannah gripped her hands tightly together. 'Nick has asked me to marry him, but I wanted more time before giving him an answer.'

'Then you do not love him?'

'I care for him passionately,' she defended hotly. 'He has shown me that I do not want to spend the rest of my life alone. I had forgotten how much I used to laugh, and work feels more like play when I am with him. He is good with the children and does not mind the rigours of farm life.'

'But do you love him? Enough to forgive his restless nature or his womanising if it occurs in the future? Enough to forsake all others? For nothing less than that will make you happy.'

Hannah did not answer and absently rubbed the nose of a foal that had thrust its muzzle against her shoulder.

'Your silence speaks volumes, Niece. You must be honest with him and not keep him waiting.' Elspeth dusted the sugar crumbs from her fingers and fixed the young woman with a stare that was loaded with warning. 'He is a good man in many ways, but is he the right man?'

Hannah found herself unable to answer, and Elspeth nodded sagely and hobbled back to the wagon. 'Fetch young Sawle to take me home. I will not insult you by staying to chaperone you in Trescoe's company. You more than most women know what is right.'

Hannah sent Davey to inform Mark, and herself went to change into a more serviceable gown for the chores still to be done that day. Her aunt was right: her heart already knew the answer she must give Nick. She would speak with him now.

He was in the stables, stripped to his breeches and shirtsleeves as he curried a mare's coat with a brush in each hand. The long, sweeping movements showed the strength of his shoulder and back muscles. The bay's coat shone from his work and Hannah leaned against the side of the stall to watch him. His brown hair flopped forward over his brow, giving him a rakishly handsome air.

When he had finished getting the tangles from the mare's tail, he said, 'Do we both pass your inspection, ma'am?'

She laughed, but there was a catch to its sound and he looked at her sharply. Putting the grooming brushes aside, he stepped closer to her.

'Such a serious expression on so lovely a woman. What has displeased you?'

'It is not a question of displeasure.' She paused, her gaze searching his face.

His forefinger tilted her chin and his eyes sobered. 'Whatever you have on your mind you had better say now; it will not improve with the waiting.'

Had he guessed her intention? She had never been good at hiding her emotions. 'I cannot marry you, Nick. It would not be right. I love you dearly, but as a very special friend, or a brother.'

'That is more than most marriages have. Are we not good together?' His voice was husky and coercing. 'I adore you. I would never make you unhappy.'

She dragged her regard from his compelling stare; there was too much temptation in its sultry promise. 'Can you truly see yourself bound to this farm, forsaking so many pleasures? It would stifle your joy of life. I have already sensed a restlessness about you. The farm and training the horses will never be enough. I will never be enough. I am not a woman who can share the man she loves; neither could I curtail the free spirit that calls you to seek other places, other adventures. That is what makes you so exciting.'

For some moments he stared down at the dust on his boots. When he lifted his gaze, his smile was irrepressible. 'But that life has no meaning without you.'

'You say that now, but what of one year, or five years' time. The race meetings will call you and you will hanker for another more exciting world. My life is here.'

'It was a wonderful dream, you and I.'

'An unrealistic dream.'

Reluctantly he nodded. 'You will not reconsider?'

She answered softly, not trusting her voice to stay firm. 'You will always have a special place in my heart, Nick, but not as a husband. There is no reason why you should not stable your mares on your father's estate. You have taught Mark a great deal about exercising the horses correctly, but when Japhet returns it is for him to train them if he wishes them to race.'

'I will take the mares with me this afternoon. They show great promise and will win many races. Japhet's reputation as a horse breeder is assured.' He touched a lock of her hair that had fallen to her shoulder and his eyes were tender as he bent closer.

She did not resist his kiss. The sweetness of his lips kindled a fire of longing that took all her willpower to hold in check. Her hands rested on his chest and he drew back.

'Something for me to remember you by,' he said with a grin. 'And whoever wins your love will be the most fortunate of men.'

'Goodbye, Nick.'

She walked rapidly into the house, ignoring the calls of the children as she headed straight for the solitude of her room. Had she made the biggest mistake of her life?

Five hours later St John was allowed back into the chamber and a beaming Felicity kissed the brow of the baby, who was crying lustily.

'He has good lungs,' St John said by way of greeting.

Felicity's smile did not falter. 'Husband, come greet your new daughter. Is she not beautiful? So small and delicate but perfectly healthy.'

Somehow he managed to say the right things and agreed that the child was to be named Thea, but inwardly St John fumed. He could not get away quickly enough. He ran down the stairs, and when Adam came to congratulate him in the hall, he pushed past him.

'She's given me a damned girl. Am I not already plagued with a household full of women?'

'Felicity is young and healthy. Your next child will be a boy.' Adam was shocked at his twin's reaction. 'We will drink to the baby's health.'

'That is all right for you to say. You have two sons. I do not intend to work all my life to blithely hand Trevowan over to young Rafe.' He shouted for a servant to bring his greatcoat. 'Keep your drink. I am going to get drunk and it will not be to wet the baby's head.'

'Where are you going?' Richard appeared, his face bright with interest.

'Anywhere there is good drink and gaming to be had.' He snatched his greatcoat from the hands of the servant and stormed from the room.

Richard ran after him. 'I'll come too.'

Joshua regarded Adam. 'You should go with them.'

'Nothing I say or do will make any difference. It will probably make the situation worse. He will return tomorrow with a sore head and hopefully his purse will not be too much lighter. It is Richard I am concerned for. I would not have him getting into bad company.'

'The lad needs to sow a few wild oats. He returns to naval duty soon.' Joshua had been told of Richard's addiction. 'We have to trust him. Once away from home, every temptation will be waiting for him. We must pray the lad has learned his lesson. Your twin too. His love of gaming is no less an addiction than young Richard's craving for opiates.'

In the next month life returned to normal on the farm. The first bite of winter was in the air and plans were being formed for Christmas. Diplomatically, no one in the family mentioned Nick's departure from the farm with his horses. With the shorter days there was much to occupy Hannah, but always there was a sense of loss and of incompleteness. To overcome her feelings she decided to have a barn dance and hog roast for the family. It would be a way to show her appreciation for all the support and help they had given her since Oswald's death. It would also be a pleasant diversion as the days shortened in the month before Christmas.

The idea was greeted with enthusiasm by the family, and everyone offered to contribute some delicacy to the feast. There were still two days of cooking to be completed, and Hannah had been up since first light to ensure that the last of the pies and cakes were prepared and baked. The kitchen had become hot and stuffy, and she stood by the open door drinking a cooling cup of buttermilk. It was almost midday. The sky was clear and the sun was bright, but the first frost that had whitened the trees and meadows still lingered in the shaded parts of the fields where the sun failed to reach. Luke was sliding on an icy puddle when he suddenly gave a whoop of joy and ran off down the track. Hannah had come out of the buttery and turned a puzzled stare in the direction her son had taken. It was early in the day for even Elspeth to visit. A solitary rider in a tall hat and greatcoat was silhouetted against the bare branches of the oaks. It was not until a smaller figure leapt to the ground from the front of the saddle and ran towards Luke that Hannah dared to hope that she was not imagining the scene before her.

'Luke, Luke! It's me!' the boy shouted as he rushed towards his friend.

Hannah could not drag her stare from the rider. She felt as though the air had been knocked from her lungs and she gripped her hands together when she realised that they were shaking. How foolish to feel nervous. But she did. Her throat dried and a knot of anticipation corded her stomach. She did not move until he towered above her, his horse snorting in the cold, its breath forming clouds around its muzzle.

'Good morning, Hannah.'

His voice jolted her back to reality. This was no apparition. Sam had returned. But a Sam unlike all her memories. His triple-caped greatcoat was of the finest navy wool, and a gold buckle adorned his high-domed beaver hat. Only the finest bootmaker would have made the boots that moulded so perfectly to his strong calves, and his tawny hair was shorn fashionably short.

She swallowed against the dryness of her throat and gave herself a mental shiver to bring herself to her senses, then she laughed, her voice cracking with huskiness. 'Your pardon, Sam. My wits have gone begging. This is a surprise, a wonderful surprise.'

He dismounted and threw the reins of his gelding to the new groom, Kit Martyn, who had accompanied Toby Keswick from the hayloft. The milkmaids and Lillith and Aggie were standing in doorways giggling as they witnessed Sam's arrival.

Hannah clapped her hands. 'Get back to your work and bring some mulled wine and cake into the parlour for Mr Deighton and some lemonade and biscuits for Charlie and Luke.' Luke was dragging Charlie into the barn to see some week-old kittens.

Toby Keswick and Sam eyed each other assessingly before Hannah introduced them and also Kit.

'I needed another groom,' she explained, and spoke of inconsequentials as they walked through to the parlour. There she turned to study Sam, who had removed his hat and coat. 'You look well, and Charlie has grown so much in the last year. Were you reconciled with your family?'

'It is a long story. The farm has prospered. I should be mortified that I was so easily replaced.'

She ignored the taunt and self-consciously patted her hair. 'I look a mess. I was not expecting visitors other than my family, but I am delighted to see you. Give me ten minutes so that I can change. You will be staying for lunch, will you not?'

'I would like that. And you look lovely as you are. I worked for you for over three years, remember; this is how I remember you best.'

It was not the flattering image she would have liked him to remember her by. She was unaccountably tongue-tied as she handed him the mulled wine and sipped at her own glass.

He was at ease, his presence filling the low-ceilinged parlour as he said, 'I noticed the milk herd was larger and there were more foals in the paddock.'

'A legacy from Uncle William allowed me to increase the herd. There are new faces here but old ones were missed and not easily replaced.'

'That is heartening to learn.'

His stare swept admiringly over her in such a way that every inch of her flesh blushed in a thrill of anticipation. She cleared her throat to steady her voice. 'Tell me of your year. It has been so long, Sam. So much must have happened. I hope all turned out well for Charlie with your family.'

He told her of all that had passed, speaking through lunch as they ate alone in the dining room and Luke and Charlie played happily together.

'You must have been delighted to learn that Catherine was married to her cousin,' Hannah said. 'But for Charlie to be Lord Eastley's heir must have been a shock. How did his lordship receive Charlie? And what of your father? Does he accept the new situation?'

'My father refuses to speak with Charlie or me. His lordship saw little of the boy. He was bed-ridden for four months and died six weeks ago. I have been attending to legal matters until now.'

'So what is to happen to Charlie? Are you still his guardian?'

'That was the sting in the tail of his lordship's acceptance of my remaining Charlie's guardian. Charlie, or Charles as Eastley insisted he be known, is now Lord Eastley and is to be brought up at Highcroft

Manor unless he is away at boarding school. He finds his new life daunting and misses the friends he made here. He has been pestering to see Luke for months.'

'So it is to see Luke that you have come?' Hannah hoped the disappointment did not show in her voice.

'Not entirely. Did you think I would not return for you?'

The intensity of his gaze set her pulses racing. She held her breath; it was too soon to hope that there was more behind this visit than two friends catching up on news of each other. His stare was hooded, concealing his emotion. After a year apart, they were as awkward together as strangers, yet each glance from him could set her blood on fire.

'Your time for mourning is over.' He did not falter in his stare but his own voice was uncertain. 'I heard that two men vied for your attention this summer, and that one had captured your heart. I did not know if it was appropriate for me to visit.'

'An old friend of Japhet's was often here. He had purchased two of the horses and taught Mark how to train the others so they would be ready for racing when Japhet returns.'

'I heard that he hoped to be more than a friend.' Sam twirled his wine glass as he stared deep into her eyes.

'Nick would never have made a farmer. This is Davey's future, as Highcroft Manor is Charlie's.'

They were verbally dancing around each other, saying everything but saying nothing that really mattered. She had dreamed of, waited for this moment for so long, and they were both so formal, so uncertain in each other's company. She cursed the recklessness that had allowed her to encourage Nick and believe that no harm could come of it.

His military bearing made him seem even more remote. 'You make it sound like a bridge that can never be crossed. There is always compromise.'

'How can there be compromise?' Her heart leapt with a traitorous expectation, making it harder for her to say. 'Do I understand it aright that you must also live at Highcroft Manor until Charlie's majority?'

'Yes.'

The fragile hope that he had come to make her his own turned to dust. She summoned a smile, though her face was so stiff it felt it was cracking. 'Then Charlie is a lucky boy. You will never fail him.'

'Neither will I sacrifice the happiness of any I love. Marry me, Hannah.' He grimaced. 'That is not how I meant to ask you.' He slid down on one knee and took her hand. 'I love you. Will you honour me by becoming my bride?'

'How can I marry you, Sam?' Her expression was haggard. Fate was mocking her. This was so cruel she almost wished he had not come. Her gaze devoured him and she forced the words out through her longing: 'My home is here and you are bound to Highcroft Manor.'

'Not for twelve months of the year.' His grip on her hand tightened as he continued with passion: 'Charlie goes to school next year. The bailiff has run Highcroft for twenty years. He can do so in my absence whilst Charlie is away. Most of the year will be spent here. And Highcroft is not so far, for it borders the Tamar.'

He raised her to her feet and his arms slid protectively around her. 'We can make it work. I have still to get my father and brother to accept Charlie as his late lordship's heir. With you at my side, Highcroft Manor will be a house of laughter and love, not the empty mausoleum it is now.'

Her senses were reeling. This was so much more than she had expected. Her tiny world had just exploded. The challenge Sam had offered her was immense. Her palms were against his chest and she could feel the strong, assured beat of his heart. Then before she could speak his hands tightened possessively around her, binding her in a passionate embrace, and his lips captured hers in a poignant hunger. He kissed her until she was breathless, his mouth travelling to her eyes, and then his breath was hot against her ear. 'This is not the future either of us planned, but we cannot forsake Charlie. It will not be without its challenges, and I vow now that your children will never lose out. This farm is as important to me as Highcroft. I will not fail you or the children. We can make it work, Hannah.'

Her heart was too full of emotion to speak, her eyes stark with her love. He went on as though a reply was irrelevant. 'The hardest decision of my life was to leave you last year. I knew then that you were the only woman for me, but you were not ready to admit that another could share your heart with Oswald. I do not expect you to love me more than him. Our love will be different, but equally abiding.'

The adoration in his eyes humbled her as he lovingly ran his fingers over her hair. 'Sam, you had left but a week when I realised how much I missed you, how much I had come to love you. Loyalty to Charlie and your family had to be honoured, and if you had turned your back on your responsibilities then you would not have been the man I had fallen in love with. But I fell in love with a man who was also committed to my family and farm. This is my home.'

It took all her willpower to move away from him. His proposal was the answer to her dreams, but when a dream is realised it rarely comes without a price. From the moment she had married Oswald and Rabson Farm had become her home, she had never aspired to be more than a farmer's wife. This was her children's home and heritage. To forsake it would be to betray Oswald in the cruellest way.

'How can we marry, Sam? I will not have this farm managed by strangers. I owe Oswald more than that.'

'Anything is possible if you have faith that our love and our future were meant to be.'

It would be so easy to accept the dream he offered, but she was no love-struck maiden who believed in fairy-tale endings. She stared helplessly at him, her heart torn asunder. All she could see were the problems. Her allegiance would put her children's interests before her own. This was not a decision she could make on impulse.

Chapter Forty-two

The smell of the hog roasting over the outside spit was a tempting aroma chasing away the more unpleasant farmyard smells. The house was filled with the scents of cooked pies and cakes and freshly baked bread. The barn had been swept and the floor scattered with dried thyme, rosemary and lavender, which when trodden underfoot would sweeten the air. Trestle tables were covered with linen sheets and the children had scoured the hedgerows for the last of the wild flowers to place in vases. Some hardy nasturtiums and honeysuckle had escaped the frost. Benches were arranged each side of the tables for the diners, and the walls had been decorated with sprigs of laurel and holly. Two barrels – one of mead and the other of cider – were placed on stools.

Even the weather was kind to them. It was a glorious clear, sunny day that lifted everyone's spirits and chased away the previous day's frost with its foreshadowing of winter. To keep the children amused, ninepins had been set up in the garden, and there would be prizes for sack and three-legged races. As the family arrived, no one commented on the dark circles around Hannah's eyes. They all assumed that the hard work of the last few days had taken its toll.

While the children played blind man's buff in the garden, cups of hot mulled wine were handed round as the family paused by the paddock to look at the foals. They were skittish in the bright sunshine and seemed to sense the excitement in the air. As they trotted around the meadow, their proud Arabian heads were tilted, their tails held high and manes flowing. Last year's stock were more dignified and followed the mares, questing for sugar tidbits or apples from their admirers.

'It breaks my heart that Japhet is not here to see the fine horses he has reared.' Cecily dabbed a tear from her eye.

Hannah put her arm around her shaking shoulders. 'Mama, do not upset yourself. This is a day of gratitude for all the good things that have happened this year. We have something of Japhet with us.'

335

'Sometimes I wonder if I will ever see him again. He has achieved so much in the new land. From his letters he clearly loves the country and the freedom of life as a settler. It is a land of opportunity and Japhet was ever an opportunist.'

'Japhet is a Cornishman. He will never forsake his homeland,' Elspeth clipped out, but there was a catch to her voice that was not usually present.

Hannah shrugged and her own voice was sad. 'He has been away so long. So much has happened. So much has changed.'

Joshua put his hands on his daughter's and wife's shoulders. 'Change is inevitable.' He laughed to dispel the moment of melancholy. 'Are we not supposed to be celebrating triumphing over the adversity we suffered this year? Japhet will return or he would have insisted that Tor Farm and the foals be sold.'

'We do have much to celebrate.' Adam added his voice. Everyone missed Japhet but he did not want the day to be spoiled. His cousin had worked hard to pay this tribute to her family. 'Hannah should be proud of the foals and her expansion of the milk herd. We have all over-come adversity this year, and though she has never complained, it has been harder for her than most. Not only does the milk herd thrive but her sale of dairy goods has trebled.'

She waved aside his praise. 'The year started badly for us all. Yet our troubles did not defeat us – they united us. We should be grateful to Harry Sawle for that. He did everything in his power to destroy us, yet we triumphed over his evil and he paid the ultimate price. And I want to thank you all for your help and support when you all had busy lives and your own problems to contend with.'

'That is what families are for,' Adam assured her.

Joshua smiled at St John and Adam. 'Your father would have been proud of you both this year. Trevowan and Boscabel are free from debt. St John has a delightful new wife and daughter and Adam has won an order that will ensure the security of the yard.'

Adam nodded appreciation at his uncle's words. The onus of respon-sibility for the shipyard had been a heavy yoke for his shoulders. It was not until it had eased that he realised how much he had feared failing his father's belief that his guidance would bring the yard to greater glory. He still had some way to go to achieve so much, but he was confident in his ability.

He was concerned that St John did not respond to Joshua's praise. He stood apart from his wife and the atmosphere was strained between them. Amelia had linked her arm through Felicity's and led her towards the warmth of the barn. It was good that the two women seemed to have formed a close relationship now that Sophia Quinton had stopped her visits to Trevowan.

It made Adam appreciate how fortunate he was in his own marriage. He glanced at Senara, who stood with Bridie as they watched Rowena order the younger children into two teams so that they could race each other across the lawn whilst bowling a hoop. The boys protested, with Joel's voice the loudest. He picked up a ball and kicked it to Nathan.

'Play football,' he shouted. 'Lovedays against Rabsons.'

'Girls do not play football,' Rowena protested.

'Then play with your stupid hoops.' Luke tackled Joel and ran off with the ball. Davey, Nathan and Joel yelled excitedly as they sped after him.

Rowena stamped her foot and put her hands on her hips. 'Why do they have to ruin everything?'

'Let the boys have their silly rough game, Rowena,' Abigail placated, her expression worried lest her cousin threw one of her increasingly frequent tantrums. 'You and Charlotte can be against me and Florence.'

Rowena continued to scowl as the excitement from the boys grew louder. She hated not being the centre of attention. Then she frowned as another boy ran out from the back of the farmhouse to join the others. The rest of the girls had not noticed as they were practising with their hoops. Wasn't that Charlie? If he was here, then surely Sam was with him. She lost all interest in the hoop race. She had overheard much gossip from the women as they speculated on the relationship between Hannah and her overseer, who had left the farm so suddenly. She was bored with childish games. She wanted to be part of the grown-up world. And if Sam was here, why had he not joined the family?

A fiddler had struck up a tune in the barn and she saw the last of the adults disappearing through the entrance. She broke into a run to tell them her news and was furious to discover that they were already gathered around Sam, who must have been inside all along, and greeting him with laughter and surprise. Losing interest, she helped herself to a honey cake from the table and returned to her cousins.

'Why did you not tell us that Mr Deighton was here?' Cecily frowned at her daughter.

'He insisted that I show you the foals first and thank you for all your support this year.'

Amelia whispered rather loudly to Felicity: 'Why should Hannah tell us if her overseer has returned? He ran the farm extremely well, but how Toby Keswick will take his arrival is another matter. I suppose Hannah intends to replace him.'

Hannah coloured at hearing the remark. 'Sam is not here to replace Keswick. Charlie has inherited Highcroft Manor and the title of Lord Eastley from his grandfather, and as his guardian Sam will manage the estate until Charlie comes of age.' She rushed on before they could interrupt, moving towards Sam as she spoke. 'Sam has also asked me to marry him, and after talking all through the night as to how we could honour our obligations both to the late Lord Eastley and to Oswald, I accepted his proposal.' Her eyes shone with happiness and love and she gazed up at Sam. 'We shall marry a month from today, at Christmas. We have lost so much time together. I hope you all approve and that this celebration will now be a betrothal feast.'

'Your happiness is our only concern, my dear,' Joshua answered. 'But we will miss you when you move away.'

'But that is what we spent the night discussing. We will spend at least a third of the year here. I want Davey to be a part of the land he will inherit, and Sam agrees with me.'

Senara had poured glasses of mead for all the family and passed them round. 'It is wonderful to have another Christmas wedding. Adam and I married at the winter solstice. May you be blessed with the happiness we have shared.'

Adam raised his glass. 'After a year of turmoil, what better way for it to end than with a wedding? Congratulations to you both.'

'You will have your work cut out, Deighton.' St John's eyes narrowed. He could barely control his envy that the man who had been his cousin's overseer would now have a fortune in his control as his nephew's guardian. The Rabson farm was also a valuable asset. His jealousy increased as he saw the love and respect in the eyes of the betrothed couple. He had never loved Felicity in that way.

Cecily hugged her daughter, hiding her fears about her happiness. 'Yet the marriage will not be without its problems. Was there not some feud with your father, Sam? Was it resolved, or do you face a court battle over Lord Eastley's will?'

'It is not yet resolved, but I am hopeful that my father will come to see reason,' Sam replied. 'I promise you all that I take my responsibilities to Hannah and her children equally as seriously as I do my guardianship of Charlie.'

'You have never failed Hannah in the past,' Joshua agreed. 'Yet your responsibilities now are very different.'

'When is life not without its challenges?' Hannah waved her mother's doubts aside. 'It is how we cope with them that is important. We have all faced hardship and danger this year and have survived. Adam almost lost the yard but his fortitude overcame his hardship. The challenges are what set us apart and make us who we are. I welcome them, and I know that with Sam at my side we can triumph.'

Elspeth had been regarding the couple in silence. Now she cleared her throat and peered at them over the top of her pince-nez. 'Sam has proved he is a man of honour and integrity. I applaud this marriage. Hannah should have a break from the arduous work on the farm. Her new life will be rewarding and fulfilling. There are enough of us to ensure that the welfare of the horses and the running of this farm does not suffer in her absence. I give you both my blessing.'

'I drink to that.' Adam lifted his cup. 'To the challenge of life and our success for the future. Now where is that delicious hog roast that has been tempting us to eat since our arrival?'

The toast was drunk and Peter stepped forward. 'Indeed this is a day for giving thanks and gratitude for the blessings bestowed upon us. We have triumphed over those who would bring us down and become the stronger for it. Let us rejoice in the good fortune and happiness of this day. Our enemies are defeated and we are at peace.'

Senara savoured the moment of happiness. They were indeed at peace. Or as close to peace as they could be. A rare event amongst the turbulent lives of the Lovedays. Although the family were united in a way they had not been for years, it would not last. What was it about even the most magnanimous and worthy of this brood that they attracted contention into their midst? Yet their valour and solidarity always overcame it, and nothing would daunt them whatever misadventures lay ahead. That was their strength.